BENEATH THE ICE

ALTON GANSKY

D1166978

BARBOUR
PUBLISHING

ISBN 1-58660-674-3

Cover created by Lookout Design Group.

Published by Barbour Publishing, Inc., P.O. Box 719, Uhrichsville, Ohio 44683, www.barbourbooks.com

Our mission is to publish and distribute inspirational products offering exceptional value and biblical encouragement to the masses.

 Member of the
Evangelical Christian
Publishers Association

Printed in the United States of America.
5 4 3 2 1

To my best friend and wife, Becky.

PROLOGUE

Dr. Harry Hearns struggled to place the plastic-coated electric lead into the tiny copper socket. He failed for the third time. Anyplace else, any other time, this would have been a simple task, but this was not just any place or any time.

The lead slipped from his hand, and he swore at the stateside engineers who designed the sensitive instruments in warm, comfy offices.

"Hey, Doc." The voice scratched out of a microphone/speaker attached to the lapel of Hearns's parka. *"We're gonna go bingo fuel if you don't cart your academic fanny back in here."*

More swearing. Hearns released the lead, raised his hand to the mike, and keyed it. "You're welcome to come out and help," he snapped. "Assuming the wind isn't too much for your sensitive skin. . ." He returned his attention to the device before him.

"Speaking of wind, it's picking up, and we pilots are kinda sensitive to that."

Hearns chose not to respond. They would wait. They had no choice.

Pulling his gloves tighter, he took another stab at connecting the wire. It was like doing surgery while handcuffed. Once again he fumbled the small connector, and it slipped from his fingers. For a moment he considered removing the glove, but he had been around too long to do something so foolish. It wasn't the cold he feared as much as the metal box and pole before which he knelt. He had no desire to place bare, moist skin next to metal that had been exposed to temperatures so far below zero that most people could not fathom the effects.

The wind picked up, taking ice crystals airborne and swirling them around like motes of precious gems. The first time Hearns saw what scientists called "diamond dust," he stood in stunned amazement, moved by its beauty. Now, though, bone-weary, cold, and facing a recalcitrant electronic component, it just annoyed him.

"Too many years on the ice," he said to himself. The puff of mist that escaped his mouth with the words froze to his gray-brown beard.

The breeze stiffened, carrying with it the sound of ocean slapping the sides of the ice. Hearns knew the ocean was a half mile away and 150 feet lower than the plateau he stood upon. He also knew the ice extended 1300 feet below the surface of the frigid waters.

"Seriously, Doc. Mrs. Larsen didn't raise her little boy to be stupid. We've already made two extra stops for you. It's time to head back."

He looked to his right at the Coast Guard's bright orange and white HH-60 Jayhawk helicopter that waited for him fifty yards away. "Get off my back, Lieutenant Larsen. I'll be there as soon as I can."

The surface beneath his feet shifted, and the ice roared as if in pain. The small toolbox he had brought with him danced on the ice.

Okay, now I'm getting nervous.

Hearns keyed the mike again. "We're on an iceberg, Lieutenant, and icebergs move—which is why I'm here."

That *was* why he was there, he reminded himself. He had made icebergs the object of twenty years of study. This berg, B27, was especially interesting, the second largest iceberg known, second only to B15, which calved off the Ross Ice Shelf in March of 2000. B15 had been nearly 4,200 square miles, a little less than the size of Connecticut—170 miles long and 1,000 feet thick. B27, or "Kong" as it was known to the engineers and scientists that made this part of Antarctica home, was eighty-five percent of that but well worth studying. It might be only the second largest berg, but it was still three times the size of Rhode Island.

Hearns had studied icebergs with the National Ice Center for most of the last two decades. His specialty was formative ice structures. No one knew more about how bergs formed. What he didn't know was why they broke apart—calved—like they did.

Kong had calved from the ice shelf four weeks before and had been slowly moving out to sea. Hearns knew that Kong would split soon. B27 had done so just a few weeks after it dropped into the ocean. Not even an iceberg the size of Kong could defeat the unrelenting pounding of the sea. It would last years, but not many. Bit by bit it would fragment into smaller and smaller pieces. The berg would become two, then four, then a dozen, until it disappeared into the ocean, its majestic white grandeur indistinguishable from the cold, churning sea.

Now the iceberg was beginning to break in two. Hearns wanted to know why.

Two weeks after the B27 separated from the ice shelf it had been part of for more years than could be numbered, Hearns and his team had placed instruments along the length of it. Those instruments monitored temperature, wind speed and direction, barometric pressure, and much more data. More important to Hearns, however, they monitored the iceberg's position. A GPS monitor in each instrument station took periodic readings and radioed the information to McMurdo Station, Hearns's home base.

Two of the GPS stations on Kong had quit broadcasting; Hearns was sure that had to do with cheap transmitters. *Can't do real science when they pinch pennies,* he thought.

He took a deep breath and shut out the sound of the wind, the moaning ice, and the distant water and made another attempt to secure the tiny connection. "Someone is going to hear about this," he promised himself.

It slipped in.

"Finally," he said to the rising breeze. He stood, shut the metal box, and secured the lid. He took one last lingering look at the triangular aluminum mast that held the antenna, gave the support chains a tug to make sure they were snug, then jogged toward the helicopter.

"That's what I'm talking about, Doc. Put some heart into it."

The ice shook and rumbled. *Icequake.* Hearns lost his footing. He tumbled to the hard ice in a heap; the toolbox skittered across the surface. The ice groaned in agony.

"You okay, Doc?"

Hearns struggled to his feet. Hot bolts of pain fired up his back and down his leg. He took a tentative step: pain, but not severe. That was good. The last thing he needed out here was a broken hip. He trundled on, this time with a limp.

The ice shuddered again, and Hearns stopped, turning to his left. A crack had appeared—right where he had expected it, right where he had predicted it! Although he had been right about the place where the calving would happen, he had been wrong about the time. His calculations showed that it would be at least another week before an appreciable hunk split off.

Another quake; the gap in the ice widened.

"Doc! Move it!"

For once, Hearns agreed with Lieutenant Larsen. Despite the pain in his hip, Hearns broke into a full run. The cold air bit his lungs with each inhalation. He felt as if he were gulping angry bees.

Each step crunched the ice beneath his boots. The wind rose another notch and pushed against his form. The helicopter had been fifty yards away when he started. Any closer and the constantly turning rotors would have stirred up ice in Hearns's work area. Now he wished he hadn't been so cautious.

"This baby is splitting up, Doc. Run!"

He was running, but he was running with a box of tools in one hand and heavy boots on his feet. He was in good shape for a man of fifty, but the Antarctic climate didn't care. It could send the strongest man to his knees without warning.

At last he reached the helicopter. The side door slid open, and a pair of strong hands seized the parka he was wearing. A half-second later, Hearns was inside, and the loading door slammed shut.

"Strap in," flight mechanic Neil Russo commanded. Then he spoke into the microphone that hung from his orange flight helmet. "He's in. Feel free to bug out."

Hearns sat in the nearest jump seat and pulled the safety harness across his chest and lap. The engine began to whine as the rotors came up to speed. Dr. Hearns slipped on his helmet. He would now be able to hear what the crew said over the roar of the engine and the pounding of the rotors.

"Hold on," Larsen snapped. "We done wore out our welcome."

Hearns's stomach dropped like a stone as the chopper took to the air. He hated flying, but this time it was a welcome feeling.

"Oh, baby," Larsen said. The words poured through Hearns's helmet earphone. "I was getting just a touch nervous there."

"Just a touch?" Russo asked.

"Okay, maybe two touches."

Hearns ignored the banter. He waited a moment until the helicopter had settled into a gentle ascent, then released his restraints and made his way to the windowed door. The iceberg receded from them as the craft continued its rise. Below was the familiar shape of Kong, a white mass of ice as far as the eye could see. What wasn't familiar was the growing crack that had only been a supposition before.

"Camera," he whispered.

"What's that, Doc?" Russo asked.

"My video camera. . .where is it?" Hearns didn't wait for an answer. He lurched toward the seat he had occupied on the flight from McMurdo. The helicopter pitched slightly but not enough to slow Hearns's movement toward the seat. Next to it, fastened in like a passenger, was the worn backpack he carried on every trip. Yanking it open, he plunged a gloved hand inside and removed a small video camera. He paused, then reached back into the satchel for his digital camera.

"What are you planning, Doc?" Russo wanted to know.

"Take this," Hearns ordered. "Turn the switch on top until it points at the camera icon. Start snapping."

"What—"

"Do it, man. We're missing it." He tossed the camera in Russo's lap and returned to the window. He activated the video camera and adjusted the zoom. Through the eyepiece he saw the fracture become a split and the split a crevasse.

"Wow," Russo said. "Are you seeing this, Lieutenant?"

"Roger that. Looks like we bailed just in time."

"Spin us around," Hearns said, pushing back the hood of his parka.

"No can do, Doc. I told you, your extra stops have eaten up more fuel than we planned. We're headed home."

"If you wanted to play it safe, you should have become a plumber," Hearns shot back. "Now turn us around."

"I joined the Coast Guard thinking I'd be patrolling the beaches of sunny California, not hopping from iceberg to iceberg in the Antarctic. I'm not here by choice."

"Turn us *around!*"

Hearns felt the chopper bank to the left. His heart raced more from what he was seeing than from the threat he had just escaped. Kong was separating, calving into several smaller icebergs. Scientists had seen it happen before, but not Hearns and not from a helicopter flying overhead. He had no intention of missing his chance to record it.

"Looks like you finished up just in time, Doc," Russo uttered, the camera pressed to his eye. "How many shots do you want?"

"Fill the memory stick," Hearns answered. "I can study them later. . . ."

"Hey, Doc. What's that?" Russo didn't explain. He didn't need to.

Hearns pressed the ZOOM button and tightened his shot. He closed his eyes and shook his head. It had to be wrong.

"Do you see it, Doc?"

"I see it. I just don't believe it."

"It sorta looks like—"

"Lieutenant, take us closer to that dark object," Hearns ordered.

"The one in the crevasse?"

"Yes."

The helicopter dipped and banked. "Make it quick, Hearns. You got sixty seconds. . .no more."

"We'll leave when *I* say," Hearns barked.

"Unless you plan to come yank the stick out of my hand, we'll leave when *I* say."

"Then put me down," Hearns said. "You can send another chopper after me."

"That'll cost me my commission. No can do."

Hearns swore but kept the camera taping. "Lower."

Nothing happened.

"Listen, Larsen!" Hearns shouted. "If Kong cleaves, the smaller piece is certain to roll, and we'll lose sight and access to it."

"And you wanted me to set down," Larsen said. "What is that thing, anyway?"

"I can't be sure unless we get closer," Hearns admitted. "I don't want to speculate."

"I'll speculate," Russo said. "It looks like a building."

"Impossible," Hearns said. "It's close to fifty meters down in the crevasse, maybe more. Ice builds up at two centimeters per year. Do you know how old that makes the object?"

"I don't know nothin' about that, Doc," Russo said, "but it still looks like some kind of building to me."

Russo was right. It looked like a building—and a large one at that. That was nonsense. It had to be. Researchers had found fossil trees and other plant life in Antarctica but nothing showing a human presence—and buildings were distinctly human things.

"It's an optical illusion of some kind," Hearns said, "but we need a closer look. Lieutenant, I insist you put us down."

"I'll pull closer—I'll hover over it—but I will not set down. Is that clear?"

"Yeah, it's clear," Hearns growled.

"How close do you want me to get?"

Hearns thought for a second. "I'm worried about what the rotor blast might do. If you get too close, then the props will kick up ice particles, and we won't be able to see squat."

"Roger that," the pilot said.

"Pull just a little closer, but be prepared to pull away if I say—"

Even over the noise of the helicopter's engine, Hearns heard the crack, the rumbling, the shearing squeal of tons of ice rubbing against tons of ice. It was if the earth itself had split open. Hearns felt his heart tumble to a stop then skip back to life. Thirty meters below them, the ice chasm widened and deepened. Kong was now two icebergs. The berg shuddered before Hearns's eyes, and then the smaller section began to roll on its back like a dying whale.

"Up!" Hearns shouted. "Take us up. I need more altitude to keep my eye on it."

The helicopter shot up fast enough to make Hearns feel sick. He pushed the nausea away and focused on the dark object.

"We're losing sight of it," Russo said.

"Veer north," Hearns said. "Quick, man!"

The object disappeared from sight, and Hearns felt ill again.

"I'll stay this course until we're feet wet, Doc. Maybe you can see where it went under—if it went under."

"It went under," Hearns whispered.

"How can you be so sure?" Russo wondered.

"Because Kong didn't cleave down the middle. It's only half a mile or so to the berg's edge. That means that the new berg is top heavy. It rolled. The ice we can see now used to be under water."

"You want me to keep going or not, Doc?" the pilot pressed.

"Yes. We'll drop a die marker and come back. Maybe we'll find something."

Hearns turned off the camera and stared at the ice below.

No matter how hard he tried, he couldn't deny what he had seen. *Maybe it's better this way*, he thought. *Maybe it's best if we don't know.*

CHAPTER 1

I hope you're kidding," Perry Sachs said. He shifted in his seat, trying to find a way to be comfortable dressed in clothing far thicker and heavier than he was used to wearing.

"Maybe I should have mentioned this before," Jack Dyson said. "You know how shy I am."

Perry laughed. He looked at his friend's smiling face, lit by the overhead lights that lined the C-5 Galaxy aircraft as it bumped along through the twilight-tinged air. Jack Dyson was a tall, broad man who looked as if he could have a stunning career in the NFL. His black face was accustomed to smiling, and his eyes danced with humor. Too often those meeting him for the first time assumed he was a dumb jock, as if a large body made for a small mind. The assumption always led to their embarrassment. Jack was the sharpest man Perry knew, and Perry knew and worked with the brightest.

"Shy. Yeah, that's you, all right," Perry replied. "I don't know how many times I've had to draw you out of the shadows."

"I'm a sensitive soul," Jack said. He turned and looked out the window. "Sure looks cold down there."

Perry leaned over and looked past his friend. The light in the cabin returned a thin reflection from the plastic pane. For a moment, Perry's own image distracted him. Gazing back was a handsome man with hair one shade lighter than coal, weary blue eyes, a narrow face, and two days' growth of beard. At thirty-nine, Perry was easing into middle age. His lean body stood six-foot-two—when he got to stand. Since leaving Seattle a week earlier, he had been on one aircraft after another until he had arrived in Christchurch, New Zealand, the day before. After he'd grabbed a warm meal and six hours of sleep, Jack had joined him, having taken his own series of red-eye flights from a job site in Canada.

"Antarctica looks cold to you?" Perry said. "You *are* a sensitive soul."

"Even Canada was warm."

"Spring is just ending in Canada, my friend. Down here winter is just around the corner."

"That I know," Jack said. "Like I said, I don't like the cold, and it's only going to get colder."

"That's why we have to work fast," Perry said, leaning back in his seat. "We have to leave before winter sets in, or we'll be stuck down here for more months than I care to think about."

A whining noise filled the long bay in which they sat. "We're descending," Jack noted. He looked at his watch. "Right on time. These flyboys are punctual."

A voice came from behind them. "That's because the sooner they land this beast and unload, the sooner they get to go back to McMurdo." The passenger who'd spoken rose and stepped into the narrow aisle formed by the cargo boxes that ran the long axis of the aircraft.

"I thought you were sleeping, Commander," Perry said.

"I was, but that last bounce told me that I had too much coffee—if you catch my drift. I'm gonna hit the head before we land." Commander Trent Larimore, United States Navy, passed a hand over his thin face. Two years older than Perry, Larimore had dark hair lightened by too much gray for a man his age.

"Better make it quick, sir," a fresh-faced young man said, making his way back from the front of the large plane. He was the load-master for the trip. "The skipper wants everyone in their seats. We've begun our descent."

"Never fear," Larimore said. *"Semper paratus."* He moved aft, leaving the young loadmaster looking puzzled.

"Always prepared," Perry translated.

The young man nodded and moved along the aisle repeating the information about landing.

"I should have asked him for peanuts," Jack said. "He'd make a good flight attendant."

"Don't tell him that," Perry replied. "You might hurt his feelings."

"I thought the navy handled these flights," Jack said. "Or at least the air force."

"The navy used to, but they stopped in 1999. These days the New York Air National Guard handles supply flights. They were available, so we arranged a ride."

"Frankly, I'm tired of riding. The sooner they put wheels—I mean, skids—down, the better."

Perry agreed. He had tired of sitting and was ready to ex-change the crowded cargo plane for some open air. He thought about the work before them, the task they had been retained to do—something never done before. The familiar mix of anticipa-tion and anxiety stewed in Perry. It was a sensation he had come to love, and one he had felt on many occasions. It was what made him feel alive.

As vice president and senior project manager, Perry had traveled the world for Sachs Engineering, an international construction com-pany founded by his father decades before. Since 1975 Sachs En-gineering had erected buildings and structures across the globe, many for Western governments. Secrecy was a valuable commodity, and Perry's father, Henry Sachs, knew how to market it. When a situation demanded nontraditional construction—such as underground facili-ties—Sachs Engineering was often the first called.

Perry had never known another job. He worked on small, local projects while in high school and filled summers off from college working in deserts, swamps, and on mountainsides. He worked his way up through the ranks. Being Henry Sachs's only child bought him no favors. Dad insisted that advancement came with experience, education, and production. That was fine with Perry.

"Look at Gleason," Jack said, nodding forward. "I'll bet he's read that file a dozen times since we went airborne."

"Did you expect otherwise?" Perry asked, and Jack shook his head.

Gleason Lane was the head techie of the group. He specialized in making electronic equipment do more than designers imagined. Like Perry and Jack, Gleason was an MIT graduate. While Perry took a degree in architecture, and Jack a degree in civil engineering, Gleason had studied computer science. It didn't take him long after graduation to realize that pounding computer keys in a cubicle wasn't for him. Perry arranged a field job for him, something at which he excelled. His reputation had made him a much sought after consultant.

"We're asking him to do the impossible," Perry continued. "Of course, he'd be offended if we asked anything else."

"So what did you promise his wife this time?" Jack asked. Perry and Jack had remained unmarried. They traveled to places they couldn't discuss to do work they couldn't explain—and not return home for six months. It was difficult to keep a woman interested in that kind of relationship.

Gleason, on the other hand, had married during his senior year in college and now had two preteen children. Any time Perry required Gleason to leave home for more than two weeks, he sent gifts to the family. Fortunately, Gleason was seldom required to be gone as long as Perry and Jack. He came in, did his work, and left. It took less time to set up a computer system than it took to tunnel out a mountain or build a bombproof building.

"I sent the kids a new video game player and got the missus a DVD recorder. That way she can record all the shows she likes to watch with Gleason."

"She's an understanding woman," Jack said. "Not many around like her."

"Feeling lonely in your old age?"

"Old? I'm a good deal younger than you, Pops."

"Three months cannot be defined as 'a good deal younger,' not even in your world."

"Yeah? Well, at least I'm still pretty. You, on the other hand. . ."

"The only thing pretty on this flight is Sarah Hardy, and you ain't her."

"Ah, the lovely NASA robotics expert," Jack said with a smile. "Thinking of asking her out for dinner and a movie?"

"For the next few weeks, dinner will be coming out of a can or plastic pouch. And as for movies, I didn't think to pack a theater."

"Just as well. You know how you are around women."

Perry looked at his friend. "And just how am I around women?"

"You know, tongue-tied, intimidated, and—let's be honest— you can be a little irritating."

"Not me, buddy. I'm as soothing as hand lotion."

"I believe last year a certain small-town mayor named Anne Fitzgerald planted the palm of her hand on the side of your face."

"She tried, but failed," Perry rebutted. He had met Anne in Tejon, California, the previous year. She had been a problem from the beginning, interfering with a project that Perry was doing his best to keep undercover. Before it was all over, she had saved his life and he hers.

"Do you still see her?" Jack asked.

"From time to time," Perry said, but offered no more. The truth was, there was nothing more to offer. She had continued on with her mayoral duties, and he had gone back to Seattle, then to Japan for an extended period.

"Did I miss anything, gentlemen?" Larimore asked as he returned to his seat.

"Just the in-flight movie," Jack quipped.

"Yeah, right," Larimore said. "I wasn't gone *that* long."

The plane banked left and continued its descent. The load-master was making a final check of the onboard crates, inspecting the lines and cargo netting.

"Doesn't seem right," Jack said, "a plane this large with this much equipment landing on ice. Doesn't seem natural."

"Don't sweat it," Larimore said. "I've been in these things when they've landed on sea ice only six feet thick. Ice is incredibly strong. It's done all the time."

"Thanks. I feel better now," Jack said.

"Sarcasm," Larimore said. "I recognize it."

"Jack never outgrew it," Perry said.

The conversation lulled as the plane dropped through the cloudless sky toward the barren continent of ice. Perry stole another look out the window and was glad he was not the pilot. They were flying over a featureless terrain that made determining altitude impossible. He leaned his head back and closed his eyes.

It seemed a good time to pray.

Touchdown was as smooth as any Perry had experienced, except for the unusual sensation of the plane moving along on its skids. Instead of the roaring of rubber wheels against fluted concrete runway, he heard the whisper of a quiet gliding action.

The engines powered down, and a few moments later, the load-master appeared again. "Time to open the door, folks," he said, and a chorus of groans greeted him. The nearly 250-foot-long C-5 was capable of carrying 270,000 pounds of cargo. They had come close to that, and this was the second flight in. An earlier flight had landed on-site two weeks before to set up crew quarters, communications, and monitoring equipment. Now Perry and his team would begin their work.

Commander Larimore led the exit, followed closely by Perry, Jack, Gleason, and Dr. Sarah Hardy. Larimore's team of navy personnel poured out a moment later.

It was a different world.

It was a painful world.

Perry had tried to prepare himself for the moment. He had read everything he could find and had been briefed by experts on Antarctic conditions. Mental preparation was one thing; experiencing the harsh reality was something else.

Perry and the others wore clothing designed for the subzero conditions, but he immediately felt frozen to the marrow. He walked down the ramp that lowered from the rear of the C-5 and strolled from beneath the tail that towered six stories above the ice.

His heart pounded; his breathing was irregular. He caught himself panting. His lungs hurt, and his lips burned. A slight wind blew past his face, fluttering the fur lining of his parka hood. The breeze felt like a thousand razor blades across his skin.

"I. . .hate. . .the. . .cold," Jack whispered.

Perry tried to respond but only managed a nod.

In front of them a wide dome rose fifteen feet from the surface, as well as two large structures that looked like cargo boxes on steroids. All three buildings were flown in on the previous C-5. A door opened in the dome, and two figures garbed in dark blue snowsuits approached. They walked with their heads down until they stood before the gathering.

"Good day," one of them said. He seemed unbothered by the cold. "I'm Dr. Griffin James, chief scientist for this project. Welcome to the bottom of the earth." He threw his arms wide. The other figure stood a few feet to his right and a couple of steps behind. "This is my sister, Dr. Gwen James. She is our associate director, so you'll want to treat her well."

"I'm Perry Sachs—"

"You may have noticed that it's a little chilly here," Dr. James went on. "That's to be expected. You're not far from the place where the coldest temperature was ever recorded—a negative 89.2 degrees Celsius. That's 128.6 degrees *below* zero to you nonmetric folks. It makes today seem positively balmy, doesn't it?"

The weather didn't feel mild to Perry. He felt frozen. His legs were beginning to shake.

"Dr. James—" Perry began again. His lungs tightened, and his chest began to hurt.

"By now you may have noticed that your lungs hurt," Dr. James continued. "That's because of the altitude. You are standing on the highest, driest, coldest, windiest, and emptiest place on the planet. Beneath your feet is 70 percent of our planet's fresh water, and below that—well, that's why we're here, isn't it? We're at over twelve thousand feet above sea level. Not much oxygen, just extreme cold and mildly filtered ultraviolet light. Be sure and wear sunblock when tanning." He laughed at his own joke. He laughed alone.

Perry turned to look behind him. Heavily garbed men, the men assigned to Larimore, unloaded the plane. They worked efficiently. Most, he knew, would be returning with the plane as soon as they had finished offloading everything. For a moment he envied them.

"If you develop headaches, dizziness, disorientation, then tell Gwen immediately. She's our paramedic. Altitude sickness can be a serious problem. Most of you will adjust just fine."

Perry drew a ragged breath, and then said, "Dr. James, may we go inside?" He motioned toward the large, squat geodesic dome.

"I'm not finished," Dr. James protested. "As chief scientist, I am in charge of this operation. Questions and comments should be directed to me, and no work should be commenced without my approval."

"Who does this guy think he is?" Jack whispered.

Dr. James stopped and directed hard eyes at Jack. "Who do I think I am?"

"Uh-oh," Jack said.

"Five minutes on the ice and you're already in trouble with the teacher," Gleason chided.

"You're John Dyson, right?" Dr. James asked with clipped words.

"Everyone calls me Jack." Perry saw his friend flash his best winning smile.

"Everyone calls me Dr. James and—"

"That's it," Larimore snapped. "If it's all right with you, Perry, I'm going in."

"I haven't dismissed anyone," Dr. James said.

"Listen, little man," Larimore said. "As a military man, I'm well acquainted with chain of command. According to my orders, Mr. Sachs is in charge, not you."

"I'm the chief scientist—"

"So you keep saying," Larimore shot back. "And just so there's no confusion, I don't care. My orders are to serve as military liaison and assist this man—" he motioned to Perry with his thumb— "in whatever way I can. I handle military personnel, Ms. Hardy handles robotics, and you and your sister advise us on issues of science. Sachs oversees everything. Got it?"

Perry studied the navy commander for a moment. He seemed unfazed by the cold or thin air.

"And if I don't get it?" Dr. James asked.

"That plane leaves in an hour," Larimore replied. "As far as I'm concerned, you can be on it. It makes no difference to me."

Griffin's jaw tightened. Larimore took a step forward.

"Griffin, don't," Gwen James said. Her words carried concern and annoyance.

"Thank you for the warm welcome, Dr. James," Perry interjected. He took another deep breath before continuing but felt like he was sucking oxygen out of an empty jar. "Let's continue the party inside. Perhaps you'll give us the ten-cent tour, Dr. James." He started forward, but Griffin remained rooted to the ice. "All right then, maybe the other Dr. James will provide the tour." Perry stepped around Griffin and trudged across the white surface toward the warmth of the dome. He didn't look over his shoulder until he reached the thick door. Larimore, Jack, Gleason, and the others were right behind him. Bringing up the rear of the pack was Gwen.

Perry didn't wait for her; he opened the door and waved his companions in as if he owned the place. It was too cold, Perry decided, to stand on ceremony.

Thirty minutes later, key personnel gathered in a semicircular room in the center of the dome. Dr. Gwen James had given the group a tour, showing them the sleeping quarters, bathrooms, and galley. It was a tight fit. The six men—all navy Seabees—were housed in one of the square buildings a few feet away from the dome. The other rectangular structure Perry saw held food, medical, and other supplies for six months. If things went well, they would be on-site less than a third of that time.

Heavy coats had been sloughed off, but warm clothing was still the order of the day. Perry wore a white, long-sleeved undershirt, thick pants, and boots. The others wore something similar.

With the parkas and thick, fur-lined hoods gone, Perry could better see the faces of the others. Nonleadership personnel had been asked to give the team leaders some space and privacy. Perry, who always worked aboveboard with his crew and who encouraged participation from every worker, felt guilty for sending the others from the room, but on this trip, he wasn't making the rules.

The room, with its dark, insulated dome ceiling, made Perry feel like he was in a spacecraft. The furniture was utilitarian, designed to be unfolded and set up on a moment's notice and with as little effort as possible. Everything about the place was Spartan and indicated the hasty setup.

Dr. Griffin James entered the room last, noted where Larimore was seated and took an open seat farthest away. Larimore studied him for a moment, then smiled and offered a tiny nod. It wasn't a friendly gesture. Everyone who needed to be there was present. It was time to get to work. Perry stood.

"You've all received files on our mission, including biographies for team leaders," Perry began. "I expect you have all reviewed them, but let's introduce ourselves to make sure we're all on the same page."

"I get it," Jack said. "It's like a party, and this is the icebreaker."

A few people groaned.

"Wouldn't want another misunderstanding," Dr. James growled.

"No, we wouldn't," Perry responded, unfazed by the snipe. "Since you spoke up, Dr. James, let's start with you."

"Everyone met me outside, remember?"

Perry felt his patience with the man growing thin. According to James's personnel file, Griffin was thirty-two years old, never married, and a rising star in his field. Perry judged him to be five-ten and 160 pounds. His hair was sandy blond, his eyes dark blue. His mouth turned down as if chiseled in that position. Perry could tell Dr. James was a man who didn't laugh much.

Griffin frowned then said, "Dr. Griffin James, glaciologist, Ohio State—chief scientist." He offered no more.

"Dr. James will provide guidance about the ice and the problems we may face." He smiled and nodded at Gwen James. Her hair was dark, a shade lighter than Perry's. Smooth, alabaster skin covered a serious face. Unlike her twin brother, she struck Perry as less impressed with herself. She took the cue.

"Dr. Gwen James, biologist, University of California, San Diego. Griffin and I have been working on subglacial bioforms. I've been retained to monitor and record any discoveries indicating microscopic life. I'm also the team paramedic. It's not my forte, so stay healthy."

"Thank you, Dr. James," Perry said, then asked, "Since we have two Dr. Jameses, may we call you Gwen?"

"That would be unprofessional," Griffin said.

"Shut up, Griffin," Gwen shot back. "It's not unprofessional, and it will go a long way to make communication error free."

Perry pressed back the urge to smile. There was fire in the woman, and, apparently, she was used to handling her brother.

Skipping over his own crew for the moment, he turned to Larimore. "Commander?"

Larimore sat up in his chair. "Commander Trent Larimore, United States Navy. I oversee a team of six Seabees. Our job is to erect the exploration module, maintain environmental parameters, and generally be the life of the party."

"Seabees?" Gwen asked.

"We're the construction arm of the navy, ma'am," Larimore explained. " 'We build, we fight' is our motto."

Next, Perry turned to a brown-haired woman with cover-girl cheekbones and hazel eyes.

"Sarah Hardy, robotics, King's College, London." There was a slight twang to her words.

"You don't sound British," Jack said with a wink.

She smiled. "I'm not. I grew up in Austin, Texas. My family moved to England when I was a teenager. I'm with NASA."

"Thank you, Sarah," Perry said. "Jack?"

The large man stood, bowed, and then said, "Jack Dyson, civil engineering, MIT, and all-around swell guy." Perry saw Dr. James roll his eyes. "My job is to make sure Perry doesn't make a mess of this operation."

"Translation: He's the other project manager," Perry explained.

"Gleason Lane," Perry's friend said without waiting for a cue. "Like Perry and Jack, also MIT, except I majored in a challenging discipline—computer science. I handle all the tech stuff except robotics. That's the lovely Sarah Hardy's expertise."

"Perry Sachs," Perry said. "Project director, Sachs Engineering, architecture, MIT."

"Architecture!" Dr. James exclaimed. "You've got to be kidding. Why would Pentagon honchos send an architect to Antarctica?"

"Because he's the vice president of Sachs Engineering," Larimore said before Perry could reply. "They have built things in places you can't even imagine. They're a known quantity at the Pentagon."

"That's something else that bothers me," Dr. James said. "What does the Pentagon want down here? The International Antarctic Treaty of 1959 prohibits any military action or bases."

"Which is why a civilian is leading this project," Larimore said.

"It's just like the military," Dr. James complained. "I'm at the bottom of the world and have been given only the barest of information. If we're leaders on this team, then why don't we have the whole story?"

"That's why we're meeting right now," Perry said. "I'm going to bring everyone up to speed, but it probably won't satisfy you. Right now, I know more about this project than anyone in this room, and I can tell you: It's not much.

"Six months ago," Perry continued, "a radarsat image of Lake Vostok was taken by NASA as well as another aerogeophysical survey by aircraft. These have been done before, but a change was noted." He folded his arms. "As you know, we are situated over an under-ice lake named for the Russian research center many miles east of here. There are nearly eighty under-ice lakes in Antarctica. Lake Vostok is, by far, the largest."

"It's roughly the size of Lake Ontario," Dr. James interjected.

"*Was* about the size of Lake Ontario," Perry corrected. "It's larger. It's grown."

"Not possible," Dr. James said with a dismissive wave. "Things move slowly in this environment. The ice cap below us is moving at one centimeter per day. That means that one year from today, our camp will be four meters closer to the ocean. Four meters—that's all. Vostok could not have grown by any perceptible amount since the last survey. Maybe it's just a misinterpretation of data."

Perry shook his head. "NASA doesn't think so. The Pentagon doesn't think so. The lake is 10 percent larger. Three months ago, another survey was done, and the lake had changed another 2 percent."

"That would mean the ice above the lake is melting," Gwen said.

"And melting fast," Jack said. "Relatively speaking that is."

"Are you suggesting that the Antarctic ice cap is melting below our feet, Mr. Sachs?" Dr. James asked. "That's not possible, not in any time less than millions of years." He paused for a moment, shaking his head as if attempting to convince himself. "It's absurd. It can't be." He released a humorless chuckle. "Of course, it would be bad if it were true—really bad."

"What do you mean?" Gleason asked.

"Studies have been done," Griffin explained as if speaking to a class of undergraduates. "There's always someone out there who can't resist running a worst-case scenario computer model. One study showed that if just the east ice sheet of Antarctica were to melt, the world's water level would rise two hundred feet."

"That can't be good," Jack said.

"Not good?" Griffin said. "A two-hundred-foot rise in the ocean would destroy billions of dollars of homes and buildings, displace millions of people, and have unimaginable impact on ocean life. For example, you could kiss all of Florida good-bye. Only divers would be able to visit Disney World."

"Is that what's happening?" Sarah asked. Perry could see the lines of concern crease her face.

"No one is saying that the ice cap is melting, but something is going on. Our job is to find out what."

"That explains the secrecy," Larimore added. "Imagine what the media could do with that information. By the time the press was finished, the world would believe the end was coming next week."

"So what are we supposed do?" Gwen said. "We can't monitor such changes from here. Such things are better done from space."

Perry started to answer when Griffin leapt to his feet. "Wait a second." He glanced around the room, looking each person in the eye. "You can't be serious."

"Sit down, Griffin," Gwen said. "He hasn't said what we'll be doing."

"Don't be dense, Sis. Think." He pointed around the room. "Military specialist, construction experts, and—this is the real giveaway—a robotics expert." He spun to face Perry. "You're planning to puncture the ice sheet. You want us to help you bore down to the lake."

"That can't be it, Griffin," Gwen said. "That's insane."

Perry said nothing. He stared at the biologist.

"Oh no, you don't," she said. "I. . .I won't allow it. That water is pristine. It hasn't seen the light of day for four hundred thousand years. No one has figured out how to study it without contaminating it."

"I have," Perry said.

"That explains all the specialized equipment you made me bring," Larimore said.

"Wait until you see what's coming next week," Perry remarked.

Gwen was on her feet. "You're not going to do it. I won't let you. We are not going down in history as the ones who contaminated the largest, purest, most undefiled water on the planet." She began to pace. "We've found microbial life forms beneath the ice. Who knows what might be living in the lake or how it has changed over the centuries? The moment you touch that water you could be dooming entire and yet unknown species to extinction."

"Didn't I read somewhere that the Russians bored into Lake Vostok?" Sarah asked.

"No, you didn't," Griffin said. "No one has bored into the lake. The Russians stopped drilling a hundred meters above the lake's surface. To keep the hole from freezing over, the idiots pumped the hole full of Freon and aviation fuel. There are over sixty tons of toxic chemicals hovering over the lake. We don't need to repeat their error."

"We're not going to repeat anyone's error," Perry said. "The environmental considerations have been factored in. One reason you were chosen for this mission was your well-known commitment to keeping Antarctica clean."

"It's already been defiled." Griffin's expression hardened. "What you're suggesting is sheer hubris. I don't plan on participating."

"That goes for me, too," Gwen said.

Perry paused, then said, "I assure you that we will not contaminate the lake, but understand this: We are going beneath the ice. You can help us, or you can leave on the plane. But you have less than an hour to make up your mind."

He watched them for a moment. He had feared the twin scientists would respond this way. What really bothered him, however, was the way they might respond when they heard the rest of the story.

CHAPTER 2

Perry's head pounded as if a spiked ball were bouncing around inside his skull. He stepped into the camp's central building. Jack had dubbed the place Dome Sweet Dome, but everyone else called it the Dome. He paused long enough to peel back his parka hood and remove the dark goggles that protected his eyes from the cold, wind, and ultraviolet light. He bent forward, rested his hands on his knees, and took several long, deep breaths.

"I bet you thought you were in shape," Jack said. He sat with Gleason, three of the Sachs crew, and three of the Seabees.

"This working at altitude is killing me," Perry confessed. "I feel like a man with one lung running a marathon—uphill."

"Should I tell you what you look like?" Jack quipped.

"No need," Perry said, then took several more deep inhalations. "I've seen you after your thirty-minute shift." He stripped off his parka then walked to an empty wood chair and plopped down.

Jack snickered.

"Your team is up, chuckles," Perry said. "We'll talk about pain when you get back."

Jack rose as did the others in the commons.

Perry watched Jack slip on his cold weather gear. Jack paused, then said, "Seriously, buddy, are you okay? Some people have problems with elevation. One of the navy boys is down with altitude sickness. Gwen ordered him to bed and put him on O-two."

"I'm fine—just a headache and shortness of breath. I'm adjusting. Another day and I'll be playing soccer on the ice." Perry looked up at his friend and saw concerned eyes studying him. "I'm fine, Jack. Just go out and see if you can match what my team did."

"Match? We're holding back so you boys will have something to do. We wouldn't want you to feel left out. Gleason is sitting this shift out. He has some reading to do."

"No, I don't," Gleason shot back. "No one's going to accuse me of not carrying my own weight. . . ." He trailed off, catching Jack's intent. "Of course, there is that report—"

"Knock it off," Perry ordered. "I don't need a nursemaid. Now, get out there and get to work. The sooner the Chamber is up, the sooner we can get down to business."

Jack hesitated then nodded. A moment later, he led Gleason and the others out into the icy wind.

For a few moments, Perry was alone in the wide, concave room. He leaned his head back and stared at the dome overhead. The ribbing of the geodesic structure made Perry feel as if he had been swallowed whole by a massive, ancient creature. Light fixtures had been screwed into supports, their electrical cords tied into place by nylon straps. The light in the room was stark and uninviting. He reminded himself that this place was home for the next few weeks.

He had been many places in the world, but this was by far the strangest. Outside, bits of ice flew on a bed of rising wind—wind that bit the face and froze every exhalation. Ice everywhere, yet, technically, Antarctica was the driest place on earth. Very little precipitation fell at the bottom of the world, but when it did, it remained as crystals of frozen water. The image of the vast ice sheet filled his mind. He had seen it in pictures, studied satellite photos. . . . The starkness was almost frightening; the white reflection almost painful. Cobalt blue sky bowed overhead touching the ice softly on the horizon. It was beautiful but ominous.

"Are you drinking water?" a voice asked.

Perry raised his aching head and saw Gwen James seating herself on a nearby bench. The modular bench, like all the furnishings, had been flown in when the Dome and associated barracks were set up. Almost everything was assembled on-site, everything but the building he was now in. It had been airlifted by massive Sikorsky helicopters and set in place as a single unit. The cargo-crate dormitories had arrived in the same way. Very little assembly was required. Griffin James had overseen the installation, but Sachs Engineering employees did the work. The assembly team left three days prior to Perry's arrival. Perry had made sure a bonus check was waiting for each man upon his return to the States.

"Yeah, I keep pouring it down," Perry replied.

"It's one of the best ways to battle altitude sickness. You should be drinking three or four quarts per day. And your urine output should be copious and clear."

"I don't talk about urine output until the second date," Perry said, smiling. "I'm fine, but thanks for the concern."

Gwen and Griffin, despite their objections to the project, had decided to stay. Perry was glad. It would have been difficult to replace them on such short notice.

"The work is going okay?"

Perry nodded. It made his head hurt more. "It's grueling, but the Seabees are tough, and my men are used to adverse conditions. The Chamber should be finished soon—two or three days more, if the wind doesn't get worse."

"I'll confess to being impressed," Gwen said, pushing back a strand of dark hair. "It's a big structure, and a handful of men are piecing it together in less than a week."

"That's the advantage of modular construction. All we have to do is match part *A* to part *B* and—voila!—instant dome. Well, almost instant. Besides they've built this before."

"They have?"

"Three times. We did it as practice. Three teams working in thirty-minute shifts. It's almost second nature to them."

"Including the cold?"

Perry sat up and rubbed his eyes. "No, not the cold. That was one thing we couldn't duplicate. If we had had time, if we weren't racing the onset of Antarctic winter, we might have trained on-site at altitude and in the cold. I did make them wear gloves while working so they could get used to handling the tools. They hated it."

"I bet no one is complaining now."

Perry laughed. "If they are, I haven't heard it."

"You never will. The men respect you. That's easy enough to see. I doubt they'd dare disappoint you."

"They're good men, every one of them."

The conversation lulled, then Gwen said, "I suppose I should apologize for my behavior, and for my brother's. We're. . .passionate about our science."

"No apology needed," Perry said. "You expressed your opinion, and it was heard. We need you here. I'm just sorry we didn't get off to a good start."

"It doesn't matter now. Time can't be unwound."

"Where is Dr. James?"

"In his quarters, reviewing what little information we have on this area. He's opinionated, gruff, and often rude, but he is also brilliant."

"He just needs to know that we are not the bad guys. We're cautious, and we're good. Things will be done right."

"I hope so. You may be destroying something very nearly perfect. Did you know, Mr. Sachs—"

"Please, call me Perry. I would be much more comfortable."

"Very well. Perry, did you know that pollution has found its way down here? We're only a few hundred kilometers from the South Pole, yet we can find traces of human pollution. The largest creature native to Antarctica is a fly, the wingless midge, which grows to only twelve millimeters—less than half an inch. Beyond that, there are microscopic animals such as nematodes and tardigrades, but that's it. A great deal of life comes to Antarctica—penguins and sea lions, for instance—but they are not native to the land."

"I do know that," Perry replied. "We've made it a priority to leave this area as clean as we found it. All waste is collected and packaged for removal. Even the buildings will be removed. I can promise you we won't leave a single candy wrapper behind."

Gwen studied Perry. He felt as if the biologist had put him under a microscope. "You haven't told us everything, have you?"

"What do you mean?" Perry asked.

"Scientists are observers by nature. We are fascinated by the details. I've been watching you. I think you know more than you're telling."

Perry matched her gaze, his mind spinning with possible answers. He settled on the simplest. "I do know more than I'm telling."

Gwen's eyes widened. "I'm surprised you would just admit it."

"My only other choice is to lie to you. I'm not comfortable with that."

"A man of morals? You're a rare breed."

"Not really. There are more of us than you think." Perry closed his eyes and tried to push the headache to a back corner of his skull.

"What aren't you telling us?" A new voice.

Perry opened his eyes to see Griffin standing a short distance away. "In good time, Dr. James. In good time."

"Why not now?"

Perry sat up. The last thing he wanted was another confrontation with Griffin. "Let me ask you something. How much do you talk about your research, especially your findings?"

"That's different. Science is very competitive, and it's not unprecedented for research to be stolen. A good scientist is a cautious scientist."

"You're right. It is different, but not entirely. I have reasons for withholding information. Believe it or not, it's for your own good."

"Ignorance is never good," Griffin said.

"That's where you are wrong, friend," Perry said, standing. "Sometimes ignorance is bliss." He started for his room then stopped. "This may not come easy for you, Dr. James, but you're going to have to trust me."

Eric Enkian gazed into the cerulean sky, where the late spring sun hung like an enormous heat lamp, baking everything it touched. Las Vegas was hot. It was always hot, and the temperatures would continue to rise with each passing day. He removed his hardhat and wiped his brow. Frowning, he turned back to the thin man in the gray suit and white dress shirt. A white hardhat rested on his narrow head. He wondered why a man would wear a suit to a job site so exposed to the hot sun but decided he didn't care enough to pursue an answer. Architects were a breed unto themselves.

"I know this may sound like heresy to a man such as yourself," the architect said, "but using synthetic stone will speed construction and save you a great deal more than pocket change."

Eric forgot the sun for a moment and looked deep into the man's eyes. They were weak eyes—eyes that went with a weak body. His mind was his only redeeming factor. Stewart Teller was the finest and most sought after architect in the western United States. His high-rise buildings were as innovative as they were beautiful. It was this skill that forced Eric to tolerate the man.

"You see," Stewart went on, "the synthetic stones are designed with ribbing on the back and interlocking channels to make installation easier. They're virtually indistinguishable from the real thing. So the building will be just as beautiful but will go up faster and for less money."

Unlike the architect, Eric wore comfortable slacks, a yellow T-shirt, and expensive sneakers. He hated suits and generally hated those who wore them. At six-feet-four, Eric towered over the shorter man. His well-muscled frame and square jaw made both men and women take a second glance—the former with envy, the latter with lust. He was closing in on sixty, but a meticulous diet and rigorous exercise left him looking a decade younger.

Turning from the expensive architect, he focused his attention on the metal skeleton that stretched for the blistering sky. Steel girders spanned the distance between their vertical counterparts, forming an imposing matrix that towered thirty-three stories above the bustling Vegas boulevard. There were two towers of equal height—sixty-six floors altogether.

Always sixty-six.

Workmen moved at an even pace around the building like ants on a discarded watermelon rind. They worked with purpose and steady determination. Eric liked that. It was the way things should be. Purpose. Determination. Production. The ancients knew the formula and had built structures that boggled the twenty-first century mind.

"I know that mining is your business, Mr. Enkian," Stewart said, "so naturally you'd have a predilection for natural stone, but we can achieve our goals faster and more economically with this slight change. I'm sure you see my point. Perhaps we can use some stone from one of your mines on the interior. In fact, I have some art ideas—"

"Stone," Eric said. "I'll provide the stone."

"Um, that's not my point, sir. I'm saying that synthetic stone panels would allow us to move ahead of schedule and provide a structural enhancement that would benefit—"

Enkian stopped and turned dark eyes on the man. "Stone. My stone. You tell me the dimensions, the needed density, the ideal porosity, and whatever else you think is important, and I will find it and provide it. But the exterior will be natural stone—taken from ground I own."

"I have no doubt that you can provide the very best, Mr. Enkian. I mean, a man with as many and as varied mining interests as you have around the world can certainly bring beautiful material to the project, but it will slow things down."

"Stone is more than decoration, Mr. Teller. It is the heart of our planet, and it will be the skin of my new building. Is that clear?" Enkian watched the man squirm then acquiesce.

"I'll have the structural dimensions and requirements sent to your—to which office should I send it?"

"I leave today for Mexico City. Send it electronically."

Stewart said he would see to it. "It's going to be a grand building, Mr. Enkian. Photos of the EA Mining towers will grace all the architecture magazines around the world. It will make you famous."

"I care nothing about fame. I am not so shallow. This building is a response to my growing mining concerns in Nevada, nothing more." Again, Enkian studied the metal skeleton. EA Mining had a dozen such buildings around the globe, each one designed by the best architects and engineers, each one a testament to the mining empire he headed. In Nevada he pulled gold, copper, tungsten, barite, and gypsum from the ground. In other countries, he scooped out coal, gravel, platinum, uranium, and even diamonds. Marble was sliced away in quarries and iron hauled to the surface. Not even the sea floor was safe. Enkian had helped design a process of manganese nodule mining that was cost-effective, making EA Mining one of the first companies to harvest the ocean floor profitably.

For decades EA Mining had been one of the most successful mining operations in the world; now it was second to none. That gave Enkian a large measure of pride. It also made him one of the richest men on the planet. His name appeared annually in *Forbes* magazine's list of the world's richest people. Their estimate of his wealth was only 10 percent correct.

Noise from the workers snapped Enkian back to the moment. Whistles and catcalls joined the sounds of hammering, humming heavy equipment, and the crackle of welding. He turned to see what he had expected. His assistant, Tia Matteo, was walking toward him.

Tia was younger than Enkian by a decade and a half, slim and tall with black hair that reached her belt line. She moved with the grace of a dancer and the power of an athlete. Her jawline was smooth and met in a delicate curve at her chin. Her blue eyes broadcast her intelligence and a delicate nose graced her face. Enkian knew she could cause more whiplashes by walking down the street than a fifty-car pileup on the freeway. It humored him to watch how men responded to Tia. *If they only knew,* he thought.

"Hey baby, why don'tcha bring some o' dat over here?" one of the workers called. Enkian recognized him as one of the foremen. Laughter and more wolf whistles followed.

"I'm sorry, Mr. Enkian," Stewart said. "I'll put an end to this right now."

Enkian raised a hand stopping the man midstep. "Wait."

"But. . ."

"I said, *wait.*"

"Don't walk by, sweetheart," the foreman said. "I got what ya want right here."

Enkian watched as Tia stopped and turned toward the man. She flashed a smile that made the sun dim, then walked over to the worker.

"Look out, guys!" someone yelled. "He's reeling her in." Laughter floated in the hot air.

Tia stepped to the man and leaned over to whisper in his ear. "That's it, sweetheart, tell Daddy what you want."

She did.

Enkian could not hear what his assistant had said, but he didn't need to. Whatever words she uttered drained the blood from the foreman's face. Tia turned and resumed her course.

"Hey, boss," a welder called out. "Did she give you any good ideas?"

The foreman didn't respond immediately. He stood as still as the steel columns behind him.

"Come on, boss, share with the rest of us."

"Shut up! Get back to work. The next guy who talks will be drawing unemployment." The foreman walked away, his face red, his head down. Slowly, stunned workers returned to their jobs.

Enkian smiled as Tia approached. They exchanged knowing glances. Again, she leaned forward and whispered, this time in Enkian's ear. He nodded, then asked, "Everyone? You're certain?"

"Yes," was all she said.

Enkian smiled. "Good. Very good."

She raised her hand to adjust the hardhat she wore. Despite having seen it many times, Enkian couldn't help noticing the tattoo on the back of Tia's right hand. He stared at it. The dragon seemed to stare back.

Enkian turned to Stewart. "That foreman. Have him fired."

"He doesn't work for me, Mr. Enkian. He works for the general contractor."

"Then have the general contractor fire him. Fire the construction company if you have to. That man is not to set foot on this site again."

CHAPTER 3

It had taken four days for the small group of Seabees and Perry's crew of six to erect the dome that would house their activities. Unlike the dome that had been set up the week before, this one contained only two rooms: the four-thousand-square-foot work area and a bathroom.

Perry, Jack, and Gleason had designed the structure from scratch. In some ways, it was one of the most challenging designs Perry had ever faced. When first presented with the difficulties of working in Antarctica, Perry assumed warmth and protection from the wind and ultraviolet light would be the most important considerations. He had been wrong. The more he learned of Lake Vostok and the need to keep it uncontaminated, the more he realized sterility was the most difficult job before him. He had requested and received consultations from scientists working for the Centers for Disease Control in Atlanta as well as microbiologists throughout the country.

The number of bacteria, viruses, and microbes associated with the human body surprised him. Simple exhalation could be an ecological contaminant in a pure environment such as that found under two miles of ice. Microscopic creatures lived on the skin, in hair, mucus, saliva, and under fingernails and toenails. A simple cough could have unforeseen consequences.

The reverse was also a problem. No one knew what might be living in the lake beneath the ice. For all he and the experts knew, the lake could harbor a virulent and deadly strain of bug that could kill them all, though few thought that likely. Infectious disease had a complicated host-disease cycle, something not likely to be found in the ice-capped lake. Still, the idea couldn't be dismissed.

Perry stood in the center of the dome and waited for the last of the team to enter. This was a practice run. To keep the Chamber as free of human contaminants as possible, each worker had to enter a "suiting" cubicle and don a "clean" suit and respirator that filtered all exhalations. A negative-pressure locker prevented air exchange between the Chamber and the "normal" facility.

Jack was the last person through the locker. "Sorry to keep everyone waiting. I couldn't decide what kind of tie to wear."

Perry smiled through the full-face shield that rested in the hood of his clean suit and looked over the others. Each wore a metallic silver suit with an antiglare face mask.

"You look marvelous," Gleason joked. "Personally, I would have preferred something in blue."

"Are they always like this?" Larimore asked Perry.

"You have no idea," Perry replied. "If I can have everyone's attention, please." A short-range transmitter carried his voice to the others. "Welcome to the Chamber. We will be spending a great many hours in here. We'll consider this a clean room. We're meeting in here so that each of us can practice donning our suits and passing through the various locks designed to keep the air uncontaminated."

"A noble effort, Mr. Sachs," Griffin said. "But what of the structure itself? Was it decontaminated before it was erected?"

"It was, Dr. James," Perry said. Griffin's attitude had settled into forced civility. Perry was thankful for that. "There are two domes overhead. One, as you saw from the outside, is made of translucent paneling. It will allow sunlight to pass through, warming the inner, second dome. External mechanical equipment keeps the air temperature a few degrees below freezing."

"So the ice doesn't melt," Sarah said.

"Exactly," Perry said. "We don't want to be sloshing around in here, but we want it warm enough that we don't have to wear thick, heavy clothing. Your suits come equipped with small electric heaters. You won't roast, but you will be able to maintain an in-suit temperature above fifty. Warm clothing should handle the rest."

"What are those doors?" Griffin asked, pointing a silver-gloved hand toward the far west wall.

"Equipment air locks," Perry said. "The air lock system you came through connects the Dome with the Chamber, but it's too small to admit larger supplies. Those doors lead to a larger area, where equipment can be assembled or disassembled as needed."

"How high is the ceiling?" Griffin asked.

Perry knew where he was going. "Twenty-five feet. You're wondering how we're going to drill with a low ceiling overhead."

"You have over two miles of ice to drill through," Griffin said. "Unless you have some engineering magic up your sleeve. . ."

"I don't, but Sarah does."

All eyes turned to Sarah Hardy. Perry saw her smile through the large faceplate.

This was Sarah's big moment, and she was flooded with apprehension and excitement. A quiet woman, she preferred solitude to gatherings. Now she was the center of attention, not of a party's guests, but of several brilliant men and women. She blinked in disbelief. To think that she, a fifty-hours-a-week lab rat, was standing on an ice sheet at the bottom of the world, garbed in a clean suit was almost too much for her to take in.

She saw Perry through the plastic face shield; he was smiling. Her heart skipped, and she felt a sudden wave of embarrassment. She forced herself to focus.

"Well, as you know," she began, "my specialty is robotics. Over the last few years, I've served as chief engineer on an ambitious NASA mission. One of NASA's directives is to learn if there is life on other planets. Not little green men, but microbial life. Earth is the only planet that has life, so far as we know. However, there are some interesting possibilities fairly nearby."

"I assume you're talking about Europa," Gwen said.

"Exactly. Europa is a moon of Jupiter and is roughly the size of our own moon. It's one of the ten largest satellites in the solar system. What makes it interesting is that its surface is covered in ice—water ice. We think that three miles beneath the surface is slushy ocean, maybe sixty miles deep."

"Sixty miles!" Larimore exclaimed. "Our ocean is. . .what?"

"About three miles deep on average," Griffin said. "There are areas a mile or so deeper, but nothing like sixty miles."

"Exobiologists think Europa is a likely place to find microscopic life," Sarah added.

"Isn't Europa too far from the sun?" Gleason asked. "Doesn't life have to have some heat?"

"Yes, it does," Sarah said, "but as Gwen can tell you, some microscopic life can thrive in unimaginable conditions. They're called extremophiles and have been found in everything from boiling water to ice."

"Including the ice beneath our feet," Gwen added.

"Europa is warmed from the inside—thanks to Jupiter, whose gravity pulls at it constantly. Europa orbits Jupiter every three and a half days. It is bathed in radiation from the planet and subject to extreme tidal forces. The end result is that the moon has a warm core that heats the water under its surface. My job was to help design a device that could travel through space, land on Europa, and bore through three miles of ice, while all the time sending back data. It's called a cryobot."

"I didn't think that program would be available for years," Gwen said.

"We have an advantage," Sarah explained. "We don't have to travel 380 million miles to do our job. We can control everything from right here."

"You plan to send a robot down through the ice?" Griffin said, his disgust apparent. "I don't know how to make this any plainer. The waters of Lake Vostok have not seen the light of day for millennia. It has been sealed off from external contact. It is unspoiled, but you want to change all of that by dropping a mechanical device into the waters. That is the height of stupidity."

"Griffin—" Perry began.

"Listen, you pompous pig," Sarah countered. "You're not the only one concerned with such things. At NASA our greatest fear was introducing an organism into the environment of Europa. We want to know what's there, not deliver something. Hairy is cleaner than an operating room."

"But there is always the chance of leaving behind oil or some other substance," Griffin said. "We are talking about a machine."

"It's been thought through," Sarah said. "My life is invested in this thing. I haven't overlooked a single detail."

"Wait a minute," Jack interjected. "Did you call the thing *Hairy?*"

"Yes," Sarah said. Her embarrassment was detectable even over the speakers in Perry's suit. "It's a nickname. . .sort of."

"Doesn't sound too sterile to me," Griffin chided.

Sarah exhaled loudly then said, "A short article in the April 1995 issue of *Discover* magazine described hairless ice moles that could melt ice with their heads. The article said they were discovered by researcher Aprile Pazzo. Her name is Italian for April Fools'. It was a joke, but it caught on and appeared in other publications. Some called them 'naked hotheaded ice borers.' The hotheaded part stuck in my mind."

"So you call your cryobot Hairy," Gleason said. "Well, it does roll off the tongue a little easier."

"When do we get to see this hairless ice-boring mole of yours?" Griffin asked.

"No time like the present," Perry said. "Give me a hand, Jack."

It took only ten minutes to cross the Chamber and open a plastic box that had been set near the equipment door. Perry and Jack pulled tools from a sealed plastic pouch and removed the metal bolts that locked down the lid of the container. Once the top was removed, the sides folded down like a flower opening to the sun. Perry pulled back plastic sheets to reveal a torpedolike device resting on a curved stand.

Hairy was six feet long and wide enough to hold a man. The front of the cylinder sported a shining copper cap. The rest of the device was bright orange.

"You were going to send that to Europa?" Larimore asked.

Sarah laughed. "No. The space-traveling version is much smaller. I was told that we needed a big hole, so I brought this pup."

"Why a big hole?" Griffin asked.

"I'll hold that answer until later, Dr. James," Perry said. "Just know that I'm the one who asked for it."

"Figures. More secrets," Griffin snapped.

"You don't get it, do you?" Larimore said to Griffin. "This is going to happen whether you like it or not."

"I may not be in the U.S., but I still have the right to express myself." Griffin turned to Perry. "How are we supposed to contribute when you keep so many secrets?"

"Trust," Perry said, knowing that it would do nothing to alleviate Griffin's suspicion. "Soon you'll know everything, but not now." He paused and looked at his team. They were an odd mix, and he was asking them to trust someone they'd never met to do something that had never been done. Perry couldn't blame the man. The truth was, he was having trouble trusting Griffin.

"How does it move?" Gwen asked, filling the sudden silence.

"Gravity," Sarah answered. "There is no motorized drive for the descent. It is, however, equipped with various sensors and water jets for maneuverability."

"Camera?" Gleason asked.

"Several," Sarah replied. "Real-time video and digital stills. We control everything by cable and joysticks."

"Do you have any experience doing that?" Griffin pressed.

"Yes. I've controlled this unit and others like it in a pool and in open sea. I also practice with a computer program that throws variables into the formula. It keeps me on my toes. It's very much like a video game."

"I've never played a video game," Griffin said. "Waste of time if you ask me."

"That explains a lot," Larimore said.

"Enough bickering, gentlemen," Perry ordered. He started to speak again when a rumble vibrated the Chamber's dome. Powerful propellers thrummed the air, shaking the arched structure. Perry grinned. "Last plane in and out, folks. Let's go see what Santa has brought."

CHAPTER 4

Perry pulled on his parka, slipped on his shaded goggles, cinched his hood around his head, and stepped out of the protective dome onto the dim, cold, eerie ice. He rounded the Chamber in time to see the same C-5 aircraft that had chauffeured them to the barren ice taxi to a stop.

"The limo's here," Jack said. "Do you suppose anyone thought to bring pizza?"

"More gear and supplies," Perry replied. "Oh, and one other important addition."

Larimore's Seabees and Perry's work crew trotted out to the mammoth plane as its tail ramp descended. They disappeared up the ramp in a line. They waited for no orders. They knew the task before them. Perry marveled at the crew's dedication.

As the propellers slowed, a stepped ramp lowered, and a man emerged. He wore a bright blue parka and the same cold-weather garb that hung from Perry's frame, but unlike Perry, this man was short and round. He waddled down the stairs, awkwardly creating a drama with each step.

"That kinda looks like. . . ," Jack began. "You're kidding."

"No humor here, buddy," Perry said. "And I don't think Dr. Curtis will find any joy in this." Dr. Kenneth Curtis packed 250 pounds in a five-foot-nine-inch body. He moved slowly but always with purpose. While his rotund shape and balding head might have kept him from appearing on the cover of a fitness magazine, his mind had earned him several mentions in scientific literature.

Perry walked toward his friend, a wide smile on his face. Jack and Gleason followed. Dr. Curtis wore no smile. "Welcome, Professor," Perry said. "Glad you could make it."

Curtis huffed. "There is now a standing order at my house. 'If a man named Perry Sachs calls, I'm not in.'"

"But then your life would be dull," Perry said. "You'd spend all your time in a safe Boston classroom teaching fresh-faced students who don't appreciate your true genius."

"Smack-dab in the middle of nowhere and he's still trying to play me like a violin," Dr. Curtis grumbled. "You may have killed me this time, Perry. I can't breathe, my head hurts, and I'm losing all sensation in my extremities."

"Just like the rest of us," Jack interjected. "It's not that bad, Doc. It's just like Boston."

Perry watched Curtis raise his head and narrow his eyes. "Boston has a symphony. Does this place have a symphony. . .or a library. . .or a decent restaurant?"

"How about a transistor radio, Gleason's comics collection, and a can of sardines?" Jack laughed at his own wit.

"It's a good thing I like you boys," Curtis said, "or there would be real trouble." He winked at Perry.

Despite his bluster, Perry knew Curtis to be kind, thoughtful, and deeply spiritual. But he did love to complain. "I assume it's warmer inside than outside." He nodded at the Dome.

"A little," Perry said. "The dome on your right is called, well, the Dome. The square buildings are dormitories, storage, and the like. The larger dome on the left has been dubbed the Chamber. That's where the work goes on."

"Let me guess," Curtis said. "Jack named the buildings."

"It's a hobby," Jack said.

Curtis shook his head. "For a big man, you have a tiny imagination. Let's go." Curtis took several quick steps.

Perry looked at Jack. "Same old Professor Curtis. You gotta love him."

"I can't wait until he and Dr. James butt heads. That'll be worth the price of popcorn."

Perry jogged a few steps until he caught up to Curtis. "I appreciate your coming down."

"An archeologist in the heart of Antarctica!" Curtis said. "Makes no sense—it makes no sense at all!"

"Then you why did you come?" Perry prodded.

"Because, Perry, in your hands, the absurd somehow becomes real. I don't want to miss that."

Enkian strode into the conference room, pushing aside custom-made teak doors. Tia was a single step behind. His entrance caused the three men and one woman sitting at the conference table to bolt to their feet. Enkian ignored them, marching to the glass wall that looked over the cityscape of Mexico City. The sun was setting, blazing bright orange as its light struggled through some of the worst smog seen on the planet. It was foul air made fouler by the repeated belching of the volcano Popocatepetl just a few miles away. It was rumbling more these days, spewing gas on a daily basis and occasionally ejecting ash into the already polluted air. To some, it was a seventeen-thousand-foot eyesore with a two-thousand-foot wide crater at its peak. To Enkian, it was the power of the earth. The sky grew darker and the air thicker. Seventeen million people lived in the city, most so poor they were incapable of dreaming of the kind of wealth and power Enkian wielded.

Lights from the city stabbed at the encroaching darkness, but the darkness could not be dissuaded. It had come to do what it did every day—cover the city in blackness. Mexico City was a modern city—the capital of the country and its cultural heart. Its influence dominated the land. Seven centuries before, Enkian thought, the city had worn a different name, and its citizens could not trace their lineage back to Spain.

Tenochtitlán, its name the better part of a millennium ago, sat upon an island in Lake Texcoco. Here the Aztecs found their administrative and military strength, an influence felt far into Central America. Temples and pyramids of stone, gleaming white and red in the hot sun, dominated the city.

The city was divided among the *calpulli,* and these clans held sway until Hernándo Cortés lowered an iron fist upon it. Eighty-five days later, Tenochtitlán had fallen. War, conquest, and a series of epidemics from European diseases gutted the city of its 200,000 inhabitants, leaving only 30,000. Now a great city spread out before him, but despite its size, it was a pale thing in comparison.

Enkian turned his attention from the window to the spacious room. Dominating the area was a conference table made of Pentelic marble. From a chemical point of view, the material was nothing more than compressed limestone, but in the hands of an artist it was so much more. Phidias had secured his place in history because of what his hands could do with marble. Enkian touched its smooth, polished surface and felt its coolness creep up his fingers. This white stone had been quarried from the Penteli mountains north of Athens. He had chosen the piece himself and followed every detail of its removal, polishing, and sculpting.

He caressed the table again. To others it was lifeless, albeit beautiful, stone. To Enkian it was more alive than those who stood around its perimeter.

"Sit down," he said, while he remained standing. Tia sat at his right hand. She carried nothing in her hands, yet he knew that she would recall every word spoken. "What do we know?"

"If I may, sir," a man said. He was rail-thin and wore tight-fitting wire-rimmed glasses that rested on a beaklike nose. Enkian nodded at Jeffrey Tottle, vice president of EA Mining's European offices. The others around the table held similar positions. Caesar Rivadavia handled South America; Rich Aldington oversaw all operations in Australia and New Zealand; Jean Sedlar reigned over work in Asia and Indonesia.

Tottle rose, producing a remote control from his pocket. He pressed a button and the wall to Enkian's left parted, revealing six large plasma monitors. Each shone with EA Mining's logo, a three-row, six-block stepped pyramid. Above the pyramid's pinnacle was a sunburst, as if heaven were spilling through a gash in the sky. A button-push later, the first screen filled with the image of a hand-some dark-haired man.

"Perry Sachs," Tottle said crisply. "Senior vice president and project manager for his father's firm, Sachs Engineering."

"I know the firm," Enkian said without emotion.

"Yes, we used them in South Africa when we encountered a touchy digging problem in one of our chrome-ore extraction centers. They redesigned one of our automated diggers. They're resourceful." Tottle returned his attention to the screen. "Perry Sachs is a bit of an adventurer. Not the careless type, but he can't resist a good mystery. This is well-known among military types. Sachs Engineering does a great deal of secret work for the U.S. military and a few U.S.-friendly countries. The company has deep pockets. Although not as wealthy as our. . .as your company, Mr. Enkian, they have a brain trust that rivals our own. They are formidable."

"Go on," Enkian said. Tottle was a superior businessman and a loyal follower, but he did tend to ramble.

"Our investigators have learned that Sachs is leading a team of experts in some effort in Antarctica." Pictures of people began to appear on the screens: two women, five men. "These are the core operatives. They know what we know, that Lake Vostok is growing."

"As the prophecy said it would," Enkian said.

"Precisely." Tottle advanced the images. "There's an interesting mix of skills present at the site. Sachs, his partners John Dyson—he goes by Jack—and Gleason Archer are all MIT trained. Also present are Dr. Griffin James, a glaciologist; his sister Gwen James, a biologist specializing in extreme bioforms; and Sarah Hardy from NASA."

"NASA?" Enkian said.

"Robotics expert." Tottle pushed the button again, and a map of Antarctica appeared. He zoomed in on the Lake Vostok area.

Enkian leaned forward. He saw something special. It was a photorealistic map, but it showed only white ice. In his mind, though, Enkian could see through the ice. It was there. It had to be. Why else would such an eclectic band of explorers be sent to such an inhospitable spot?

"They have been easy to track, but hearing them has been difficult. They encrypt all E-mail and maintain nonspecific radio communications. Still, we can assume—"

"They're going under the ice," Enkian said.

"Yes, sir. Of course, that is a slow process, so we have some time."

"No, we don't," Enkian said. "We have no time to waste."

"It took the Russians months to core as deeply as they did."

"Sarah Hardy," Enkian interjected. "She tells us what we need to know. They're not coring. They're sending a drone through the ice. It's an ingenious idea, but they must not succeed in my absence. Does everyone understand that?"

Heads nodded, accompanied by general assent.

Enkian fell silent, and the enormity of his thoughts weighed on him like the world on Atlas's shoulders. "The time has come. We are the blessed. Generation upon generation of our forefathers has kept the faith, the dream alive. You received it from your fathers as I received it from mine, and he from his before. But now—" his voice choked—"now the time is here. We are the chosen. We are the six—

six of the sixty-six. Nothing will ever be the same. We will see to that. The prophecy."

"The prophecy," they repeated in unison.

"The prophecy."

"The prophecy."

He turned to Tia. "We have operatives in place?"

"They have begun their work."

"You have reports from them?"

She shook her head, her long black hair shuddering down her shoulders. "No."

"We've lost contact with them? Compromised?"

"No," she said. "They've been busy."

Enkian nodded, then smiled. Rising, he tilted his head back and raised his arms. He could hear the chairs sliding back from the marble table as the others joined him. He began to sway like wheat in a gentle breeze. He began to hum. The other joined him until the room sounded like a hive of colossal bees. Then Enkian spoke, his eyes closed so tightly that flashes of light danced in his vision.

"Most honored are you above all the gods. Your decree is unmatched by men and gods. You, Marduk, are the most honored of all gods. Your decrees are unquestionable. For now and forever, your declarations are unchangeable. No one from the gods can transgress your boundaries. Marduk, you are our avenger. You are our avenger. Our avenger. Avenger."

CHAPTER 5

Sarah could not enter her room without feeling entombed. The space served as her bedroom and private office, but it was the size of a small hall bath. The builders had placed a cot to one side, and a three-foot-wide desk—little more than a flat surface on folding legs—sat next to the curved surface that formed the wall and ceiling of the Dome. A folding wooden chair was the only other piece of furniture. "I've seen larger graves," she had joked when Dr. James had shown her the cubicle that would be her home for the next few weeks. The sight of it gave her a chill that had nothing to do with the cold beyond the curved wall.

Living near the South Pole was a challenge—she had expected that, but expectations seldom measure up to reality. She spent as little time in the room as possible, preferring to sit in the larger shared area everyone called the Commons. There was one thing to be thankful for: She had a room to herself. The military workers and Sachs employees shared a dormitory space with bunks hastily made from two-by-fours.

It wasn't just the diminutive room that bothered her; it was the confinement. Back in her normal life she had an office and work area in the Jet Propulsion Laboratory in Pasadena, California. There she could come and go as she pleased. Often she walked the tree-lined street in front of her ranch-style home, gazing at the stars that could still fascinate her. Here, she could move from room to room, building to building, but time outside was limited—especially when the wind blew. It blew a lot, roaring, squealing past, separated from her only by the wall of the Dome.

She was beginning to feel claustrophobic.

"This is nuts," she said to herself as she pushed the POWER button on her laptop, which whirred to life. There were other taxing conditions. Water was available by the acre, but it was in the form of ice. The energy necessary to convert it to liquid then warm it enough so it wouldn't freeze tender skin was costly. As a result, showers were to be taken in two minutes or less. Two minutes! That wasn't enough time to get wet as far as Sarah was concerned.

The computer finished its warm-up, loading all the necessary programs. Sarah moved the mouse and clicked on an icon. A new program loaded, filling the screen with the JPL logo and the words CRYOBOT SIMULATIONS 2.3. She pulled two joysticks from the table and set them on either side of the computer. Sarah reminded herself that she was not playing a video game but training for a mission. In a few days, she would be seated at a table in the Dome, guiding the large cryobot through the ice and into a lake that no one had ever seen.

She would be at the controls, performing every move under the scrutiny of several pairs of exacting, demanding eyes. Millions of dollars of equipment and thousands of hours of work rested in her ability to manipulate the joysticks just the right way. "No pressure," she muttered.

As she thought about the watchful eyes, one pair of eyes pushed to the forefront, eyes that gleamed with intelligence and sparkled with kindness; eyes that revealed a no-nonsense attitude but were still quick to laugh. Dark eyes made light by something she had not been able to identify.

Sarah worked with the brightest minds in the world. The JPL

and Caltech were bastions of brilliance. Knowledge, skill, and superior intelligence did not intimidate her. She saw it on a daily basis. But Perry Sachs was somehow different. In some intangible way, he exuded—what? A rare confidence? That was true. A refreshing honesty? Again true, but still not on target. She shook her head. Whatever quality had caught Sarah's attention, its definition remained a few inches out of reach. Whatever it was, it was real and. . .endearing.

The program began to run. The display was similar to a commercial jet's instrument panel except altitude was measured in negative numbers, speed was measured in centimeters per hour, and orientation included displays for vertical as well as horizontal bearings. Other virtual gauges indicated interior and exterior temperatures, "nose" heat—the temperature of the heating element that would melt the ice below Hairy—and a half dozen other instruments. The program was designed to create problems at random. So far, the program had won every contest, something she wasn't willing to admit to the others.

The descent was the easy part of the "flight." Hairy would melt its way down through layers of ice until it punctured the boundary of ice and liquid water. Then the difficult task of controlling the device began. She advanced the program until it was seconds away from breakthrough. That was the hard part, the challenge no one could anticipate. It was where she always failed.

No one knew what to expect. Did Vostok have currents? Surely it did. The temperature difference between surface water and deep, near-thermal water would move the water in a circular fashion, the warmer rising, the colder sinking. But there could be other factors yet unanticipated. It was in the unknown that danger lurked. There was the excitement and the frustration of field science. No matter how well one planned and practiced, the unexpected could blindside the most prepared. She was determined to be ready for anything and everything.

I wonder what kind of preparations Perry's been making? she thought. *There's no doubt he's thorough.* She could tell that just by talking to—

The computer sounded an alarm, and the instruments froze. "What the—" Sarah studied the readings then realized she had let her attention wander and allowed the speed to increase to a rate faster than the winch could handle. She had broken the connection.

Good thing this is just practice, she said to herself as a feeling of embarrassment rose in her. Feeling like a schoolgirl, she was grateful that no one was around to see her blunder. She reset the program. *I need to get Perry out of my mind.*

She reset the computer and wondered if she would ever get it right. Instead of starting the program, she pushed away from the simple desk, rose, and left her monastic cubicle.

I wonder what Perry is doing?

Gwen James stood to one side as Perry, Jack, and several of the workmen struggled to erect the first of two tubular aluminum towers. The tower stood ten feet tall, was triangular, and held in place by four-foot lengths of rebar pounded deep into the ice. She watched the men grunt, struggle, lift, and push until the tower was exactly where they wanted it—a job made more difficult by the clean suits they wore.

Perry was in the middle of it all. She had assumed he would stand off shouting directions from a safe location, but he was clearly a man more comfortable when his own hands were involved in a task.

"I show level on this axis," Gleason said.

"The bubble's in the middle here," Jack added.

"Let's take a look," Perry said, stepping back.

"It looks like a gantry for some kinda rocket," Jack said.

"In a sense, it is," Perry agreed. "Except we're going down and not up." He took several deep breaths, bent over, and placed his hands on his knees. "Growing old isn't for sissies."

Gwen smiled. Perry was far from old and, based on what she had seen over the last two hours, very fit. "How's the head?" she asked.

Some people never adjusted to high altitude. For some, exertion at this altitude and temperature could be fatal. It was one reason she was hanging around. As the camp paramedic, she was responsible for everyone's health—even that of the sometimes exasperating Perry Sachs.

"Not bad," he replied. "The pain is almost gone, but this thin air makes me feel like I've just run a marathon."

"You wouldn't lie to me, would you?" Gwen asked. "Men have this weird sense of bravado."

"I think she just said you were weird, Perry." Jack flashed one of his famous smiles. Gwen could see that the big man was sucking in air by the barrelful.

"She wouldn't be the first," Perry said.

"This is all very sweet," Griffin said. He had been standing a good distance away as if getting too close to physical labor might tarnish him. "But I still don't fully understand. The tower is the support for the cryobot? It doesn't seem strong enough. More to the point, how do you plan to load that thing on a vertical surface? It's huge; it must weigh a ton."

Gwen frowned at her brother. She loved him dearly, but more days than not, he was a serious pain.

"It does weigh a ton," Perry explained. "Hairy is an amplification of a prototype. Sarah's space-bound version is much smaller, but we wanted big, and big requires support. This tower is a secondary guide."

"That doesn't explain how you plan to lift such a heavy and awkward device," Griffin complained.

"That's why the world needs engineers and not just scientists," Jack quipped. "We like heavy and awkward. It makes life interesting."

"If you don't have an answer. . . ," Griffin prodded.

"We have more than an answer," Perry said. "Follow me."

Gwen watched as Perry released his workers for a well-earned break. They had worked in shifts day after day and hand in hand with the Seabees to erect the Chamber, unload equipment, and do work that Gwen's degrees in biology had not equipped her to understand.

"You were eyeing him, weren't you?" The voice came over the comm system in Gwen's hooded suit. She turned to see Sarah standing just behind her.

"How long have you been here?"

"Just a minute. Long enough to note where your gaze was directed."

Gwen returned her attention to the small group of men as they gathered around a large, plastic-wrapped wood crate. "I don't know who you're talking about."

"He's a hunk and a half, isn't he?"

"You mean Mr. Sachs?"

"Yes, I mean Perry. Don't feel bad, I can't get him off my mind either."

Gwen started to object but remained silent. Each protestation that came to mind rang hollow. She felt warmth around her cheeks. "My brother has questions," she said changing the subject.

"Your brother always has questions," Sarah said. "Are they opening the tractor?"

"I don't know. Griffin was asking about what they were going to use to lift the cryobot."

"Oh good," Sarah said with obvious joy. "I've only seen this on paper. Come on." To Gwen's surprise, Sarah took her gloved hand and began to tow her in the direction of the others. They arrived in time to see Perry, Jack, and Gleason prying off the lid of the wood container.

"This was fabricated by the boys at CAT," Perry was saying.

"The company that makes the big tractors?" Griffin inquired.

"Exactly. They've customized things for us before. Our construction needs can be unique. We often rely on the engineering prowess of others. The people at Caterpillar are experts at blending heavy engines with heavy steel."

"I'll check the battery," Gleason said. Sarah watched him move away.

Perry and Jack lowered the sides of the container to reveal an amorphous blob of plastic sheeting that formed a translucent cocoon. "Everything has been sanitized," Perry explained, "even the heavy equipment."

Gwen estimated the covered object to be as long as a car but not as high. She couldn't see it clearly, but she was sure she had never seen anything like it.

Perry began stripping away the sheeting and, with Jack's help, uncovered the mechanical beast.

"Where is Larimore when you need him?" Jack asked.

"His Seabees are loading the plane for its return trip," Perry said. "Division of labor and all that."

As the last sheet of plastic was removed, folded, and set aside, Gwen saw a strange device. It was painted a bright yellow and had a pair of two-foot wide tank treads. Unlike a tank, it had no true top to it. Instead, it was low and flat with its upper surface a scant thirty inches above the ice. Resting on the mechanism lay a tower similar to the one just raised by Perry and the others. Perry had a slight smile on his face. Gwen could see the pride he felt for the device.

"Shall I?" Gleason asked.

"Absolutely. Let's see what this thing can do." Perry stepped back as Gleason removed a box from its holder at the back of the tractor.

Perry looked at Griffin then at Gwen. Smiling, he asked, "Ever been to the Kennedy Space Center in Florida?"

Both said they hadn't.

"You should go," Perry said. "There's a lot to see. When the space shuttle is moved from the V.A.B. to the launch site, it is moved by a device like this, only much, much larger."

"V.A.B?" Gwen asked.

"Vehicle Assemble Building," Sarah said before Perry could reply. "The shuttle is moved to the launch site in a vertical position on the Mobile Launcher Platform."

"Right," Perry said. "It's moved along a special road designed to hold the weight of the shuttle and its transport vehicle. We're moving something much smaller, but we have to do it in a closed environment with little overhead space."

"What do you call this thing?" Griffin wondered. He was frowning.

Jack answered. "After much soul-searching we've dubbed it 'the Crane.'"

"Inventive," Griffin said, shaking his head.

"It has flair, doesn't it?" Jack said. "We could name it after you. How does the Griffin Grappler sound?"

"I think I'll pass on that honor." He turned to leave.

"You don't want to see how it works?" Perry called after him.

"I'll let you boys play with the toys; I've got some real research to do."

He strode away. Even through his face shield, Gwen could see the exasperation on Perry's face.

CHAPTER 6

Perry was exhausted, and his persistent headache was tightening the vise on his brain again. His body protested each movement. He was accustomed to physical labor. His father had made him work various construction sites all through high school. He was as happy driving a nail or operating heavy equipment as he was sitting at a drafting board and, more recently, a computer. He lived with the perpetual dissatisfaction that came with the sense that he was missing something. When sitting in an air-conditioned office, studying construction drawings for a large project, he felt cheated that he could not be in the field making it happen. When he was in the field doing hands-on work, he wondered if he couldn't be more use reworking plans. He was seldom bored.

Ninety minutes before, Gleason had adroitly controlled the crane, moving it through the large space defined by the Chamber dome until he felt sure enough to try a lift. Electronics was Gleason's forte, and Perry let him have full rein.

It was amazing to watch. The flat vehicle scooted smoothly along the ice, its treads leaving tracks in its wake. Perry had watched Gleason raise and lower the mast that would pick up Hairy and position it over the target area. The crane was designed like a mobile derrick with a steel mast hinged to the tractor base. The mast could be cantilevered over the front end of the base. To keep it from tipping while under load, a pair of hydraulic outriggers extended from the center structure. The outriggers had wide metal plates that served as feet and spread the load over a wide area.

Perry knew every inch of the design and the physics behind it, but he still stood in amazement as the ten-foot-long mast bowed like a gentleman until it was parallel with the ice-shrouded surface. Gleason had extended the boom over Hairy then activated a set of iron pinchers that wrapped around the cryobot as gently as a mother hugging her child.

Perry and Jack crawled around on hands and knees checking the boom's grapples. Convinced the cryobot was not in danger, Perry gave the thumbs-up to Gleason, who sent the radio-control signal that would raise the boom. It rose at a pedestrian speed, and Perry had to work to quiet his impatience.

The sound of powerful electronic winches pulling steel cable through tackle at the end of the mast filled the dome. The dome's concave surface amplified the sounds more than Perry expected. The noise of it reverberated in his bones. He could also feel the vibration in the ice. Five minutes later, Hairy was vertical, its nose pointed down. Gleason then guided the tractor to a spot opposite the fixed tower the men had raised earlier. It took several tries, but Gleason positioned it perfectly.

A new noise caught Perry's attention—a noise he felt more than heard. The ice was vibrating in resonance to the sound. Perry knew what it meant, and as if confirmation were needed, Larimore's voice came over the radio in Perry's clean suit: "If you want to say bye-bye to your babies, you better jump to."

Perry acknowledged the message and hustled to the air lock, where he changed into his outdoor gear. Five minutes later he jogged across the white surface to the aircraft that awaited him. He ran up the back ramp and wished each man on his crew a safe journey, thanking them for the sacrifices they had made to make the project a success so far. He then exited and watched with the rest of the team as the loadmaster raised the ramp.

"Did any volunteer to stay?" Jack asked.

Perry laughed. "Not a one. They all looked eager to get back to the home fires, snuggle with their wives, and play with their kids."

"You're just trying to bring a tear to me eye," Jack said with a wink.

"And then there were eight," Larimore said. "Our number has been cut by more than half."

"They did their jobs," Perry said. "Your Seabees broke a sweat even down here."

"They're good men," Larimore said. "Every last one of them."

Perry watched the large plane taxi away and then turn toward the wind. This had been part of the plan. Resources had been allotted for the work crew, but only for a few days, just long enough to set up the chamber, move cargo, help with equipment, and unload the three aircraft that delivered crew and freight. After that, the men weren't needed; everything that remained could be done by the remaining eight. Fewer people meant fewer resources spent providing food and water and better use of the shelter. It also meant increased security and preserved secrecy.

Perry gave a brief wave even though the aircraft was now too far away for anyone on board to see. Still, the gesture made him feel better. He glanced at the seven others around him. Even Griffin James had come out to say farewell. It was a gesture borne not of civility but of shared understanding that leaving was just as dangerous as arriving.

The roar of the engines filled the frigid air and soon the plane was sprinting along the ice. Several long moments later it lifted into the air, its nose pointed at the cobalt sky.

"How's it feel to be the only military man this far south?" Griffin asked. "You have no underlings to order about."

Perry watched Larimore turn to face Griffin and prepared

himself for more verbal fireworks. The passing days had done nothing to alleviate the stress that had been sparked the moment the two met.

"There are always underlings, Dr. James," Larimore replied. "Always."

"Don't look at me, Commander," Griffin shot back. "I'm no one's inferior."

"Shut up," Gwen snapped at her brother. "That was uncalled for. You're even starting to get on my nerves."

Larimore shifted his eyes from Griffin to Gwen. He nodded politely. "It's my turn to cook," he said and began to walk away, then stopped. "Hey, Griffy, what kinda poison do you want in your stew?"

Perry shook his head. They needed Larimore because he was the on-site military liaison. Since the Pentagon had funded the project, they wanted someone on the scene who could give direct, eyewitness reports. For a moment, despite his admiration for Larimore, Perry began to wish the commander had been on the plane.

"My shift's over," Jack said. "I'll help peel potatoes."

Perry turned to Gleason. "Let's finish the electrical hookup."

"Right," Gleason replied. "Sarah wants to do a sensor check as soon as possible. If things go well, we can start descent a little after dinner. If you're ready, I mean."

"I'm more than ready," Perry replied, slapping Gleason on the shoulder. "My curiosity is killing me—"

The ice shuddered.

A second later a *boom* rolled over the camp.

Perry spun. It was a sensation he had felt before. Henry Sachs had taken Perry, then just twelve years old, to San Diego. Henry was there for meetings, but he saw it as an opportunity for father-son bonding. Perry waited by the hotel pool for his father to return from a meeting at the Naval Training Center in the heart of San Diego. As Perry hovered just above sleep, the lounge chair he sat in moved with a jolt. His first thought was earthquake, but nothing followed. Others around the pool murmured and looked around in bewilderment. Then Perry saw it: a short distance away, a rising plume of dense, obsidian black smoke.

His father arrived at the hotel an hour later than expected, and he brought with him the horrific story of a Boeing B-727 that had crashed not far away. That September day was still fresh in Perry's mind, as was the thought of the 137 people who had died in the plane. Seven more had died on the ground, and two others in a Cessna 172 practicing approaches at Lindberg field. Perry never forgot the abrupt jolt he felt from the crash even though he was several miles away.

The jolt he had just felt was similar. Turning, he saw what he did not what to see: a column of smoke in the distance. For the briefest moment, Perry's mind struggled with alternate explanations, but desperate as his mind was to avoid facing the hideous truth, it could not sweep away reality. There were no houses burning or forest fires because there were no houses or forests.

There was only one explanation. The C-5 had gone down and, unlike in San Diego all those years ago, there was no fire department, no military rescue, no anything.

Larimore and Jack sprinted back outside, both pulling on their parkas.

"What was that?" Jack asked.

Before Perry could respond, Larimore called it, "The plane. . . Oh, dear God, the plane went down."

A stiff, cold wind pierced Perry.

Okay, think, Perry commanded himself. "How far?" he wondered out loud.

"It can't be too far. The plane just took off," Sarah said. Her face was as white as the ice she stood on.

"Farther than you think," Larimore said. "The C-5 isn't a fighter jet, but it travels at a good clip."

"How far?" Perry pressed.

Gleason answered. "Assume three hundred miles per hour. . . that's five miles a minute. The plane took off—what?—five minutes ago? So it's maybe twenty-five miles from here."

"Not so far," Jack said. "It couldn't have gotten up to speed yet. Plus much of the distance would be vertical. I'm guessing less than ten miles."

"I think you're right, Jack." Perry turned and jogged toward the supply module next to the Dome. He slid to a stop in front of a wide pair of doors. He fumbled with the latch, his gloves hindering his movement. A moment later, he swung the doors wide and plunged into the dark room. He flipped a switch. Sealed lights overhead sprang to life, bathing the room in white light. In front of Perry was the Antarctic equivalent of a garage. Large tools, two portable generators, and a pair of snowmobiles filled the small space.

"What are you thinking?" Jack's voice said behind him.

"I'm thinking the same thing you are," Perry said.

"I figured as much. I'll take the one on the right."

Perry and Jack moved forward when Griffin and the others rounded the corner.

"You can't be serious," Griffin said. "You can't go out there. Not that far. Not with your lack of experience."

"There may be survivors," Perry said.

"I doubt that," Griffin said. "I haven't the slimmest of hopes that such is the case."

"I do," Perry said. "Now get out of the way."

"Hold on," Larimore said. "You can't go alone."

"He's not," Jack said. "I'm keeping him company."

Griffin was furious. "Committing a double suicide won't help those poor souls out there."

"This isn't suicide," Perry said. "It's what a man does for his friends and those he's responsible for."

"Your friends are gone, Sachs," Griffin snapped. "Face it."

Perry turned and marched to the scientist. "Six of those men are down here because I asked them to be. Every one of them has a wife at home, and most have children. I'm going to have to face those families. When I do, I want to be able to say I did everything I could."

Griffin shook his head. "You won't be able to say anything because you will be frozen in the ice, dead as dead can be. Don't you feel the wind? It's kicking up. It's a katabatic, a hurricane on ice. It will freeze you then blow your lifeless body across the continent. You won't survive. Be logical."

"I am," Perry said. He returned to the snowmobile and mounted up. "Someone get on the radio. Let McMurdo know what happened, and tell them to send help."

"I'm going, too," Larimore stated. "Those snowmobiles are designed to carry two each."

Perry shook his head and started to object, but the logic was too sound. Two men could do little if there were survivors. Every hand would be helpful. Besides, Larimore had lost as many men as Perry. How could he refuse? He gave a quick nod.

A sound behind Perry made him turn. Jack was hooking a tow-sled, a simple device designed to hold equipment or tools, to the back of Perry's snowmobile. *Always thinking, Jack.*

"Sarah, Gwen, gather up blankets, spare parkas, and the med kit." Perry watched them disappear around the corner.

"I can't tell you how unwise this is," Griffin said. "You've not seen what the wind can do."

Perry hadn't experienced severe winds in the Antarctic, but he had done his research. The katabatic was a downslope wind, moving from the center of the continent out and becoming stronger toward the coast. He hoped they were far enough inland to avoid the worst of it. Wind combined with extreme cold was a two-edged sword cutting twice on the way into its victim. It seemed a horrible way to die.

That thought made Perry more resolute. The image of an injured man lying with just the cold-weather suit to protect him chilled Perry far more than ice-laden wind could.

He pulled the snowmobile out of the equipment garage, dragging the skid-supported trailer behind him. Jack followed suit the moment he had finished attaching his own tow-sled. They stopped just a few yards from the garage, dismounting to help Gwen and Sarah load the requested items.

"We brought what we could," Gwen said. "I hope it's enough."

"It will do," Perry said. He remounted the snowmobile.

"Oh, all right, all right," Griffin said. "I'm coming, too."

Perry looked at him with surprise then turned to see the same expression on Jack's face. "Griffin, you don't need—"

"Yes, I do. I have more Antarctic experience than all of you combined. It's my duty." Before another objection was raised, he straddled the seat behind Perry and pulled his hood lower. He said something Perry couldn't make out, but he didn't ask the scientist to repeat it. Seconds were wasting, and every moment an injured man spent on the ice was another moment closer to death.

Perry gunned the throttle and set his course to the plume of smoke. He just hoped there was someone to rescue.

CHAPTER 7

The Learjet rolled down the runway with ease then turned its nose skyward, slipping into the night. The yellow lights of Mexico City glistened like jewels spilled on blacktop but soon gave way to the dark of unpopulated desert. The ground below the aircraft receded in feet then in miles as the jet banked south. Overhead, stars blinked as if winking at the speeding craft.

Tia didn't care for the stars tonight any more than she cared for them any other night. They were burning balls of gas hanging hundreds of light-years away that might or might not even be there. What concerned her was what lay ahead—thousands of miles ahead.

She leaned her head back onto the white leather seat and closed her eyes. She was tired, wearied from the day's work. That was all the emotion she would allow. Tired or not, it didn't matter. The goal mattered. The prophecy mattered. Pleasing Eric mattered. Everything else was incidental—including her life.

Still, rest would be welcome, and there was little else for her to do. She inhaled deeply and thanked the gods for the next few hours of near solitude.

Solitude was her friend, her treasure, her lifelong goal. Solitude was sweet, a delicious aloneness that most avoided but that she thrived on. Her world afforded her little of the precious commodity.

Even now she was not alone. Two pilots directed the aircraft on its course; two others waited their turn. Five other people were aboard, people who were as dedicated to the prophecy as she, trusted workers whose roots could be traced through centuries and whose dependability had been proven many times. They were people with a single goal and no conscience to hamstring them—people just like her.

The Learjet was full, but not one person would bother her. None dared unless the disturbance was sufficiently important to risk her wrath.

Unlike commercial aircraft, the business jet was equipped with tables, a workstation, and a luxurious office. Tia sat alone in a seating group of four, two seats separated by a maple-and-cherry-wood table from two facing seats.

The phone on the table rang.

What drowsiness circulated in Tia's head evaporated before the bell sounded again. She snapped it up and said, "Matteo."

It was Eric. She listened then set the phone down. The conversation lasted less than sixty seconds. Again Tia lay her head back and closed her eyes, keenly aware of the jet's movement through the clear air. She wondered what it was like to feel one's aircraft tumble from the sky. She had no way of knowing, but she had learned nearly twenty people had just experienced the sensation.

Of course, they weren't talking.

Tia had no idea how Eric knew of the crash, but she never asked such questions. She was the second most powerful person in the organization, but there were still things she did not know. Eric was not prone to trust anyone, not even her. Most likely, Eric had another operative involved. He had operatives everywhere.

The smoke rose from the ice as if someone had cracked open a gate to Hell. Perry knew that jet fuel had combined with wood crates, fabric, nylon, plastic, and a hundred other things that terrified him.

The plume was black as oil and roiled and folded upon itself like the contents of a witch's cauldron. Acid churned in his stomach and burned his throat. His heart hammered like a race-car piston, and his neck tightened into a wad of muscles. He had one nearly over-powering desire—to turn around, to avoid seeing what he knew lay before him. Images of the carnage flashed like a strobe in his mind. He fought them back, but they always returned more powerful, more garish, and more horrible.

Perry had seen enough airline accidents on television for him to envision what lay a few miles ahead. Images he had seen on the news that day in 1978 in San Diego and others floated like ashes on the wind in his brain. Lockerbie, Florida, the Iranian airliner shot down by a navy ship, and bodies—bodies on the ground. . . bodies floating on the water.

Perry accelerated. One hope drove him to face what no man would ever want to see—the possibility of a survivor. No matter how badly injured, no matter how slim the chance of life, Perry would do his best to bring him home.

Only the cold and the wind expurgated the images of destruction. Griffin had been right, the wind was picking up, and with it the windchill dropped. Added to that was the "created" wind from Perry's pushing the snowmobile faster and faster over the ice.

Perry was a man of prayer—spontaneous prayer. His faith had seen him through the best times and the most miserable. He had no formal time each day when he prayed, but his mind was heaven directed always. He was praying now, but there were no fine words, no beautiful phrases. The tragedy had reduced him to the most basic of all prayers, the kind of intercession that was rooted in abysmal despair and grounded in shock. "Dear God. . .dear God. . . dear God. . ." They were just two words, monosyllabic, but they said more than most preachers could intone. It was a plea from the heart, from where soul was stitched to emotion. It was simple; it was needy; and it was genuine.

Perry felt his parka tighten. Griffin, who rode on the seat behind him, had once again tightened his grip.

"It does no good if you kill us on the way there," Griffin shouted over the noise of the gas engine and the roar of the wind.

"Minutes may mean lives," Perry shouted back. *Minutes may mean lives.* Did he believe that? Was he so naive as to think anyone could be alive in the inferno that lay ahead?

Perry pressed on, fighting the growing wind, battling his own fear. He turned and saw Jack to his left and less than three feet behind. Jack's face, covered with goggles, his head encased in the parka hood that had been pulled down tight to prevent its slipping, told Perry that the jovial giant was intent on getting to the site. His jaw was tight, his lips pressed into a tight line, and his chin pressed forward. Perry had seen the look before, and it gave him some comfort. Jack was a jokester, but he was also the bravest man Perry knew.

Behind Jack was Commander Larimore. Perry could see none of his face. Larimore had his head down and pressed into Jack's back, using the big man as a shield against the unforgiving wind.

Perry's skull felt as if it were about to split open. His breathing was labored, made all the more difficult by shock and wind so cold it threatened to freeze his lungs solid with every inhalation. He should slow down. He knew that, but images of men in pain lying unprotected on the ice field refused to let Perry go.

Perry stepped up the pace.

The column of smoke widened as they approached. The wind was no one's slave, not even that of a burning cauldron of jet fuel, and it pushed the noxious mixture around, spreading it like tar on the open air. Perry tried to judge the distance, but the borderless expansion of white made it impossible.

The smoke had taken on a life of its own, its folding, seething billows shaping itself into frightening images. For a moment, Perry thought he saw a gigantic face peering down at them from the top of the column—a devilish face with a wicked sneer. It was as if the fire mocked them, as if it were greedy for four more lives that were willingly giving themselves over to its clutches.

The wind picked up loose ice crystals and began painting the air with sparkling flecks of white, which rode the rising breeze—white diamonds of ice, a black curtain of smoke, and a crystal blue sky.

Easing up on the accelerator, Perry watched as what had been a column of smoke now morphed into an obsidian wall. Black snow joined the ice dust, thickening the air. A moment later Perry realized he was seeing not black snow but soot from the plane fire. The air was cooling the roiling smoke so that if fell back to the surface.

Perry's gut twisted as he approached the wreckage. He slowed the snowmobile to a crawl and let his eyes survey the destruction.

Pieces of the aircraft were scattered in a long stretch as far as Perry's eyes could see. Most of the metal was unrecognizable, but some pieces were too large to miss. The tail section lay upside down, half its height driven into the ice. Packing crates lay in splinters. Wire, hydraulic line, cable, and aluminum skin from the fuselage were strewn about. Perry pressed on until he came to a crater in the ice. Fracture striations radiated from the impact point across the ice surface. A wad of sheet metal and titanium ribs filled the crater like the carcass of a prehistoric bird to be dined upon by others.

The fire burned too hot for Perry and the others to approach, but he could see that the impact crater had been enlarged by burning fuel and material. Perry tried not to dwell on the fact that that material included human flesh.

Steam rose from the pit and mingled with the black smoke.

"The smoke is turning gray!" Larimore shouted.

"The water from the melting ice is smothering the fuel," Griffin said. "In the end, the ice wins. The ice always wins."

"The debris field has to be a mile long," Jack said. "Maybe we should split up."

"Too many hazards," Perry said. "We stick together. Jack, you and the commander move fifty yards off our flank, and Griffin and

I will search closer. We'll circle the debris field once, then again more slowly. You know what we're looking for."

"I know what we're going to find," Griffin said.

So did Perry.

The sound of cracking ice and crackling fire was unnerving. The rain of black soot and ice particles made Perry feel as if he were driving a snowmobile on a distant planet's surreal landscape.

Checking Jack's position to his right, Perry pressed on. He steered around a jagged piece of fuselage then around a small pool of jet fuel. Twenty feet ahead he saw something he recognized—a chair. Coming up from behind he could see the shoulder straps still in place. Perry stopped the snowmobile and dismounted. With Griffin close behind, he approached the chair and stepped to its front.

Griffin bolted. A moment later, Perry heard him vomiting. Perry closed his eyes and tried to drive away the image of the headless, legless torso strapped to the seat.

Gwen James paced around the Dome's communication cubicle. Anxiety ran roughshod through her. The sight of burning wreckage in the distance had shaken her to the core, but hearing her brother volunteer to accompany Perry to the site had shaken her more. Griffin was a smart man, an intellectual, and brilliant in his field, but he was no hero.

Worse, Gleason sat at the communication table trying to make contact with the outside world, but nothing was working.

"Is the power on?" Gwen asked.

"Yes," Gleason said patiently. "It was the first thing I checked."

"This can't be right," Gwen said. "The system was working this morning. How are we going to reach others for help if our radio doesn't work?"

"One thing at a time," Gleason said. "Why don't you try one of the walkie-talkies while I work on this?"

"The handhelds aren't designed to work with that kind of range. You're just trying to keep me busy."

Gleason looked up from the communication console and made eye contact with Gwen, and then he looked at Sarah, who stood to one side observing. "What I'm trying to do is contact McMurdo Station. I know the handheld radios won't reach that far, but they might reach Perry and the others. They may be too far away, they may not. I know only one way to find out."

"Do you want me to do it?" Sarah asked.

"No, I'll do it," Gwen snapped. She felt a moment's guilt for her rudeness, but patience wasn't a family virtue. She stepped to a wood rack—a simple plywood board with dowels attached to its surface. The rack held six walkie-talkies. Four were gone, carried by Perry and the others. She snatched up the first one, turned it on, and keyed the mike. "Griffin, this is Gwen. Do you hear me?"

Nothing.

"Griffin, this is Gwen at base. Do you hear me?"

More nothing.

"It's not on," Sarah observed.

"Of course it's on," Gwen shot back. "I turned it on."

"There's no red light," Sarah added.

Gwen turned her attention to the top of the radio. The power light was dark. She tried the ON switch again but the light remained cold. She grabbed the other handheld and activated the power switch. It, too, was dead.

"I don't like this," Sarah said. "Something stinks." She moved toward Gwen and took one of the radios, then pulled the plastic back cover off to reveal the empty battery compartment. She looked at Gwen.

Gwen's heart flipped. She followed Sarah's example and stripped off the cover of her walkie-talkie. The battery compartment was empty.

"Could someone have forgotten to put batteries in?" Gwen

wondered. That didn't seem right. Everything on an expedition like this was checked and double-checked.

Gleason turned and faced the women. "I know we brought more batteries for those things." He searched the small room and found nothing. "I saw them in here before."

Gwen's chest tightened. "But you have power to the main radio, right?"

"Yeah," Gleason said. "At least the light is on, but I'm not getting output."

"The satellite phone. . . ," Sarah suggested.

Gwen knew right where that was and grabbed it from its charger stand that rested on a small fold-up desk. As with the radio, she activated the power switch and felt her heart drop like a rock in a well. No power. She opened the back and again found an empty place where a battery should have been.

"What's going on here?" she asked, tears welling.

She watched as Sarah raised the handheld to her ear and shook it. There was a tinkling sound. "That can't be good," she said.

Gwen shook the radio in her hand and heard the same thing. She repeated that action with the satellite phone. More noise.

"I need a screwdriver," Sarah demanded.

"What are you doing?" Gwen demanded.

"I'm taking this thing apart."

"You'll ruin it," Gwen protested.

"I think someone has done that for us."

"I'll open the radio," Gleason said.

"Turn the power off first," Sarah said.

"Yeah, that's the first thing they taught me at MIT."

"Sorry, Gleason," Sarah said. "I'm a little edgy."

"No sweat. I'm a little nervous myself."

"I'm not sure we should be doing this," Gwen admitted, but she had no better idea.

"Let me work," Sarah said. "I'm a robotics expert, so I know circuits. I know electronics."

Gwen wanted to object, but her rational mind told her Sarah was right. She watched as Gleason and Sarah stripped the casing off the equipment.

"I don't believe this," Sarah said, holding out the radio. "It's been sabotaged."

Looking at the radio Sarah held, Gwen could see loose parts broken off from the circuit board.

"Same here," Gleason said.

"How? Why?" Gwen asked. Her voice caught on the words.

"Acid," Gleason said. "It wasn't enough to take the batteries or clip the power cord. Someone wanted to make sure the radios never worked again. I can see where some kind of acid was squirted on the circuits. Let me see your radio." He took the handheld from Sarah's hand. "Same thing. It looks like they squirted the acid through the notch where the battery wires run between the battery bay and the electronics."

"Who would do that?" Gwen asked.

"That is the big question," Gleason replied.

Gwen's knees went weak, and the blood drained from her face. "That means. . .that means. . ."

"The plane crash was no accident," Sarah said, uttering the thought Gwen could not put words to.

"The others may be in trouble," Gwen exclaimed. "If we don't have radios, then they don't either."

"It's worse than that," Gleason said. "If the plane crash was intentional, I doubt the party responsible would have boarded."

Gwen looked at Gleason then blinked several times. "You mean that the saboteur is one of us?"

Gleason nodded, and his face darkened.

Outside, the wind screamed around the Dome as if in a fury of pain.

CHAPTER 8

Perry felt sickened. Not by the gruesome sights—and there had been plenty of those—but by his failure to find a single survivor. So powerful was the crash that he had been unable even to find a whole body. Body parts—arms, legs, hunks of flesh—were abundant, but he'd seen nothing to give him a thread of hope to cling to.

Leaning into the rising wind, Perry looked into the faces of the others, each bearing the scars of shock. He made eye contact with each one but said nothing. Nothing could be said. It had been a fool's errand from the beginning, but it had been necessary.

Perry bowed his head. He could hear only the sound of the wind whipping around his body and the thundering of his own heart. Never had he felt so helpless; never had he felt so sad. Thousands of miles to the north, wives waited to hear from husbands, and children were eager to tell Daddy the latest news from school and the neighborhood. Mothers, fathers, brothers, sisters, and friends were a phone call away from horrific news—news that would leave a scar not even time could remove.

And Perry felt responsible. No one would blame him. No inquiry could ever say that he had been careless. But the fact remained: Six of his best employees were dead, burned and scattered across a desert of ice.

His throat tightened, and he felt broken inside as if pieces of his being had frozen, shattered, and fallen into an unrecognizable heap. Emotions bubbled. He was brokenhearted and furious, depressed and despondent. He stood in the cold, in the barrenness, unable to do anything else. Grief had paralyzed him, welding his feet to the ice. Since his mind could not pray, his heart did.

Moments crept by, then he felt something across his shoulders. He didn't need to look up to know his friend Jack had put his beefy arm around his shoulders. It said more than any poet could.

Perry took several deep breaths then said, "Someone contact base and let them know what we found."

"I'll do it," Griffin said softly. It was the first time Perry had heard the man speak in a whisper. He stepped several yards away, and Perry watched as he put the handheld radio to his lips, then raised it to his ear to hear better.

"You okay, buddy?" Jack asked, shouting against the wind.

"No," Perry admitted. "I don't think I'll ever be the same." He looked along the field of debris. To his left he could see the inverted tail section, to his right the conical nosepiece lying on the ice like a rounded pyramid.

"None of us will ever be the same," Jack said.

"That's for sure," Larimore added.

"There's something wrong with the debris field," Perry said, forcing his mind to work on facts instead of stewing in emotion.

"Yeah, I noticed that, too," Jack said.

"I know crash reconstruction is a specialty best left up to FAA and NTB types, but the pattern of debris is. . .unexpected."

"What do you mean?" Larimore asked. "How should it look?"

Perry glanced up and down the rubble again. "At first, I thought the crater was where the plane hit, but that can't be. The tail section is behind the crater, and the nose section is on the leading edge. If the C-5 had nosed in, then I'd expect to see the front end of the plane in the hole or at least having created a long gouge."

"But the front of the plane is in the front, and the back is in the back," Jack said.

"Meaning?" Larimore pressed.

"That it came apart in the air," Perry replied. "The debris runs out to the side more than I expected. And the bodies. . ." Images of bodies ripped into pieces and falling to the ice inundated Perry's brain. "We didn't find a single intact body. Not one."

"It blew up in midair?" Jack said. "Is that what you're saying?"

"Exactly."

"There weren't any explosives on board," Larimore said.

"None that we know of," Perry countered.

Griffin jogged over to join the others. "Something is wrong, guys. I can't raise the base. My walkie-talkie is dead."

Perry examined his radio. "I know I turned this on when I left." He checked the power switch. It was in the ON position but the indicator light was dark. He brought it to his lips. "Check. . .check." Nothing. "We should be hearing that over your radios."

The others quickly checked their units. All of them were silent.

"I don't like this," Griffin said.

"Neither do I."

"It gets worse," Jack said. "The wind is picking up. Going back we'll be driving into a headwind. It was hard enough when it was behind us; I don't think we can make it going head-to-head with it."

"Which was my initial concern," Griffin retorted.

"Well, we can't stand out here," Larimore said. "I can't feel my feet as it is."

"We didn't bring shelter," Griffin complained. "If you had listened to me—"

"We'll have to make shelter," Perry said. Then it occurred to him. "Follow me." Without wasting a moment, Perry mounted his snowmobile, Griffin behind him.

"Where are we going?" Griffin asked.

"You'll see." Perry accelerated and moved toward the distant end of the debris field. Moments later, he stopped by the inverted nose section of the downed C-5. It towered above the flat ice. The front landing gear skid lay ten yards farther along.

"What are we doing here?" Griffin asked.

Perry waited until Jack and Larimore joined them. "If we can find an opening, we can use the nose section for shelter against the wind."

"Great idea," Jack replied and dismounted. It took only a minute to find a tear in the skin large enough to crawl through. Perry was relieved. He had no desire to dig through the ice to tunnel underneath. Fortunately, the opening was on the leeward side. Wind wouldn't be pouring in, but it would make itself known.

Perry crawled in. The others followed. It was dark, but without the wind pounding them, it felt warm.

"A metal igloo," Jack said, as he crawled through. "Any port in a storm as they say."

Perry nodded in the darkness and struggled with the irony that surrounded him. Not long before, this piece of fuselage had been part of the deathtrap that took the lives of six of his men, six Seabees, and the C-5's crew. Now it was the one thing that separated them from death. It was like making a lifeboat out of the *Titanic*.

"Who would do this?" Gwen asked.

It was the third time Gleason had heard it, but he said nothing. The woman was controlled but well stretched into her fear zone. It was normal. It was to be expected. Gleason wasn't sure if he was telling himself that to feel better about Gwen or to comfort himself about his own fears.

"We have no way of knowing," Sarah said. "At least not right now. What we need to do is remain calm and focus on the problem."

"Who made you queen?" Gwen groused. "For all I know, you're the one who did this. You said it yourself. . .you know electronics."

"You're a better suspect than I am," Sarah said. "You and your whiny brother have made it clear from the beginning that you're opposed to the mission. Makes me wonder why you're even here."

"Because we didn't know you were going to puncture the ice sheet. Had we known, we would have turned it down flat."

"Feel that strongly, do you?" Sarah prodded.

"Absolutely."

"Strongly enough to do something about it? Strongly enough to—oh, I don't know—destroy our communications equipment?"

"How dare you!"

"Easily. You're the biologist. It would be easy for you to obtain enough acid to do this."

"You sniveling little—"

"Enough!" Gleason had tolerated all he could. He was shocked by his tone. A quiet man, he had trouble remembering the last time he raised his voice. "If you ladies want to duke it out, then take it outside. If not, let's pull our collective brains together and think this through."

"What is there to think about?" Gwen complained. "My brother may be on the ice with someone responsible for not only sabotaging our radios but bringing down an airplane full of people."

"Maybe," Gleason agreed, "maybe not. The perpetrator may have been on the plane."

"And killed himself?" Sarah interjected.

"It's been done before, and that's assuming the crash was intentional. It may have been an accident."

"Do you really believe that?" Sarah asked.

Gleason frowned. "As much as I want to, no. Arguing isn't going to unwind time. We need information. We need communication."

"You're right," Sarah admitted. She turned to Gwen. "I'm sorry. I guess I'm more on edge than I realize."

Gwen stood silently, fire smoldering in her eyes. Gleason saw Sarah shrug then turn her attention to him. "Maybe we can build one good radio out of the ones we have here. You know, piece one together."

"Perhaps," Gleason said, "but we need to do something else first." He started for the door. "We need to find out if we are alone or if someone chose to stay behind."

"I suggest we stick together," Gwen said. Gleason noted that her words were missing some of their former heat.

"Agreed," Gleason said.

"No argument here," Sarah added.

Gleason led them from the communications cubicle.

It seemed wrong to Perry. The discomfiture was rooted in emotion; he knew that. Still, taking shelter in the damaged remains of the C-5's nose section—a nose that had been amputated only a few hours before—struck Perry as a cruel irony. The shelter was needed. The wind continued to race, to scream, to claw with invisible fingers at the four men who huddled among wires, cables, metal struts, and things too difficult to identify with the meager light that puddled in through the sheet-metal tear.

To insulate themselves from the ice floor, Perry and Jack had gathered bits of broken crates from outside and carried them back into the makeshift shelter. Each man sat on some arrangement of wood.

The sun was still up, hovering over the horizon like a balloon that had lost too much helium to climb any higher. It would stay up not for hours, but for weeks. Since arriving in Antarctica, Perry had not seen the sun set. He was glad it wouldn't be setting today.

The sight of wreckage and dismembered bodies haunted Perry's thoughts. He tried to push them away, to perform a mental, emotional exorcism of the demon images, but his normally disciplined mind failed. The images would be with him forever.

"I think I accounted for all my men," Larimore said. He sat

crossed-legged on several pieces of wood. His head was down, his shoulders slumped. The body said it all. "Best I could tell anyway." His words sounded like a whisper against the wind's clamor.

Perry looked at the man. "Did you know them well?"

Larimore shook his head. "No. Not really. It was a new command for me, a new station. I knew their names, read their files and proficiency reports, but hadn't had time to get close. You're not supposed to get close to those under your command. It makes it hard to send them into harm's way."

"Still, you're human," Jack said.

"Yeah, that's the hard part." Larimore sighed. "I've never lost a subordinate before. Never. Working with the equipment we do, there are bound to be injuries. I have had a few of those, but no deaths. I'm afraid I feel. . .awkward."

Perry understood. Like most men, he was uncomfortable with certain emotions. Larimore was the same. Awkward was a good word. What Perry was feeling—an emotional stew of shock, sadness, grief, anger, and a dozen other emotions he couldn't identify—was impossible to describe. It was beyond definition, but it was real.

"What about you?" Larimore asked. "From what I saw, you were close to your men."

Something stuck in Perry's throat. "As close as life would allow. Sachs Engineering has over a thousand employees, so I can't say I know every one of them. I chose these six, however. I had worked with them before on one project or another. They were the best and most trusted men I could find."

"How trusted?" Griffin asked. His tone was spiced with suspicion.

"What do you mean?" Perry asked.

"I've been thinking," Griffin explained. "I think you're right. Something isn't right about the way the plane came down. The crater is wrong, the debris is wrong, and the bodies—" he shuddered—"the bodies are wrong."

"So now you're a crash expert?" Larimore said.

"As much as anyone in this. . .place. Why don't you get off my back?"

"Someone needs to be on your back. You've been nothing but a pain in our rear ends since we landed."

"And you're a pompous military elitist who—"

"Say it, and they will be the last words you utter!" Larimore shouted. He reached for Griffin but was cut off by Jack's outstretched arm, an arm that moved with unsettling speed and grabbed a fistful of the commander's parka. Larimore wasn't going anywhere.

"At ease, Commander," Jack said evenly. "When we get back to base, I'll build you two a boxing ring. Right now we need cooperation, not combat."

Larimore settled back into his seat. "You're right. I'm sorry. This thing has me. . .I'm not myself."

"I doubt any of us are," Perry said. "Go on, Dr. James, but keep the snide remarks to yourself."

"Okay, okay," Griffin said. "I'm not very good in social settings." He looked around the shelter and let slip a small laugh. "If you can call this a social setting."

"You were talking about things not looking right," Jack prompted.

"Perry said it earlier. It looks like the plane blew up in midair. How does that happen? Planes like this have been the workhorse of the Antarctic. Their safety record is excellent. If there weren't explosives on board, then how did it blow up?"

"A spark in the fuel," Larimore suggested.

"Possible, I suppose," Griffin said, "but while you were combing the field of debris for survivors—and clearly there could be none—I spent a little time looking at what's left of the fuselage. This is way out of my field, but I know enough physics to recognize a hole caused by an explosion."

"You found such a hole?" Perry asked.

"More than one," Griffin said.

"A fuel explosion would do the same thing," Larimore said.

"Fuel is kept in the wings, right, Commander?" Griffin asked.

"Right."

"The holes I'm talking about are in the cargo and seating area. Furthermore, the metal skin is bent out, not in."

"That would mean the explosion took place in the cargo cabin," Perry interjected.

"Precisely," Griffin said. "That's the problem. We have no need for explosives on our mission site, therefore none should have been on the aircraft. I didn't requisition any. Did anyone here?"

"No," Perry said.

"Then how does an explosion take place?"

"An explosion that would tear the craft apart while it was flying," Jack said.

"You see the problem."

"You're saying someone maliciously planted a bomb on the C-5 for the purpose of killing all on board." Larimore shook his head. "What would that achieve? To keep the area pristine, we're required to cart off all waste. The only cargo was trash, leftover packing material, empty crates. . . There was no scientific information. Why destroy a plane that was essentially a flying garbage truck?"

"But there was something on board," Griffin said. "Knowledge."

The statement struck Perry hard. "Someone wanted to kill witnesses?"

"Yes," Griffin said. "Can you extrapolate my next point?"

"I can," Jack said. "Whoever did this will be after us next."

"You got it," Griffin said. "You get an A for the day."

"That would explain the radios all being out at one time," Larimore said.

"What I can't figure out is how someone detonated an explosive in flight, unless they were on board themselves," Griffin said.

"An altitude switch," Jack suggested. "When the craft reached a certain altitude, the bomb would go off."

Perry shook his head. "The airplane flew from McMurdo to our base. It would have reached that altitude on the way over and been destroyed."

"Maybe it was connected to a timer," Jack said.

"Perhaps," Griffin said, "but that seems a bit risky, doesn't it? I mean, the plane was carrying supplies and would be unloaded as soon as it landed."

"Maybe it was meant for us," Larimore said. "Maybe it was supposed to blow up on-site."

"That's possible," Jack said. "But we're left with the same problem: How does the bomb know when to go off?"

"If the bomb was inside the cabin, which it seems certain it was," Griffin said, "then the bomber runs the risk of someone discovering it beforehand. The loadmaster checks everything multiple times before takeoff. He knows the inside of that plane better than the designers. So does the crew. Surely he would have noticed something out of place. The bomber would know that."

Perry's mind was racing, and he didn't like the track. "You're assuming the explosive was loaded at McMurdo."

"Where else?" Griffin asked.

"What I mean is, we're assuming someone at McMurdo planted the bomb. But it might have been done closer at hand."

"Whoa, wait a minute," Larimore said. "That would mean one of the flight crew, one of your men, or one of mine set the bomb. They were all on the plane. That'd be suicide."

"That's not what I'm suggesting," Perry said.

"He's suggesting one of us did it, Commander," Griffin said. "And I agree."

CHAPTER 9

Eric Enkian stepped from the limo without waiting for the chauffeur to open the door for him. He hated such displays of arrogance. He could open his own doors. The limo was a business decoration, something to impress clients—especially foreign clients.

The drive had been slow through Mexico City's clotted traffic and then up the steep road that led to his hillside home. Enkian not only owned the home but the hillside itself. There were no neighbors—just the way he liked it. He dismissed the driver for the evening and walked up a path decorated in Mexican red pavers, pavers made from material pulled from the earth by EA Mining. Flowers lined the walk, and trees dotted the hillside. A gentle breeze pushed leaves around in a chorus of whispers. The sky overhead was void of clouds and shone a hazy blue, tinted by Mexico City's infamous smog.

Enkian paused a moment and looked at the spacious home before him—eight thousand square feet of simple luxury blended with the latest technology. Its roof was flat and its walls a mix of glass and stone. No wood adorned the exterior, and only minimal wood on the interior. Enkian found the coldness of stone more comforting than wood. Stone made the single-story structure secure, and he was certain the building, if left alone, would stand for a thousand years.

He walked up the five steps that bridged the vertical distance between grade and porch. The stairs and porch were made of blue granite and buffed to a glasslike shine. He entered a code into a keypad to the left of the front door then placed his thumb on a small, transparent plate. The door unlocked, and Enkian entered the home he had not seen for the last two weeks.

It was good to be back from Las Vegas. He enjoyed mining and building, but he enjoyed being alone more than anything.

The door opened to a small foyer, which in turn led to an expansive room. Gold-veined black marble covered the floors, and the walls boasted limestone from an ancient seabed. Fossil fish and plants were imbedded in the wall. The roof was reinforced concrete tinted blue.

It not only looked good to him, but *felt* good. The stone brought security and a connection with the past—a past too long forgotten and soon to be remembered.

He removed his shoes and felt the smooth marble beneath his feet, and once again he began to feel grounded to the earth. Leaving his shoes in the foyer, Enkian crossed the great room and passed the kitchen to his home office. Stretching the width of the home, the office was roomy and open. Glass walls formed three sides of the room. The window walls were equipped with remote-controlled blinds that rose at the touch of a button. Enkian left them down. He had another room to visit.

A decorative metal door was centered in the one solid wall. He pressed his thumb on a sensor identical to the one at the front door. The metal door whispered open, and Enkian stepped in. To the right of the door were two buttons, one above the other. He pressed the bottom button and spoke, "Eric Enkian," and then looked up to a glass panel above the door where he knew a camera was directed his way. It took less than two seconds for the voice-and-face-identification system to verify his identity.

The door closed, and the elevator began a smooth descent. When it stopped, Enkian emerged and motion-activated lights illuminated a subterranean room that had been built to his dimensions: sixty-six feet by sixty-six feet.

Unlike the polished floors of the home above, this room's floor was covered in black sand. Enkian felt the warmth of it on his feet as he walked toward the center of the room. There were no chairs, no sofa, and no tables, but the room was filled. At its center was an arrangement of stones, one carefully set upon another. Enkian set a loving hand on the top layer. Sixty-six stones from various places in the world: Egypt, Mexico, Iraq, several African nations, China, Japan, Central America, Canada, and the United States. Blue stones set upon white stones shouldered to green and yellow, rising from the sandy floor.

He patted the stones then looked around the room. No matter how many times he moved into this microcosm—he had done so more times than he could count—he felt a sense of pride and connection to the past. He was proud of this room, but it was just a container for things more important.

Enkian took a deep breath as he let his eyes trace the only other structures in the room. Black onyx pedestals stood like sentinels, each topped by a glass case. Each case glowed with the light of the small halogen bulbs hidden in the base. He stepped to the closest one, bent, and peered in. The red-brown cylinder within—identical to the cylinders in every case—was adorned with writing that hadn't been used for millennia. Sixty-six cylinders, each one more valuable than gold.

"The prophecies," he said aloud, his words echoing off the stone walls. "The time is near."

He thought of Tia, now somewhere in South America. Soon he would follow.

He returned to the stone column in the center of the room then slowly removed his shirt and tossed it aside. On top of the stones—on top of the altar—lay a flint knife. He took it in his right hand

and studied its sharp edge and lethal point.

Closing his eyes, Enkian ran his left hand over his torso, feeling each scar on his chest, then over his belly, which bore even more scars. He began to hum, then chant in a language few knew, and then he raised the flint blade to one of the few unmarked areas of his body, placing the stone blade against his flesh just above his navel.

With great care, he pressed the blade into the tender flesh—chanting, chanting, chanting. When he felt blood begin to ooze between his fingers, he bent forward and laid his body on the stone altar.

"All of me I give. . .all of me I give. . ."

Dr. Kenneth Curtis took a seat next to Gwen. She looked at him briefly but gave no other acknowledgement. She didn't want company. She didn't want conversation. She wanted her brother back in the safety of the Dome. The structure shuddered under the wind's onslaught. The Dome's shape made the wind roar instead of shriek as it did around sharp corners. She wished she found some comfort in that.

"We've just finished a second check of the buildings," Curtis said. "Everything looks normal. Gleason and Sarah are trying to cobble together some communications."

"Good," Gwen replied. It appeared a conversation was coming her way whether she wanted it or not. She considered going to her room.

"Give me your hand," Curtis said, extending his own. His fingers were short, his nails trim, and his palm wide.

"What?"

"Your hand, young lady—give it to me."

The request took her aback. "Why? I don't understand."

"Indulge me."

Reluctantly, she complied. His hand was warm and firm, though she had expected the rotund archaeologist to have soft, pudgy flesh.

He closed his fingers, taking her hand in a gentle grasp. "Do you feel that?"

"Feel what?"

"My hand, of course." He smiled, and his eyes brightened.

"Of course I feel it. Shouldn't I?" *This is stupid,* she thought and began to pull away. He tightened his grip. "What are you doing?"

"So you do feel my grasp?"

"I said 'yes.' So what?"

"I'm older than you by about twenty years," he began. His tone was even and somber. "I've seen things. I've experienced things."

"Are you coming on to me? Because if you are—"

"A wise person knows when to listen. You feel my hand because I'm here. That's what I want you to know. I'm here. Gleason is here. Sarah is here. You are not alone."

"I know that."

"No you don't, Dr. James. . .Gwen. You've been sitting alone at this table, shutting everyone else out. I can understand the desire, but not the practice. You're worried about your brother."

"You figured that out all by yourself?" Gwen was surprised he didn't react to her words.

"Yes, I figured it all by myself. I am worried about Perry and Jack. We have a right to be worried, and we would be fooling ourselves to pretend otherwise. We must believe the best and pray for the rest."

Gwen blinked. Had she heard correctly? "Believe and pray? You're suggesting we pray? Believe in what? Pray to whom?"

"Believe that when the wind settles, your brother, Perry, Jack, and Commander Larimore will all walk back in here. Pray to God that it will be so."

"And that will make it happen? I'm a scientist. Facts are my food, not faith."

"Isaac Newton was a scientist, and he wrote more on theological matters than mathematical. You can add to the list Louis Pasteur and a thousand more. I am a scientist, too; it is why I am a person of faith."

"Faith didn't save the people on the transport plane."

"I am not suggesting faith keeps bad things from happening. I *am* saying faith enables us to deal with bad times."

"So that's it," Gwen said. "Sarah said Perry was different in some way. Is he like you?"

"A believer? A Christian? Yes, he is—unapologetically, I might add."

"And you think that will keep him warm in sixty-mile-an-hour winds?"

"Perry is the most resourceful, intelligent, and determined man I've ever met. When he's on a project—any project—he takes care of those around him. If your brother were injured, Perry would carry him back if he had to."

"My brother is pretty resourceful, too. He has years of experience on the ice."

"That, too, gives me comfort," Curtis said. He squeezed her hand. "Just know, Gwen, that you are not alone." He released her hand, rose from the table, and walked in the direction of the communications cubicle.

Gwen stared at the blank wall and tried to process all she had heard. *Prayer couldn't hurt,* she told herself, then shook her head. "Ridiculous," she said to the empty room. She looked at her hand and admitted that for those few moments, it had felt good to share her fear.

The men sat huddled in a tight circle, hoping their exhaled breath would warm the air a degree or two. Jack had engaged Griffin in a discussion of how many bodies it would take to warm the temperature ten degrees in their emergency shelter. Griffin had resisted, but Jack pressed the right button: "You're right; it's the kind of thing an engineer could figure out." The debate began with the men batting mathematical formulas back and forth like shuttle-cocks in a badminton game.

Perry followed the discussion for awhile but left the two men to their folly. He tried to nap, but each time he drifted off, he was awakened by an image of a burned leg lying on the ice, or a hunk of identifiable flesh mixed among the wreckage. Each vision made his heart leap and breath catch.

"So," Jack asked Griffin, "how bad can these winds get?"

"They're faster on the coast. Katabatic winds have been meas-ured close to two hundred miles an hour. Hurricane speed. We've got it easy, really."

"Doesn't feel easy," Larimore said.

Perry glanced out the tear that was their door and noticed more light. The wind had picked up shards of ice and snow, creating a whiteout condition, but now Perry could see more.

"Listen," he said.

"To what?" Larimore asked.

"The wind is quieter." He turned to Griffin. "Is this just a lull in the storm, or should we be thinking about heading home?"

Griffin listened. "You're asking my advice?"

"That's exactly what I'm doing."

Griffin seemed pleased. "It's too early to tell, but the wind can leave as quickly as it came."

"Give us a bottom line, Dr. James. Go or no-go."

"I say give it another thirty minutes. If it continues to drop, then go. I just suggest we go fast when we do."

"Roger that," Larimore said with near glee.

Perry felt thankful. The waiting was over. It was time to do something. The question was, would someone try to stop him?

CHAPTER 10

Tia sat in the passenger seat of the Toyota Land Cruiser as it bounced down the road from the Carlos Ibanez de Campo International Airport toward Punta Arenas. The flight had been long enough that she felt fully rested despite the lateness of the hour. It had also been long enough to make her glad to be free of the confines of the Learjet. Two men sat in the seat behind her. Another Land Cruiser followed a few yards behind.

"Would you like refreshment, *Señorita?*" Oscar, the driver, asked, his accent thick. "Your trip has been long." The driver was younger than thirty but looked older. Eric had told her he was a supervisor at one of the copper mines in the country.

"We had plenty of refreshments on the plane, Oscar," Tia replied. Her eyes traced the dim road ahead. They had flown far enough south that the sun barely set beyond the horizon. The twilight was confusing, her internal clock telling her it must be close to midnight. To her left she saw the dark blue stretch of water called the Strait of Magellan.

"I know a place not far from here where the beer is good." He paused and ran a hand through dark hair that already showed touches of gray. His features were Spanish, but some sharp edges around the face told Tia that some Native American blood coursed through his veins. "I think of the men—a chance to stretch their legs before checking in at the hotel."

Tia turned to the two companions who rode silently in the back. One raised an eyebrow but offered no words. They were due to check in at the hotel and spend half of the next day touring the copper mine, waiting for final preparations to be made for the next leg of their journey. She had no interest in seeing the gaping hole in the ground, but it was necessary to keep up appearances. Covertness came with a price.

Turning back to the road ahead, she gave it another moment's thought. She had no desire to sit in a hotel room. She nodded. "Beer it is."

Oscar grinned broadly. Tia was certain he was thinking of more than just the men.

The cantina was off a back street in the north part of town. They passed through an industrial area, past a few small shops, and pulled onto a gravel parking lot, where a lone clapboard building stood. A hand-lettered sign identified the establishment as SEBASTIAN'S. Yellow paint peeled from the wood, and the shingle roof looked in need of repair. The blue water behind it gave it the kind of quality landscape painters loved to capture in oils.

"It is not much to the eyes, but the *cerveza* is the best in all of Magallanes."

"I'll have to take your word for it," Tia said. Her five travel companions poured out of the vehicles, stretched, and made their way to the door which hung awkwardly on its hinges. Tia followed and entered last, except for Oscar, who stood to one side and waved her in with a gallant motion.

The inside of Sebastian's was little better than the exterior. Abused wood tables, some leaning precipitously, dotted the dirt-caked wood floor. Tobacco smoke filled the air, stinging Tia's eyes and chewing at her throat.

The driver stepped to her side. "Many of the miners come here.

For many, here is better than home."

The rocky tables, worn booths, and long, scarred bar were filled with men. Dirt clung to their clothing and sweat to their skin. Outside, the air was cold. Punta Arenas's average temperature was a mere forty-four degrees, much colder when winter arrived. Two hundred inches of precipitation fell every year, mostly snow. Inside, the bodies of patrons and an overworked heater had raised the temperature beyond the level of comfort.

When Tia first entered, the bar was reverberating with Spanish rock music and the cacophonous hum of forty simultaneous conversations. The sight of seven men entering dulled the roar—and Tia's presence quenched it.

Most of the patrons were male, but a few provocatively dressed women were scattered around the room. Tia was sure their trade had nothing to do with mining, manufacturing, or anything similar.

Tia stood out. Her height and waist-length black hair made her irresistible to the eyes of many men. She had grown used to it. Men had been undressing her with their eyes since high school. It had ceased to bother her. The five men with her and the two drivers moved to the battered bar, and Oscar ordered beer for everyone in his charge.

Tia stood next to Oscar at the bar. "You come here often?" she asked and wondered why anyone would.

"On *Sábado*," he said. "Saturday nights. It is the only day I can leave the work at the mine."

It was Saturday; apparently Oscar did not want to waste his one free night. The bartender, a pudgy man with dark skin, a week's worth of stubble on his chin, and a shiny bald head, set a chipped glass of beer before Tia. She eyed it then took the mug in hand.

A man sidled up to her and said something in Spanish. Tia set down her beer and turned. "Excuse me?"

"Americano?" the man asked. He tapped the small glass in his right hand on the marred bar top. The bartender pulled a bottle of

tequila from beneath the bar and filled the man's glass. She judged him to be in his early twenties, and he stood as tall as she. Muscles bulged beneath his worn beige shirt. She was certain they were formed by hard work and not membership in a gym. His breath was sour from bad gums and alcohol. Tia decided she didn't like the man.

"I'm from America," Tia said. "What of it?"

"Please, *amigo*," Oscar said, "this is a private party."

"Too good for us?" the man asked.

"No—" Oscar began.

"Yes," Tia interjected and turned her back on the man. She caught sight of her crew, each one smiling but not making eye contact.

"That's a pretty tattoo," the interloper said. "It is some kind of dragon, no?"

"Yes. Now go away."

"I go where I wish to go, pretty *Americano*." He raised his voice. "Eh, *amigos?*" The others in the bar cheered in agreement.

Tia looked at Oscar, whose face had gone white and his eyes doubled in size. She knew what he was thinking, that he had led his employer's representative into a dangerous situation. *"Amigo,"* he said, "please let us drink our beer in peace. We don't want trouble."

"I don't want no trouble, either," the thick-armed man said. He leaned forward and sniffed Tia's neck. "I want something else."

"Please," Oscar said, his voice shaking. "Do not do this. You do not understand."

"I understand enough." He reached forward and gently stroked the dragon tattoo on Tia's hand. "Such a pretty tattoo for such a pretty lady."

"Do you use that hand?" Tia asked.

"For many things," he cooed. He sniffed her neck again. Two of her crew pushed away from the bar, but she shook her head. They returned to their previous position, their eyes fixed on the drunk man. "Would you like to see what I can do with this pretty hand?"

Tia's movement was so swift the man could not have responded if he had been sober. She grabbed the man's fingers and squeezed like a vise. Before he could release a cry of pain, she slammed his hand to the bar, raised her mug, and then brought it down like a mallet, its edge digging into the man's flesh. She heard the bones in his hand snap.

Then came the scream of pain. Spanish began to flow from his lips in what Tia assumed were curses, but she didn't try to translate. Instead, she spun, her arm outstretched, the glass mug still in her hand. It struck the man hard on the cheekbone. The cursing stopped, and he dropped to the floor. He shuddered and shook as blood ran from his nose and the gash on the side of his head.

Another man sprang from a nearby table and charged Tia, but she saw him coming. A quick side step, and her extended foot sent the would-be assailant to the ground. Tia shattered the mug on the back of his head. The man did not move.

Hearing a sound behind her, she spun to see the bartender pull a baseball bat from somewhere beneath the counter. He took one step, then his direction changed. One of her team had seized the barkeep by the front of his shirt and dragged him over the counter. One punch later, he became the third man on the floor.

The men in the bar shot to their feet as if choreographed but stopped before they could take a step, their eyes fixed on Tia's five-member crew. All five had pulled identical nine-millimeter pistols from beneath their coats. Five guns were pointed at the heads of various patrons. Only the rock-and-roll song could be heard.

Tia looked down at her hand, which still held the handle of the shattered mug. "A waste of beer if you ask me." She tossed the glass handle and walked to the unconscious bartender. She studied him for a moment then reached into the back pocket of her jeans and removed a thin billfold. She extracted an American hundred-dollar bill and tucked it into the bartender's shirt. "Perhaps we should call it a night, gentlemen."

She walked to the door, patrons parting before her like water before the prow of a ship.

The wind had settled some, but it was unwilling to release its grip on the flat expanse of ice. Perry leaned forward over the steering bars of the snowmobile, trying to lower the profile of his body and present less surface for the wind to press against. Perry could feel Griffin mimicking the position behind him. A glance at the other snowmobile showed Jack and Larimore doing the same thing.

The cold was bitter and angry. The moist air left Perry's lungs and froze against the stubble on his face. Breathing was difficult as the wind slapped around his parka's hood. His jaw hurt from chattering, and his body protested the odd position, but Perry pushed on. He had no choice.

The realization that one of the remaining eight could be a saboteur gave him a different kind of chill. He corrected himself. Not eight. He could vouch for Jack, Gleason, Dr. Curtis, and, of course, himself. That reduced the number of suspects to four: Larimore, Griffin, Gwen, and Sarah. Not one was a likely candidate. Larimore had lost six of his own men. Griffin might have some hidden motivation, but the scientist didn't seem the kind to resort to mass murder. Gwen and Sarah seemed even less likely. Perhaps he was showing his male chauvinism. A woman could make a bomb as easily as a man. He strained his memory to recall any news story about a female bomber. While he may have seen one, none came to his mind.

Perhaps it had been a suicide bombing. Such things were no longer rare. The Middle East, Europe, and other countries had their share. And who could forget the airliners crashing into the Trade Towers on September 11 just a handful of years before?

Maybe it had been an accident. After all, they were ill equipped to judge what caused the explosion. Perry certainly wasn't skilled in evaluating aircraft accidents. Perhaps something on board had exploded because of some unfortunate circumstance. He hoped that was the case. He doubted it was.

The thoughts boiled in Perry's brain. If one of the remaining eight were a saboteur, then he was facing the most dangerous situation in his life. There were no police to call, no security detail to ease his mind. He and the others would be sleeping with a terrorist. An icicle ran through Perry's mind. *Or terrorists.* The deed could just as easily have been done by more than one person.

Perry consulted the GPS monitor mounted on the snowmobile. Fifteen miles to go, a short distance in most circumstances. Today, it seemed half a world away.

Perry wondered what he would find when, Lord willing, they pulled up at the Dome.

CHAPTER 11

The snowmobile's motor sputtered to a stop in the equipment bay where Perry had found it the day before. The bay seemed warm, but Perry knew it was just the absence of the chilling wind, a wind he had been facing for too long. He was breathing hard, his joints ached, and his muscles burned.

He waited for Griffin to dismount then swung his own leg over the snowmobile. It felt good to stand, and he would have taken his time stretching, but he had other things on his mind. Without a word, Perry left the bay, rounded the Dome to the entrance, and plunged in.

His skin felt like it had caught fire when the heated air struck him. He knew that by most standards, the room was cool, but the difference from the outdoor temperature made the sixty-degree compartment seem like an oven.

"Gleason," Perry called out. No reply. Jack, Griffin, and Larimore poured through the door.

"No welcome-home party?" Jack asked.

Perry shrugged then called out again. "Gleason? Sarah?"

"Maybe they're in the Chamber," Larimore offered.

"Here comes someone," Jack said. Perry looked down the narrow hall that led to sleeping cubicles. Gwen was approaching. Even in the dim light of the building, they could see that something was wrong.

Griffin stepped forward. "What's wrong, Gwen? We tried to raise you on the radio, but—"

Gwen walked past her brother straight to Perry. Her face was drawn and colorless.

"Gwen?" Perry began.

"Um," she said, "Gleason would like to see you in the back."

Perry studied her for a moment, recognizing abject fear when he saw it. He removed his gloves and started down the corridor. He heard the others behind him. To either side were the small rooms that served as private berths. In the very back was the restroom— the head, as Larimore called it. The Dome had two bathrooms; the worker dormitory had one large facility. The rooms were small and had been built as modular units that could be easily assembled on-site. Since the rooms were modular, they contained only two toilets separated by a curtain and two small sinks. A simple cabinet held typical bathroom items. Team members took showers in a separate room.

Slipping into the small space, Perry found Gleason and Sarah hunkered down, staring into the cabinet. Gleason was sweating, something Perry hadn't seen anyone do since arriving in Antarctica. Seeing Perry enter, Sarah stood and stepped aside. Like Gwen, she was pale.

"What's wrong, Gleason?" Perry asked softly as he approached.

"See for yourself."

Perry dropped to one knee and peered in. His mind seized at the sight.

"Tell me it's just a really ugly spider," Jack said, his humor unconvincing.

"I wish," Perry said. "It's a bomb, and its counter seems stuck." Perry studied the device. It looked like a lump of gray clay with an electronic clock stuck on top. The clock showed four red numbers—00:00.

"Kinda makes you wonder why we're still here, doesn't it?" Gleason said. His throat sounded dry. Perry couldn't blame him.

"Better let me have a look at that," Larimore said. Gleason moved aside to give the commander some room. He lowered himself to a knee beside Perry. What followed was a series of curses and oaths strong enough to peel paint. He took several deep breaths, calmed himself then said, "C-4 plastic explosive. Enough to destroy the Dome. I've used this stuff to clear construction sites in battle conditions."

"Why hasn't it gone off?" Perry asked.

"I don't have an answer." Larimore shifted to two knees, placed both hands on the floor, and moved closer.

"Is it wise to get that close?" Griffin asked from his place in the doorway.

"If it goes off now, Doc," Larimore said, "a few inches won't make a difference. I'll be scattered over the ice."

"*We'll* be scattered over the ice," Sarah added.

Perry rose and looked at the others. He was calm, focused, but felt his body shutting down. He recognized it as a defense mechanism. Emotions were useless at this point, something the others must have realized, too, since he could detect no panic, just controlled terror.

"Okay, I think it's best if everyone goes into the Chamber. That's as far away as we can get without being outside. Griffin, you lead the group. Make some room behind the remaining wood crates. I don't know that they will provide much protection, but as far removed from this site as they are, they might help."

"What are you going to do?" Jack asked. "I'm not leaving you here to baby-sit a bomb."

"Not to worry," Perry said. "I have a job for you and Gleason."

"Oh goodie," Gleason said. "I was afraid you were going to leave me out."

Perry addressed Larimore. "Can you disarm this thing?"

He shook his head. "Normally, I'd say yes, but the counter has me spooked. If it were still counting down, I'd just pull the detonator wire from the C-4. No electricity, no boom. But the fact that the counter is at zero makes me think there may be a short somewhere. If I pull the wire, I may bridge that short, then it's bye-bye, everybody."

Perry blew a steady stream of air through his lips. "In that case, I want you to go with the others."

"I'm not deserting my post," Larimore said. "I'll take my chances with you."

"I appreciate that, but the team will need a leader if things. . . don't go well. I need Jack and Gleason to help me try something."

"Forget it," Larimore said. "I'm staying."

"So much for chain of command," Jack said.

"You can file a grievance from the Great Beyond if we're killed," Larimore quipped. "I can tell when a man has a plan. What are you thinking?"

"It may be the dumbest thing I've ever considered," Perry said, "but here's what we're going to do." He explained his thoughts and was greeted with thick silence. "Anyone have a better idea?" No one did. "Okay then, let's do this."

Gwen struggled to keep tears of frustration in check. Everyone around her was as calm as if they had received news no more important than the mail had arrived. She wanted to scream, to run, to give in to the near irresistible panic. She fought the urge. At the moment, her mind was the most important tool she had. Emotion could be released later.

"Let's go," Griffin said, taking his responsibility seriously and marching back down the corridor.

Gwen followed on his heels with Sarah on hers. A sense of guilt percolated within her. She felt as if she were running to hide while brave people remained behind.

"Perhaps we can help," she said to her brother.

He shook his head but didn't turn around. "Perry's no pal of mine, but he knows more about this kind of thing than we do. I've learned one thing about him: He is resourceful. Besides, it does no one any good if we all get killed."

"You're all heart," Sarah snapped.

"I'm all brain, ma'am, and right now we need more brain than emotion. The best thing we can do is get out of the way."

Gwen wished she could do more, but she knew Griffin was right. If the bomb killed Perry and the others, and she survived, at least she could tell the story—assuming Antarctica didn't kill her first.

Perry left Larimore to study the bomb more and helped Gleason, who was using a wrench to remove the bolts that held the exterior panel to the Dome's geodesic skeleton. They had power tools, but Perry was afraid they would create a vibration that would be transferred to the bomb's electronics. If Larimore was correct and a loose or broken wire had created a short, then a vibration or any movement might set it off. The explosive had to be moved, but Perry was determined to minimize that as much as possible.

Gleason worked rapidly but with great care. Each movement was the result of directed thought. Perry held the panel as Gleason finished removing the bolt. As he did, Perry heard a noise just beyond the wall. Jack had arrived on schedule.

Slowly, Perry pushed the lightweight composite panel out and felt it tugged away by Jack. The frigid wind that had been their adversary blew through, a weaker version of what they had endured over the last fifteen hours.

The air bit at his face and bare hands. He pulled his gloves from his pockets and quickly slipped them on as Jack set the panel to the side. Behind Jack was the snowmobile he had ridden less than an hour before.

"Good work, Jack," Perry said. "Gleason is going to help you with the rest."

"Come, Glees, ol' boy," Jack said. "Let's show Perry how to customize a snowmobile."

Gleason gave a nervous chuckle and stepped through the new opening. Perry returned to the lavatory and saw Larimore seated cross-legged on the floor. "I assume from the draft that you were successful."

"The remodeling is underway," Perry said. "Anything new?"

"No," Larimore said. "I've been playing with ideas, but I'm not thrilled with any of them."

"Let's hear them." Perry stepped around and saw the electronic clock still frozen at zero.

"I was thinking that we could join the others in the Chamber and just wait for the battery to run down. There's a small battery pack on the back of the package."

"Dead battery means no explosion," Perry said. "But you dismissed that idea?"

"Yeah, I did. The clock doesn't draw that much energy, so the battery could last days, maybe weeks."

"I have clocks at home that run for months before I have to replace the batteries."

"Precisely," Larimore said. "I don't think we could live that long with this thing and remain sane. Most likely it would go off before the battery was drained."

That had occurred to Perry as well. "Gleason tells me the batteries are missing from the base's radios, too. There's a good chance that one or more of them are on the bomb."

A tearing sound floated in on the wind. Perry was glad to hear it. It was almost time.

"It's tempting," Larimore said.

"What?"

"To reach in there and just pull out the wires. It might work."

"We'd better stay with the plan. The less we move the wires the better off we are."

"I hope you're right," Larimore said.

"I pray I'm right," Perry replied.

Gleason reappeared. "The chariot awaits," he said.

"Okay," Perry said. "You and the commander should make your way to the Chamber and join the others."

"I'd rather stay," Gleason said.

"I can't risk it, buddy," Perry said. "The others are going to need you if things go bad. Besides, I'm nervous enough. The fewer distractions I have, the better."

"So now I'm reduced to a distraction."

"You know what I mean," Perry said.

"Yeah, I do," Gleason said. He put a hand on Perry's shoulder. The gesture was simple, but the communication was profound.

"Get out of here, Gleason, and take this navy swab with you." Larimore started to protest, but Perry cut him off. "I insist, Commander. The fewer people around, the better this will go."

Larimore rose and extended his hand. Perry shook it. "Godspeed, Perry."

Perry replied with a silent nod. The two left, and Perry stepped to the opening. "Time for you to beat feet, pal."

Jack's expression became serious. "Sorry, I can't hear you."

"I said it's time for you to head to the other dome."

"Too much wind. I can't make out a word you're saying. Besides, there's a twelve-inch drop from the floor to the ice. The Dome is raised to allow room for insulation, remember."

Perry remembered. He also knew that Jack was hearing every word. "I can do this alone."

"What?" Jack raised a hand to his ear.

Perry shook his head. He could force his will on almost anyone but Jack. Jack made up his own mind about things. Perry glanced over his friend's head and saw the snowmobile two yards away from the Dome. He could also see strips of gray duct tape running from the handlebars to the side of the vehicle, locking the steering in a straight direction. On the seat was a cardboard box with the words CANNED BEEF printed on the side. Jack must have snatched the box from the galley on his way to retrieve the snowmobile. Another strip of duct tape hung limply from the throttle.

"What say we stop wasting time," Jack said. "You hand me the package, and I'll deliver it."

There would be no arguing with Jack, and time was slipping by. It was time to act. Perry shook his head and returned to the bathroom, bent over, and placed his hands on the side of the gray brick that he knew to be one of the most powerful explosives around. If the bomb went off in Perry's hands, there would be no pain, no awareness of his failure. Nor would there be much of him to bury.

"It is appointed for men to die once and after this comes judgment." The Bible verse made him wonder if his appointed date had arrived. Images of his father and friends flashed into his mind. He smiled. He planned to live a very long time, but if his life ended in the next second, it didn't matter. It had already been a great life.

Perry closed his hands on the bomb and lifted it from its place in the cabinet. He was surprised he was still alive. "Step one," he whispered to himself then turned toward the door, moving slowly, thinking about every step before he took it. Five steps later he was facing the cold blast of wind as it shot through the recently made opening. Jack stood just outside, his normally jovial face drawn tight. The wind whipped the fur lining of his hood, but Jack stood solid as a rock.

"I think I can do this myself," Perry said as he approached the opening.

"Just give me the thing," Jack said. "The sooner this is over, the better I'll feel."

"Even if we get blown to tiny little bits?"

"Yeah, I hear Heaven is real nice this time of year."

"Any time of year," Perry said. The conversation helped keep him calm and focused. Bending at the waist, Perry handed the deadly device to his closest friend and felt guilty the moment he did. He should have found some way to make Jack leave.

"Got it," Jack said. "Not as heavy as I thought it would be." He turned and took a step toward the idling snowmobile.

"I don't suppose I should remind you that you're walking on ice."

"Thanks, chum. Up until now I didn't have anything to worry about."

Perry waited until his friend was a few steps away, then he jumped the short distance to the ice. Jack moved very slowly. Perry jogged around him, giving him a wide berth, and reached the vehicle first. He watched Jack take a step, twisting his foot from side to side to make sure of his footing before taking another. It was like watching someone walk underwater—excruciatingly slow. Perry used the time to double-check the system Jack had set up on the snowmobile. Duct tape ran from the handlebars to the body. The cardboard box was also secured with the tape. The flaps had been torn off, leaving just the four sides and the bottom. Perry hoped the famous fix-it-all tape could stand the abysmal temperatures a little longer.

Jack arrived and gently set the explosive device in the box, pushing it to the rear—a good idea, Perry realized. If the bomb slid, then it might explode while it was close enough to do real damage.

Jack released his grip and took a step back. "Your turn."

Perry nodded, took the piece of tape that dangled from the accelerator handle, and turned the handle enough to rev the engine just above idle. Then he secured the tape.

"Now the scary part," Perry said.

"The other part wasn't scary?"

"Step back," Perry ordered, and to his surprise, Jack did.

Perry reached forward, dropped the snowmobile in gear, and prayed that it wouldn't lurch. The engine chugged a moment, wanting more fuel, but then slowly pulled away. Perry had no desire to play spectator. He sprinted for the opening with Jack a step behind. When he reached the hole in the wall, he dove through it and rolled forward on the floor. He heard a thud behind him. His big friend had taken the same approach.

Staggering to their feet, they turned and watched the snowmobile crawl along the ice.

"How far do you think it will go?" Jack asked.

"There's some rough ice a hundred yards or so ahead of it. If Larimore—"

The slow-moving vehicle erupted into a ball of fire. Perry and Jack hit the floor and covered their heads.

CHAPTER 12

I t's time you came clean," Griffin said.

The entire group sat in the common area of the Dome. It had been two hours since the snowmobile carried away the bomb. Perry had called for another search of the facility, and they had searched every corner, nook, and crevice twice more. Gleason had filled Perry in on the acid-injured radios and how he, Sarah, Gwen, and Dr. Curtis had begun searching the area and found the bomb. It had not been an idea that first occurred to them, and Gleason bemoaned the fact. They had spent hours trying to construct a single radio that would work. He and Sarah had cannibalized all they could with no success. It was in desperation that they began the search, hoping to find some clue as to who might have done such a thing.

Perry looked at Griffin and wondered how to respond. Perry was weary from the previous day's expedition—seeing the horrific loss of life, searching wreckage for life he knew wasn't there, enduring the windstorm huddled in a makeshift shelter, riding back against a still too powerful wind, and then finding the bomb. What Perry really wanted to do was go to bed and forget, at least for a few hours, all that he had seen in the past twenty-four hours. That was not to happen. He would not allow himself that comfort. Not yet.

"Come clean about what?" Dr. Curtis asked.

"Perry has admitted to withholding information," Griffin said. "I think the situation is such that we need—that we have a *right* to all the information available."

"We have more pressing problems," Sarah said. "From what Perry has told us, we may have a killer among us."

"We don't know that," Larimore said. "The plane may have been brought down by a bomb, but there was a bomb here as well. Would someone plant such a device in the only shelter available to him. . .or her?"

Perry had told them of the crash and his suspicion that it was no accident. The bomb in the bathroom was an exclamation point to it all.

"It's not fair that you and your buddies have all the secrets," Griffin said. "We're out here risking life and limb, just like you."

"Ease up, Grif," Jack said. "I don't know any more than you, and if that's the way it has to be, then there will be no complaints from me."

Perry looked around the room. Seven faces looked back, faces that made no secret of their exhaustion. "Dr. James is right," he said. "This is as good a time as any. I had planned to lay out all the cards once the construction crew was gone."

"You didn't trust my men?" Larimore asked.

"It's not a matter of trust, Commander, it's a matter of secrecy and need-to-know information. No one on the crew had a need to know."

"I sure need to know," Gwen said.

Perry stood and clasped his hands behind his back. He paused, organizing his thoughts. "You already know of the surveys done by satellite and aircraft. I told you when we arrived that Lake Vostok, the body of water that is two miles beneath our feet, is expanding, indicating an under-ice melting that has yet to be explained. That, of course, is true."

"Of course," Griffin said.

"What you don't know occurred a few months ago. Dr. Harry Hearns—a scientist with the National Ice Center—made an unusual discovery in an iceberg."

"Don't you mean *on* an iceberg?" Gwen corrected.

"No, I mean *in* an iceberg," Perry responded. "Dr. Hearns specializes in icebergs and how they calve. While studying a particular berg—the second largest ever seen, as I understand it—the berg split, and he shot video of it."

"Nothing unusual so far," Griffin said.

"No, it's not," Perry replied. "There are plenty of such events on video, but what made this one so different was *what* the video captured. The ice split, and Hearns, who was in a helicopter, saw a dark object. Once the calving was complete, the new berg, the portion that split off, was top-heavy and rolled into the sea."

"What did he see?" Sarah asked.

"A building," Perry answered, then waited for their response. Silence. The seven looked from one person to the other.

"A building?" Griffin said with disbelief. "He saw a building on the ice?"

"Not on—in. He filmed a portion of a stone structure that was, according to his report, 150 meters below the surface of the ice, entombed."

"That's impossible," Griffin said.

"That's right," Perry said. "By today's scientific understanding, that is impossible."

"That's very old ice. Ice is laid down at about two centimeters a year, and you're talking fifteen thousand centimeters. That's seventy-five hundred years ago. Not possible. There's some mistake. There are seventy million cubic miles of ice on the continent, and it didn't get here suddenly. It took millions of years for this ice sheet to form."

"Then explain Hearns's house or whatever building he saw," Larimore said.

"As I said, it's a mistake," Griffin said with a dismissive wave. "I've met Dr. Hearns, and he seemed a very serious and capable scientist. Someone has twisted something he said. I bet he's furious over it."

"He's not," Perry said. "He's dead."

Griffin's hard expression softened. "What?"

Perry explained. "He wasn't satisfied with the brief glimpse he had from the helicopter. He made arrangements to dive on the inverted iceberg. While he waited for the ship and two-man submersible that would allow him a closer look, he studied the video and still photos, sending them via satellite to several colleagues. Those colleagues put pressure on the National Science Foundation and the military to provide Hearns with the necessary equipment. It worked."

"It also clued in the military," Sarah said.

"Right. Hearns got what he wanted, but something went wrong on the dive. It appears that the pilot sailed the craft right into the ice. Maybe the controls jammed, but the collision breached the hull, and the submersible was flooded with freezing water. They drowned."

"That's horrible," Sarah said.

"Ghastly," Gwen agreed.

"Further suspicions were raised when two Coast Guard pilots died in a fatal crash."

"Let me guess," Jack said. "They were the pilots who were flying Hearns's helicopter when he saw the structure."

Perry nodded. "Exactly."

"And this is what you've been holding back from us?" Griffin asked.

"There's more." Perry handed out manila folders to the team. "You each received brief packets before you left your homes to come here. All the information you needed was contained in those packets. What wasn't in them is the information you now need." Perry waited as the other seven opened the thin folders. He watched their expressions.

"This is another radar survey of the lake below the ice," Curtis said. "It looks different than what I saw before. For one thing, the lake seems larger than the last image—"

"What is that?" Griffin asked.

"That is why we're here," Perry said.

"It looks like some kind of mound," Sarah suggested. "An upheaval of the crust along the edge of the lake?"

Perry didn't answer. He was standing in a room filled with great minds: scientists and engineers from various fields, each considered an accomplished expert in his or her field. They would get it given time.

"It's awfully uniform," Curtis said. "It's difficult to be certain, but it seems symmetrical and shows strong perimeter lines."

"Nonsense," Griffin said. "That would suggest design. It has to be a natural phenomenon. Why didn't we see this before?"

Perry was waiting for that question. "As you know, you're looking at a radar image taken from a plane. Using sixty megahertz radar data, which measures the change in ice thickness, we have determined that the ice shield has been melting faster than previously thought. As it melts, new details can be seen. We combined all the information—data from radar, satellite imagery, InSAR interferometry, and more—and developed a three-dimensional model. That's on the next page."

Papers rustled and then—

"This is a joke," Griffin said. "This is your idea of humor."

"Oh my," Curtis said, staring at the image. He leaned back in his chair and stroked his chin.

"Wow," was all Jack said.

"Dr. Curtis?" Perry prompted. "What do you think?"

"I think my world has just been turned upside-down."

"It's not real," Griffin said, springing to his feet. "First you tell this kindergarten tale about a stone building in an iceberg, and now you expect me to believe that there is a. . .a *pyramid* below my feet."

"Ziggurat," Dr. Curtis corrected. "Essentially the same thing, but with some marked differences."

"Call it what you will," Griffin snapped. "But I call it foolishness. If this were true. . ."

"It's true," Perry said after a moment. "And we're going to take a look at it."

"I refuse to participate in such a waste of time," Griffin said.

"Where you going to go?" Larimore asked. "What are you going to do? Sit in your room and fabricate new ways to deny what your eyes tell you?"

"The commander has a point," Gwen said, breaking a long silence. "We're stuck here. It's not like we can walk home. There's no plane, and one isn't due for weeks."

"When the transport doesn't show up on schedule, they'll come looking for it," Griffin said.

"That's true," Perry said. "But in the meantime, I say we occupy ourselves with the original task."

"Aren't you forgetting something?" Sarah intoned. "The plane didn't go down by accident, at least that's your contention. And the plastic explosive in the bathroom certainly was no accident. There's still a killer somewhere."

"Unless he blew himself up on the plane," Gwen said. "That wouldn't bring a tear to my eye."

"If one of us were the killer," Larimore began, "then why would he or she blow up the only means of survival?"

"That very question has been on my mind," Perry said. "Things don't add up. Not yet. Still, we can't sit around looking at each other. Let's carry on with our mission."

"When?" Jack asked.

"Right now," Perry said. "It's time to unleash Hairy."

The twin turboprops of the Casa 212 airplane knifed through the thin Antarctic air. The wing-over-body craft was painted a white that matched the terrain below. Minutes before, Tia and her team had watched the blue waters of the southernmost Pacific Ocean, where Pacific became Atlantic, turn icy white. The ground below swept by at nearly two hundred knots. The speed seemed greater since the pilot was skipping along at an altitude of less than a hundred feet. It was not safe, but it was what Tia had ordered.

To the right rose the Ellsworth Mountains; to the left was the wide expanse of the Ronne Ice Shelf. Ahead lay more ice.

Ahead lay the future.

"You know me, buddy," Jack was saying. He and Perry were watching Gleason and Sarah make the final connections to the cryobot called Hairy. The rest of the team stood nearby wearing the clean suits. "I'll believe just about anything you say, but this one has me wondering. A pyramid below the ice? Ice that most people in the know say was laid down long before anyone could have sailed here?"

"I didn't make it up, Jack. It's there, and yes, it looks like a pyramid—or ziggurat, as Dr. Curtis reminded us."

"What's the difference?"

"Shape," a voice said. Dr. Curtis approached. "Pyramids have straight sides while ziggurats are stepped. Usually the word *ziggurat* is applied to Mesopotamian structures, but the term can be used more widely. A ziggurat starts wide at the ground and each layer up is smaller until it reaches its peak."

"So you think one of these ziggurats is below the ice," Jack said.

Dr. Curtis shook his head. "I'm sorry, Perry, but it's too much to believe. I've seen strange things in my day, including that find of yours in the Tehachapi Mountains that still has me answering questions from universities all around the world, but this pushes my credulity a tad too far. I have to agree with Dr. James. It's a mound of some sort that coincidentally looks man-made."

"Sensible conclusion, Dr. Curtis," Griffin said. "At least I have one other reasonable person around."

"Don't count me too far on your side, Dr. James," Curtis said. "I'm willing to admit that I've been surprised before."

"We all have, but not by the likes of this," Griffin objected. "Buildings mean humans, and it is simply impossible to think that humans ever inhabited this region—or anywhere in Antarctica. The largest native animal here is the wingless midge. Anything larger than that insect could never survive the hostilities of the land. Sure, penguins, seals, and the like make their way to the shoreline, but nothing moves inland."

"But Antarctica has changed," Perry said. "What we see today is not the way it's always been."

"Everything changes, Mr. Sachs. Nothing is stagnant."

"Except old ideas," Perry countered.

"Excuse me?" Griffin said, looking injured.

"Humans have a tendency to latch onto a truth and cling to it no matter how much evidence tells them otherwise."

"You mean like your faith," Griffin said. "My sister tells me you're a Christian. Is that so?"

"It is."

"That goes for me, too," Jack said.

"And me," Curtis said without embarrassment.

"Really?" Griffin said, looking at Curtis. "That surprises me. I can understand how these two might succumb to such myths, but you're scientifically trained. And in archaeology at that."

"I have found science deepens my faith," Curtis said. "And don't sell these men short. You're too intelligent a man to be shackled by scientific chauvinism. Perry, Jack, and Gleason are no fools."

"Thanks, Doc," Jack said. "I think you're just swell, too."

Curtis sighed. "No matter how much they may act it." He returned his attention to Griffin. "Science is the pursuit of reality. We struggle to describe what was, what is, and what may come to be. Once we cease to test, to reexamine, then we become the keepers of the old, not the explorers of the new."

"I don't think you can accuse me of being a keeper of the old," Griffin said.

"Really?" Curtis asked. "An hour ago in the Dome, when Perry revealed the news about poor Dr. Hearns's find, you pooh-poohed it out of hand. When presented with the possibility of a human-made structure where no such structure could possibly be, you refused to participate in a search for the truth."

"But you said you didn't believe it to be what it appears," Griffin said.

"That's true. I don't see how any structure, pyramidal or not, can be there. The difference between us is I want to ascertain the truth."

"Science is science, and stupidity is stupidity," Griffin remarked.

"Sometimes it's hard to tell the difference," Jack said.

"You know as well as I," Perry said, "that Antarctica used to be very different. All we see is cold and ice, but life existed here—life much larger than the wingless midge. The fossil record shows the presence of forests of the southern beech tree, *Nothofagus*. Fossil leaves of a plant similar to the ginkgo biloba have been found as well. Conifer remains are present, including one that stands twenty-three feet high. On the Antarctic Peninsula the remains of a giant, flightless bird have been unearthed. In recent years a crested carnivore fossil was found, as was a duck-billed hadrosaur. Evidence of small dinosaurs exists, too, such as the *Leaellynasaura* and later marsupials. On Seymour Island, near the Antarctic Peninsula, scientists found a fossil of an armadillo the size of a Volkswagen."

"That's a long way from an established human civilization," Griffin said.

"My point is, life used to be here in abundance," Perry said.

"So what changed?" Jack asked.

"You want to take a crack at that, Dr. James?" Perry asked. "It's your specialty."

"I'll concede that complex life used to make its home here, but that would have been when Antarctica was part of Australia, which was part of a single large continent, the supercontinent Gondwana."

"Okay, I'll bite," Jack said. "Gond-what?"

"Gondwana or Gondwanaland," Griffin said. "Three hundred million years ago the continents of South America, Africa, Australia, and Antarctica were part of a single land mass. The name comes from Eduard Suess, an Austrian geologist. He wrote a book around the turn of the twentieth century called *The Face of the Earth*."

"The original Dr. Seuss, eh?" Jack joked.

"Whatever," Griffin said. "His concept is now called plate tectonics. That's the idea that the continents are not stationary. There was a time when all the continents were one. That land mass is called Pangaea. At least, that's how the theory goes. It's still hypothetical."

"As much of science is," Curtis commented. "That explains the need for an open mind and desire for truth."

"Let me ask something," Perry said. "Why is Antarctica so cold?"

"Two reasons, primarily," Griffin said. "First, location: Antarctica does not receive much direct sunlight, and most of what it does receive is reflected back into space by the white ice. Also, there are months near darkness where very little light reaches the surface."

"And the second reason?" Perry prompted.

"The Antarctic Circumpolar Current."

"The ocean makes it cold?" Jack said.

Griffin nodded. "This continent is surrounded by ocean, like a huge island. The oceans affect weather everywhere. At the higher latitudes the water is warmed by the sun, and currents move that warm water around, which transfers that energy to the climate. The Antarctic Circumpolar Current never gets to the higher latitudes, so it remains cold—extremely cold. It is the main reason for the freezing conditions we find ourselves in."

"If the continent were part of a larger land mass, then the current wouldn't be stuck in the circumpolar loop, right?" Perry said.

"Right."

"Therefore, the continent would be warmer."

"True," Griffin said, "but all of this happened hundreds of millions of years ago."

"Perhaps," Perry said. "Perhaps not."

Gleason and Sarah approached, closely followed by Gwen, who had been caught up in the work.

"We're ready, Perry," he said. "Just give the word."

"Consider it given."

CHAPTER 13

Thomas Mahoney snapped an order to the young sailor who stood at the state-of-the-art control console of the 420-foot Coast Guard cutter, and the sleek vessel began a slow turn, just as it had a few miles before. He let his gray, sun-bleached eyes trace the water's surface. He saw nothing new, and his frustration increased.

"Is it just me, or is something out of whack?" his executive officer, Ray Seager, asked.

Mahoney thought for a moment, wondering if he had detected something wrong with the ship, something that had slipped by him. The diesel-electric propulsion system seemed normal. If anything was wrong with the thirty-thousand-horsepower engines, his crew would notify him immediately. Then he caught his XO's meaning.

"You mean the missing plane?" Mahoney said.

"Exactly. It doesn't seem right."

It doesn't seem right, Mahoney thought. They had received word of a missing C-5 overdue at McMurdo Station. The *Healy*, an icebreaker and scientific platform, was pressed into search duty. It made sense. No one knew the cold waters better than an ice-breaker captain and his crew. This was Mahoney's second year as CO, and although far from home, he loved the duty. Most days the powerful ship cleared channels for supply ships or aided researchers in scientific exploration. Cutting through ten-foot-thick sea ice was a combination of skill, experience, and brute force. The captain and thirty-one-member crew provided the former, the *Healy's* mass and engines provided the rest.

"What's bothering you, Commander?" Mahoney asked. Off the bridge he would have referred to his XO and longtime friend by first name, but never in front of other crewmen.

"Everything, Captain." Mahoney was taller than Seager by two inches and weighed a good fifteen pounds more. Those pounds wanted to settle just above his belt, which annoyed him. "We've been at this for ten hours now and have found nothing, not a single piece of wreckage, not the tiniest pool of fuel or oil on the surface. I don't think she's out here."

"Neither do I," Mahoney admitted. "It would take the world's worst pilot to overshoot McMurdo and fall into the sea without a distress signal or radio communication."

"I suppose it could have been mechanical failure," Seager said.

"What kind of mechanical failure could cause an aircraft to fly past its intended landing area and drop into the sea? The crew would have be asleep at the wheel. And weather isn't a consideration. The sky was clear and the katabatic didn't hit the coast until the craft had been overdue by two hours. I agree, something isn't right."

"So what do we do?"

"We follow our orders, Commander," Mahoney said with crisp, military diction. "We search until we're told to stop."

The Sachs Engineering building rose from the concrete and asphalt of downtown Seattle like a stately redwood, reflecting the late afternoon sunshine back to the cloud-adorned blue sky. Below Henry Sachs's twelfth-story office's window, commuters clogged the narrow streets. It made no difference to Henry; he wasn't planning on returning home until just before bedtime. With his wife

Anna visiting her sister in Florida, there was little need to rush home. Instead, he settled in his large leather chair.

Henry Sachs was not given to ornamentation or fine art. A simple metal desk in a quiet room was all he needed to lose himself in his work. His office, however, was far from Spartan. Rich red-oak paneling covered the walls, leather chairs and a sofa marked off a casual meeting area, and halogen ceiling lights bathed the umber carpet in the purest white light. Paintings hung proudly from walls, displaying projects his firm had erected over the years—at least the ones that carried no top-secret classification.

He sat behind a desk made of quilted maple. The desk was his pride and joy. Not because it was one of a kind but because of the artist who made it—his son, Perry. In fact, Perry was responsible for the whole office. Henry had been overseas for extended business and when he returned, he found his office made over in *Architectural Digest*-fashion. "Happy birthday," Perry had said. The thought still brought tears of joy to Henry's eyes, tears he was quick to hide from others.

On Henry's desk were several file folders, a thin computer monitor and keyboard, and a family picture. He picked up the picture and studied it. The photo had been taken at a local restaurant, where Perry had taken Henry and Anna to celebrate forty years of marriage.

On the glass pane that protected the picture, Henry saw the pale reflection of his face. He had grown older. He acknowledged the fact, but he refused to allow it any seat in his mind. The reflection that stared back was of a man with white hair combed back in easy waves, a deeply tanned face, and a mouth comfortable with smiling. Just beyond the glass was the picture of his wife—dark hair, dancing blue eyes, a petite nose, and lips parted to reveal a row of white teeth. She was stunning when he met her, and she still made his heart leap when he looked at her.

He missed his wife.

He missed Perry, too. His son's image, a younger version of himself dressed in black coat over gray shirt and tan pants, gave Henry pause. He was proud of his son in more ways than he could count, but seeing his picture filled him with concern. It was a nebulous sensation that something was wrong. He had the vague feeling that Perry was in danger. There were no facts to justify the fear, but it was there nonetheless.

The phone rang, startling Henry.

He answered. He listened. He began to pray.

"When?" he asked the caller. "That was almost a full day ago. . . . You'll keep me advised? Good. Thank you for calling."

Henry Sachs hung up the phone and wondered what to do next. Ironically, the call had come from Seattle, from the Coast Guard base. The base commander had taken it upon himself to notify Henry of the downed plane. He knew Perry was scheduled to stay on the project site for several more weeks. He felt some comfort in that. What brought him no comfort was what he had to do next—phone six now-bereaved families.

CHAPTER 14

Perry stood to one side of the hole in the ice. Over the last few hours Hairy had made significant headway, moving faster than expected. Perry checked the rigging again, just as he had five minutes before. The support structure they had erected earlier remained rock solid, and the cable that connected Hairy to the surface moved easily along its guides.

Again Perry leaned over the four-foot-wide hole and stared into its open maw. It was remarkable that Hairy could do what it was doing, melting the ice before it and sinking through the slush left behind. A thick-walled hose trailing after Hairy carried water out of the hole so that it wouldn't refreeze and close off the opening.

"It's a patient man's game," Larimore said. "I'm afraid I'm ill-equipped to play it."

"Moving through two miles of ice is going to take some time," Perry said. "Too much energy to the heating elements could cause problems with the onboard sensors."

"It's hard to believe," Larimore added, "that this robot is moving downward under its own power."

"Its own weight," Perry corrected. "There are small tractorlike treads on the side that keep it centered in the ice shaft, but they provide no appreciable forward movement."

"And they plan to send one of these to Europa?"

"Yes. According to Sarah it will be much smaller and will have to work without all the rigging we've hooked up. We have an advantage that the space-going cryobot doesn't. We can pump out the slush, provide an unlimited power source for the heating element in the head, and, once it breaks through to the lake, control it in real time. By comparison, this is a walk in the park."

"Some park," Larimore said. The navy commander seemed alien and somehow different in his clean suit. "Do we really have to wear these? When we were putting some distance between us and the bomb, we didn't bother with these things."

"That was an emergency situation," Perry replied. "We had no choice. We want the Chamber as unpolluted as possible. Breaching protocol once for an emergency situation doesn't change our goal."

"You got that right," Gwen said. "It may be a moot point. No matter what we do, we're bound to introduce something to the lake that wasn't there before."

"I bathed, I promise," Larimore said, as if trying to lighten the moment.

"You can't bathe enough," Gwen said seriously. "Human skin is covered with microscopic animals. Even our breath is loaded with bacteria. We're all walking worlds for microscopic life. It has always been that way."

"Suddenly I feel dirty," Larimore quipped.

"You are," Gwen said. "We all are. And now we're going to plunge a mechanical device into pristine waters. There'll be no going back."

"Hairy is cleaner than an operating room," Perry said. "Sarah saw to that."

Gwen shook here head. "It may have been clean when it started down, but there are microorganisms in the ice."

"You mean we're taking microscopic bugs from the surface

down with the device?" Larimore asked.

"That's right," she said with a sigh. "That's been the big problem all along. It's impossible to make the journey without taking unwanted passengers with us."

Perry understood her point and felt badly about running such a risk, but he also knew that it had to be done. "The lake may not be as pristine as you think, Doctor. It's my understanding that there is still some uncertainty about how these lakes form. Isn't it possible that the water could have percolated in from below and not be the result of melted ice?"

"It's possible," Gwen allowed.

"And the geological heat source is certainly contributing something to the water. If the water remains liquid because of ground heating, then the geothermal heat may also be contributing to the water."

Perry turned to see Gwen scowling at him through her face shield. "If there's a pile of garbage on your front lawn, should I feel free to dump my waste there as well?"

Perry laughed. "Point taken, Gwen."

"Those things you describe may have created a closed-system environment. They're not contaminating what's there; they may be maintaining it."

"Quarter mile," Gleason announced. He was standing behind Sarah, who was seated before a table that held two computer monitors. Her hands were folded in her lap. There was little for her to do but watch the electronic readouts. It was going to be a long vigil, one that would have to be shared. Sarah had estimated, based on the ice densities given her by Griffin, that Hairy would take forty-eight hours to core through the ice sheet. That estimate assumed a speed of over three feet per minute, a speed she had told Perry was remarkably fast.

"Where's your brother?" Larimore asked Gwen.

"He got bored and went to his room. There's little to do here but wait for the outside world to find us." She paused. "I think he's planning on leaving with the next plane, which he assumes will be here soon—once someone realizes that the C-5 didn't arrive."

"I see," Perry said. "What about you? Will you be going with him?"

"No," she said quickly enough to surprise him. "I don't approve of what you're doing, but you have my interest. If you're going to breach the ice sheet anyway, I might as well be the scientist who sees it first."

Perry smiled. "Curiosity wins out again."

"A scientist without curiosity is like a car without wheels," Gwen said.

"For once, I think your brother had a good idea," Larimore said. "I'm useless here. I think I'll hit the rack for awhile. What are you going to do, Perry?"

"I'm going to try and split them up," he answered, nodding at Gleason and Sarah, their eyes glued to the monitors. "They need to take shifts. Staying up for forty-eight hours won't do them or the project any good."

"Good luck," Larimore said and headed for the air lock.

Once Larimore was out of the Chamber, Gwen turned to Perry. "Do you think it's wise to leave him alone?"

"Commander Larimore?" Perry asked.

"Yes. He's the most likely suspect for putting the bomb on board that plane."

"Perhaps," Perry said. "But then again, you could have done it, or your brother, or Sarah."

"Or you," she snapped.

"From your point of view, you're correct." Perry thought for a moment. "I can't keep an eye on everyone at all times and neither can you. There's only one person who knows if the bomber is among us, and I doubt that person will volunteer the information."

"So we just give up? We just surrender to the situation?"

"We remain vigilant. The only other option is to lock everyone in their rooms, and that would be useless. The doors don't even have locks."

"I'll confess to being. . .uncomfortable," Gwen said. "I'm not sure I'll be able to sleep again until I'm in my own bed with all the doors locked and bolted."

"Understandable," Perry said. What Gwen didn't know, and what Perry didn't feel compelled to tell, was that he had already had a conversation with Jack, Gleason, and Dr. Curtis—the three men Perry trusted completely. Together they would keep an eye on the other team members. After Griffin had left the Chamber, Jack and Dr. Curtis followed. Perry had not gone with them but knew they were "chatting and snacking" in the commons area, but they were also tracking the movement of the others into the Dome. Perry and Gleason covered the Chamber. It would be a tag-team effort, but two of his team would be awake at all times and able to account for the whereabouts and activities of the others.

Their work had just doubled.

The dials Sarah watched were virtual. There were no metal hands pointing at letters painted on a disk, just light green lines "drawn" on the computer monitors. There were two monitors. The one to her right displayed the onboard camera's view; at the moment, it showed only milk white and occasional bubbles. The one on her left displayed six gauges. To her right sat the joystick controls she had been practicing with over the last few days. At the moment the joystick was as useless as a paperweight. Hairy was following its program of melting its way through the ice. Gravity provided the propulsion, and since it was moving in a shaft just a hair larger than itself, there was no room to turn.

Sarah shifted in the uncomfortable seat.

"We should have brought a padded chair," Gleason said.

"A nice rocking chair would be good," Sarah said, then smiled at the image of a wooden rocking chair resting on the ice.

"This is one slow video game," Gleason said.

"Don't tell me you're one of the men who wastes hour upon hour with a game controller in your hand."

"It builds character," Gleason said. "Besides, I have kids, and Perry is always buying them some new game. Someone has to teach them how to play."

"You're close to Perry, aren't you?" Sarah asked. She noticed a tingling in the back of her brain, and her stomach dropped.

"Yeah, we go way back. He's good to me and mine."

Sarah turned her attention to the gauges. The tingling in her brain was moving forward as if crawling along the inside of her skull. *Not now,* she said to herself. "How. . .how many children do you have?"

"Two. A twelve-year-old boy and a girl who's eleven."

"A girl," Sarah said. Her vision blurred, and she felt her eyes begin to roll back. "You'll. . .you'll have boys coming by. . .soon."

"I plan on buying a big ugly dog to sit on the front doorstep," Gleason said. "If they get past the dog, then they'll have to get past me."

"You sound like my father. He said I couldn't. . .date. . .until I was. . .thirty. . . ." The gauges disappeared. The monitors melted away. The world ceased to exist.

"Smart man. Was your father an engineer, too?"

She could hear his voice, but her mouth would no longer work.

"I asked if your father was an engineer, too."

The darkness deepened from gray to purple-black.

"Sarah? Are you all right?"

The Nothing had swallowed her.

"Perry!"

Perry snapped his head from Gwen to Gleason.

"Perry, I need you!" Gleason was kneeling beside Sarah, who had been seated a moment ago.

Perry closed the distance between them quickly and dropped to his knees. "What happened?"

"I don't know," Gleason said. "We were talking, and she slumped over. I caught her before she hit the ice."

"Did you notice anything strange before she fell?" Gwen asked. Perry was glad she had followed him.

"Not really," Gleason said. "She was asking about my family, and then her speech became slurred and halting. Next thing I knew, she was keeling over."

"Let me in," Gwen ordered, and Gleason stepped aside.

Perry watched as Gwen laid a gloved hand on the fallen woman's neck. She shook her head.

"What?" Perry demanded. "No pulse?"

"I can't tell. These gloves are in the way." Gwen stripped off her clean-suit gloves then the thinner pair she wore beneath. Again she pressed her fingers to Sarah's throat and nodded. "Pulse is strong and regular." Her eyes drifted to Sarah's chest and lingered. "Breathing is even." She bent over and placed her face shield close to Sarah's. "She's moving her lips, but I can't hear anything."

"We should get her into the Dome," Perry said.

"Agreed."

"Take her feet, Gleason."

Before Perry could slip his arms under Sarah's, he saw her eyes snap open. She blinked a few times then sat up.

"Are you okay?" Gleason asked.

"Yeah. Yeah, I'm fine." She started to get up.

"Take it easy," Perry said. "You passed out."

"Nonsense," Sarah said. "I'm fine. I must have fallen asleep."

"It looked like more than sleep," Gleason said. "You fell off the chair."

"I've been pretty tired. I think the thin air is getting to me."

Perry looked at Gwen and could tell she wasn't buying the story. Sarah shrugged off Perry's grasp and stood up. "See, I'm fine. I just let myself slip off. I've always been able to go into a deep sleep." She sat down at the table again as if nothing had happened. "Did I miss anything?"

"I don't know," Gleason admitted. "I was preoccupied with you."

"I want you to take a break," Perry said. "And I want you to let Gwen have a look at you."

"No need. I'm fine."

"I insist," Perry said. "In fact, I'm pulling rank. I was coming over here to suggest that you two split shifts anyway. Now is as good a time as any to start."

"But I need to monitor—"

"Gleason will keep an eye on Hairy and will let you know if there are any problems or changes. Now go." Perry looked at Gwen, who nodded. "If Gwen gives you the okay, you can come back after a few hours' sleep. Got it?"

"There's really no need. . ."

"Got it?"

"Yes, sir!" Sarah jumped to her feet and snapped a salute. Perry saw the anger on her face. She marched off, and Gwen had to step fast to keep up.

CHAPTER 15

Because it's none of his business," Sarah snapped after she and Gwen had reached her small room. "And quite honestly, it's none of yours."

"You couldn't be more wrong, and you know it," Gwen replied in the same tone. "I don't know where you think you are, but death is just outside those walls. We're not in a comfy apartment with a hospital around the corner should we need it. We're in the middle of no-man's-land—no-woman's-land, if you prefer. What happens to one of us happens to all of us."

"You're overstating the issue," Sarah said.

"Oh, really? And you've spent how much time on the ice? My time on the continent adds up to two years. Yours? Two weeks. And do I need to remind you that we have no communications with the outside?"

"No, you don't need to remind me." Sarah moved to her bed and plopped down.

"Good, now let's start from the beginning. What just happened?"

"I told you. I fell asleep."

"You expect me to believe that?"

"It's the truth," Sarah said, her voice softening. "In a manner of speaking." She was being evasive, and she didn't know how to stop herself. She had been making excuses for herself since she was a child.

"What do you mean, 'in a manner of speaking'?" Gwen's face darkened in thought. "Wait a minute. Are you telling me you have narcolepsy?"

"More like it has me." There, it was out, and there was no taking it back.

"Ah," Gwen said. She pulled the room's lone chair from under the tiny desk and sat down. "That does shed some light on things."

"I've had it since I was a teenager." Sarah felt a tear brim the edge of her eye. Confessing weakness was not something she did well. "Medication has kept it in check, but stress sometime sets it off."

"Stress? You mean like living in the world's coldest place, knowing that a plane full of people went down ten minutes after you waved good-bye? Something as simple as that?"

Sarah chuckled. "Yeah, I'm sensitive that way." She took a deep breath. "It's not all that rare really. One in two thousand people are affected. Many are undiagnosed. It's what kept me out of the astronaut corps."

"I can't believe Perry would let you come out here with a condition like that."

"He doesn't know. I've worked hard at keeping it under wraps. This project needs me, and I need it. I couldn't let the opportunity slip by. In one way, I'm lucky. I know I have it. The average span between onset and proper diagnosis is fourteen years."

"Fourteen years? You can't be serious."

"I'm serious about most things. I'm especially serious about my disease."

"I'm afraid this is a little beyond my paramedic training," Gwen confessed.

"There's nothing you can do, or should do. Mine is a moderate case. I can drop off at anytime, but my meds keep things in check. I haven't had an episode like what you saw in months."

"Any other triggers besides stress?" Gwen wondered.

"Not for me. Some people go under when they feel strong emotions, such as surprise or amusement."

"And the symptoms?"

"They range from extreme daytime drowsiness to sleep paralysis."

Gwen shook her head.

"Sleep paralysis," Sarah explained, "is an abnormal episode of REM sleep atonia. The victim can't move for a few moments and may suffer hypnagogic hallucinations. You know those people who claim aliens visit them while they're asleep in their beds?"

Gwen nodded.

"There's a good chance that what they're experiencing is sleep paralysis with hallucinations."

"Do you hallucinate when you have an episode?"

"No. I just slip under for a few minutes."

"What should I do if it happens again?"

"Nothing. It probably won't happen again, but if it does, just leave me alone. It never lasts more than five minutes."

"What about your medication?"

"I take Protriptyline. It's an anticataplectic compound."

"Any side effects I should know about?"

Sarah was tired of talking about it. She just wanted to be alone. "Nothing serious: dry mouth, constipation, sometimes blurred vision if the dosage is too high."

"You know," Gwen said, leaning forward, "I'll have to tell Perry all this. He is the team leader, and he has a right to know."

"I'd rather you didn't," Sarah said. She was feeling sick.

Gwen smiled. "Well, here's the good news: You're already here, and there's no immediate way home. I doubt he'll tie you to the bed."

"He can and will send me home as soon as a plane arrives."

"Maybe," Gwen said. "Let me talk to him. In the meantime, it's my turn to issue orders. I want you to rest for awhile, and you are never to go outside alone. Your episodes may only last five minutes, but that could be a death sentence out there. Agreed?"

Sarah nodded. "Agreed."

"What's going on?" Griffin said, pulling Gwen into the galley.

"You're hurting my arm," she said and jerked free. "Lighten up."

"I'm sorry. . . I noticed that you were in Sarah's room."

"So?"

"With the door closed."

Gwen felt defensive. "You were listening at the door. Snooping is beneath you."

"I wasn't eavesdropping." Griffin frowned. "What do you take me for? If I had my ear pressed to the door I wouldn't be asking you questions now. Something happened, and I think I have a right to know about it."

"There was a small incident in the Chamber," Gwen said lightly. "There's nothing to get worked up over."

"Why don't you let me decide that? Something happened to the cryobot? It broke?"

"No," Gwen said, marveling at her brother's hopeful questions. "Hairy was on target and on pace when I left. Sarah just had a little spell."

"Define *spell.*"

Gwen wondered if she should continue. She was at odds with herself. One portion of her mind wanted to keep Sarah's secret private; another part acknowledged the need to be open and honest in their hostile environment. As it was, she was on her way to talk to Perry about the matter when her brother sidetracked her.

"Don't switch sides on me now, Gwen. You're not a doctor; there is no doctor-patient confidentiality here. You're under no obligation to keep secrets."

"You've always been a real pain, Griffin, and now you're starting to annoy me. I know what my duties are. I know how to carry them out, and I don't need you to act like my big brother. And you're right, I'm under no professional obligation to keep medical data private, but there is such a thing as simple human courtesy."

"So you have gone over?" He crossed his arms and narrowed his eyes.

"What do you mean?"

"I've been monitoring the interpersonal dynamic between you and the others. You're crossing over to their side."

Gwen was nonplussed, uncertain that she heard correctly. "Their side? Griffin, you idiot, there are no sides. We're a team—a team with a mission, and a team that has experienced tragedy. If there are two sides in this situation, then you're the lone member of one of them."

"So you agree with their puncturing the ice cap? How did you fall so far? I thought we were in agreement on this."

"We are. But they're going to Lake Vostok whether I agree or not. My concerns are on the record. I have fears about contamination, but I can't stop it. At least I can learn from it."

"Tell me about Sarah."

Gwen hesitated and studied her brother. He had always been the dominant of the two. They were born the same day, and both had a lifelong passion for science, but those were the only things they had in common. Griffin studied harder than anyone she had ever met, and she had attended the university with some of the finest young minds in the country. Griffin excelled them all. He had had no life beyond his studies, and now, his research consumed him. He had no friends, attended no parties; he was happiest when alone and surrounded by books and data. Still, he was her brother, and he loved her, in his own way. He never said so, but she could tell he was watching over her. They were close, tied together by an unseen umbilical that only twins understood.

"Sarah fainted."

"Fainted? In the Chamber? While at the controls?"

"Leave it to you to paint the situation in the worst possible light."

"But she was at the controls, right? So what? Did she just collapse?"

"That's what people do when they faint."

Griffin stared at her, and Gwen felt like a microbe under a microscope. "What are you not telling me?"

Gwen shrugged.

"You know I can read you like a book."

"And I you."

"Agreed, so let's put this little charade behind us. Give me the rest of it."

The turmoil in Gwen rose to a boil. "She has narcolepsy."

Gwen had seldom seen Griffin stunned, but this was such a time. "The sleeping disease? I don't believe it. Worse, I don't believe Perry Sachs would be so stupid as to bring someone with a neurological disorder to the heart of Antarctica."

"He doesn't know. She kept it a secret from everyone. I was just going to tell Perry."

"Oh, you tell him first and then decide if I'm worthy to hear the news later."

"He is the team leader. Proper protocol requires that I tell him first and let him decide the next step."

"What's the protocol for family?" he chided.

Gwen shook her head. He had reached the point where talking was useless. He was quick with his tongue, and Gwen had never been able to outthink him in a debate. She doubted she would succeed this time.

"I think you're getting too close to the others," Griffin said. "I think you're being swayed because Perry is a tall, handsome guy. You've put your brains on the back burner and are letting urges take over."

A fire ignited deep in Gwen's stomach. She took a step forward until her nose was a mere inch away from her brother's. "I am my own person. I am no one's puppet. I make decisions because I have thought them through. My urges do not make up my mind for me. Besides, my urges are my business, dear brother. And as far as family loyalty goes, it is the only thing keeping me from slapping that arrogant look off your face. That is an urge I might give in to."

"You wouldn't dare—" He stopped midsentence.

"You ever say anything like that again, and you will find out what I dare." She whirled and stomped from the room.

Perry raised his eyes as something in his peripheral vision demanded his attention. He had been watching Gleason watch the monitors, wishing that Hairy could move faster than a few feet per hour. Someone was approaching. Dressed in a clean suit, Perry had trouble recognizing the person. All he could tell was that it was a woman. He hoped it was Gwen since he had ordered Sarah to rest.

His hope was fulfilled as Gwen approached with a snap in her step he had not seen before.

"How's Sarah?" Perry asked when Gwen was in earshot.

"Fine for the moment," Gwen said. Perry thought the words were more forced than needed.

"Any idea what happened?" Gleason asked, looking up from the monitors.

Gwen looked at Gleason then at Perry.

"You can speak freely," Perry said, picking up on the unspoken question.

"Sarah has narcolepsy," Gwen blurted, then related the discussion she had had with the stricken woman and the minimal exam she had given.

Perry leaned his head back and stared at the domed ceiling of the Chamber. He had been so careful, so demanding of details. How had that slipped past him?

"She says it is a mild case and that she's been living with it since her teen years. She also said she has medication to control it."

Perry shook his head and wished he could remove the face shield and rub his eyes. "Is she in danger?"

"No," Gwen said. "According to Sarah, more people have this than we realize. She hasn't had serious problems before, and her episodes don't last long."

"I don't know why I didn't recognize it when she passed out then awoke so quickly," Gleason said, returning his attention to the video gauges. "My high school biology teacher had narcolepsy. One day while he was teaching, his speech became slurred, his eyelids drooped, and his knees went wobbly. We had a teaching assistant in the class who calmly stepped over to the man, took his arm, and called for a chair. I brought one up." Gleason laughed. "That TA was great. A college girl as I recall. Anyway, she held up a finger to quiet the class, which was naturally disturbed, and said, 'Watch.' It wasn't more than three minutes until my bio teacher hopped up and took a quick look around. Realizing what had happened, he gave us a thirty-minute lecture on the disorder. At the time, I thought it was the strangest thing I had ever seen."

"So you think it's safe for her to carry on?" Perry asked his friend.

"What choice do you have?"

Perry let that fact circulate. "All right. She shouldn't go out alone—"

"I've already her told her that," Gwen interjected. Her words carried an edge.

Perry saw a strained look on Gwen's face. "What's wrong?"

"I told you, she has—"

"I was talking about you," Perry said. "Are you okay?"

"Yeah, yeah, I'm fine." She looked away.

Perry reached out and touched her shoulder. "What's happened?"

"Nothing. I just had an argument with my brother. That's all."

"That's all?"

She sighed. "I suppose it's the stress. The plane going down, you boring through the ice to drop a machine in undisturbed water, my brother's attitude and. . .and. . ."

Perry felt Gwen's shoulders soften and saw her head fall forward. He could hear her sniffing. He searched for words and found none. Instead, he pulled her close and wrapped his arms around her. He had a fleeting thought about how ludicrous they must appear to Gleason: two people clad in sterile, protective garments, intertwined in an embrace.

"I feel so stupid," she said between sniffs.

"No need," Perry reassured her. "Either we deal with our emotions, or they will deal with us."

"Not very scientific of me," she said.

"Scientists have hearts and souls, too."

Gwen pulled back and laughed. "How does one blow one's nose while wearing one of these suits?"

"Very carefully," Perry suggested, smiling.

She pulled away. "Thank you. I'm sorry. I'm not usually given to tears."

"There's no one here to shame you over that." Perry looked up and was surprised to see someone standing a few feet away.

Griffin stared back with an unmistakable, disapproving scowl. "Isn't this sweet?"

Gwen spun around. "What are you doing in here?"

"We hadn't finished our conversation," he said bitterly, "although it seems pretty much over now."

"I don't know what you're thinking," Perry said, "but it's wrong."

"What's that?" Gleason asked.

"I know what I just witnessed, Mr. Sachs."

"Grif, you need to shut up," Gwen said. "I warned you about your mouth—"

"People?" Gleason stood.

Perry was getting angry and doing his best not to show it. He had had all of Griffin he wanted. "Do you have something to say, Dr. James?"

"Shut up!" Gleason shouted. "Listen. Does anyone else hear that?"

Perry stopped and listened. A low rumbling had worked its way into the building. It was getting louder.

"Is that what I think it is?" Gwen asked.

"It sounds like a plane," Perry said, sprinting for the air lock.

CHAPTER 16

Tia felt two emotions when the skids of the Casa 212 touched down on the ice: relief and excitement. Relief because she had grown weary of being confined in an aircraft, and excitement because of what lay ahead. Behind her, five men released their seat belts and stood, preparing themselves for the coming mission.

Tia looked out the window and saw two domes, one larger than the other, a covered walk between them, and two rectangular buildings on either side of the smaller dome.

She also saw several people pouring out of the structures to greet them. They were expecting something, and she knew why. The C-5 had been brought down in sight of the camp. Such a tragedy would certainly garner great attention, and someone would send a plane to check on those left at the site.

That's what they expected. What they didn't know, Tia thought, was that the world believed everyone was on the plane and that all were dead.

The Casa had flown over the crash site, and she had seen the carnage, the crater, and the scattered bits of metal that served as grisly ornaments on the ice.

She looked at their smiling faces. A couple applauded. *Ironic*, Tia thought.

"They look happy to see us," one of the men said. "Shall we disappoint them?"

"Yes."

Perry watched the oddly shaped craft pull to a stop fifty feet from the Dome. The airplane was white and bore no logos on its exterior. It was moved by a pair of turboprops mounted to wings attached over the passenger area.

"That's a type of cargo plane, isn't it?" Gleason asked.

"It's a Casa 212," Perry said. "I rode in one about a year ago. It can carry passengers or cargo. There's a loading ramp in the tail section."

As if on cue, a flat panel below the tail began to descend. Perry felt an odd sense of disquiet. He had been expecting a plane. One was not due for several weeks, but after the C-5 crashed, he had been sure someone would send out a search party. Still, something didn't seem right.

"Where are Sarah and Gwen?" Jack asked. "Don't they want to greet our new friends?"

"Women are smarter than men," Dr. Curtis said. "They've probably stayed inside where it's warm."

Perry looked at the round archaeologist and smiled. "You always did prefer hot weather." Condensation floated from his lips.

"Maybe they're setting up the barbeque," Jack quipped. "I could go for some London broil. It would be the hospitable thing to do for our guests."

"Fine with me," Gleason said. "Just so long as I don't have to stand outside and watch you cook it."

Perry caught a glimpse of Griffin and found the same scowl he had seen chiseled into the man's face.

"Let's not be rude, gentlemen," Larimore said. "Let's say hello to our new arrivals."

◆❖◆

"Come on, come on," Gwen said. "The men are already out there." She slipped on her parka and began working the zipper. Sarah felt no desire to move faster.

"We're women. Aren't we supposed to be late?" Sarah asked.

"No need to perpetuate a false stereotype. I'm late only half the time."

"How did he take it?" Sarah asked.

"What?"

Her stomach churned. "You told Perry about my narcolepsy, didn't you?"

"I told you I was going to," Gwen said. "It's not something you can keep secret in a place like this. Now put on your coat. I must say, you're not showing much enthusiasm."

"Why should I?"

"Because we've been cut off from the world. Our radios are useless. That plane means we're a good deal safer."

Sarah felt as if she were melting. "That's what it means to you."

"What else can it mean?"

"I may have to return on the flight. The project is going to go on without me." She heard her voice crack.

"No, it isn't," Gwen said. She stepped to Sarah and pulled her parka closed and zipped it like a mother would do for a child. "I didn't say anything about sending you home and neither did Perry. He's concerned about you, as he should be, but I don't think he's going to send you packing. After all, the cryobot is your baby."

"Gleason can run it."

"Yeah, well, I think you're worrying about something that isn't going to happen. Now let's go."

Sarah watched Gwen turn toward the door. She followed and felt the slap and sting of the world's coldest air. Gwen stopped midstep and gasped.

"What?" Sarah asked and peered over Gwen's shoulder.

Gwen took a sudden step back and closed the door. "What do we do?"

Sarah's words came quickly. "We can't help them now. We hide."

The first man emerged pointing a weapon at the group. It was such an unexpected sight that Perry was uncertain he was seeing it correctly. Perry recognized the weapon as a military-issue submachine gun—an MP-5. That gun alone could mow down he and the others before a word could be spoken. Four men and one woman followed the first man, each armed with the same weapon.

They wore white parkas that blended perfectly with the snow and wore dark goggles that shielded their eyes not only from the environment but the view of their captives. They moved with confidence and in a pattern that suggested planning and training. The men fanned out, their weapons leveled at Perry and the others. Perry knew he was facing professionals, and he didn't feel good about it.

"Not what I expected," Jack said. "Do you suppose they have the wrong address?"

"I don't think so," Perry said.

The smallest of the group, the woman, marched toward them. "Line up!"

They complied. She walked before them, eyeing each one through her dark goggles like a general inspecting his troops. She moved back down the line and stopped in front of Jack. She gazed up at him.

"I don't think we've met," Jack said.

She swung the butt of her weapon in a fierce arc, connecting with the side of Jack's head. He staggered back a step, and she sprang forward, this time jamming the barrel into the big man's stomach. He doubled over, and she brought a knee to his face. Jack fell backward to the ice, his head bouncing once. He didn't move.

Perry took a step toward his friend, but the woman pointed the barrel at his face. "First rule: Take out the muscle." She looked at Jack then back at Perry. "Are you Perry Sachs?"

"Who wants to know?"

"First the muscle," she repeated, "then the brains." She spun on a foot raising the other to deliver a devastating blow to Perry's midsection. Perry felt like he had been hit by a car. Something hard hit the back of his head, and the snowy ice came crashing up. A half-second later, Perry realized the truth: The ice wasn't rising; he was falling. He lay on the surface, the ice cold on his face, and then white ice turned to black.

Perry rolled onto his back and struggled to remember where he was. The back of his head hurt, and the skin felt tight, as if someone had surgically inserted a large rock between scalp and skull. His hair felt matted, too. He reached up to touch the sore area and noticed his hands were bound with a nylon tie. Things were starting to come back to him.

"Good to see you moving, buddy," a voice said. "You had me worried."

Perry blinked a few times and rolled to the side. It was Jack. He was seated on a folding chair. Dried blood clung to his ebony skin. Like Perry his hands were bound.

Perry struggled to sit up on the floor, and his abdomen exploded in pain. "I think we can officially say that we have been worked." His voice sounded weak in his ears.

"Yeah, and by a girl at that," Jack said.

"Help him to a chair," a woman's voice said. Perry looked up and saw a tall woman with long black hair and a marble expression standing a short distance away. She was still holding the machine gun. Two men hoisted Perry from the floor and dropped him on a chair. The movement was painful and the sudden rise from horizontal to vertical made his head pound and his mind spin.

The fog in Perry's mind lifted, and the scene came into focus. They were in the Dome's common room. His team was all bound with the same nylon ties. Each was still in their outdoor gear. The attackers, however, had shed their white parkas. Perry counted five men and the one woman. Six in all. That was how many he had counted leaving the aircraft.

"Would someone explain the meaning of all of this?" Perry asked.

"Isn't it obvious?" the woman said. "Your facility has been taken over, and you are being held hostage, left alive by my whim."

"I tried to tell them you meant to return that library book," Jack said.

"Your jokes don't hide your fear, Mr. Dyson," the woman said. "They make you seem small and petty."

"Ah, just the look I was going for."

"Shut up, Jack," Griffin complained. "You're just going to make them angry."

"You'd be wise to listen to Dr. James," the woman said.

"You know our names," Perry said. The pain was raising a storm of nausea.

"Of course I do," she said with a sneer. "Do you think I'd fly all the way down here without knowing who I was going to face? We have very accurate intelligence."

"We?" Perry said.

"Yes, and don't bother asking." She paused and walked around the group. "I'm puzzled. I see Dr. James, Commander Larimore, and you—" she studied Curtis—"you must be Dr. Kenneth Curtis. You arrived after the others. True?"

"Yes," Curtis said. He looked pale and faint.

"There is Gleason Archer, and there are your fearless, albeit inept, leaders, Perry Sachs and Jack Dyson."

"I'd give her an A for that," Jack said. "Good memory."

"We seem to be missing two people," the woman said. "Where are the ladies?"

No one spoke.

She sighed. "I am a very impatient woman. There should be two female scientists here, a Sarah Hardy and Dr. James's sister, Gwen. I would like to know where they are."

"They're not here," Larimore said.

"My intelligence sources say they are."

"All right, I'll tell you exactly where they are," Larimore said.

Perry tensed and raised his eyes to the commander, who looked the other way.

"I'm listening, Commander. Make it quick."

"You go out that door and start walking that way," he said, motioning with his head. "You'll find a big hole in the ice and a lot of body parts lying around."

"You're saying they died in the crash of the C-5?" She stepped over to him, crouched down, and stared into his eyes.

"That's what I'm saying. They're dead, most likely due to you."

She straightened. "We brought the plane down," she admitted, "but I doubt the ladies were aboard. They're essential to your work here."

"We're not at the Honolulu Hilton," Larimore said. "These are adverse conditions. Sarah came down with altitude sickness. Gwen is our paramedic. She was flying back to McMurdo to make sure Sarah arrived safely."

"How noble." She turned to the men who accompanied her. "I want a full search. Every nook and cranny. There are only four buildings here. They can't have gone far, and they're too smart to stay outside." Three men scattered. The woman stepped back to Larimore and pressed the barrel of the gun between his eyes. "You had better not be lying to me, Commander, because unlike the others, you are expendable."

From his position, Perry could see a dark green tattoo on the woman's hand. It took a moment, but he recognized it as a red-eyed dragon. "Since you know our names," Perry said, hoping to pull the woman's attention away from Larimore, "maybe you'd honor us with yours."

She turned and stared into Perry's eyes. He felt like she was sucking the life out of him. Her eyes would have been beautiful in any other context, but to him they looked flint hard and cold.

"It beats saying, 'Hey lady,' " Jack added. He smiled, and Perry was once again amazed at his friend's fortitude.

"Tia," she said. "You may call me Tia."

"No last name?" Perry said.

"You don't need one." Her voice dropped an octave, making her even more unnerving. "All you need to know is that I'm in charge; I have no sense of humor, and killing is a hobby of mine." She turned to Jack. "And I hate flippancy."

Perry watched his friend open his mouth then shut it without a word.

Gwen's heart fluttered like a butterfly, and her breathing was ragged. She wished she could blame it on the cold and the altitude, but it was fear—simple, mind-shredding fear.

"In here," she said to Sarah, sprinting across the ice floor of the Chamber. She had assumed the unwelcome guests would go to the Dome first. It seemed natural that the three-building structure with its sleeping quarters would be the first destination. It was a guess, one she hoped was right. Even if she were correct, she and Sarah had only minutes before the intruders searched the Chamber. She had no idea what they wanted, but the work site was too far off the beaten path to warrant a home invasion. Logic told her that whoever the gunmen were, they were here because of the project.

"You're kidding."

"I'm open to ideas."

Sarah had none.

Gwen moved as quickly as she could to the long wooden crate where Hairy had been housed prior to its unveiling. The box was ten feet by six feet, large enough to hold Hairy, its support equipment, and bubble plastic packing material, much of which was still in the container. Its lid lay propped to one side. "Get in."

Sarah didn't hesitate, throwing a leg over the edge of wooden box and crawling in. Gwen hesitated a moment then took hold of the rough, heavy wooden top. She grunted, groaned, and pulled until her spine felt as if it would herniate. "I need help."

Sarah was out in an instant, taking hold of the opposite end of the top. Together they hoisted it in place, leaving just enough room to crawl into the near-empty container. Sarah went first, then Gwen. Once inside, they jiggled the lid into place.

It was a desperate and probably futile attempt, but it was all they had. There were very few places to hide. Gwen hoped the lid was in the correct spot and that the others would think it an unopened crate. The hard work had calmed her nerves, slowing her heart and quieting her breathing enough to think.

"Now what?" Sarah asked.

"I have no idea." Gwen wondered if she had just crawled into her own coffin.

"At least it can't. . .can't get. . .worse. . . ."

"Sarah? Sarah?" It had happened again. Gwen was thankful the narcolepsy attack hadn't happened before they hid themselves. She wasn't strong enough to carry a limp body across ice.

In the darkness, she reached for the other woman and found her head leaning against the side wall. She traced Sarah's face with her fingers until she found her mouth. It was clear, unencumbered by the plastic packing. That was a good thing. The only good thing she could think of.

The sound of moving air seeped into the hiding place. Gwen recognized it. She had heard the same noise many times upon entering the Chamber. Someone had just entered the building.

CHAPTER 17

W e've made contact," one of the men said to Tia. Perry watched as the woman stepped to a tall man and took a black satellite phone from his hand. They were all tall, Perry realized—Tia and her five soldiers. Tall, lean, and muscular. After they had stripped off their parkas, Perry had seen biceps bulging beneath the long-sleeved cold-weather shirts and shoulders stretching the material. Something else bothered Perry, something he'd noticed when they first emerged from the plane. The men moved with a precision that came only from practice. This was no ordinary group of thugs. He suspected they were ex-military.

"Phase one is complete," Tia said into the phone. Her spine straightened as she spoke, and her head lowered an inch. Whoever was on the other end of the satellite link intimidated her.

That was a frightening thought.

Perry tried to make sense of the one-sided conversation.

"Six." She paused as she listened. "Searching now for the two women." She listened some more. "They say they were on the C-5. I don't believe them." Another pause. "No casualties. Understood. Which one? It will be done." She handed the phone back to her accomplice then returned her attention to the group. "Commander Larimore, I have just been instructed to put a bullet in your heart if those two women are not found."

Perry looked at the navy man, who showed no fear. Larimore's eyes narrowed, and his jaw set like a vise. "Bring it on," he said.

Tia studied the commander, waiting for a break in his façade. Few men could face death without showing some fear. She was disappointed that he was proving to be the exception to the rule. In fact, his resolve concerned her because it seemed to be shared by most of the others. Dr. James was beginning to snivel—that was to be expected. Dr. Curtis seemed resigned to the situation. But those who worried her most were the men from Sachs Engineering. She had done her research and had been briefed in detail. They had faced death before and survived each time. To her, that made them dangerous.

There was something else. Enkian had hired special investigators to do background checks on each of the party members. Each was exceptional in his or her own right, but three had something unexpected in common—they were churchgoers, religious men. Dr. Curtis was a surprise to her, apparently a late addition to the team, so she knew the least about him. She assumed he might share the same beliefs as his friends.

Religious people could endanger her mission. Often they were unafraid to die and were committed to ideals greater than themselves. This was something she understood, and she knew that the religion often didn't matter. An Islamic extremist might blow himself up to make a point and to enter paradise. Christians, however, had always bothered her and often in ways she couldn't quantify. She was uncomfortable in their presence. It was illogical, but nonetheless real.

"Perhaps I could change your mind, Commander, with a well-placed bullet in someone else's head," Tia said. "Maybe one of the Sachs people. There are too many engineers on this site anyway."

Larimore gave a humorless chuckle. "I doubt you're going to give any of us a free lift home after this is over. People like you kill their hostages. We're dead no matter what we say or do."

"Nothing in this building," a man with bleached blond hair said as he emerged from the galley area. His companion had no hair at all. "We checked the dormitory annex, the supply building, and their rooms. There's no one in this complex."

"That means they must be in the other dome." Tia thought for a moment. "Go help the others search—wait. We'll all go. There may be a faster way of doing this."

"I will not take no for an answer," Henry Sachs bellowed, and bellowing was something he did well. He had spent his life working with employees a third larger and twice as strong as he. Normally a soft-spoken man, he had a switch that turned him from taciturn to tyrant. That switch had been thrown.

"Sir, I don't know how your call made it this far, but we at the White House receive thousands of calls every day. The staff can't speak to every caller."

Sachs sighed then said, "Here's what you do. You put me on hold. You find Mr. Jeter and speak two words to him: Henry Sachs. That's all I ask."

A moment later he found himself on hold. He waited with impatience. Since receiving word about the missing transport plane, he had been on the phone, begging for information and calling in favors—and he was owed a lot of favors. Calls to the Commandant of the Coast Guard had garnered a promise of instant information, but Sachs wanted more. He had only one son, and he wasn't content to wait on others to find him.

"Mr. Sachs," the woman's voice said, "I apologize for the confusion. Mr. Jeter will be on the line momentarily. He was in a meeting and—"

"Thank you," Sachs said. He felt bad for bullying the aide, but he was not at his diplomatic best.

White House Chief of Staff Robert Jeter walked down the hall of the West Wing, his head hung as it often did when he was in thought.

"Mr. Jeter," an aide began, "I have the secretary of transportation on the line—"

"Not now," Jeter said with a wave of his hand. He stepped into his office and closed the door. The lights were dimmed, just the way he liked it. He kept his shades drawn and preferred dark furniture and dark wood paneling. The room was lit by a single desk lamp, the television that was never turned off and seldom moved from CNN, and his computer monitor. The president called the place "The Grand Mausoleum," but Jeter liked it. The darkness helped him focus on the hundreds of items he had to keep orbiting the administration.

He snapped up the phone. "Henry me-boy," he said with a weak and forced Irish accent. "To what do I owe this pleasure?"

"I need your help. More specifically, I need the president's help."

"I have a meeting with him and the director of communications in three minutes." He felt his stomach tighten. "What do you want me to tell him?"

"As you know, in all my years of supporting the president I have never asked for anything."

"That's true," Jeter said. "You make the rest of us look bad." Sachs had been a financial supporter of President Calvert from his first run for the Senate. It was the only reason Jeter was talking to him now.

"It's about my son, Mr. Jeter. I've been told a cargo plane went down and he was on it."

"That's horrible," Jeter said. He twisted in his seat then pulled a pad of paper from his desk drawer. He had a near-photographic memory, but he still took copious notes on everything. "Where?"

"They're telling me the plane overshot McMurdo—"

"McMurdo? He's in Antarctica?"

"Yes. Are you aware of the Lake Vostok research project?"

"Vaguely," Jeter said, regretting the lie. "Something about an underground—I mean under-*ice* lake and some debatable environmental changes. The Pentagon sent a crew down there."

"That's right. My son Perry was leading the research team."

"Really? I thought he was an engineer or architect—"

"Forgive me, Mr. Jeter, but none of that matters. What matters is that my son's plane is missing and assumed lost at sea after overshooting McMurdo."

"You're right. I'm sorry. What can we do?"

"Perry shouldn't have been on that plane. It was supposed to ferry back six of my employees and six navy Seabees. Furthermore, I'm having trouble believing that the pilot could overshoot their intended destination and then fall into the sea."

"But that's what the experts are saying?"

"Experts can be wrong. I'm an expert, and I know how often I'm wrong."

"Give me all the facts." Sachs did, and Jeter scribbled notes. "I'll share this with the president."

"I want someone to check out the research site," Sachs said, not as a request but as something that could not be refused. "I know the military has means of satellite surveillance. We built the building that houses the electronics."

"And you want the president to order that kind of surveillance?"

"Exactly."

"I'll tell the president, Mr. Sachs, and I know he wishes the best for your son. As I do."

"Thank you."

Jeter hung up the phone and reviewed the notes on his desk. He pulled the paper from the pad, turned his chair, and dropped it into the hungry teeth of a shredder. In less than a second, the paper was reduced to tiny squares of confetti.

He rose from the chair. Something on his desk caught his attention: his keys. He picked them up and noticed an adornment he had carried since college: a small oven-fired clay cylinder with six sides. Etched into its surface was a dragon.

He placed the keys in his pants pocket and left to meet with the president.

CHAPTER 18

Perry watched, concerned, as Griffin squirmed, fidgeted, and appeared to be an eyelash away from a nervous breakdown. Perry had seen what stress and fear could do to a man. Tia had just ordered them to their feet. They all rose, but Griffin began to rock like a metronome.

"Why can't you just leave us alone?" he said. "We don't have anything you could possibly want."

"Oh, but you do," Tia said. "Now stand up."

"No, I'm staying here. You have no right to do this."

Perry tried to sum up his situation. Bound, held at gunpoint, isolated at the bottom of the world, he had never been so powerless. Now he feared Griffin was going to make things worse.

"Calm down, Griffin," Perry said. "It's best if we do what they say."

"No! Don't tell me to calm down. You're probably in on this. You can't fool me. This is all part of your plan."

"Griffin," Jack began.

"Shut up! Go away, all of you. Leave me alone."

"Yeah, like that's going to happen," one of the guards said.

Griffin spit on him.

"That does it." The man raised his weapon.

"No!" Perry shouted.

The gun went off, and Perry expected to see a spray of red. Instead, he saw the guard land hard on the floor, Jack on top of him and the machine gun skittering across the floor. The guard next to Perry raised his gun but not far. Perry lowered a shoulder and charged, connecting with the small of the man's back. The man fell forward but was on his feet a half-second later. The guard spun and punched him on the side of the head, and scorching pain raced down Perry's neck. Another swing caught him in the midsection. Perry gasped for air.

Jack fared no better. Tia calmly stepped to his side and kicked him hard with her booted foot. Perry heard a rib crack. Jack rolled to his side, and Tia gave him another kick, just above the kidney.

The downed guard sprang to his feet and looked for his weapon. Tia raised a hand and stopped him. She walked over to the ownerless gun, picked it up, and brought it to the man, who said thank-you sheepishly.

Tia smiled and shot him in the chest. "I said no one is to be killed unless I order it. Drag him outside."

The two remaining guards took their fallen companion under the arms and dragged him from the room.

Perry struggled to his feet then fell into the chair he had been sitting in a few moments before. His wind was coming back, but not fast enough. Jack lay on the floor, rolling from side to side.

"I have only been here a few minutes," Tia said, "and I'm already tired of all of you." She stepped to Griffin, who stared at the spot where the dead man had lain only seconds before. His eyes were wide and his face bloodless. She backhanded him so hard he fell from the chair. "You will do as I say, when I say, and without question. Do you understand?"

"Yes. . .yes, ma'am."

"Get up. We're going to the other building."

"What? Not again."

A hand clamped over her mouth, and Sarah jumped, ready to scream when the fearful reality of her situation came back to mind. The darkness of the crate covered her, and she froze. She gently touched the hand over her mouth, and Gwen removed it. Sarah said nothing. Outside she heard movement—feet on ice. She could also hear smaller boxes being moved.

They were looking for them. It was only a matter of time before they checked the shipping crate. Would they shoot them right there, turning the wooden box into a coffin? Sarah pushed the thought from her mind.

The vague sleepiness that hovered in her mind told her she had had another episode. Coming out of it, she had almost given away their position. Her condition nearly proved to be the very thing she denied it was: a danger to others.

There was another sound: the air lock opening.

"Anything?" A woman's voice.

"No, ma'am. There's no sign of them. Maybe the navy guy was telling the truth."

Sarah wished she could see. At least then she would have more information. For now, she was blind and contained. There was enough room in the crate for them to prop up on an elbow but no more. She reached forward and touched Gwen's leg, and she felt Gwen's hand take hers and give it a squeeze.

It was silly, she thought, two grown women with Ph.D.s holding hands like schoolgirls.

Still, it gave her a measure of comfort.

Perry led the group into the Chamber. It was cold, but he felt fortunate that his attackers hadn't removed his parka before securing his hands. When he stepped through the air lock, he saw the two men sent in search of Gwen and Sarah milling around the loading area. He was relieved but puzzled that they were empty-handed. Where could they have hidden? Surely—and he prayed this was true—they hadn't stayed outside. They were too smart for that, but panic had a way of rendering the wisest people fools.

"Nice setup," Tia said. "It looks like you know what you're doing. Is that it?" She pointed to the vertical aluminum frame that had guided Hairy down the ice shaft.

"That's the ice hole," Perry said.

"How are you coring?" Tia asked. "I don't see drilling equipment."

Perry explained about Hairy and its operation. He saw no need to withhold information. It would only anger the volatile woman and gain them nothing. Tia walked to the rig and peered down the hole. "You've made headway. How deep is it?"

"The ice or the probe?"

"The probe. I know about the ice."

"I don't know. The monitors give the details." He nodded at the table. They walked toward it. He explained the monitors and their readouts.

"This is the device Sarah Hardy designed?" Tia asked. Perry said it was. "Then where is she? I find it hard to believe that you would let her leave while the device is coring."

"That's my job," Gleason said. "I'm checked out on the controls and operations. It's too much for one person to monitor twenty-four hours a day."

Tia nodded as if agreeing. "How long before it hits the lake?"

"Another twenty-six hours," Gleason said. "Assuming all goes well."

"It's autonomous?"

"At this stage, yes. There is little for us to do but make sure the power source remains uninterrupted."

"All the power comes from the surface?"

Perry nodded. "During the descent stage we provide energy to the device through the power cord you see feeding off the spool."

"And once it hits the water?"

"It jettisons the cord, which is too heavy to tow. We control its movements by fiber optics."

Tia seemed pleased. "Can we speed it up?"

"I wouldn't," Perry said. "Heat from the head radiates back along the cryobot's body. Too much heat could damage something."

"It's that delicate?"

Perry shook his head. "It's not delicate, but it's powerful. You can try it if you want, but you may end up with nothing more useful than a fishing weight at the end of the line."

She looked at her watch. "The timing is perfect." She turned and studied the building and its contents. "What's in the boxes?"

Perry hesitated. It struck him what was different about the place. The wooden crate that had held Hairy was closed. It shouldn't be. "Most are filled with packing material and debris. We planned on transporting all waste from the site when we were finished. Once a box is empty of its load, we refill it with the packing material so it will be on hand when we need it."

"But not all the boxes are empty?" Tia pressed.

"No, the ones to the left, the two tall ones and the wide, long crate that's laying flat on its side."

Tia marched toward the stack of boxes, stopping by Hairy's container.

"That one's plastic anti-impact material," Perry called after her.

Tia turned and eyed Perry. He didn't like her expression. Slowly, she reached down and took the edge of the loose lid, lifted it, and peeked inside. She let the lid fall and walked to the larger containers. "Open these. I want to see what toys they have. I'll keep an eye on our friends." She raised her machine gun.

Gwen held her breath. She had been listening to the conversation, muted by distance and the wood sides of the crate, slowly pulling the plastic packing material over Sarah and herself. It was a thin chance, a gossamer hope, but if she could blanket themselves in enough of the opaque material, they might avoid discovery, assuming no one looked too closely.

When the lid of the crate moved, she nearly jumped. She held her breath, waiting for a command or the blast of a gun. To her surprise, the lid dropped back into place.

Maybe Perry's God was watching after all.

Enkian boarded the chartered Boeing 757, taking only a moment to appreciate its sleek lines. He had other things on his mind. As he stepped through the hatch, he was greeted by a red-haired beauty who looked half his age.

"Good morning," she said with a smile that would capture the attention of every dentist lucky enough to be nearby.

Enkian didn't return the smile. "Everyone is in place?"

"Yes, sir. The team is seated in coach, and the deck crew is awaiting your permission to taxi."

"Cargo is secured?" he asked, stepping to the middle row of the first-class seating area. He was the only one of the fifty-plus passengers in the well-appointed area.

"Just as you've instructed."

Enkian nodded. "Tell the pilot it is time to leave."

The redhead nodded and disappeared into the crew cabin. She reappeared a moment later. "We have clearance to taxi. The captain says we will be in the air in five minutes. May I bring you anything after we're airborne?"

"Water with lime."

"Anything to read?"

"No." Enkian fastened his seat belt and leaned his head back against the leather chair. He needed nothing to read. His attention focused on what lay ahead. Many hours would pass, and several stops would be made before the distance from Mexico City to the extreme southern region of the planet was reached. He planned to spend the time in meditation and planning.

He thought of the cargo in the hold and smiled. The 757 belonged to Air Mexico, but the crew was his. He doubted the executives of the airline would appreciate his plans to bypass all cargo inspection. It had been difficult to arrange, but massive amounts of money made things happen, especially in countries where earning a livable wage was a luxury.

The plane began a slow taxi away from the terminal. Enkian heard the engines begin to whine as the large aircraft moved toward the runway.

Minutes later it took to the air, and Enkian had to suppress his excitement. Excitement was to be expected. It wasn't every day that a man left his home on a flight toward his destiny. In his case, the destiny had been set eons before.

⟨ C H A P T E R ⟩ 19

Robert Jeter stepped through the door that joined his office to the Oval Office. He had been chief of staff for three years—the youngest chief of staff since Hamilton Jordon guided the Carter administration—but he still felt a rush of pride each time he crossed the threshold into the president's historic office. The brown-and-tan carpet with the great seal of the president embroidered in the center, the alabaster walls, the high ceiling with its frescoed seal of the United States adorning the center, and the remarkable view out the windows gave him goose bumps. He never showed it, but they were there.

Waiting for him were four men: David Jannot, a skinny, anemic-looking man from the CIA; FBI Director Steve Belanger; the secretary of homeland security, Larry Shomer; and President Richard Calvert, who wore a charcoal suit, white shirt, and brilliant blue tie. He was seated in an overstuffed, high-back chair, a concession to the touch of arthritis in his lower back.

"Sorry to be late," Jeter said. "There was a phone call I could not avoid."

"You're not late," President Calvert said. "These guys are early. Coffee?"

"No thank you, Mr. President. I'm ready to float away as it is."

Calvert chuckled. "This nation runs on caffeine. Take a seat, and we'll get started." Jeter sat on one of the two cream-colored sofas, crossed his legs, and opened his ever-present notebook. He was the only man with pen and paper in hand. The others—except the president, who held nothing—made use of handheld computers. "Start us off, Steve."

"Yes, sir," Belanger said and gave a brief report of FBI activities. Larry Shomer added information from the Homeland Security perspective. There was little of consequence, which Jeter knew was not unusual. These meetings were held daily and often lasted less than fifteen minutes.

"I have something new," Jannot said when Shomer had finished. "NSA picked up on it. A plane went down in the Ross Sea yesterday with its crew and passengers. Presumably it sank, but a certain Coast Guard captain is throwing a fit. He thinks the whole thing is wacky."

"Ross Sea?" the president said. "In Antarctica?"

"Yes," Jannot said. "The National Security Administration monitors radio transmissions around the world. One of their listening posts picked up radio communication between the skipper of a Coast Guard cutter and his peers at McMurdo. Someone reported the plane missing, and there is an eyewitness that says he saw it hit the water."

"So what's the captain's beef?" Belanger asked.

"I haven't read the transcripts, but the reports say he thinks it's impossible for a pilot to overshoot McMurdo and crash into the sea and only have one witness. His ship was in the vicinity, and they saw nothing."

"Who was on the plane?" the president wondered. "Anyone we should know about?"

"There are many flights in the area," Jeter said. He thought uncomfortably of his phone conversation with Henry Sachs. "Probably some college professors."

"I wouldn't dismiss it so lightly," Larry Shomer interjected.

"It was an American plane?" the president wanted to know.

"NSA thinks so," Jannot replied. "I've asked them to narrow it down. It seems no one knows much about the flight. Some kind of secret."

"Secret flights over Antarctica?" the president said. "That's a multinational place. Such things aren't supposed to happen. Wait a minute." He looked at Jeter. "Didn't we get a briefing from Defense on a possible problem in that area?"

Jeter swallowed hard. "Yes, sir. About two months ago, maybe longer." Jeter watched the president's eyes dart back and forth as he recalled the meeting.

"I want more information, and I want it right away. The last thing we need is the *Washington Post* saying I don't care about Americans lost overseas. Learn what you can."

Jeter left the meeting feeling far more depressed than when he had arrived. He closed the door to his office behind him, set his notepad on the desk, and picked up his phone, dialing for an outside line.

Nearly two thousand miles away and thirty-five thousand feet above the earth, Eric Enkian took a call.

Perry watched helplessly as Tia's four men pried open crate after crate, container after container. They scattered wood chips, dropped nails, and spread packing material like children opening Christmas presents. They worked with the finesse of a nearsighted bull. Since he could do nothing else, he tested the nylon tie that bound his wrists. He felt fortunate that it wasn't so tight that it cut off his circulation, but it was clear that he wasn't going to work his way free. The thick ties were the kind used to bind electronic cable. He had also seen police use them as auxiliary handcuffs. They were light, strong, and impossible to break, and any effort to try would only cut deep into his flesh.

He glanced toward the others. Griffin was near catatonic, frightened, no doubt, beyond any of his nightmares; Dr. Curtis was stoic and appeared more irritated than frightened. Jack was studying the men as they worked, and Perry knew he was sizing them up. While Jack did not seem happy, he showed no fear. Gleason cringed each time a box was opened roughly. Larimore worried Perry. He looked furious, ready to spring into action at the slightest opportunity. That, he knew, would be the end of the commander's life.

Then there were Sarah and Gwen. He was certain they were hiding in the empty cryobot box, but Tia had given no indication that she'd seen them when she cracked open the lid.

"I'm impressed," Tia said. "Come here, Mr. Sachs."

Perry walked from his place near the ice hole toward the packing area, where the equipment had been set. He said nothing when he came close.

"These two items intrigue me," she said, pointing at the contents of a just-opened crate. "Are these what I think they are?"

"That depends on what you think they are."

"Don't get cute with me, Sachs. You've seen how patient I am. These are dive suits, aren't they?"

"They are," Perry replied.

"Deep-sea diving suits, right?"

Perry nodded. He watched his captor study the hard-shell suits. Each of them hung on a metal rack, its arms extended slightly as if reaching for a hug. The "head" was a bulbous affair with a half sphere of clear plastic.

She looked at the suits for a moment then turned toward the ice hole. "You were planning on going down through the ice?"

"We tried to plan for everything. Being where we are, it's hard to run down to the hardware store to pick up something we need."

She looked back at the ice shaft. "These are too big for that hole."

"I know," Perry said.

"Are you going to make me beat this out of you?"

"I'm not much of a conversationalist."

"Learn. Or someone, maybe your big friend over there, will get more of our hospitality."

"They're dive suits, yes. An advancement of the JIM suit, designed for additional mobility while being smaller than any suit ever developed. They are a hybrid of two suits—one from NASA and another from the navy. These suits allow us to work at depths beyond what a scuba diver can endure. They're heated, self-propelled, and carry advanced communication gear. They're designed to be used around offshore drilling rigs and in rescue situations. We had a few projects that required underwater construction. We call them Atmospheric Diving Suits: ADS I and ADS II. The designers dubbed them the Addy twins."

"I've seen JIM suits."

"Basically, that's what they are."

"You still haven't explained how you're going to get down a hole that small."

Perry nodded toward a long, wide box that Tia's men had pried open. Tia walked to it. "Another cryobot?"

"Yes." Perry watched her study the device.

"It has to be six feet in diameter."

"A little over," Perry said.

"Why not start with this one?" Tia asked. "It would have saved time."

"The larger the surface area of the heated head, the more energy it takes to move through the ice. Our plan was to open a smaller hole first, explore with Hairy, and—"

"Hairy?"

"The cryobot that's working its way toward the lake. If need be—and if it's safe—we could core out a larger hole with the bigger cryobot."

"Which should go faster and take less energy since two-thirds of the ice has been removed."

"Exactly."

Tia stared off in the distance. "The suit provides more than heat and comfort. Correct?"

"Yes. One of the problems is that we are two miles above the lake. In addition, we are at twelve thousand feet above sea level. To send a man down from this altitude, through a couple miles of ice into a pressured lake would be unwise—actually, it would be murder. Even if we could do that, bringing the person back to the surface would be fatal. The pressure change would cause the air in his blood to bubble."

"Decompression sickness. The bends."

"The world's worst case."

Tia looked at the suit again. Perry could tell she was studying the white armorlike skin. "From what I know about JIM suits," she said, "is that they're huge, more submersible with arms and legs than a dive suit. This is what—half the size?"

"Forty percent." She was intelligent, Perry decided, and that chilled his blood. Intelligent psychopaths were unnerving.

"You can maintain a stable atmospheric pressure in such a small suit?"

He nodded. "It's based on a design that NASA was considering a decade ago. They examined the feasibility of a ridged-skin space suit. Materials technology has advanced considerably in the last few years, as has machine miniaturization. We were able to strip away the bulk and make articulated joints that moved in a far more natural way."

"Depth rating?"

Perry was growing weary of answering questions at gunpoint.

"I asked you a question," she snapped.

"Three hundred meters," Perry replied.

"Nearly a thousand feet," she murmured. "Didn't the older JIM suits go deeper?"

"This isn't a true JIM suit. It's based on the same principle, but the design is unique. The bulkier suits had greater depth potential—six hundred meters to be exact—but they were, well. . .bulkier. We'd never get a hole in the ice large enough to accommodate one of those."

"And the diver breathes normal gases?"

"That's the real advantage."

"That and not being crushed," Tia said.

"And movement is fully three-dimensional?"

"As far as the tether will allow."

"So air and power come from topside."

Again Perry nodded. "The suits can operate autonomously for close to ninety minutes using onboard air and battery power. Longer dives require outside support."

"Impressive."

"How about undoing my hands?" Perry said. "I've been a good boy and told you what you wanted to know."

"You haven't told me where the women are."

"I believe Commander Larimore gave you that information."

"He's lying. I can smell it on him."

Perry frowned. "What is it you want?"

"I don't want anything, Mr. Sachs," Tia said, her face a mask of dissatisfaction. "I have it already, don't I?"

"Only you would know that."

She looked back at the suits, the large cryobot, and the other gear scattered about. "I'm very impressed. Enkian will be, too."

"Who?"

"The man who will be killing you."

CHAPTER 20

Everything is normal," Gleason said. His words caught in his throat. Tia was standing behind him, the barrel of the gun pressed to the back of his skull. Perry's heart broke for his friend. He knew that Gleason's mind must be racing to his wife and children, who might become a widow and orphans at any moment.

"You said twenty-six hours before the probe breaks through the ice," Tia said.

"At the current rate, yes," Gleason said. "It's impossible to be more specific since ice density changes with depth. It could be more; it could be a little less."

"It must be monitored?"

"It should. There's nothing to do now but watch, but yes, someone should monitor it."

"And that's you?"

"I can do it," Perry said.

"So can I," Jack interjected.

Tia pulled the barrel from Gleason's neck, and Perry watched his good friend take a deep breath.

"You're to stay with it until it breaks through," Tia ordered.

"Not wise," Perry said.

"Oh, really," Tia said. "And why is that?"

"Gleason has already been on duty for too long. He needs rest, as does the rest of my crew. If they don't eat and rest, they'll make mistakes, and this operation is too sensitive for that."

"If anyone makes a mistake, it will be their last one."

"Nice a thought as that is," Perry said, "if the cryobot freezes in place, then we'll be left with a very deep hole and a half-million-dollar cork."

"We have the other, larger cryobot," Tia countered.

"As I told you, it's designed to follow the smaller one down the hole. It's not made to move much ice, only to widen the shaft. It's like drilling a pilot hole in wood to make room for a screw—no pilot hole and the wood splits."

"I get the idea," Tia snapped.

Jack looked at the nearest of the four gunmen. "And you said she was dumb." The guard started toward Jack.

"Stand down," Tia commanded. "We have our orders."

"Who gives you your orders?" Perry asked. "Enkian? You mentioned someone named Enkian."

"That doesn't concern you."

Perry laughed. "Let's see, I'm tied up, held against my will while five automatic weapons point in my general direction, and I watched you kill one of your own men. I'm afraid I have to disagree—it does concern me."

Tia didn't respond. She turned her attention back to the computer monitor.

"Surely you can't be afraid that I'll pick up the phone and call 911," Perry said. "I assume you know our radios have been sabotaged."

Tia didn't rise to the bait.

"What about the C-5?" Perry asked. "Are you responsible for that?"

"Not personally."

"But it was one of your people, right? What about your man—the guy who planted the bomb? It was a bomb, wasn't it?"

"It was."

"Your man left a bomb to destroy the Dome, the place we live, then he carried a similar device onto the plane. Correct?"

"Close," Tia smiled.

"So what about your man? Unless he blew himself up, he must be one of us."

Tia turned to face Perry. "He sacrificed himself for a greater cause."

"He committed suicide?" Larimore asked.

"No, Commander," Perry said. "That isn't what she said. She said he 'sacrificed himself' for what he believed in. The guy who planted the C-4 in the bathroom didn't know there was a bomb on the plane, right?"

"You should have been a detective, Mr. Sachs. Your deductive skills are wasted in engineering."

"Someone else put the bomb on the plane then," Perry said. "Someone here or back at McMurdo?"

"McMurdo," Tia admitted. "It was regrettable, but necessary."

Jack turned to the same gunman he had been egging on. "Kinda strips away that sense of job security, doesn't it? One killed after doing his job, and one killed today doing his job. Tell me, pal. . .is your life insurance paid up?"

"Please don't make me kill you, Mr. Dyson," Tia said. "I'm not opposed to it, you understand, but someone wants to meet all of you. I don't want to disappoint him."

"Enkian?" Perry said the name again.

Tia fell silent again.

"So what can be so important that you'd 'sacrifice' your henchmen?" Perry pressed.

"Something you can't imagine."

"Try me."

"I won't try you, Mr. Sachs, but I will warn you one last time."

Perry looked up and saw a small movement near the open

crates. He lowered his head but raised his eyes in the direction of the movement. Something was staring back at him from the crate Tia had opened a few moments before. His stomach twisted. He couldn't see enough detail to identify which one, but he knew it had to be Sarah or Gwen. Maybe both. The wood container was large enough to hold them both. He had no idea how Tia missed seeing them, but he thanked God for it.

"Okay, no more questions, but I'm back to my original point. My crew needs food and rest. They're no good to you otherwise. Leave one of us behind to monitor Hairy's progress and let the others go back to the Dome."

"Why is it I think you're up to something?" Tia asked.

"What do you think a bunch of scientists and engineers are going to do against automatic weapons?"

Tia looked around the Chamber again. "This one stays," she said, pointing to Jack.

"He's already been on shift for twelve hours," Perry argued. "I was due up next. I've slept more recently than the rest."

Tia looked as if she were considering it. "No. Dyson stays, and one of my men stays with him. There's nothing to do but watch the computer monitor. Someone can relieve him in a few hours."

"At least untie my hands," Jack said. "It's difficult to enter computer commands this way." He held up his bound wrists.

Tia nodded at one of her men, who removed a large knife from its leather sheath on his belt. He bounded to Jack and made a vicious slice with the blade. The nylon tie fell at Jack's feet.

"Ow!" Jack jumped back, clutching his thumb. "You cut me."

"Sorry," the man said with a smile.

Perry started toward his friend but stopped when every MP-5 pointed his way.

"It's okay," Jack said, waving Perry off. "It's not deep."

"You stay with him," Tia told the man with the knife. "Everyone else into the other dome."

Perry turned and took a step, then glanced over his shoulder at Jack, who had already taken a seat behind the monitor. This was not how he had expected it to go. He had hoped to be the one left behind, to have more time to figure out some useful plan. *What now, Lord? I'm running out of ideas.*

Robert Jeter paced his plush office. His stomach was a vat of heated acid, and his jaw ached from clenching it. Small droplets of sweat dotted his brow. *This is crazy,* he said to himself. *Pure, unadulterated lunacy.*

In precisely three and a half minutes, he would have to walk through the door into the Oval Office and meet with the same people he had seen that morning and one additional person: General Brian McDivett. It wasn't going to be pleasant. The president was in a mood. . .more than a mood; he was on the verge of smashing furniture. The NSA had verified its previous belief that a C-5 had gone down and may have gone down in a place other than was being searched.

That was bad enough, but now the president had learned—thanks to General McDivett—who had been on the aircraft. If that was all there was to it, then things would not be so bad. But the president was facing an uphill reelection battle, and Jeter wanted the chief executive's image to be clear as crystal.

And there was a greater problem hovering over Jeter like an engorged thunderhead. His call to Enkian had gone south in the first thirty seconds. He made it clear that Jeter was to "take care of the matter." *How?* Jeter wanted to know. There was no sane way to take care of the matter. Now Jeter was stuck, as his mother used to say, between the devil and the deep blue sea.

He looked at his watch. Thirty seconds before the meeting, and he had no idea what to do. Normally a decisive man, quick on his feet and quicker in speech, he suddenly felt mired in fear. Something wasn't right, and he suspected it was going to get worse.

Jeter dried his palms on his trousers, pulled on his suit coat, ran a hand through his brown hair, and took a deep breath. He told himself he was ready, but he knew otherwise. A few steps later he was in the Oval Office, looking at a very angry president and four very uncomfortable men, one wearing an army uniform. "Again, it appears I'm last in," Jeter said. He looked at his watch. He was ten seconds early.

The president was standing behind his desk, and Jeter knew what that meant. Normally, President Richard Calvert was the kind of leader who offered you a comfortable seat and something to drink, then sat next to you and chatted about sports for a few minutes. When angry, though, he used the full force of his office to get his point across. He stood behind the wide desk and made his guests sit in less comfortable chairs opposite him.

"Let's get to it," the president snapped. "I want to hear from you, General, because I know what I'm hearing from CIA can't be right."

"I'm not certain what the CIA has been telling you, Mr. President—"

"Tell me about the C-5 in Antarctica," he snapped.

"Yes, sir. As you know, the Pentagon became aware that something unusual was going on over an under-ice lake called Vostok. It's about the size of Lake Ontario, and the Russians have a couple of research stations in the area. Some years back, the Russians drilled very close to the lake then stopped. Or so we were told."

"You think they were doing something else?"

Jeter stood to one side of the desk and watched the general squirm. He understood what the man was going through.

"We couldn't be sure," General McDivett said, "but it crossed our minds. With all their economic problems, the Vostok research facility was supposed to be very nearly closed down. So when recent surveys over the area showed that Lake Vostok was expanding, we thought we should take a look. Ostensibly, we teamed with the

National Science Foundation and sent a team of scientists and engineers to investigate."

"What could the Russians do to make a lake under a few hundred feet of ice grow?"

"Actually, sir, it's two miles below the ice, and the answer is, we don't know. There has been suggestion of under-ice nuclear disposal or testing."

"That sounds far-fetched," the president said.

"I agree, sir, but we have our share of paranoids."

"You're not one of them?"

The jab pained the general, who frowned. "No, sir, I am not. It might be a natural occurrence, but it demanded investigation. A melting of the ice cap would be disastrous, to say the least."

"You said you partnered with the NSF. Who else was down there?"

McDivett filled his lungs. "We sent three scientists with needed specialties, a crew of engineers and workers from Sachs Engineering—government-approved contractors—and six navy Seabees with their commander."

Jeter watched as the president's face turned crimson. "You're telling me that we lost military people on this mission?"

"Yes, sir. The six Seabees were due to be on that plane. For security reasons, we wanted to limit the number of people on the site to essential personnel. Only the commander remained behind. However, we've been trying to raise the base by satellite phone and radio, but there's no answer. We think something may have gone wrong and the team abandoned the site."

"Why would they do that?" the president wondered.

"We don't know, sir. All we know is that they're no longer responding, and that the C-5 is lost over the ocean."

"Is it?" the president said. "Our friends from CIA seem to disagree. Fill the general in, David."

"Yes, sir. I'm sure the general knows some of this, but compiling information from the NSA and other sources, we know there is a disparity between radio traffic from the Coast Guard, the airport at McMurdo Station, Antarctica, and what we have recently discovered." He removed some photos from a file he held on his lap. "These photos were taken by satellite two hours ago."

"This isn't over water," McDevitt said.

"The big ears of NSA picked up radio communication from the Coast Guard cutter conducting the search. The skipper thinks he's on a wild goose chase and the plane had to go down over ice."

A set of pictures was passed to Jeter. He studied them for a moment. The image was clear enough. He didn't need photo analysis training to recognize the scattered and burned remains of an airplane or to see the smoldering crater.

"That's it?" Homeland Security Secretary Larry Shomer asked.

"Not much left," Jannot said. "No one could have survived that, and if they did, the cold would have killed them soon after."

"So it didn't go down over the ocean," President Calvert said. "The Coast Guard skipper was right. But why would anyone think the craft was over the ocean to begin with? It was a direct flight to. . .to. . .where does one go when they leave Antarctica?"

"Usually Christchurch, New Zealand," the general answered. "Our team was to spend a few hours at McMurdo then fly to Christchurch."

"So I ask again," Calvert pressed. "If they weren't scheduled to be over the ocean, then why search it?"

"I made some calls to the Coast Guard commandant," Jannot said. "He checked things out and tells me there was an eyewitness who saw it hit the water."

"An eyewitness?" Calvert looked at the picture. "Two crashes?"

Jannot shook his head. "I doubt it."

Jeter watched his boss drop deep into thought. "Wait a minute." The president turned to McDevitt. "General, you said there were navy Seabees and a crew from an engineering company.

What company did you say?"

"Sachs Engineering," the general replied. "They've done a great deal of work for the military all around the world. Always on time and always under budget. They have some expertise that—"

"Henry Sachs?"

"Yes, sir," the general answered. Jeter saw the puzzlement on his face.

"Henry Sachs has been a longtime supporter," Jeter explained. "He and the president are acquaintances."

"You're telling me Sachs lost some of his employees in that crash?"

"Yes, sir," McDevitt said. "And worse than that. I checked the roster of workers. His son Perry was leading the mission."

Curses erupted from the president's mouth. He began to pace back and forth behind his desk.

Jeter felt his heart flutter. He knew what was coming next. He had to speak. "Mr. President, you should know that Mr. Sachs called earlier today. Word has reached him."

"And you didn't tell me!" Calvert bellowed. His words reverberated in the round room.

"I was planning on telling you in this meeting—"

Another volcanic eruption spewed from the president. "All right, here's what I want. David, I want the CIA on this. I want more and better photos. I want to know everything. Got it?"

"Yes, sir," Jannot replied.

"Tell NSA to step up their monitoring of the communications down there. If a penguin burps, I want to know about it. General, I want to know if those folks truly abandoned the site and died in that crash."

"Sir, communications are broken and—"

"Fix them! I don't care if you have to hitchhike down there yourself. I want information. I want answers, and I want them now."

Jeter took a step back when the president snapped his head

around to face him. "We'll talk later. In the meantime, this is a high-priority situation. I want this on top of everyone's to-do list. The rest of you, get me what you can."

Everyone stood.

"Now get out."

"What are you going to do?" Jeter asked.

"I'm going to call a friend who just lost his son. Now give me some privacy."

Jeter shambled from the room, feeling scalded by the president's anger. He closed himself in his office, dropped into his chair, and began to think. Hard.

CHAPTER 21

Jack studied the dials displayed on the computer monitor. He preferred real dials and readouts, not pictures of them produced by a computer. Gleason loved this stuff, but give him the real thing any day. He harbored no ill will toward computers. He could use them better than most, but he had a predilection for things that left grease or dirt under his fingernails. Computers, while useful, were also sterile. Still, he was stuck with this one, and he made sure he was familiar with the readings and the computer commands. It wouldn't do to upset the gunman who could cut him in half before he could speak a word.

He moved his eyes from one dial to the next until he had them memorized. Gleason and Perry had briefed him on its operation, but he had had little reason to believe he would actually be seated behind the controls. That was Sarah's job. . .Gleason's job.

He was thankful there was nothing to do but watch and wait. That meant there was less opportunity for him to do something wrong. It also gave him time to think about his situation. Something needed to be done. He held no optimism that these guys were going to give everybody a lift home.

For the moment the numbers were even, but the automatic weapons tipped the balances to the bending point. He had also seen how fast, fluid, and vicious the woman named Tia could be. And the incident with the man and the knife that left the thumb of his left hand bleeding drove home the point that the men were well trained.

Jack glanced up from the dials at the man in black who stood just to his left. He was a few inches shorter than Jack and weighed twenty, maybe thirty pounds less, but Jack doubted the man was anything but muscle. Take away the gun and the knife, and Jack might have a chance, but for now he could do nothing but wait.

Then there was another problem. Jack had been friends with Perry for so many years that he could read his body language and anticipate almost everything he was going to do. It had been a brief movement, the merest of tells, but Jack picked up on it. Perry saw something, something in the area of the empty shipping crates. Jack had brought his gaze to bear just in time to see someone peeking over the edge of Hairy's crate, the lid raised just enough to allow a pair of pretty eyes to scan the situation.

So there they were—he with his fanny in a fiberglass folding chair and one, probably two women hiding in a crate across the Chamber.

Then he heard it. It was slight, almost impossible to hear, and Jack would not have noticed it if he were not waiting for it. A scraping, soft and subtle. Wood against wood. If he could hear it then—

Jack stood, stretched, and yawned loudly.

"Sit down," the gunman ordered.

"My sitter is broken, pal. I need to stretch. You know how it is." Jack spoke louder than necessary. It was his only hope of distracting the gunman. He caught a glimpse of the slow-moving container lid.

"I said 'sit down.'" The man's sour face darkened and tensed.

"Come on, give a guy a break. A man can only sit for so long." Jack stretched his back and took another step to the side. The gunman's piercing eyes followed him. As he moved, Jack let his eyes drift over the man's shoulders and saw Gwen emerge from the crate, plastic packing material clinging to her parka. A second later, Sarah appeared. He didn't know what they planned, but he had to keep the guard occupied.

"So how do you get into this line of work?" Jack asked with a wry grin. "I mean, do you answer a newspaper ad or go to school for training? Acme School of Terrorism or something like that?"

"You're not funny, big guy," the gunman said, raising the barrel of the wicked-looking gun to Jack's chest. He flipped a switch and a small, red light appeared over Jack's sternum. He hadn't noticed before that the MP-5 was equipped with a laser marker.

"Now that's cool," Jack said. "You could point out things on a map with a light like that."

"You're a trigger squeeze away from death. Sit down."

"I don't think you'll kill me right now," Jack said. He caught a glimpse of Sarah and Gwen moving. He didn't look at them, fearing the guard would catch his eye movement. "Maybe later, sure. But not now. You'd have to answer to your boss, and she seems, if you'll forgive me, a little edgy. Maybe she's not sleeping well."

"I'm not afraid of her."

"Oh, sure you are," Jack said as if he were having coffee with the man. "Can't say I blame you. She's tough as nails. I mean, look at what she did to your partner in the Dome. Wow. One measly mistake and he takes one in the chest. Your boss may not be much on employee morale, but she sure knows how to motivate."

"He screwed up."

"No doubt about that. Kind of makes you wonder what the price will be for your screwup."

"I don't plan on making any mistakes."

Jack rubbed his side. "She gave me a couple of good kicks." His side ached, and each movement caused him more pain. He was sure Tia had cracked one or more of his ribs. "It hurts to breathe."

"You're gonna be feeling more pain if you don't sit down."

"Now, now," Jack said, wagging a finger like a teacher scolding a child. "Your boss said no one was to be killed. I heard her. Granted, I was on the floor rolling in pain, but my ears were still working pretty good."

The man flipped another switch on the machine gun. Jack recognized the safety being moved to the OFF position. He sighed melodramatically. "That's the problem with you terrorist types—you have no sense of hospitality."

"I'm not a terrorist."

"A rose by any other name. . . ," Jack said and began to move toward the chair, then stopped abruptly. "Do they teach Shakespeare in terrorist school? 'Cause I just quoted him, and you don't seem all that impressed."

"My patience is gone, funny man. Now put your—"

It had taken all of Jack's discipline not to look up as Sarah stepped behind the man and swung something long and dark. He heard a thud and a grunt of pain, then saw the gunman's arm drop to his side.

Jack was moving before he had time to think. In two steps he was in front of the guard, whose face was twisted in pain. The man started to turn. Jack helped him with a punch to the side of the head. The gunman went limp and crumbled.

Jack jumped into the air and reached for his fist. It was on fire. Pain radiated up his arm and into his shoulder. The movement made his ribs ignite in scorching agony.

"Are you all right?" Sarah asked.

Jack turned to see her standing two feet away with a crowbar in her hand. "Better than he is."

"I couldn't bring myself to hit him on the head," Sarah said. "I was afraid I'd kill him. Stupid reasoning, I know."

"Not at all," Jack said. "That whack you gave him on the arm is gonna leave a mark."

"Yeah, well that punch you gave may leave a trace, too," Gwen said.

"I think it hurt me more than it did him." He shook his hand as if he could throw off the pain. "You guys have been in that box all this time?"

"Yeah. Not many places to hide around here," Gwen said.

"What do we do now?" Sarah asked.

Jack bent and picked up the gun that lay next to the unconscious man. "Take control of this baby first. After that, I don't know."

A whooshing sound rolled through the Chamber, and Jack looked up in time to see Tia and Perry walk into the room. Before Jack could think, Tia raised her weapon. Perry reached for the barrel, but the round had been fired.

Jack felt the impact in his left shoulder, then his feet left the ice, and the floor rose to meet him. His breath was forced from his lungs on impact. The first pain he felt was from his damaged ribs, then his nervous system caught up with the event. Pain like a thousand hot nails radiated from his shoulder. He rolled to his side to see a red fluid spreading out on the ice like someone had spilled a quart of crimson paint. Then Jack realized the paint was his blood.

He heard a scream.

He heard his name.

Jack saw Perry's face hovering over his own. "Hey, buddy."

"Hang in there, pal," Perry said. "I'm here. I'll get you fixed. . . ."

Jack heard no more.

Robert Jeter had been in politics all his life. He had never wanted to hold office; he wanted to manage those who did. That was where the real power was. The man who could sway a king was a king himself. That had been his philosophy, but now he felt like the marionette. Someone of great power and influence had just taken control of his strings.

Jeter had prided himself on his control. At George Washington University he had graduated in the top one percent of his class. He knew more about the American political system than any ten experts combined. He knew how to work congressmen and senators. He knew how to plan a foolproof campaign. No candidate he backed had lost, including the man who now carried the title POTUS—President of the United States.

Richard Calvert was the most powerful man in the world, and as the one who stood beside him, Jeter was the second most powerful. No one saw the president without first going through him. He controlled the appointment book, and if Jeter blackballed a person, that person would never meet the president again. Control the gate and he controlled the man behind the gate.

For the most part, Richard Calvert was controllable. He played the game, and he played it well. He knew when to listen and when to turn a deaf ear. A master at conciliation, he hadn't seized the presidency; he wiggled into it in a dance Jeter choreographed.

But Calvert was also a principled man. He didn't mind compromise, and he chose his battles well, but certain things were sacrosanct to him. One such thing was honesty; another was loyalty. In one day both attributes had come into play.

Jeter knew what was going through his boss's mind. He made it his business to know. The president was feeling that someone was working behind his back. News of the crash had not reached his ears as it should have, especially since the loss of life included military personnel and the son of a friend. The searing look he had given Jeter at the end of the meeting made it clear that he was blaming his chief of staff. Serious damage control was needed.

That was just one side of his problem. The other was Eric Enkian, a man he had met only twice, each time for mere seconds. Despite the short time, Jeter knew he was deeply indebted to the man. Jeter came from a poor family. His father had been a miner in the hellish coal holes of Virginia's Cumberland Plateau. When

Jeter's mother was diagnosed with breast cancer, it had been Enkian who paid for the treatment that saved her life. He had no doubt his mother would have died under normal care, but Enkian had arranged for care at a cancer treatment center in California. Not only had he paid for it, he also had arranged the travel, rented a home nearby, and allowed Jeter's father extended leave so he could be with his wife. That was when Jeter was sixteen.

A few years later, Jeter received a letter stating that EA Mining would pay full tuition and expenses to any college Jeter chose and could enter. While he had been expecting to spend a few years in a state college, suddenly Harvard, Yale, Stanford, and others lay before him. He was told it was because of his high school achievements; he later found out that there were other reasons.

During his junior year a man from EA Mining came to visit. He was polite, dapper, and appeared extremely wealthy. This last fact became clear by the late-model Porsche he drove and the two large gold-and-diamond rings on each hand. Jeter rode in that Porsche that day, his benefactor's representative at the wheel. As they motored down the freeway, the man asked a question.

"You see these rings, boy?" the man had asked. Young Jeter said he did. He hadn't been able to take his eyes off of them. "Everything about them comes from EA Mining."

"They must pay you a lot of money," Jeter had said.

"They do, son, but you miss the point. These are not just pieces of jewelry; they're reminders. The diamonds come from our mines in South Africa, the gold from Alaska, the silver inlay from Nevada. The gold was heated in a furnace made by materials from our other mines. The material used to polish the diamonds. . ."

"From an EA-owned mine," Jeter posited.

"Exactly. Look around the campus," the man had said. "Marble from our mines, asphalt parking lots from our mines, even the chalk the professors use comes from our mines."

"Are you trying to talk me into going to work for EA Mining?"

Jeter asked. "I'm a poli-sci major."

"Mr. Enkian knows that. Political science is an important study. We're not asking you to work the mines like your father; we would like you to join us in a different way."

"What way?"

"You'll see."

Ten minutes later, they pulled in front of the Watergate Hotel, released the sports car to the valet, and walked into one of the world's most famous buildings. Jeter followed the mysterious man into the spacious, world-class restaurant and was surprised to see his father seated at a table by the window overlooking the Potomac. It had been over three months since Jeter had seen him, and he looked different. He looked frail. The suit fit a little too loosely and hung limply on shoulders that Jeter remembered as always being broad and strong.

"Dad, what are you doing here?"

"I wanted to see my son."

Jeter felt ill at ease. Something was wrong. "What is it, Dad? Are you ill?"

"I'm just getting old," his father had said. "Working the mines has taken its toll."

Jeter's heart skipped. His first thought was one that orbited the thinking of anyone who had a family member in the coal mines: black lung. "You mean. . ."

His father smiled. "No, my lungs are fine. We use the best safety equipment in the mines, son. I have colon cancer." He said it as if he were announcing the purchase of a new piece of furniture. "The doctors tell me they caught it early, and that it's in a good location. They'll perform surgery in two days. I'll go home a couple of days after that. They don't think I'll need a colostomy. That's good news."

"I'm coming home," Jeter said.

"No, you're not," Dad said flatly. "You stick with your studies. I'm going to be fine, and the company is sending me to the best doctors. There's nothing to worry about."

"But what about chemotherapy? You'll need help. . . ."

Dad shook his head. "No, I won't. The company has taken care of that, too." He smiled. "I didn't come here to talk about my surgery, but you have a right to know."

"What then?" Jeter was puzzled.

"It's time I talked to you about something I should have brought up long ago."

Food was brought, and drinks served, but Jeter had little interest. He was focused on his father.

"You come from very noble stock, Son. We have a family history that goes back farther than you can imagine."

"I don't follow, Dad."

For forty-five minutes his father explained about his lineage, about the people from which he sprang, about their skill and the nation they had formed. He also explained about their sudden downfall and effort to return to a former glory—an effort that had been underway for centuries.

"I've never heard of this," Jeter said. "In world history class, they mentioned the people you're talking about, but we didn't spend much time on it."

The man from EA shook his head. "History classes talk about the people who came after us. They know very little."

"Okay," Jeter had said, "so I'm not Italian or British. So what?"

"There's a religion behind it all," his father explained. "Some follow it closely; others, like your mother and myself, don't."

"I'm not much of a religious person," Jeter said. "You know that."

His father nodded. "I'm afraid you get that from me. It doesn't matter. Belief isn't part of our religion. It's not like the Christians or the Jews or the Muslims. But it is part of what defines us. It makes us unique."

"And that makes us a unit, a people with a single purpose," the man with the Porsche said.

"No one's asking you to join a church," his father said. "But we are asking that you help keep the system alive."

"How?"

The benefactor spoke first. "By learning who we are and teaching your children when the time comes. At times we may need help with one thing or another."

"I'm just a student. What can I do?"

"You won't always be a student, Robert," the man said. "We take care of our own. Do you want to go to graduate school? We can make it possible. Need money to start a business? We can provide it. We can help make you successful beyond your dreams."

"Wait a minute," Jeter said. "My father has been a laborer in the mines all his life. He didn't get special treatment."

"Of course I did, Son. I don't have the smarts you do. You got that from your mother. I hated school; I prefer to work with my hands. I was born a laborer, and I'm not ashamed of it. You were born for more. I know it, your mother knows it, and the company knows it, too."

"What do I have to do?"

"Just listen, and help when you can," the man said.

Jeter looked at his father, who stared back with anticipation. "This would make you happy?"

"Yes," his father said. "And your mother, too."

"When does my education begin?"

"We'll let you know," the man said. "You just keep up the good grades. Oh, and one more thing." He reached into his pocket and pulled out a set of keys and pushed them to Jeter. The key chain held a key with the Porsche emblem and a hard clay cylinder.

"I don't understand," Jeter said.

"The car we came over in—I assume you like it."

"I love it."

"It's yours."

Jeter couldn't believe his ears.

"You're giving me a Porsche?"

The man nodded.

"I'm. . .I'm speechless."

"That's a first," his father chided.

"What's this cylinder thing?" Jeter studied it. It had six sides, and the image of a dragon was etched into its surface.

"It's our symbol, our identity. The six-sided cylinder represents the sixty-six clay cylinders that contain the prophecies."

"Prophecies?"

"You'll learn more about those in time. The dragon is an ancient symbol, something else you'll learn later. For now, just know that anyone who carries one of these is family. He or she is duty bound to help you, and you to help them."

"Like a service club," Jeter said.

"In a way, but it is also much more."

Jeter turned to his father and saw a wide grin part his lips. It felt good to see his father smile. That day was the last time he saw his father smile. He died on the operating table two days later.

Henry Sachs hung up the phone and fought back hot tears. The president had been kind, very gracious, but he brought no hope. He had told Henry of the crash and been honest about the wasted search efforts conducted in the Ross Sea.

"Not that it would have made any difference, Henry. The photos of the crash make it highly unlikely that there were any survivors."

"Perry wasn't supposed to be on that flight," Henry said.

"I'm told that repeated efforts to contact the research site have been in vain. The consensus is that there is no one there to answer."

"That's not like Perry, Mr. President. Something else is wrong. I can feel it."

The president said he understood, but Henry doubted his

conviction. "I've ordered another satellite survey. We plan to look for signs of life."

"How would you tell?" Henry asked. "Unless someone happens to be walking outside, you won't see anything."

"Actually," the president said after a moment's hesitation, "we can."

When the call was over, Sachs was left clinging to a single hope: that despite the silence of the camp, Perry was still alive deep in Antarctica.

Henry Sachs noticed his hands were shaking.

Jeter stepped from the limo that had pulled up the long drive of his Georgetown home. It was a home he saw less and less, spending up to sixteen hours a day in the West Wing.

He gave the driver a cursory wave and plodded up the steps of the colonial home. The sun had set hours before, and the moonless night matched the darkness in his soul. He was a man caught between two ideals, two commitments, two loves. On one hand he had made a promise to his father two days before the old man died; on the other, he had made a commitment to the president and to his country.

"Hey, stranger," a sweet voice said from the sitting room. Jeter walked in and kissed his wife gently on the lips. The kiss felt good; it reminded him that someone in his very confused world loved him unconditionally.

If Nobel Prizes were given for patience and understanding, then Martha Jeter would have a closetful of them. Being married to a man entrenched in the halls of government was no easy task. His hours were long, his frustrations high, and his absences frequent. Martha bore the burden of household and family, almost single-handedly raising their daughter Courtney.

"You look wrung out, baby," she said. Middle age had been

kind to her. She was slim, dark-eyed, and had a mane of auburn hair that caught the eye of both men and women.

"I'm beat, and I have to be at the office early."

"That's not new. You're always at the office early." She patted the seat next to her and set aside the book she was reading. Martha seldom watched television and avoided the news as much as possible. "I live with the news," she had said many times.

"Yeah, I know. I'm thinking of quitting and going into real estate." That made her laugh. "What? You don't think I can sell town homes to freshman congressmen?"

"You'd be the best at whatever you did. I just had you figured for the speaking circuit. Can I fix you a drink?"

"A highball," he said.

"Uh-oh, the drink choice of a bad day." She rose and made her way to the wet bar situated in the corner.

"Some days are worse than others. It comes with the territory. Did you hear from Courtney today?"

"She sent me an e-mail. She's planning a weekend trip to San Francisco."

"Why she chose to go to Stanford University is beyond me. A California school of all things. I could have gotten her into George Washington."

"That's your alma mater," Martha said, returning with the mixed drink in one hand and a bottled water in the other.

"And just what is wrong with my alma mater?"

"Nothing. It's just *your* alma mater. You know how independent Courtney is."

"I've got the gray hairs to prove it." He took a sip of the drink and set the glass aside. He ran his hand through her hair. "How come I got all the gray?"

"Who said you did? You can buy magic in boxes these days. You find them in the cosmetic aisle."

Jeter chuckled. He couldn't remember the last time he had

walked into a neighborhood store. "A weekend in San Francisco, eh? Ah, to be young."

"Oh. A messenger brought this by about an hour ago."

"What is it?"

"A package—that's what messengers bring."

"Very funny. Hand it here."

She reached forward to the wide, walnut coffee table at their feet and picked up a brown envelope. Jeter saw his name and address neatly penned on the front, but no return address. He opened the envelope and removed a picture.

"So what is it? More love notes from political groupies?" He didn't answer. "Robert?"

"It's a picture."

"Of what?"

"Of Courtney."

"Really? Maybe a friend sent it."

Jeter knew the photo didn't come from friend. That was made clear by the crosshairs drawn over the image of his daughter's head.

CHAPTER 22

Sarah watched the monitor closely. "It should be soon," she said. "Maybe a meter or two." She pulled the joystick control closer.

Perry watched her carefully, hoping the stress of being confined in the Chamber with a ruthless woman and her henchmen holding guns wouldn't trigger an episode of narcolepsy. He had no idea how Tia would respond or if she would believe it was anything more than a trick.

Tia had brought the rest of the crew into the Chamber. Jack sat on one of the folding chairs. The left sleeve of his parka was dyed dark red with his own blood. Tia had allowed Gwen to examine the arm. He had been fortunate; the round that had been redirected by Perry's quick reflexes had torn a ragged hole in the upper arm. Gwen had been forced to suture the wound. Jack didn't complain. Instead, he had taken the additional pain stoically.

Griffin stood next to his sister and near the monitor. The thought of seeing a lake no one had ever seen apparently had enlivened him from his emotional catatonia.

Larimore was bracketed by two of the gunmen. He had endured a beating for lying about Gwen and Sarah. Why Tia had let him live, Perry couldn't fathom. She didn't seem the forgiving type.

Gleason and Dr. Curtis huddled nearby, and another guard watched them from a step or two away.

The room seemed to chill even more, something Perry didn't think was possible. He gazed at the open maw of ice through which a metal cable and thickly insulated fiber optics descended. The support cable was slack, allowing the weight of Hairy to pull it through the freshly melted ice. When it broke through, the cable would pull taut.

"What happens next?" Tia demanded. She was looking at Perry.

Perry was in no mood to explain anything. He was a package of anger and frustration, both of which he kept in check. They were good for emotional fuel, but such emotions could cloud the thinking if given too much sway. He took a moment to weigh the price of silence. He decided that he was willing to pay it but doubted that he would be the object of the woman's wrath. Most likely she would hurt someone else to get Perry's cooperation.

"At some point, the ice beneath Hairy will give way, unable to support its weight. When that happens, the feed line will snap tight. That will be the first indication. We should also see something on the monitor. Though not immediately, because the onboard lights won't have come on."

"Why not turn them on now?" she wondered.

"Power and protection. Most of the power is being used to heat the head that melts the ice. The lights are hidden behind protective panels. Ice is hard and sharp. It may be made of water, but it can easily rip a hole in metal."

"Just ask the owners of the *Titanic*," Jack said.

Tia turned to him and frowned. "I would think you've had enough pain for one day."

Jack shrugged.

"Go on," Tia prompted.

"The cryobot will fall a few inches," Perry said, "and a gush of air will probably shoot out of the hole."

"Air?"

Griffin spoke up. "Yeah, air. There's a good chance that some air is trapped between the lake and the ice sheet above. Of course, that's just speculation."

"Your science can't tell you for certain," Tia sneered.

"No, my science can't tell me, and neither can anyone else's. We think we know what's going on down there, but we won't know for sure until we look. Not that I approve of any of this."

"Your approval isn't needed," Tia said.

"Tell her about the water, Sachs," Griffin snapped. "I'm sure she'll find that captivating."

Perry worried about Griffin. He had lost control once, and now it looked like he might do so again. He was emotionally sensitive, something that was apparent the moment they landed and Griffin greeted them with the news that he was team leader. He had been pouting ever since. Now, under the weight of impending injury and probably death, under the constant gaze of gun barrels, he looked like an earthen dam with everwidening cracks.

"Water?" Tia said.

"Yes, water," Perry explained. "The lake is under pressure. It should be; it has a couple of miles of ice resting on most of its surface. There may be areas of ice bridging, but the lake is far too large for us to think that the ice sheet hovers over the water."

"This thing is going to gush like a geyser?"

"Of course not," Griffin chimed in. "We're over ten thousand feet above the surface."

"Someone had better clear this up for me," Tia demanded. "Someone without the attitude." She raised an eyebrow at Griffin.

Perry spoke quickly, pulling her attention back to him. "We don't know how much pressure the water is under. There are many variables to consider: the density of the water, the ability of the ice sheet to float on the surface, the compressive strength of the ice sheet, the fact that water cannot be compressed—"

"Cut to the chase."

"Best guess is that a column of water will rise up the shaft as much as a third of the distance."

"So no shower," Griffin said.

"What will that do to the probe?" Tia wondered.

"We don't know. It's another reason we have the larger cryobot. Not only will it widen the shaft, but it will serve as a backup should Hairy take a beating and cease to function. Ideally, the pressure will break through the last couple of feet of ice in the shaft and push the probe back up. If it does, we have to be ready to take up the slack in the support cable. Then Hairy will begin to sink through the water."

"There's no chance water is going to come shooting out of the shaft?"

"I wouldn't go so far as to say no chance," Perry said. "I assume you've seen film of oil gushing out of the ground. Bottom line is: We don't know. The lake has been expanding, so that may have increased the pressure. Then again, it may have an outlet that serves as a release valve."

"What precautions have you taken?"

Perry shrugged. "Dr. James doesn't think it will rise more than a third, and that's good enough for me."

"And if he's wrong?"

"Then we all take a really cold shower," Griffin said.

"We don't know what's down there," Perry admitted.

The sound of the air lock opening pulled everyone's attention to the door. Perry was confused. By his count, everyone at the site was already in the Chamber. Then he remembered Tia's comment about "the man who is going to kill you."

The door opened, and a tall, deeply tanned man stepped in. His head was held high, his stride long, and he wore a white parka. Behind him streamed armed men, who quickly surrounded Perry and the others. Having five people with guns was bad enough; now

Perry was looking at fifty or more. What little glimmer of optimism he held for escape flickered and burned low like a candle flame, leaving only a red ember at the wick's tip.

Tia suddenly stood erect, walked to the man in white, and knelt before him, bowing her head. "My lord," she intoned.

"Oh brother," Jack said.

Once again Jeter was the last into the room, this time by choice. He closed the door to the Oval Office behind him. He faced the president and the security team, the same men he had met with the night before and the morning before that. Unlike the previous night, when the president had made them all sit around his desk, they were in their usual seats on the sofas and comfortable chairs. A silver coffee urn sat on a mahogany serving tray, which rested on the ornate cherry coffee table.

"You sick?" the president asked. "You look like warmed-over death."

"I didn't sleep well last night," Jeter said. Thoughts ricocheted in his mind. He thought of the last meeting, when he had been unable to conceal the fact that he had known of the C-5 incident and hadn't told the president; of the photo of his daughter with the crosshairs drawn over her beautiful face; of his wife's tearful response; of the phone calls made to locate his daughter, all to no avail, only to have her call at 11:00 that night to say she had arrived safely and been at a loud party. Only after she went into the quiet restroom had she noticed that she missed a call on her cell phone. He had demanded she stay at the party until picked up by a man he would send. He had even given a password: "pickles." It was all he could think of at that hour. Pickles had been her childhood dog. The moment he hung up, he called the director of the Secret Service, rousing him from bed, and told him of his fears. Ten minutes later, an agent from the San Francisco office had taken

Courtney from the party to a private residence, and he and three other agents had stayed with her.

Jeter also thought of his father and the commitment he had made that day in the Watergate Hotel and the car he had been given.

"What's eating you?" the president said. "I know it wasn't yesterday's criticism. You're not that thin-skinned."

"I have a statement to make, sir." He paused. "If I may."

"Does it have to do with this meeting?"

"It has to do with everything." Jeter saw a puzzled look paint the president's face. He reached into the pocket of his suit coat and removed his keys. He set them on the coffee table. On the silver key ring was the clay cylinder.

"Hey, I've seen that before," the CIA director said. "The deputy director has one of those."

Steve Belanger, looking every bit the prime FBI agent, agreed. "So does the director of the DC office. Come to think of it, so does the director of the LA bureau."

Jeter pulled up a chair and fell into it. His mouth was dry, his stomach burned, his neck felt as if it were petrifying. He rubbed his weary eyes and explained about his ties to the group. "It has been a family thing for generations, going back to my Irish great-great-grandfather. Probably further than that. My father told me about it when I was in college. It has been nothing more than tradition to me, but it became more the other day." He explained about Sachs's call, his own conversation with the man named Enkian, and the photo of his daughter he had received. "I didn't sleep last night because I have to make a choice. I have to choose between my country and my religion."

"You mean like Presbyterian or Baptist?" the president wondered.

"No," Jeter explained. "Much, much older and something far more different than you can imagine." He paused. "We are in danger, gentlemen—as a nation and as individuals. Whoever has one of these—" he pointed at the clay ornament—"is a physical danger to you." He paused again, lowered his head, then said, "May I see your keys—all of you—please?"

"What is this?" General McDivett asked. "You want to see if we're carrying some kind of Masonic charm?"

"Not Masonic, General. This group is unlike any other."

"They're terrorists?"

"I don't know what they are, but I do know they have great wealth, tremendous power, and have had operatives in government for decades. Now, may I see your key rings?"

"Fine with me," Jannot said. The CIA man pulled out a leather key case, opened it, and set it on the table.

Belanger did the same.

"This is nuts," McDivett said. "I've given my life to this country and served in its military for over thirty years."

"Everyone in this room can say the same thing," the president remarked, his words sharpening to an edge. "We've all served and are serving our country. Show your keys."

McDivett looked at Larry Shomer. Jeter caught the exchange. The homeland security boss fidgeted. McDivett stood and pulled the keys from his pocket. Shomer did the same. A clay cylinder dangled from each. A tsunami of nausea washed over Jeter.

"Well, isn't this interesting," President Calvert said. Jeter saw the color drain from the chief executive's face. "I assume you each received a call last night?" No one said anything. "Tell me, Robert. This late night call you got from. . . What was his name?"

"I only know him as Mr. Enkian."

"What did he ask you to do?"

"My job today," Jeter said, "is to kill you all."

Jeter reached into his pocket.

CHAPTER 23

"oint five meters," Sarah announced. "Assuming our sonar apparatus is measuring the ice correctly."

Perry felt every muscle tense. He surveyed the others. Jack
was now on his feet, still holding his injured left arm. With busted
ribs and a gun wound, it was a wonder he could stand at all. Sarah's
eyes were glued to the monitor, as were Gleason's. The three aca-
demics had huddled together. Griffin looked like a man teetering
on the narrow ledge of a tall building; his sister had both hands
raised to her mouth. Dr. Curtis stood as still as a statue, as if any
movement would ruin it all. Tia stood to the side, her eyes fixed on
the one she called lord.

"History is soon to be made," the regal-looking man said. He
turned to Perry. "I've been learning all about you, Mr. Sachs—you
and your team. I feel as if we are old friends."

"My friends don't hold me captive and kill my people."

"Hyperbole, Mr. Sachs. Nothing more. I have no friends." He
stepped to Tia and eyed her for a moment. He returned his attention to Perry. "Just loyal followers. I've been getting reports about
you. You have been very resourceful. Putting the C-4 on the snowmobile was creative."

"A desperate act by a desperate man."

"It doesn't matter. It was never meant to go off."

"What?" Larimore said. "I know C-4 when I see it, and that was the real McCoy."

"Oh, it was real explosive all right," Enkian said. "Didn't you find it strange that the counter reached zero, but there was no explosion?"

It had struck Perry as strange. "Something went wrong with the clock mechanism, or there was a short in the electronics."

Enkian shook his head. "There was no short. You were meant to find it. It doesn't strike you as strange that only one bomb was found, and that it was found at the back of your living quarters?"

"I don't get it," Larimore said. "What was the purpose?"

"To get you to leave," Enkian said. "And to slow any return. You can tell by the number of men I have that I'm in need of quality shelter. You have it. It doesn't make much sense to destroy what I can take."

"You expected us to see the bomb then leave?" Perry said. "How did you expect us to leave?"

"You were supposed to find it before the transport left," Enkian said. "Apparently my man failed to plant enough hints."

"The same man that died in the crash?"

"His life counted for something," Enkian said.

Larimore croaked out a small laugh. "I thought Griffin planted it."

"I was thinking you did," Jack said. He then asked Enkian, "Why kill all the radios if you thought we'd be leaving?"

"Contingency, Mr. Dyson. No plan is complete without several layers of backup plans. There was always the chance that someone like you or Mr. Sachs would stay behind with the equipment. Your exploits precede you, you know."

"I guess your backup plan failed," Larimore said.

"I'll admit the first one did. But I have more. Many more."

"And here we were suspecting one another," Perry said.

"I'm glad to have provided you with some entertainment,"

Enkian remarked. "Of course, now you have a bigger problem, don't you?"

"But the bomb did go off," Gwen said. "It exploded on the snowmobile."

"That's why children aren't allowed to play with explosives," Tia said. "Most likely the vibration from the snowmobile made an unintended connection."

"I think this is it," Sarah said.

Perry stood close enough to see the monitor but not as close as he would have liked. The onboard camera showed nothing but darkness.

A minute passed. Another.

Perry let his eyes drift to the aluminum support structure and the support line that was attached to Hairy two miles below. It snapped taut, then went slack. The pulley system was robotic. As soon as the line went slack, it began to reel in the extra line. The steel cable and black, plastic-coated fiber optics wrapped around the drum pulleys. The whine of the motors filled the Chamber. Gwen and Griffin took a step back.

"We're through!" Sarah shouted. "We did it!"

Then came a whistling sound. Air was being driven up through the shaft, air that had not been to the surface in eons. In an odd moment of detachment Perry wondered if it would have an odor. He prepared himself for an onrush of wind. It didn't come. Instead of a windstorm there was a slight breeze which diminished a moment later. It was as if the ground burped.

"As I expected," Griffin said. "There was a chance of a large quantity of trapped air, but the odds favored less air. Of course, under pressure, much of the gas would be in solution."

"Hairy is coming up," Sarah said.

Again, Perry found himself holding his breath. They had broken through, according to Sarah, at negative 3,642 meters. Sarah began to count the numbers off. Hairy's depth was decreasing.

"Thirty-six hundred. . .thirty-four. . .thirty-two. . ."

"It's rising like a cork," Jack said.

"Three thousand. . ." She paused. "Slowing. . .twenty-eight hundred. . ."

"That would be some elevator ride," Gleason remarked, his eyes fixed on the dials.

"Twenty-five hundred. . .holding. . .holding. It's stopped."

Perry began breathing again.

"A third of the way," Griffin said. "Just as I predicted."

The retaining line slowed to a stop.

"How's the probe?" Perry asked.

"Hairy is. . ." Sarah studied the display. "Fine. We have readings from all the sensors."

"Gleason, the rigging?"

"Perfect. No splaying and no crimping. The autoreverse worked as designed."

"Shall I activate the lights?" Sarah asked.

"Yes," Enkian snapped. "And let's remember who is in charge."

"Whatever," Sarah said. "I've been through too much today to care."

It was an odd response from her, and it took Perry a second to realize what she was doing. She was cultivating a sense of apathy. If she could trick herself into indifference, then maybe she could ward off another narcolepsy attack. It was a brave front, but he doubted that she could pull it off for long.

The large plasma screen had been filled with virtual gauges and dials. A small heater kept the screen functioning in the freezing Chamber. The pale, solid background gave way to black.

"Camera remains." She entered a few keystrokes. Enkian had ordered her hands freed, as well as the others'. With over fifty armed men surrounding the research team, there was little need for restraints. "Light shields retracting." She paused as if for effect, her finger hovering over one of the keyboard's function keys. Perry didn't need to be a psychic to know that she hesitated out of reverence for the moment. They were about to see what no one had seen before.

She tapped the key.

Jeter was reaching inside his suit coat when Steve Belanger seized his arm and pushed him back until the chair flipped backward. The two men fell to the plush carpeting.

"What are you doing?" Jeter demanded.

"Mr. President, get out!" Belanger called.

"Get off me!" Jeter shouted.

Doors to the Oval Office sprang open and four Secret Service men rushed into the room, guns drawn. Jeter turned and saw the confusion on their faces. Wordlessly, two of them grabbed the president's arms and pushed him from the Oval Office, his feet barely touching the floor.

"Wait a minute," Calvert said. The Secret Service disobeyed and continued to remove the president.

"He's reaching for a gun," Belanger shouted.

Jeter felt the cold barrel of a gun pressed against his forehead. He also felt the weight of the FBI director suddenly removed from his chest.

"Sit down," the agent ordered Belanger.

"How dare you!" Belanger protested. "I'm the director of—"

"I know who you are, sir. Sit down. No one moves until I say." He raised a small radio to his lips. "Close us down."

Jeter knew that at that moment, every key person in the West Wing was being shuttled to a safe place. Every gate was being locked. Tour groups were being told to leave. Secret Service agents were swarming the halls and the eighteen acres of grounds. He didn't move. Not with the business end of a handgun pressing against his scalp.

The agent above held the gun steady with one hand while

patting Jeter's chest and side. Jeter could see his perplexity. Holding a gun on a man he had seen every day, a man he knew was the president's right-hand man was something he had never expected. Jeter also knew that the men and women of the Secret Service took their work very seriously. The safety of the president was their primary concern. Everyone else was secondary—including the chief of staff.

Next, the agent opened Jeter's twisted coat, reached into the pocket, and removed two envelopes. He handed them to his partner as other agents descended on the location.

Seconds passed like hours as Jeter was searched top to bottom. Only then was he allowed to stand. He saw the others being searched as well. The agents were efficient, serious and nonplussed. They had just held at gunpoint and searched the persons of the directors of the FBI and CIA, the secretary of homeland security, and the chairman of the joint chiefs of staff. None of the men complained. It would have done them no good.

Twenty minutes later President Calvert stormed into the Oval Office, accompanied by two agents whom he let know in the most colorful of terms his displeasure. "Yanked from my own office like a rag doll. There's no honor in that."

"Sir, we were only doing our job."

"I know, but I'm angry and you're close by. I would like to be alone with my security staff please. It was all just a misunderstanding."

The agents left, but Jeter knew they weren't far away.

"You had better explain yourself," the president demanded. "I just had both arms dislocated because of you and Steve."

"I thought he was reaching for a weapon," Belanger complained. "What was I supposed to do?"

Jeter answered for the president. "You did the right thing. I would have done the same." He reached for the two envelopes and handed one to the president, who opened it without hesitation and with adrenaline-driven animation.

"This is your resignation," he said, surprised.

"Yes, sir, it is."

"What's in the other envelope?"

Jeter hesitated then handed it to his boss.

Calvert opened it and removed a folded photo. He studied it a moment then said, "It gives me chills." He passed it around, and each man looked at the image of Courtney and the crosshairs.

"By telling me all this, you may be choosing your country over your daughter?"

Tears ran from Jeter's eyes, but he was too tired, too frightened to care. He just nodded. "I can't do what they ask. They have done wonderful things for me, but I can't do what they ask—not even to save my daughter."

"Help us find these people," the president said.

"I don't know how," Jeter admitted. "They're everywhere: in Congress, in the various departments of government. Two are standing right here."

"Yes," the president said. "What am I going to do with you boys?"

"Wow," Gleason said.

"Amen to that," Jack said.

Perry inched closer to the monitor. The area was crowded with Enkian, Tia, and his crew vying for a direct line of sight. Perry was looking at a sight from another world. Light from Hairy's nose streamed through crystal-clear water that was dotted with floating bits of white.

"It's like having tunnel vision," Jack said.

He was right. The strong light pierced the water and illuminated the white ice walls of the shaft. "What's that floating in the water?"

"Let me see," Gwen said.

"Are those white things alive?" Gleason asked.

"It's ice," Griffin said from his position at the back. "While your machine has been melting its way down the shaft, its metal sides have scraped off some ice, most likely when the water propelled it back up."

"He's right," Gwen said. "They look like small animals, but they are nothing more than ice chips. Can you magnify the image?"

"Sure," Sarah said. "The camera has some telescopic capabilities." She zoomed slowly until several small white flecks came into sharp focus.

"Ice," Gwen said. "Nothing more, at least not macroscopically. Microscopically. . .who knows?"

"Take it down," Enkian said. "I didn't fly all the way down here to look at an ice tunnel."

Sarah frowned but entered the keystrokes that would allow Hairy to descend.

"How much movement will be available to us?" Enkian asked.

Sarah moved her head from side to side as if thinking. "A fair amount. Once Hairy exits the shaft, a portion of the outer hull will separate, decreasing the probe's weight and exposing the small propellers that will allow it to move in any direction we direct."

"How do you maintain buoyancy?"

"Hairy is naturally buoyant in the water. It's one reason it is as large as it is. There are several empty, sterile compartments that I'm flooding with water. We didn't want to introduce anything from the surface, so we use Vostok water to decrease buoyancy. Once we emerge, I activate onboard canisters filled with purified air. That air pushes out enough water to bring about zero buoyancy. Then we're free to tour as long as we like."

Enkian nodded. "Descent time?"

"Much faster than through the ice, of course, but we still want to move slowly. I estimate we'll make it through the eleven hundred meters in about thirty minutes. That's a descent rate of—"

"Nearly forty feet a minute," Enkian said. "Let's waste no more time talking. Get on with it." He turned to Tia. "Let's use this time.

Take some men and unload the plane. Bring everything but personal supplies in here."

Tia nodded and moved toward the rear air lock, where large crates passed through. She chose several men who followed without discussion.

CHAPTER 24

It's dim," Enkian said.

"Hold on," Sarah replied. "We're back to the underlayer of ice."

Perry watched with such rapt attention that he forgot for a moment that he was a captive. The plasma monitor displayed the video image returned by Hairy. There had been nothing new to see—just the vertical, white walls of the ice shaft and bits of ice that flickered like stars at night. The minutes ticked by as the probe began a slow, measured descent to the point where it had first broken through. To Perry's relief, the sudden impact of water and the over-three-thousand-foot rocket ride the probe had taken had left the device undamaged.

"We are seeing what no man has seen," Dr. Curtis said. "Water and ice laid down millennia ago."

Enkian snickered. "You know nothing."

"It is bad enough that you hold me at gunpoint. Must you also ridicule my scientific credibility?"

"Science has gotten so much wrong," Enkian said. "Especially you archaeologists. You have little more than a thimbleful of knowledge, and from that you make great pronouncements you cannot back up."

"What do you know of science?" Griffin said. "You're little more than a thug."

Tia started for Griffin. Perry took a step to intervene, but Enkian waved his lackey off. "You would be wise to watch your words, Dr. James. My patience has boundaries. To answer your question, I know more than you think."

"One meter," Sarah said. All eyes returned to the monitor.

The light from the cryobot reflected off the ice shaft, forming a white ring on the monitor. Dead center was the end of the shaft: a black hole. Light—natural or artificial—had never pierced that darkness.

"All systems are green," Sarah said. "I assume we all want to see what lies beneath the ice." She looked at Perry.

"I don't see any need to hesitate," Perry said. This was far from what he had expected. A hundred times he had played this moment over in his mind. Sarah would be at the controls, his team surrounding her, making excited comments and observation. Instead, unexpected guests had come to the party. What had been meant for a party of eight was now for well over fifty. Perry resented everything about it. Despite his anger over the situation, he could not draw his eyes from the monitor.

"Tally ho!" Sarah said, taking control of the joystick.

"Wait," Griffin said.

"What's wrong?" Sarah asked.

"Do you see the ice crystals just beyond the opening?"

"Yes," Sarah said. "It's a pretty tight fit in the shaft. Hairy has pushed some of the floaters ahead of it. It's to be expected."

"Do you see how they're moving?" Griffin asked, pointing at the monitor. "From our relative position, they're moving from right to left."

"So?" Sarah asked.

"So you had better be prepared for a stout current. It's to be expected."

"Explain," Enkian demanded.

"Lake Vostok is not static," Griffin said. "Geothermal heat close to the lake bed keeps the lake liquid while the ice cap freezes the surface water. That new ice accretes at the surface. Unfrozen but cold water descends, and warm water rises and creates a vertically circular current. If you drop the probe into the water without taking that into account, the current might pull the device away before you're ready."

"I thought you were opposed to all of this," Larimore said.

"I am. We should not have done this. We have committed a crime against nature and against the scientific community. But if you persist in moving on—well, you might as well do it right."

"Believe it or not, Dr. James," Sarah said formally, "I've considered that. . .but thanks. I'm afraid I let it slip my mind. I'm a little nervous."

"You've been practicing," Perry said. "No need to be nervous." He imagined her keeling over in narcoleptic sleep. He doubted Enkian and Tia would be sympathetic.

"Yeah, well, I didn't practice under gunpoint." She laughed lightly. "This is weird. I'm in the coldest place on earth, and my palms are sweating."

"Enough talk," Enkian snapped. "Get on with it."

Perry saw Sarah swallow hard, tighten her grip on the joystick control, and take several deep breaths.

On the monitor, the black hole grew until the shimmering walls of the shaft disappeared altogether.

"The nose is through," Sarah said. "We'll be floating free in a minute."

It was a long minute. Seconds plodded by.

Sarah's hand was over a switch on top of the controller. She rubbed it with slow, gentle strokes. She had briefed Perry on the device. It looked much like a joystick for a video game except larger. Several buttons were positioned near where Sarah's thumb rested. The device reminded Perry of controls he had seen in a jet fighter. Her other hand remained free. She drummed her fingers on the table. A few seconds later, she began to bite her lower lip.

"Any second now," she said.

The cable pulled tight with a snap. Sarah pressed the red button without looking at it. Her eyes were welded to the screen.

"And there's our current," Griffin said.

"Come on," Sarah said. Then, "Props extended, blowing negative."

Bubbles rose before the video lens. She pushed forward on the stick a half-second later. "Props are responding. We have propulsion. Water ballast is clear. We have zero buoyancy."

Griffin leaned over her shoulder and studied the gauges. "Fresh water," he said.

"How can you tell?" Larimore asked.

"The gauges tell me. Buoyancy is a function of water density. An object is more buoyant in saltwater than in fresh."

"Testing controls," Sarah announced. She moved the stick in various directions. "Everything is perfect. Hairy is responding like a sports car."

"I don't see anything," Tia said.

"There's no light down there," Griffin explained. "We're looking at a world that hasn't seen light for a very long time."

"Activating stereoscopic cameras," Sarah said. The dim light that had been pushing valiantly against the abysmal blackness suddenly had help. The monitor lit up and the image sharpened.

"What did you do?" Enkian asked.

"We've been looking through a single camera lens," Sarah explained. "Because the probe was in a shaft, the only place we could place a camera was in the nose, but most of that area was taken up by the heating element. Hairy has stereoscopic cameras and lights, one set on each side of its hull. The lights give us better illumination, and having the cameras separated by Hairy's width gives us the advantage of binocular vision."

"Depth below?" Perry asked.

"Two hundred meters," Sarah said.

"I thought the lake was deeper than that," Larimore stated.

"It is," Griffin explained. "It's well over five hundred meters at its deepest point, but we're stationed over the shallow end. The lake bottom slopes."

"There's an object below the ice, near the waterline on the southern shore," Enkian said. "Head there."

"How do you know that?" Jack asked.

"I know many things."

"I should run some exercises before I send Hairy on an extended trip," Sarah said.

"Exercise on the way," Enkian ordered.

"How far is it?" Sarah asked.

"Don't embarrass yourself playing games," Enkian said, his tone dark. "You're here because of that object. This place was chosen because of its proximity to it."

Perry frowned. Enkian knew too much, more than anyone should. Perry had even kept his closest friends out of the loop until they were on-site. Someone up the chain of command was talking about things meant to be secret.

Sarah looked at Perry as if he had a choice.

"Do it," was all he said.

Henry Sachs sat on the sofa in the living room of his spacious home. At five thousand square feet, it was far too large for just him and his wife, but it served its purpose. Entertaining clients was part of his duties as president of Sachs Engineering. Senators and generals had walked the halls of his home, but those corridors were empty now except for the ghosts of memory.

Sachs pulled his wife of decades closer, tightening his embrace and listening to her soft sobs. He had kept the news from her as long as he could, but she had a right to know about her son. "We don't know that he was on that plane," Sachs had said, but the words reverberated with pessimism. He had reminded himself of Perry's resolve, intelligence, strength, and faith, and he shared all of that with her. It was all hollow and as empty as the house that shrouded them in darkness, the house where Perry had grown up. A tree house he insisted on building himself remained in the large oak that shaded the backyard. It had been saved in hopes that Perry would settle down one day and provide Mom and Dad with grandchildren to spoil. Now it was a monument to an ended life.

Henry Sachs grieved in a way he never could have imagined. He hurt with a pain that could not be described. The ache was so deep he was sure his soul had shriveled like a grape left on the vine. He also knew that the woman he held grieved far more deeply than he could. It was what mothers did.

The phone rang, but Sachs ignored it. He didn't want to talk to people. No one had words that could bring relief. None would sympathize in a way that would ease the pain.

It rang again. And again. The wireless phone sat on the table, refusing to be ignored. Sachs snapped it up. "What?"

"Please hold for the president," a sweet voice said.

A moment later: "Henry?"

Sachs was surprised but too crushed to care. "Yes, Mr. President."

"There's a military transport waiting for you at the airport. I want you to come for dessert."

"Thank you, Mr. President, but there's no need. I appreciate the kindness but. . .but we're just not up to it."

"I understand, but you should come anyway. If you leave now, we can have pie by midnight."

Something wasn't right. Pie? "Sir, I don't understand."

"A driver will be at your door in the next five minutes."

"But sir—"

"Henry, come to Washington."

"I'm worried about running aground," Sarah said. "The bottom is rising pretty fast."

"Keep going," Enkian said.

Sarah sighed. "I'm pushing against the current, which makes the device more difficult to control."

"I said, keep going."

Sarah nodded and held in check what she really wanted to say. She was sure this Enkian jerk had a very short fuse, and if he didn't, his long-haired associate certainly did.

She pushed the stick forward, and it resisted. The control system was designed to give real-time feedback and sensory response. Sarah felt as if she were piloting the cryobot from inside. She focused on the readouts before her. The cameras were good, but no matter how high-tech, they were two-dimensional. After the initial exposure, the images lost clarity. Blackness was pierced by high intensity lights.

The lake bottom was rising, and she pulled the stick more. As the depth decreased, the force of the current subsided. Griffin had remarked that such was to be expected.

"She needs to stay off the bottom," Perry said. "If she doesn't, she might foul the line."

Sarah took a quick look at him. He seemed composed, firm, and focused, but she could see the stress in his eyes. She didn't know the man well, but he was unlike anyone she had met. He had showed courage and determination, but his most attractive quality was his concern for those around him. She could tell having his team in the grips of a gun-toting mob was weighing on him.

"She's doing fine," Enkian said.

A gauge reading grabbed Sarah's attention. "Odd."

"What?" Perry asked.

"My readings show that the bottom is rising, so I've decreased Hairy's depth. We sound off the ice above. That distance, the distance between Hairy and the ice lid above, should be decreasing, but it's not."

"It's following the slope of the lake bottom?" Perry asked.

"No," Sarah answered. "It's rising. In fact, it looks like. . .well, it looks like there is an airspace above the water and below the ice."

"Let's see," Enkian ordered. "Take it up, but don't damage the device against the ice."

Sarah hated taking orders from the man. He had no hand in designing the cryobot, had done no work or planning to make all this happen. He had just shown up with his thugs. She pulled back on the stick. A moment later, the camera broke the surface of the water. Instead of an eerie and dark underwater scene, the monitor now showed a cavern with a ceiling of ice in the distance.

"Wow," Gleason said. "It looks like a frozen Carlsbad Cavern."

"Not nearly as large," Perry said, "but much larger than I expected."

"Turn to your left," Enkian said. He seemed unimpressed with the ice cavern. "Quickly."

Sarah pushed the stick to her left, and Hairy's propellers redirected the view.

"There it is," Enkian said.

"I don't believe it," Dr. Curtis remarked quietly. "It can't be."

"It is," Enkian said. "Just as the prophecies said."

Sarah turned to see Griffin's jaw drop, then she looked at Perry, who stared at the image with unblinking eyes.

Looking back at the monitor, Sarah studied the rock formation that had captured everyone's attention and blinked.

"You were right, Perry," Jack said. "It's a pyramid under the ice."

"Not a pyramid," Enkian said. "Something far more impressive—a ziggurat. *The* ziggurat."

"You can't mean—" Dr. Curtis said.

"Bring the probe up," Enkian ordered. "Prepare the other cryobot. I want it working in the next hour."

"That's impossible," Perry said.

Sarah couldn't see her captor's expression, but she heard it in his voice. "Make it possible."

CHAPTER 25

Perry was breathing hard, his body trying to suck more oxygen out of the thin, icy air. His back hurt, but it was only a tingle compared to the pounding in his head. Recent events had kept him from drinking the water and taking the pain relievers he needed to ward off the altitude sickness that always seemed to be at arm's length.

Despite being winded, despite the jackhammer rattling in his skull, he kept working. Enkian had been serious about loading the larger cryobot in place and having it done in the hour. It was not an easy task. Perry had allowed a full day to make the switch, but Enkian cared nothing for Perry's schedule.

Additional rigging was attached to the aluminum support frame, and larger guides had to be installed to allow for the greater circumference of the new probe. Despite the cold in the Chamber, sweat began to bead on Perry's brow. Gleason and Jack were working just as hard, with Dr. Curtis, Griffin, and Gwen helping what little they could.

Guards hovered over each worker, offering no help and saying nothing. Wherever Perry moved, two armed men went with him. He tried to enlist them to help him carry a large bracket that would hold the cryobot until it was ready to be lowered. The gunmen just stared.

"It's your boss's project, you know," Perry had said. "He might give you a bonus." The men just raised the barrels of the machine guns a few inches.

Perry looked up from his place by the shaft and saw Enkian and Tia standing over Sarah and giving her orders about the position and direction of Hairy. He struggled to reconcile what he had seen on the monitor with everything he previously believed. He had known they were looking for an enigmatic object below the ice, one never before detected, but actually seeing it had quaked his soul.

"We need to name this," Jack said.

"You and your penchant to name things," Gleason said with a slight shake of the head.

Jack ignored him. "Hairy II seems so impersonal."

"It's an impersonal object," Gleason replied.

"You see there?" Jack retorted. "That's your problem. You're too academic. Did you ever name a car? What'd you call your first set of wheels, Perry?"

"Ford."

Jack shook his head. "I'm immersed in a romantic black hole." He looked at the now-vertical cryobot which looked much like an upside-down rocket. "I dub thee *Slick.*"

"Slick like ice?" Gleason asked.

"I had a dog named Slick," Jack said. "It's the best I can do. I don't do my best work under the gun—if you catch my drift."

"Wait a minute," Dr. Curtis said. He stepped to the monitor and looked at the even rows of stones, one laid upon another. Hairy was close, and Sarah had, at Enkian's order, zoomed in the cameras for a tighter shot. He studied the image and then began to mutter. "Enkian and Tia. . .Tia and Enkian." He stopped and turned to Tia. "What's your last name?"

"Why?"

"Humor an old academic," Curtis said. "It's not like you're going to let us out of here alive anyway. Besides, I doubt it's your real name."

She looked at Enkian, who was smiling. He nodded.

"Matteo."

"Enkian and Tia Matteo," Curtis repeated. "Why does that sound so familiar. . . ? Enki and Tiamat!"

Perry watched his friend closely. He also watched Enkian, whose wan smile unnerved Perry.

"That's right, Dr. Curtis," Enkian said. "You're good at puzzles."

"I know those names," Perry said, "but I can't place them. What am I missing?"

"They're the names of Babylonian gods," Curtis said. "In the Babylonian pantheon, they are the top dogs."

"Don't mock the gods, Dr. Curtis," Enkian snapped, his smile dissolving in an instant. "I have no patience with such things. And not Babylonian. Pre-Babylonian."

"Hold on," Jack said. "Why would someone take the names of ancient gods?" His words ground to a halt. "You're telling me that thing is. . .is the Tower of Babel?"

"Not a bad guess," Enkian said.

"I can't believe that," Curtis said. "It's in the wrong place. Maybe it's just another pyramidal building. The Aztecs built them, the Egyptians, and others. Pyramid shapes are found all over the globe—they're considered sacred shapes in many religions—but that's a far cry from the Tower of Babel."

"Is it?" Enkian said. "Do you think I would travel this far, spend this kind of money, take this kind of chance for just another pyramid? If I wanted to see ziggurats, I'd have flown to Iraq."

"This is nonsense," Curtis said. He looked at Perry. "I'm not buying it. It's impossible, Perry. It's beyond impossible. We're at the South Pole. Babylon prospered in a land far from here."

"What you believe is of no consequence to me," Enkian said. "You can believe your eyes or not. I don't care." He turned back to Sarah. "It's time to launch the new cryobot."

"We have to pull Hairy back up," she said.

"Disengage the power and optic lines," Enkian said. "We no longer need it."

Sarah turned, the color seeping from her face. "You're not

serious. You want me to just leave Hairy down there?"

"That's exactly what I'm ordering. Now do it."

"We can't do that—"

"Yes, you can," Enkian said. "When you explained the operation of the device to me, did you not say that it could be operated remotely through transmitters?"

"Yes, but we can't transmit radio through two miles of ice, not with enough signal integrity to operate intelligently."

"I don't care about that. I'm assuming that the device is designed to release its umbilical. Is that true?"

Sarah didn't answer.

"Your silence is answer enough," Enkian said. "Cut it loose."

"It won't take that long to pull it up," Sarah said. "We might need it later."

"Don't question me!" Enkian raised a hand to slap her.

Perry was there before the enraged man could begin his swing. Perry clamped a hand on the raised arm. A sharp pain pierced his side, and Perry dropped to the ice. He looked up to find Tia glaring down at him, the barrel of her gun pointed at his head—the same barrel she had just thrust into his ribs. "You are now expendable," she said. Perry saw her finger tighten on the trigger.

"No. I have a job for Mr. Sachs." Enkian directed his eyes to the dive suits.

"You can't be serious," Perry said, struggling to his feet.

"You're the one who brought the suits."

Perry chose not to respond. Enkian nodded at Tia, who stepped over to Griffin and placed the barrel of her gun to his throat.

"Ease up," Perry says. "I'll do it."

Wide-eyed, Griffin rubbed his throat.

Perry stood next to one of the AD suits and examined it closely. The hardshell suit was going to be his lifeboat. Like an astronaut, he was going to be fully dependent on the suit. There were a dozen different ways in which he might die. If the suit's heater failed, he'd freeze before they could pull him to the surface. If the suit had a flaw in its specially designed skin or in its articulated joints, then the high pressure of the lake could push freezing water in through the smallest of holes. It would be an unpleasant way to die. Other death scenarios floated in the dark waters of his mind, but he pushed them away. It was better to think of life.

A sound behind him made him turn. He saw Jack walking his way. With him were Griffin and Gleason.

"How you doing, buddy?" Jack asked, his face chiseled with concern.

"I'm okay." He didn't feel okay.

"Why don't you let me go?" Jack said. "That woman gave you a pretty hard jab in the ribs."

"You're more busted up than I am," Perry said. He looked at his friend's blood-soaked sleeve. "And my ribs have fared better than yours did. Besides, I don't think you'd fit in the suit."

"I'd make it fit," Jack said.

Perry nodded. "Yeah, I know you would, but I can't allow it. From the beginning, the plan was that I would go down."

"That's only because you didn't include us in the planning," Gleason said.

"I'm sorry, but it had to be that way."

"Then let me go," Gleason said. "We're about the same size. In fact, I'm a little smaller. I'd fit in the suit easily."

Perry shook his head. "We're not calling the shots. Besides, I'm the one who practiced in the suit before we came down. You're not qualified."

"I don't believe this," Griffin said. "You guys are trying to elbow out one another for the privilege of dying first."

"We've always been a little competitive," Perry said. He began to examine the suit, which hung on a metal support. "Batteries are charging, although I hope I won't need them." Power from the surface would supply the energy the suit needed to operate. The batteries were for backup. Perry thought about how quickly and easily Enkian had cut off Hairy. He was sure the man would cut him off with no more thought.

"I don't understand," Griffin said. "When they held the gun to my head, you didn't hesitate to say you'd go down the shaft. I can understand why you'd do it for these guys, but why me? You don't even like me."

"I never said that, Griffin," Perry said. "You're a good man, just too full of yourself. Purpose and happiness aren't found in knowledge."

Griffin choked. "It's the only thing I've found that brings me any peace."

"Then you haven't looked far enough," Perry said.

"This is about your faith, isn't it?" Griffin said. "You think by sacrificing yourself, you'll be in good stead with God."

"Not at all," Perry said. "My standing with God is based on Jesus' sacrifice, not mine."

"Then why do it?"

"Because Jesus did it for me," Perry said. "And because it makes the most sense. We're in a tough situation here. We need to do what we must to survive as long as we can. Maybe something will happen to our benefit."

"You mean God might intervene."

"That's exactly what I mean. We stay alive as long as we can, and we look for opportunities to save ourselves."

"And this gives you comfort?" Griffin shook his head.

"It gives me much more than that."

"Such thinking is nonsense," Griffin said.

Perry met Griffin's eye. "Do I look like a stupid man to you?"

"Well, no. . ."

"What about Jack? He kids a lot, but have you seen anything to suggest that his intellect is weak, or that he's subject to superstition?

Or Gleason here? He's one of the smartest men I know. Dr. Curtis leads his field, but he finds faith in Christ reasonable and compelling."

"Rejecting the spiritual doesn't make one intelligent except in his own eyes," Jack added. "To refuse to see the truth of faith is the real insult to intelligence."

"I'm after truth," Griffin said.

"No, you're not," Perry retorted. "You're after truth that fits your view. You dispel everything else. Take that object below the ice. I don't know if it is the Tower of Babel, but I know it's there, and that means I have to consider what at the moment seems unreasonable. That ziggurat is there whether I believe it is or should be." He turned back to the suit. "In a few hours, Lord willing, I'll be touching it."

"Why does he want you to go down there?" Gleason asked. "I can understand why you brought the suits. Taking samples of the object would be helpful."

"I don't know what his motivation is," Perry said. "He sees himself as the servant to some ancient Babylonian gods."

"He may think he is one of the gods," Jack said.

"That's a frightening thought," Gleason said. He paused. "I have some bad news."

Perry shrugged. "Another log on the fire, eh?"

"Slick is making better headway than we thought. Enkian has it working at full steam, and it is moving twice as fast through the opening. In another few hours it will be down to the water column. I estimate it'll break through six hours after that."

"That should give the batteries enough time to fully charge," Perry said. "Let's set up the other suit too. It's here, so it might as well be ready."

In college, Perry's physics professor had told the class something Albert Einstein had said. "To paraphrase the great thinker, time is relative. Time spent with a pretty girl moves faster than time spent sitting on a hot stove." Perry understood Einstein's point all too well. Time spent in pleasure passes much faster than that spent in pain—as does time spent in fear. Time was passing quickly for Perry, too quickly. When Hairy began its descent through the ice, it seemed like an eternity before it would reach the lake below. Slick was making the distance in a third of the time.

Now something was eating at Perry, something he couldn't put a finger on. The last day had been filled with thoughts of survival, his mind working to find a solution that would save him and his friends. In the midst of thoughts that swirled like leaves in a tornado was the undying inkling that something wasn't right, that just behind the veil of ignorance was a revelation of great importance—a dangerous revelation.

"Suit up," Enkian ordered. Perry looked at the tanned man with the hard face. There was a malevolent intelligence in his eyes, and determination was tattooed on his face. It was that determination that unsettled Perry. Enkian was a man with a cause. Perry didn't fully understand yet, but he knew the most dangerous men in the world were those driven by causes. Causes made suicide bombers commit horrible acts against innocents; they sent the unstable into murderous rages; they sent nations to war.

What was Enkian's cause? And what was Perry missing?

The thoughts continued to spin as Perry approached the dive suit. He had watched as the apparatus was moved into position near the ice shaft. The sound of cable being wound around its drum pulled his attention away. Slick was being raised. Enkian had ordered it lifted the moment it touched the lake. The shaft was now large enough to accommodate a man in the newly designed, hardshell dive suit. Slick would be back in the Chamber soon, and Enkian was wasting no time. Perry was to begin his descent as soon as possible.

The suit rested on its stand, its torso separated from feet and legs like a robot cut in half at the waist. Jack stepped to Perry's side. His dark skin seemed darker, and the twinkle that lived in his eyes was missing. Perry had never before seen Jack truly frightened. Now he had.

Jack helped Perry remove his parka and the rest of his cold suit. The frigid air assaulted him, stinging his skin and sinking into his body like water into a sponge. He shivered.

"Let's get you into this tux before you freeze," Jack said. Perry was wearing nothing but his thermal underwear. Jack handed him a rubberized suit, similar to a dry suit worn by cold water divers. It was more formfitting and would help keep his body temperature stable.

A bar hung over the lower portion of the dive suit. Perry slipped on gloves, took hold of the bar, and pulled himself up so he could swing his legs into their intended opening. He felt a hand grab his left foot. Jack was guiding him. Then he felt another hand grab his right ankle. Perry looked down and saw Gleason on his right.

Perry wiggled, shifted, and squeezed himself into the leg openings. Unlike older, bulkier JIM suits that allowed more room for the diver but were unwieldy and difficult to handle, the AD suit was close to formfitting. Perry had just enough room to shift while in the suit and for warm air heated by onboard heaters to circulate. Gel pads pressed against Perry's legs.

"I still don't know what you want me to do," he said to Enkian.

"I want a stone from the ziggurat."

"A stone? Those things are huge. I can't lift one of those."

Enkian shook his head. "You weren't paying attention, Mr. Sachs. Do you know the Bible?"

"I have an acquaintance with it."

"The first book of the Bible is Genesis. Chapter eleven tells the story." He closed his eyes and began to quote: " 'Now the whole earth used the same language and the same words. And it came about as they journeyed east, that they found a plain in the land of Shinar and settled there. And they said to one another—'?"

" 'Come, let us make bricks and burn them thoroughly,' " Perry finished the quote. " 'And they used brick for stone, and they used tar for mortar.'"

"I'm impressed. The larger stones of the ziggurat are made up of smaller elements. For all intents and purposes they are bricks. The large building blocks are composed of smaller bricks. You should have no problem."

"How could fire-sealed mud bricks have endured next to a lake?" Griffin asked. "The water would have destroyed them."

"Oh, the ziggurat shows some damage. That is to be expected. But remember, Dr. James—" Enkian raised a finger as he spoke. "The structure has not been *in* the lake; the lake is rising to meet it. It's been encased in ice until now. Now it is being revealed, just as the ancient prophecies predicted."

The platform upon which Perry stood was slightly elevated, giving him a better view into the shaft. The cable continued to be drawn from the hole and wrapped around a large drum. Two miles of cable took up a lot of space. But it wasn't the cable that caught his attention. It was the back end of Slick emerging into the Chamber.

Enkian turned and watched the large, torpedo-shaped device surface. "Your mission begins as soon as your friends move the cryobot out of the way."

Perry felt a chill that had nothing to do with the air temperature. He looked at Jack, who had not left his side. Jack couldn't return the gaze. Gleason stood on the other side, shoulders slumped like a man who was holding up the world.

It took half an hour to clear the entrance to the shaft, a phenomenal speed made possible only with the ordered aid of Enkian's men. It was clear that Enkian was becoming impatient.

Perry used the time to adjust his suit, check the systems for the fourth time, and prepare his soul. There was a good chance he would fail, and if he failed, he would die. If he died, Enkian would certainly send someone else down to retrieve a brick. Perry reminded himself that his failure would probably mean the death of a friend.

"It's time, pal," Jack said.

"I know."

"We're praying for you. You know that."

Perry nodded. Gleason stood by Jack and Dr. Curtis. A few steps behind them, Griffin, Gwen, and Sarah huddled together. He could see tears in their eyes.

"Cheer up, everyone," Perry said. "Remember, I planned to go down anyway. It was all part of the mission."

"Not like this," Jack said. "Not with these murderous clowns standing around with their guns. We should run tests first."

Jack was right. Perry had intended to spend a week in testing: sending the suit down empty and monitoring its life support systems, its reaction to current, and a dozen other parameters.

The top half of the suit was lowered over Perry, and he wiggled his arms into place and shifted his shoulders until he was in the tight space. The helmet was 50 percent clear, high-strength plastic that gave the illusion that the world was suddenly curved more than it had been a moment before.

He had been in the suit dozens of times, practicing in the same tank NASA used to train astronauts for EVAs—space walks. That pool was heated, and rescue divers were never far away. In a few moments he would be lowered into a tight-fitting hole and descend through two miles of ice.

Jack and Gleason tightened the metal ring that sealed the top half of the suit to the bottom. Perry was fully encased. He turned his head in the bulbous helmet to catch another view of his friends. The tension was palpable.

"Radio check," a voice said over the speakers in his helmet. It was Gleason. Perry could see him standing near the computer and monitor. He was wearing a headset. Perry knew his voice was coming over speakers attached to the monitor, but the headset provided the microphone necessary for Gleason to talk to Perry.

"Check."

"O-two feed looks nominal."

"Roger that."

"Heat?"

"Toasty."

There was a jerking motion, and Perry felt himself being lifted from the platform. A small crane would move him over the hole and lower him. A plastic-coated support cable was attached to a metal loop just behind the helmet. Power feed and optic lines ran from onboard cameras along the support cable.

He could see the shaft approaching, but once over it, he lost sight of it. The helmet kept him from looking down.

The motion changed. He was no longer moving over the ice floor but was descending. As he was lowered, he came to eye level with those in the room. The armed men stood around, faces as stoic as ever. Sarah had joined Jack and Gleason at the controls. Gwen and Griffin stood side by side, Griffin's arm around his sister. Enkian was closest, anticipation clear on his face. Tia was by his side. He caught a glimpse of Dr. Curtis, who gave an out of character wave and then closed his eyes.

Perry was jostled as his feet entered the hole. He had peered down the hole and knew that blackness was waiting to engulf him. As he inched his way down, he caught sight of Commander Larimore standing a few steps away from Enkian.

He was smiling.

For a moment, Perry assumed the smile was an offer of encouragement, but it didn't look right. It appeared more sneer than smile.

Perry looked for his friends. He needed to see them, to draw strength from the knowledge that there were people who cared enough to support him, and more importantly, to pray for him. Gwen and Sarah both looked frightened and on the verge of tears. He flashed a smile their way. Then he caught a glimpse of Jack. Friendship was not defined by the laws of physics and nature. Perry could feel the man's concern, sense his fear—a fear not for himself but for Perry. Jack mouthed something. It took a moment for Perry to decipher the lip motions: "Go with God."

Perry would go with God. He had no other choice.

" 'From the breath of God ice is made,' " Perry said, " 'and the expanse of the waters is frozen.' "

"What was that?" Enkian asked.

Jack fixed him with a steely glance. "You asked if Perry knew the Bible, didn't you? That's a passage from the book of Job." Jack turned back to the sight of his friend descending into the shaft. "Godspeed, my friend. Godspeed."

The Chamber with its artificial light and human inhabitants gave way to the glistening white of ice. Perry had no room to move. Slick had carved out just enough space for the suit to fit. His hands, encased in the rigid arms, were folded in front of him, his feet dangled above nothingness.

A passage from Psalms came to mind:

> *Where can I go from Your Spirit? Or where can I flee from Your presence?*
>
> *If I ascend to heaven, You are there; if I make my bed in Sheol, behold, You are there.*
>
> *If I take the wings of the dawn, if I dwell in the remotest part of the sea,*
>
> *Even there Your hand will lead me, and Your right hand will lay hold of me.*
>
> *If I say, "Surely the darkness will overwhelm me, and the light around me will be night,"*
>
> *Even the darkness is not dark to You, and the night is as bright as the day.*
>
> *Darkness and light are alike to You.*

He was about to test the truth of that passage.

CHAPTER 26

enry Sachs was shown into the kitchen of the White House, his wife Anna by his side. They were led to the unexpected place by a young Hispanic man who introduced himself as the president's "body man."

"I'm the personal aide to the president," the man said and smiled. "I do the grunt work. . .and I love it."

Sachs saw the president seated at a country-style wood table. He was wearing khaki slacks and a blue polo shirt. He looked tired.

"Come in, Henry, come in," he said, waving. "I hope this isn't too informal for you. Pie always tastes better in an informal setting."

"It's fine," Sachs said, puzzled. He and Anna had just flown from Seattle to Washington, D.C., at the request of the president. They were worn, wearied by travel and worry. The body man pulled out a chair for Anna, and she took it. "Mr. President—"

President Calvert raised a finger and shook his head. "I appreciate you making the trip on such short notice. I know you have a great deal on your mind and that things are difficult."

A man in a chef's uniform stepped forward and placed three plates before them. Each held a slice of cherry pie and a small mound of vanilla ice cream. He then served coffee.

"Leave the pot, Bob," the president said. "And you better leave the pie."

"If you would like an additional piece, I will be happy to serve it," the man said.

"No," Calvert replied. "Just leave everything on the table and make sure everyone has left the kitchen. I would like some private time with my friends."

"But, sir—" the worker objected then changed his tone. He nodded and said, "Yes, Mr. President."

"You have cooks in the White House at this hour?" Sachs asked.

"It's one of the benefits of being president. The hours are long, and meetings can occur any hour of the day. It's nice to have someone who can brew a pot of coffee when you need it." He waited a few moments before speaking again. "I grew up far from Washington. My roots go back to Iowa farmers. Growing up, most of my meals were eaten in the kitchen. It was where the family gathered and where friends felt at ease. This job requires that I wear a tuxedo to many meals. A man can't eat properly when wearing a tuxedo."

"I understand, Mr. President," Sachs said.

Calvert looked around the kitchen. "Please eat." He took a bite of the pie and then looked at Henry and Anna. "I have information for you. One of our eyes in the sky was able to take a few photos of the site where your son was working. As you suggested, we didn't see anyone wandering around outside."

Anna raised a shaky hand to her forehead, and Sachs placed his hand on her knee. "I guessed as much."

"There are, however, more ways of seeing. Satellite technology has come a long way. You're a man of technology, Henry, so you can understand that. I can't give you details because the apparatus is still highly classified. In fact, what I'm about to show you is a breach of secrecy, but you have a right to know. Besides, it's very hard to fire a president." He reached down by his chair and pulled a manila folder to the table. He opened it and slid it to Sachs, then he took another bite of pie.

Sachs pulled the folder close and immediately recognized what he was looking at: a photo of barren ice with two domes and two square buildings. "I recognize the domes. I helped design them."

"That first photo shows the site is still intact and apparently functioning. There isn't much to see: just the buildings and one other thing. It's the other thing that is interesting."

Sachs looked at the photo again, and Anna leaned in from his side. "I don't see anything unusual—just the domes and other buildings and the plane. . ."

The president nodded. "Look at the aircraft. Does it look familiar?"

"No."

"That's what I thought."

"No aircraft should be there. The aircraft that crashed was supposed to be the last flight in or out for weeks. It was part of the security precautions. Who does it belong to?"

"That's part of the mystery," Calvert said. "Look at the next photo."

Henry did. The unknown airplane filled the paper. He could count the windows and read the numbers on the tail. "Can you trace the registration number?"

"Yes. In fact, we already did, and it's registered to an oil company out of Houston. The kicker is, that plane is sitting in its hangar. I sent men to check it out."

"You mean the plane is in two places?" Anna said.

"No," Sachs explained. "He's saying the number is in two places. The number on this plane—" he pointed at the picture—"is stolen."

"Why?" Anna asked.

"So we can't do what we're trying to do," Calvert said. He sipped his coffee. "We can't trace the aircraft from the photo. Someone knew we might be looking."

"What someone?" Sachs asked.

"Wait, there's more I want you to see." Calvert reached across the table and turned the page.

This time Sachs saw the domes again, but they were marred by red blotches. He studied it for a second. "Infrared?"

The president nodded. "The red smears are people. If they were outside, we might have a decent look at them, at least enough to recognize someone we know, like your son."

"You can see faces—?"

"Don't ask," Calvert said. "We're not going to discuss such things. Just know that if your son were strolling across the ice, we'd be able to identify him."

"Henry?" Anna said. "Does that mean Perry is alive?"

Sachs studied the photo closely, counting the red dots. "There are too many," he said, lifting his eyes to Calvert. "There should only be eight people there. I count double that."

Calvert raised an eyebrow.

"The plane," Sachs said.

"Exactly," Calvert said. "Someone came to visit. There's more. Keep going."

Sachs turned the photo over, revealing yet another shot from space. This time there were two aircraft. "Another plane." On instinct he turned the page again to find another infrared shot. The number of dots was now over sixty. "What is going on?"

"One aircraft leaves, supposedly with your son and crew on board, and it goes down. Search and rescue crews begin looking for the downed craft hundreds of miles from where we now know it crashed. Why? Because someone was dictating information to throw everyone off track."

"But why?" Sachs stared at the president.

The president leaned forward. "I'm going to tell you a strange story, Henry. You're not going to believe it, but my source is good. Very good. I know, because he was connected to the group that is doing this. Not deeply, but others in my administration are. This is one for the conspiracy books." He looked around the kitchen and, seeing no one, continued. "Right now, I have some key people under guard, people who until today have been trusted advisors. You don't need to know who they are. All you need to know is that something big is going on, and the people behind it have their tentacles in every major government on this planet. They have reached closer to the Oval Office than I want to talk about. I know this because someone is making a frightening sacrifice to reveal this information."

"But what about Perry?" Anna asked.

"Good news and bad news, I'm afraid. First, I think he's alive and still on-site. I can't prove it, but I think he's one of those red dots you see. The bad news is there's very little we can do immediately. Apparently your son was in the wrong place at the wrong time."

Henry Sachs thought for a moment. "Perhaps he is in the right place at the right time."

"But certainly you can command a rescue," Anna implored.

"It's not that easy, Anna," the president replied. "The problem is, I no longer know who I can trust. Any order I give might be circumvented down the chain of command, or at the very least, someone would sound a warning."

"You can't just sit back and do nothing," Anna pleaded. "Please tell me you have a plan."

President Calvert smiled. "I always have a plan."

Gwen felt her heart stall as the top of Perry's helmet disappeared down the shaft. She felt tears washing over her cheeks, and her breathing became ragged. Images of horror filled her mind. She saw the support cable snapping and Perry plunging down two miles of ice. She could envision him becoming stuck partway down and Enkian leaving him to die. More images came like flies, and she tried to shoo them away.

"I don't get it," Griffin said. He stood beside her, his arm around her shoulders in a rare display of affection. "He didn't even hesitate. It's not like I'm family or even a friend, yet when that goon put the gun to my head. . ."

"There's something about him," Gwen said, "something deep inside him. I think it's his faith."

"You know I don't believe in that nonsense."

"I know, but it's good for us that Perry does."

Sarah sat at the computer monitor with nothing to do, and it was driving her crazy. Before, she had to control Hairy and then supervise Slick, but the joystick was useless now. She thought of the brave man in the ice tomb. The thought of doing what he was being forced to do weakened her knees, but he seemed to do it fearlessly. Certainly that was an act, a bit of bravado to keep their spirits up, but even as she mulled that thought, she knew it wasn't true.

"He's a remarkable man," she said to Gleason.

Gleason keyed off the microphone. "He is that."

A movement to her right caught her attention, tearing her eyes from the image of white ice that filled the monitor.

"Give me the headset," Tia ordered as she approached. "I'll handle communications."

"No," Gleason said flatly.

"It's not a request," she said.

"You will have to shoot me where I stand and pull the set off my dead body."

"Maybe I will." She took a step back and raised her gun.

Sarah leaped from the chair and backpedaled, and Gleason turned to face Tia.

"I said, give me the headset."

"No."

Sarah's breath caught in her chest as she watched Jack move to Gleason's side. He straightened his spine and folded his arms over his wide chest. "The man said no."

Dr. Curtis waddled forward and took a spot in front of Gleason. Then Gwen pulled away from her brother.

"What are you doing?" Griffin asked with surprise. The answer came when Gwen strode forward to join the others.

Sarah felt her stomach turn and heart skip as if jolted by a car battery. Despite raging terror, she joined the others.

Tia's face hardened like cement. She sneered and raised her weapon.

"Leave them alone," Enkian said softly.

"We don't need them anymore," Tia complained.

"We don't know that," Enkian said. "Leave them to their work. We are not barbarians. We know friendship."

"Coulda fooled me," Jack quipped.

"I let you win this round, Mr. Dyson. Don't give me reason to regret it."

Sarah returned to her seat. Her mind was aflame, thoughts shooting like bolts of lightning through her skull. Then the electricity began to fail. The lights dimmed, the sounds faded, and Sarah knew the narcolepsy was forcing its way through the door.

CHAPTER 27

Perry took slow, deep breaths, forcing his mind to take charge of his body. A sense of panic was threatening to choke out his reason. He laughed to himself. What was reasonable about this? He was descending through an ice pipe to a world more hostile than the reaches of space. He was encased in a life pod made of plastic, metal, and rubber, warmed by heating elements spread throughout the suit and circulated by small fans. He could do nothing but wait. He doubted there was another situation in which a man was more helpless. Climbing to the top was impossible, and falling thousands of feet into frigid water was far more likely.

He could feel himself tensing and his heart galloping. Sensors in the elastic garment he wore relayed that information to the top.

"You okay, Perry?" Gleason asked, keying the mike.

"Yeah," he answered, wishing he could see the face on the other end of the connection. "Did I mention I'm claustrophobic?" Above, he knew everyone in the Chamber heard his words over the speakers.

"Um, no, I didn't see that on your job application."

"I must have forgotten to include it."

"Seriously, bud, how are you doing?"

"I'm adjusting. It's a tight squeeze, but I seem to be sliding down like Grandma's homemade ice cream."

"Your heart rate is up, and your respiration is climbing."

"Nothing to worry about," Perry said. He didn't need anyone to tell him his heart rate was up. "I'm just testing the sensors."

"They work fine, Perry. Take a few deep breaths and think of your favorite beach."

"Will do. How are things topside?"

"Fine," Gleason said. "Sarah was considering a nap but decided against it."

Perry picked up on the message. Sarah had started an episode. It was something Perry had feared; he was also surprised it hadn't already occurred. Gwen said that undue stress could trigger spontaneous sleep. He was sure Sarah was under more stress than she had ever been in her life.

"Soon as she heard your voice she perked right up."

"Odd," Perry said. "I usually put women to sleep."

"Are you kidding? I hear you're a two-cup jolt of caffeine to the ladies."

Perry smiled. Gleason was no Jack Dyson when it came to humor, but he knew when a well-placed quip was needed. "Tell her she owes me dinner."

"She accepts," Gleason said. His tone cooled. "You're a third of the way there, pal."

"Roger that," Perry said.

He fell silent.

A third of the way—over three thousand feet. About the same distance below him was the column of water that filled the lower 30 percent of the shaft; below that, Lake Vostok.

The image of the ziggurat flashed in Perry's memory. Enkian truly believed the structure was the real Tower of Babel. He even quoted a portion of the biblical account. Perry had known from the beginning that an abnormal structure was below the ice. Satellite imagery and radar readings from an air survey had shown the widening lake and the massive object. But the Tower of Babel?

Dr. Curtis had been skeptical, too, and Perry couldn't blame him. Even now he was having trouble believing that people had populated the continent under the ice. Scientists had discovered many animal and plant fossils. Current theory was that Antarctica had once been further north and part of the larger continent, Gondwana, that he had told the others about. But even given that, it was hard to believe.

"Hey, Gleas," Perry said. "Put Dr. Curtis on the horn."

"Dr. Curtis?"

"Yeah, I have a question or two for him."

A moment later: "Perry, it's Dr. Curtis."

"Do you still carry that handheld computer with you?"

"I do."

"Didn't you tell me it had a Bible program on it?"

"Yes, among other things."

"Pull it out and find the Tower of Babel story. The one our new host quoted." Perry could imagine Dr. Curtis reaching into his parka pocket and pulling out his Compaq handheld computer. Perry often carried one. In fact, he had one in his quarters. Like a regular computer, it contained a set of programs: spreadsheets, word processing, calculators, address books, and even Internet connectivity—if they were close to any wireless Internet access sites.

"Got it."

"Help me pass the time," Perry said, focusing to remember the story. "All of this happens after the flood, right?"

"That's right. We don't know how long after. It's at least several generations."

"If I remember right, a group of people settle in some valley and decide to build a structure to keep them from being dispersed."

"The land of Shinar," Curtis said.

"Which is modern Iraq."

"That's right," Curtis said.

"And the tower was to keep the people unified?"

"Partly." He began reading. " 'Come, let us build for ourselves a city, and a tower whose top will reach into heaven, and let us make for ourselves a name, otherwise we will be scattered abroad over the face of the whole earth.' "

"So pride was the real problem."

"And disobedience."

"Right," Perry said. "They built the tower so they wouldn't be scattered, but they ended up being scattered anyway."

"Exactly. God scatters them."

"That's what I'm curious about. Does your Bible program have links to the original Hebrew?"

"Of course," Curtis said. "You want me to look up the word *scattered?*"

"I do."

There was another pause. "Got it. The Hebrew word *puts* is a *hiphil* verb, imperfect *waw* consecutive, third person masculine singular."

"Meaning?"

"Well, it means God did the scattering."

"The people didn't scatter because their language had changed. That was part of the judgment, correct?"

"Yes. The verse reads: 'So the Lord scattered them abroad from there over the face of the whole earth; and they stopped building the city.' "

" 'Scattered them abroad,' " Perry repeated. " 'From there over the face of the whole earth.' " He thought for a moment. "Say, Doc, you don't suppose. . ."

"That God literally transported people from one place to another? Well, it could mean that. But to put them in Antarctica. . . well, no one can live down here, especially a primitive people."

"What if 'down here' wasn't down here? What if, like geologists have said, that Antarctica was part of a larger continent?"

"That's the prevailing theory."

Perry wished he could scratch his head, a simple feat made

impossible by the suit. "After that account comes the table of nations. Isn't there someone with a name that means 'to divide'?"

"Yes. Peleg is listed in the genealogy that follows the Babel account, but the verse you're thinking of comes sooner. Let me check. Here it is, Genesis 10:25: 'Two sons were born to Eber; the name of the one was Peleg, for in his days the earth was divided; and his brother's name was Joktan.' Is that what you had in mind?"

"What was Peleg's brother's name?" Perry asked.

"Joktan. It means *smallness* or *to make small.* Wait a minute. Are you implying that Peleg's name is a reference to the splitting of the continents and that his brother's name refers to the newer, smaller continents?"

"I'm just hanging around killing time, Professor."

"Perry, most scholars believe Peleg's name refers to the splitting of earth for irrigation. You know, he dug water canals. To go beyond that is absurd."

"Hey, Doc, what am I doing right now?"

"You're being lowered down. . .an ice shaft. . .to take a brick stone from a. . ."

"Yeah, that's my point." Perry changed tones. "How about it, Enkian? Is that your plan? You want to finish what your ancestors failed to do? You want to build a new nation centered around the old Tower of Babel?"

Perry heard a muffled sound over the speakers, then, "I suggest you focus on your work."

"I'm just asking a question."

Pain pierced Perry's ears as a loud crack came over the speakers. He recognized it as a gunshot.

"Doc? Doc! Gleason? Jack?"

"It's all right, buddy," Jack's voice said. "Our friend just wanted to make a point. He fired a round with the barrel near the mike."

"No kidding? My ears are ringing like a fire alarm. Is everyone okay?"

"Yeah, there's a nice hole in our pretty ceiling, but that's the only injury. However, I think the Bible study is over."

"I understand." Perry thanked God that no one was lying dead three thousand feet above his head—at least not yet.

Jack slipped off the headset and handed it back to Gleason. "That was a little over the top, don't you think?" he said to Enkian.

"You don't know what *over the top* means. I am growing impatient."

"If you don't like our work, you can go down there and do it yourself."

Enkian turned from Jack and faced Tia. "Bring the items in. It's time to set up."

Tia nodded and chose twenty men to accompany her.

"Set up for what?" Jack asked.

"Church," Enkian said with a smile.

"Somehow I think our ideas of church are very different."

"You're coming up on the water," Gleason said.

Perry acknowledged the transmission and felt himself tense. His rate of descent didn't slow. The only sensation he had was something pressing against his feet. He steeled himself as if the frigid water were about to pour over him. He felt no change in temperature, but the fans that circulated the warm air in the suit sped up.

"Feet wet," Perry said. "Descent unaltered." The suit was designed to be slightly heavier than the surrounding water displacement, allowing him to sink. He tilted his head forward and watched as water lit by his helmet lights rose to his face shield. Bits of slush floated on the surface.

"All sensors are operating, Perry. External temperature is. . . cold. Suit temperature remains constant. Still comfy?"

"Still?"

"We're with you all the way, buddy."

"I know," Perry said. "Next stop, Lake Vostok."

"Bring me a postcard. You know how my kids love to get postcards."

"If we survive this, Gleas, I'm taking everyone to the Bahamas. I'll have to dock Jack's wages to do it, but he won't mind." Perry heard something distant.

"Jack said he does mind."

"Descent seems to be slowing," Perry said.

"We show it constant up here. It may be an optical illusion. You're surrounded by water, so your reference points may look different."

"The only reference point I have is the ice in front of my face."

"That's what I mean."

"You'd think there would be a few road signs." Perry closed his eyes and tried to relax. He wondered what was happening on the surface.

Jack stood next to Gleason and watched as men carried boxes through the loading air lock. Tia had disabled the air lock by jamming the outside door open. "So much for a clean environment."

"That ended the moment they walked in," Gleason said. "To think we wasted all those hours in clean suits."

Griffin marched up to Jack. "It's bad enough that they left a mechanical device filled with batteries, cable, plastic, and who knows what else on the lake bottom, but now this. Are you going to allow this to go on?"

"What do you expect me to do, Griffin?" Jack asked.

"Stop them."

"How?"

"I. . .I don't know," Griffin stammered. He looked around then marched to Enkian.

"Don't do it," Jack whispered.

"Enkian, this is an outrage. You're contaminating the work field more than you already have done."

"Then it doesn't matter," Enkian said, looking down at the shorter man.

"I doubt those boxes have been sterilized—"

"They haven't," Enkian said.

"At least Sachs took special precautions. You're—"

The slap caught him off guard. Griffin fell backward onto the ice, his hand to his jaw.

"Griffin," Gwen screamed and ran to his side.

Jack started forward, but Gleason grabbed his arm. "Don't escalate things, Jack. Griffin will have a bruise, but that's all. We have to pick the battles. Let this one go."

Jack pursed his mouth then closed his eyes. Gleason was right. "That man's mouth is going to get him killed. Us too probably."

"What do you suppose they're doing?" Gleason wondered.

"Beats me, but it's bound to be weird." Jack watched as the men brought in box after box, struggling under the weight of them.

"Those boys better be careful," Gleason said. "Unless they're used to working at altitude, some of them are going to start keeling over."

"What do you suppose Enkian would do then?"

"Drag them outside. He's brought plenty of spares."

"He's about to enter the lake," Sarah said.

Jack and Gleason turned back to the monitor. Gleason keyed the mike. "You're almost there, Perry. A few feet more to go."

"Understood." The voice was loud and strong, but it still sounded far away. Jack prayed for his friend below the ice.

CHAPTER 28

The ice wall disappeared, and Perry felt himself falling. He was surrounded by black, the lights on his helmet pressing against a darkness they could not expel. He jerked and raised his arms to balance himself, but it was a useless gesture. The sudden loss of all visual clues slammed the accelerator on his heart. Panic was tempting him.

He took several deep breaths. He wasn't falling. The cable was still attached to his suit. The motion he had felt was the pressure of the current that Griffin had described earlier. It had pushed Hairy around a little; of course it would push him.

"You okay, pal?" Gleason's words oozed from the communication system. They sounded good but far too distant. "Your heart rate just went through the roof."

"Yeah. . .yeah, I'm fine. Just startled when the current hit me."

"Take a minute," Gleason said. "There's bound to be some disorientation."

"You think?"

"I don't need to tell you where you are, Perry. You're in a place no one has ever been before."

"Except the guys who built the ziggurat."

"Yeah, well, they haven't been around for a while. Tell us what you see."

The comment puzzled Perry at first. They were seeing what he was seeing. The video feed traveled from cameras on his suit to the surface. Then it hit him: Gleason was making an effort to get Perry to focus, to talk, to calm down. He wished he were a character in an adventure novel. Those guys never showed any fear. But he wasn't. He was a human pendulum swinging in the dark at the end of a very long cable. Perry decided talking was a good idea.

"It's dark. Really dark. My lights are penetrating only a few feet—no, wait, scratch that. I think it's an illusion. There's nothing for the light to fall on. I'm getting no bounce-back."

"That's our take on it, Perry. I should have thought of that after seeing the images from Hairy."

Perry tried to focus his eyes, but there was little to focus on beyond his helmet. He raised a hand and saw the suit's white shell appear. There was no hand to see, just the manipulator which operated from within the suit. The pressure would be too great for a mere glove. The light bounced back with such intensity that it hurt his eyes. "The water is so clear it's as if I'm floating in space. I was expecting some particles in the water. This stuff is cleaner than tap water."

"How do you feel about kicking up the power on the lights?"

The suit was designed with several sets of light banks. Each bank carried two groupings of halogen bulbs. Perry couldn't have them all on while descending the shaft. That much light reflecting off the ice would have blinded him. "Will do."

Slowly—Perry had no other way of moving—he reached for the control panel on his left wrist and activated the other lights. The buttons were protected from the pressure and water by a plastic shield.

The area around Perry lit up. He was centered in a sphere of light. He let slip a nervous laugh. "I feel like a UFO." This time, he could see bits of white floating in the distance. "Ice specks."

"We see them. Griffin says you pushed out ice bits when you emerged, just like Hairy did."

"Makes sense."

"You should press on," Gleason said. There was an edge to his voice. It didn't take much imagination to guess that Enkian was growing impatient again. "Sarah says you should orient yourself ten degrees north and proceed straight ahead. Depth below you is 220 meters, but that will decrease as you move forward."

"Understood," Perry said, glad to have something to do. "Activating heads-up display." He pressed another button on the control panel and several orange displays appeared around the periphery of the face mask. He could see the outside temperature, which was well below freezing, the water being kept liquid by the high pressure. He could also see that the temperature inside the suit was a comfortable sixty-one degrees. He found the compass indicator and took a bearing. "Engaging props." Small propellers positioned at his shoulders and waist began to move him forward. An onboard computer gauged Perry's vertical orientation and automatically adjusted the speed of the independent propellers to prevent him from tumbling like a sock in a dryer.

"Sarah says propulsion is normal."

"Yeah, it's working fine," Perry said.

Gleason came back on the line. "Our friend wants you to make the best speed possible." His words were terse.

"This thing only has two speeds: slow and slower. If he has any complaints, he can come down here and show me how to do it."

There was no response. Perry focused on steering the suit through the water with a control built in the left arm. When the propulsion system was activated, the left-hand manipulator became the equivalent of a steering wheel. By twisting the wrist left or right, up or down, he could control his motion in three dimensions. It had taken hours of practice in the NASA tank, but he had finally gotten the hang of it. Here it was different. In the test tank, Perry could see the bottom, the surface, and the tank's walls. Under the ice, Perry could see several meters in front of him, but with nothing to reflect his lights, he was flying in a fog. Like a pilot at night, he was maneuvering by instruments alone.

"Depth is now 175 feet and rising," Gleason said. "The bottom is rising quickly."

"Fine with me," Perry said. "Cable is feeding well?"

"Perfect."

"I'm going to kick it into high gear."

"Noted. Don't get any speeding tickets."

"Okay, Dad," Perry quipped. He set the propulsion system to the next level, increasing his speed through the water another knot or two. He was moving against the current but still making headway. *At least the trip back will be faster.*

Something swam past, and Perry jumped in the suit. "Did I just see that?"

"Sarah let out a whoop. She must have seen it too. What was it?"

"I don't know. I didn't get a look. . .wait, there's another one. Wow! Is Gwen seeing this?"

"Oh, yeah. She's bouncing like a cheerleader." Perry could hear excited yammering over Gleason's words. "She wants you to get closer."

"It's in my path, so I have no choice." Before Perry was an amorphous blob of white. It pulsed. As he neared, Perry could see long strands of tissue hanging from beneath it. It also had pale green lights along its tentacles. "It looks like a jellyfish of some kind."

"Gwen says she doesn't recognize it."

"The thing is the size of a softball," Perry said. "How can it live down here?"

"I don't. . .wait. . ."

"Perry, it's Gwen." Her excitement carried over the distance. "This is remarkable. This is unbelievable. I never would have guessed.

It's an unknown species of cnidarian, a very simple form of life. The cnidarians we know of have only two layers of tissue—no head, gut, or brain."

"It's pretty. . .in its own way."

"The lights are bioluminescent. Now that you're closer I can see the lights moving. The comb jellyfish does something similar. The lights run along its body. The interaction of luciferin and luciferase produce flashes of light."

"It doesn't seem bothered by me."

"It doesn't think, Perry. It's mostly water and about one percent tissue. The rest is. . .ow!"

"Gwen? Are you there, Gwen?"

"It's Gleason again, Perry. Mr. Enkian isn't keen on all the PBS talk."

"Understood," Perry said, biting his tongue. They were the first people to see this new form of life, and they were being forced to ignore it.

"Depth is one hundred feet and decreasing."

Perry moved forward.

Jack turned his attention from the screen to watch the action taking place near the center of the Chamber. Boxes, some made of cardboard, others of wood, and still others of plastic had been carried in from Enkian's plane. The crew opened each box with an unexpected delicacy. Unable to contain his curiosity any longer, he stepped away from the monitor and approached two of Enkian's men who were opening one of the plastic boxes. Two guards walked with him.

"Lunch?" Jack asked. "I hope you brought enough to share."

The men ignored him. Instead they reached inside the container and gently removed an object.

"A rock?" Jack said with surprise. "You guys transported rocks to Antarctica?"

The water remained clear, and Perry could see the bottom rising to meet his feet. He slowed the propulsion system and cut it off once his feet touched the soft, sandy surface. "Feet down," Perry said.

"What's the surface like?" Gleason asked.

"Sort of a sandy-mud. It's a little slippery, but I'm having no trouble standing." He looked around him. Bits of the bottom floated in front of his helmet. Perry wondered how long the bits of debris had rested on the bottom before he came along to disturb them. "I can see the surface. It's maybe five feet over my head." The powerful lights reflected off of the shimmering surface, making it look as if a layer of mercury had been dumped on the water.

He took a step and felt the lake bottom give slightly under his feet. The suit responded well, but he still felt as if he were strolling though syrup. Like Armstrong on the moon, he pushed himself through the alien territory, but unlike the lunar astronauts, Perry felt not only his own weight but that of the water. It was work, despite his having adjusted the dive suit's buoyancy.

Each step brought him closer to the surface. He stopped to take a couple of deep breaths. "This is a little like work," he said.

"Take your time, pal," Gleason said. "That thing has been down there a long time. No need to press things now."

Perry saw something to his left, a large cylinder he knew well. "My navigation is pretty good. I found Hairy." The cryobot lay lifeless on the bottom. Sarah had guided it close to shore and raised it so that its camera broke the surface that was just a foot above Perry's head. "It seems to have slid back a few feet. Probably happened when the cable disconnected."

"Makes sense," Gleason said.

Perry took a few more steps. The work was getting more difficult, and he was feeling a tug on his back. The cable that kept him connected to the surface was becoming deadweight. The plastic lines that shielded the fiber optics and communication lines had been designed to counter the weight of the cable. They carried enough buoyancy per foot of length to cancel the weight of a foot of metal cable. Even so, Perry now had to tug much of it behind him.

"Maybe I'm too old for this kind of work," he said. "I feel like the Creature from the Black Lagoon. Did you ever see that movie?"

"No, but I read about it in the history books," Gleason joked. "I wish there was something we could do."

Perry looked up. The surface was just inches above his head. "Okay, here goes." Perry took two more strides, and his helmet broke the surface, water pouring off his faceplate in sheets. The lights that had been struggling against water were now set free in an open area of air. "Wow," Perry said, lifting his head. It was the same scene he had seen through Hairy's electronic eye, but the best video image could never replace the created human eye.

He was standing neck deep in Lake Vostok, his helmeted head above the surface like a beach ball. Fifty feet above him was an ice ceiling that arched down to either side. He estimated the distance from wall to wall was three hundred feet. Perry felt as if he were trapped in an upside-down bowl.

"Amazing," he whispered. Straight ahead about fifteen feet away was the side of a building, a brick wall that sank beneath the shore and rose until it disappeared into the ice ceiling. The scale of it was impossible to take in. The wall's edges disappeared into ice on either side. From the surveys conducted before the mission began, Perry knew the ziggurat covered several acres. He was standing at the base of a man-made mountain. The receding ice had only laid bare a small portion of the ancient structure, but it was enough to knock Perry back on his heels.

There was a scratching sound that pulled Perry's attention back. "I'm getting some noise on the line."

"Sachs, this is Enkian. Press on."

"What, no 'please'?" Perry moved up the gentle slope, the water level moving down his suit. The cable became heavier as more of it was pulled from the water. The suit was becoming a problem. It wasn't designed to stroll around on dry land. Perry pushed forward, grunting with each step. After what seemed like a mile journey, carrying a backpack of concrete, Perry stood close enough to touch the ziggurat.

"How I wish I were you right now," Enkian enthused. "You are about to touch what has been hidden for millennia."

Perry was sweating, and his heart was slamming. "Yeah, well, I'd trade places with you if I could." He leaned forward and laid his left-hand manipulator on the surface. The only sensation was of resistance. He wondered what the building felt like. "The surface is largely intact. You were right. The larger stones are made of smaller bricks, and a few of them are loose."

"Pick one up."

Fortunately, Perry did not have to bend over far. Sections of the wall had crumbled, leaving bricks at the base sticking out from the sloped surface. Perry found one in easy reach, closed the three-fingered manipulator hand around the brick, and pulled.

"Gently!" Enkian ordered.

"I'm doing my best. Back off." Perry wiggled the brick until it came free. "It appears to be smooth, almost glazed."

"That's how the Babylonians did it. The outer surface was covered in glazed brick. There are several ziggurats still standing, so we know this to be true. Turn it over."

Perry did as ordered, twisting the manipulator so the various sides of the object could be seen in the artificial light.

"*Stop!* Turn it back around."

Perry did and saw what caught Enkian's attention—writing. "It looks like a bunch of lines and dots."

"It's a type of cuneiform. It predates Hebrew and any other script you know about."

"So we can't read it," Perry said. He looked at a string of marks.

"I know what it says," Enkian remarked. "It's the name of an ancient god—Marduk."

Perry brought the brick to his waist and dropped it in a thick plastic bag. This would keep him from having to hold on to the artifact while being towed back to the surface.

There was a *pop*.

The lights went out, suffocating Perry in abysmal blackness. "I've lost lights," he said calmly. There was no response. "I say again, I've lost lights." Nothing. Just the sound of his own breathing. "Um, hello. Anybody there?"

Nothing. The sudden darkness had startled Perry, but the next realization terrified him. He couldn't hear the fans that circulated warm air though his suit.

The suit had lost all power. Perry began to sweat as the cold began to seep in.

(C H A P T E R) 29

The sound of alarm bells filled the Chamber, rebounding off of the curved walls and ceiling. It was deafening.

"Power failure!" Gleason shouted. "The suit has lost power. He's in trouble."

There was a pause of disbelief, then Jack sprung into action. "Talk to me, people."

Sarah started. "I have no telemetry at all. No communication, no video feed, nothing, but my computer is still up. Gleason is right. The suit must have lost power. It doesn't seem to be on our end."

"Gleason, you're with me." Jack spun on his heels and ran toward the support gantry. "Maybe something came loose. You take the electronics; I'll take mechanics."

"Got it."

It was only a few steps to the open hole in the ice, but it seemed like a mile to Jack. He had made three strides when, for a reason Jack couldn't fathom, a guard stepped in front of him and raised his weapon. Jack didn't slow. He slapped the gun aside with his left hand and seized the man's parka with his right. In a single fluid motion he shoved the gunman as hard as he could. The man's feet left the ice, and he landed on his back, sliding several feet. Three additional steps and Jack was by the support structure. First he traced the cable that was attached to his friend. It seemed normal. A gauge measuring line tension read well within safety parameters.

"Connections are good on this end," Gleason said. "Maybe it's the generator. The systems generator runs independently from the ones that power the facility."

"Good idea. Check that. I'm pulling him in." He reached for the control that would begin rewinding the long cable.

The room went dark.

"I've lost everything," Sarah shouted. "Computer is completely down."

"What's going on?" Enkian asked.

"I wish I knew," Jack said. "We've got to get the power back up. Gleason, go."

"Wait," Enkian ordered. "How do I know this isn't a trick?"

"Because my best friend is freezing to death," Jack said. "Either help or get out of the way."

"Why would the power go out?" Enkian demanded to know.

"That's a good question, and I have another one for you: Why haven't the backups kicked in?"

Perry's air had been cut off, and it was already getting thick. He raised his left arm and looked at the control panel. Without his lights, he could see nothing except a small red dot in the bottom left corner. He tapped it and the fans came back to life, air began to circulate, and his lights were restored. The emergency batteries and oxygen were working, but they would not last for long.

How had he lost power so suddenly? He checked the projected gauges on his faceplate. Batteries were just under 100 percent, but they would drain fast. He did the one thing he didn't want to do: He turned off the lights. The Stygian gloom swallowed him whole.

A sense of helplessness washed over him. There was no place to go, no way to help himself. He couldn't swim to the surface. He might make it to the hole, but he could never climb it. He was dependent on Jack and the others to bring him up.

He weighed the possibilities. Once his air was gone—and he only had thirty minutes in reserve—he would die. He toyed with the idea of removing his helmet in hopes that the ice cavern was filled with breathable air. He doubted it was. It was possible that there was oxygen in the chamber but equally possible that the gases surrounding him were noxious. These were things they would have tested had they been given time. Enkian had put an end to that. It was a moot point anyway. Perry had no way to take off his helmet. Getting into the suit and exiting required help. Aside from smashing the face mask, he was stuck, and if he did something so foolish he would be imprisoned in the small cavern. It would only be a matter of time before the cold killed him.

He thought of Hairy lying useless a few feet underwater. There was oxygen on board the probe, a tank used to control buoyancy by expelling water to help it dive. But that tank was deep in the device, and he had no tools to open it.

His hope lay above him, in the hands of friends, and beyond that, in the hands of God.

Jeter hadn't been told so, but he was sure there was more security around him, and they were there not to protect him but to monitor his activities. He leaned back in his chair and rubbed his eyes. He had just received word that his daughter was still safe in the care of the Secret Service, but he couldn't rest easy. The ancient cult had fingers all the way into the White House, and he was just one small intrusion. It still amazed him that Larry Shomer was part of the conspiracy. The man was the head of Homeland Security. Add to that the head of the Joint Chiefs, General McDivett. He felt sick just thinking about it.

He opened his eyes to dispel the nightmare that was beginning and saw President Calvert standing in the doorway. His tie was loose, his collar was unbuttoned, and he wore no suit coat. He did, however, wear a worn and pained look. He had not been to bed since the previous night.

Jeter sucked in a deep breath then let it out. He picked up the phone and dialed for an outside line. A moment later he said, "It's done." As he hung up, he noticed his hand was shaking.

"It was a brave thing to do," Calvert said, entering the room.

"Do you know what I just did?"

Calvert nodded. "Yes, I do. Your country appreciates it. Even more so, I appreciate it."

Jeter rubbed his chin nervously. "She's the only daughter I have. We wanted other children, but it was never in the cards."

"You haven't lost her," Calvert said. "I've ordered extra security. She's being flown home right now."

"How long?" Jeter asked. "How long can we count on that extra security? At some point it runs out, and then what? For all I know, her greatest danger may come disguised as an agent of the Secret Service. Just yesterday morning two members were sitting on the sofa opposite you."

"Those two will be no immediate trouble," Calvert said. "They're vacationing at Camp David until I can figure out what to do with them."

"But they weren't alone," Jeter said. "I never thought of this organization as anything more than a type of lodge, but here they are in the upper reaches of our government and probably significant governments around the world." He shook his head again. "Everywhere. They are everywhere."

"And so are brave men like you."

Perry turned and walked back into the water. Death was rounding the bend, but he had no intention of waiting on it. He had activated the lights long enough to get his bearings and reenter the frigid waters. It was a simple plan, one most likely to fail. To do nothing, though, made failure certain.

Once in the water, he fixed his gaze on the line that hung limply in the current. It was the current he was counting on. From the moment he emerged beneath the ice, he had been battling the moderate flow. Now he would use it. His hope was that he could make it to the hole. Perhaps Jack and Gleason would figure out a way to reach him.

He sighed. It was a stupid plan.

There was a tug—a slight tug at his back. He started to turn when the suit spun 180 degrees. He was being pulled—pulled by the lifeline.

"Way to go, boys," he said, knowing no one could hear him. Perhaps they were reeling him in. It made sense. They had lost contact with him, so their only course of action was to bring him up.

He wished they'd do it faster.

"That's not going to work," Griffin said to Jack.

Jack continued to pull on the cable, putting the strength of his back into it. "I'm not leaving him down there." Utter terror pushed the searing pain from his wounds aside. A greater pain had replaced them.

"I understand, but this is a waste of time."

Jack grunted and pulled on the cable with all his might.

Griffin frowned. "Listen to me, Jack. You're an engineer; do the math. If that cable weighs as little as two pounds per foot, then you're trying to muscle ten tons. And even if you can move Perry to the bottom of the hole, you won't be able to lift him. He weighs 180 and is wearing a suit that weighs at least that much. Do you really think you can tow him up a two-mile-long shaft?"

"I'm not giving up on him!"

"I'm not asking you to," Griffin said.

"Then what?"

"I'm asking you to think like an engineer."

Jack lowered his head and, with a reluctance conquered only by will, released the cable. He had managed to pull up several feet of the cable, which snaked down the hole the moment he let go. Griffin was right, and it pained him to admit it. Footsteps behind him made him raise his head. It was Gleason, looking as white as the ice he stood upon.

"Sabotage," he said, his breath coming hard. "Something's been done to the generators. I can't get them restarted, and even if I could, the cables have been cut in at least three places."

"Who would do that?" Griffin wondered. "Why would someone do that? It's suicide."

Jack's mind was spinning like the wheels on an Indy car. *Think. Think.* "Look for simple answers to hard problems," he muttered.

"What?" Gleason asked.

"Something Perry always says. Look for simple answers to hard problems." He paused. "Even if we get the generators going, we can't run the power through severed lines. Perry will freeze by the time we get things running again, if we can get them running."

He looked around the Chamber—there was nothing that would help. His mind took a quick inventory of everything he had seen in the camp. He shook his head. Nothing. Nothing. He forced his mind to reevaluate the situation again. "We have two choices: Either we get power to Perry, or we get him up here fast."

"That's been taken out of our hands," Griffin said.

"I want answers!" Enkian strode to the three men, his face red with rage.

"I got nothing but questions myself, chief," Jack said. Then he stopped. He quickly explained what Gleason had found. "I'm assuming there are those in your personal army that know something about engines. Find them and get them to work on the generators."

Enkian didn't move.

"You do want your precious brick, don't you?" Jack said.

Enkian growled then called for Tia, who jogged to his side. "Get some men working on the generators."

"Don't let anyone work alone," Jack said. "Put people in groups of three or four. Our saboteur is still around."

"You can't be suggesting that one of my own did this?"

"That's exactly what I'm suggesting, because I know my crew didn't. It's our man down there. There isn't one of us. . ." He paused then shook his head. "When was the last time anyone saw Larimore?"

"He went to the head," Gleason said. "A guard went with him."

Jack looked at Enkian. "Is your guard back?"

"I'll know soon enough."

"One more thing, pal," Jack said. "I need your pilot, and I need him now."

"No one leaves."

"I'm not going anywhere," Jack said. "Just get me your pilot." He turned to Gleason. "Gleas, I need a few things."

"Give me a list."

" 'A friend loves at all times, and a brother is born for adversity,' " Perry said into his helmet. His breath fogged the faceplate. Without the circulating fans operating at speed, the mist stuck, obscuring a large portion of his vision. He tried to relax, to slow his breathing. Of one thing he was certain: If he died down here, it wouldn't be because Jack and Gleason had failed to try. His life was in their hands now, and he was content to leave it there and with God.

The tugging he had felt earlier had stopped a minute after it had begun. Perry had waited for it to resume, but it didn't happen. That's when he chose to make his way back to the entry point, to the hole. It had taken battery power to run the propellers, but he had been patient and the current helped.

He wondered why he bothered to make the trip. He had no idea how being near the entry point to the lake would aid him, but it was something he felt he needed to do. Perhaps he wanted to be as close to his friends as possible. Or maybe they would lower something down the shaft. What that might be, he couldn't imagine.

Perry floated. Perry waited.

Once he had followed the line back, he clamped a manipulator hand on the cable and went limp, trying to conserve oxygen. He was on his back, the ice ceiling inches from his head.

The journey had brought bad news. He had used more power than expected. That puzzled him until he realized that he was not only moving himself but towing a quarter mile of cable behind him.

He waited. And waited.

Something squirted by his helmet, startling him. It disappeared then returned. Perry smiled.

"Well, hello," he said to the small fish that hung suspended near his visor. It was only an inch long, as white as the ice, and had no eyes. A ribbon of bioluminescence ran from gill to tail. It moseyed over the plastic shield, occasionally pecking at the smooth surface. It made Perry's eyes cross. "You like my heads-up display? The amber lights, is that it?" He admired the beauty of the tiny fish and wondered how a fish without eyes could sense light. Some light-sensitive organ, he imagined. "I know someone who would like to meet you," he said. "Her name is Dr. Gwen James. Of course, she's a biologist, so she might want to cut you open."

The fish swam away. "Was it something I said?" He giggled. The comment was funny, but Perry had reduced the airflow in the suit as much as possible. He was getting light-headed. He shivered, and his bones hurt in the marrow. Another muscle spasm. Another pain. His lungs protested the lack of air.

Waiting was such grueling work.

"Got it," Gleason said as he tightened the last nut on the large U-bolt he had placed around the support cable. Gleason slid it up and down. "That should hold."

Jack glanced at the work. Gleason had raced with Jack to the utility shed that held tools, spare parts, bolts, screws, wires, cable, and other supplies left over from the construction of the two domes and two support buildings. They wasted no time in cobbling together the new means of raising Perry to the top.

"We're ready on my end," Jack said. He looked over his shoulder and checked once again that the steel cable he had pulled from the shed ran unobstructed from the gantry through the Chamber and out the loading door, which had been propped open.

A rumble reverberated its way into the dome. It was a sweet sound to Jack.

"Are you sure this is going to work?" Griffin asked. "It looks a little iffy to me."

"I'm open to other ideas," Jack said. "Got any?"

Griffin shook his head.

"How about prayer?" Dr. Curtis said.

"That hasn't stopped, Doc," Jack said.

"Let's get on with it," Enkian said. He stood just a few steps away, his eyes never leaving Jack and the others. Several of his armed men stood behind him.

Jack raised a hand radio to his mouth. It had been given to him by Enkian, something Jack knew he wouldn't have done if Perry wasn't hanging on to something he wanted. "Radio check," Jack said.

"I've got you," the pilot's voice came back.

Jack walked to the open door and looked out into the dim light.

The Casa 212 airplane Tia and her crew had used sat a short distance away. His first thought had been to take power off the plane's electrical system, but Enkian refused to let him dismantle anything. The next best thing was to attach a cable to the back skid and run it to the steel ring around the support cable that was hooked to Perry's suit.

"This is a lousy way to do business," he grumbled to himself. He raised the radio again. "Slowly. Please make it slow."

The props began to roar, and the aircraft moved forward a few inches, then a few feet.

Gleason joined Jack. "Now all we have to do is hope the tow cable holds."

"And that the pilot doesn't taxi too fast, or too far, or that Perry doesn't hit the hole at an angle. . ."

"Okay, I got it."

"I don't think I've ever been this frightened," Jack admitted.

"Me either."

The plane moved forward, and slowly the support line began to feed over the gantry pulleys. The feed drum was locked down so only the cable that was strung over the support frame moved. The ring slid smoothly along the line as the plane taxied forward.

Jack returned to the shaft and watched as the line began to feed upward. "Hang on, my friend," he whispered. "Hang on."

CHAPTER 30

The darkness around him thickened, pressing in on his dive suit. Perry's chest expanded as he struggled to pull oxygen from the air. He had reduced the oxygen flow as much as he thought he could stand and remain conscious. Consciousness was proving to be the problem. Several times he had drifted into the darkness of his mind only to pull himself out by a sheer act of will. He raised the control panel and elevated the airflow. His head was pounding as if a demolition ball were swinging in his skull.

The fish was still there with its running lights of color streaming along its side. The creature hovered just above his face shield, lit by its own light and the meager illumination from the heads-up display projected on the edges of the plastic. Scripture came to mind. Before leaving on the mission, Perry had been studying the book of Job. It was fascinating, puzzling, and profound, the story of undeserved suffering. " 'Speak to the earth, and let it teach you; and let the fish of the sea declare to you.' " He smiled. "Is that what you're doing, little buddy? Declaring the power of God?"

A spasm quaked through him, making his aching muscles protest and his joints scream in pain. His jaw shook uncontrollably. The cold was winning.

The batteries were dying faster than expected. Maybe it was the depth, or the cold, or bad design; Perry didn't know. Nor did it matter. Death was coming in the blackness, its arms stretched out like tentacles. Perry didn't fear it. He had no desire to die, but he knew that all men faced it. It was just that he never expected to die this way, alone under miles of ice. Another thing bothered him: Death would free him, but his friends were still in danger. That truth ate at him like acid.

Perry looked up, but with his lights off there was nothing to see. He strained his eyes and noticed an area of black that was a shade lighter than the rest. It was round. It took a moment for his sluggish mind to realize he was looking at the bottom of the hole he had passed through when he entered the lake. The light from above was miniscule, and he would not have recognized it had he not been bathed in darkness for so long.

"So near, yet so far."

He shuddered again, coughed, and wondered what heaven was like.

Then he felt a tug.

Jack hovered by the opening, his mind miles below the ice sheet. Few things upset him. He had faced danger, been gravely injured—far worse than the ribs and grazing gunshot wound he now sported—and been close to death a few times. All part of life's experience to him. It was watching others suffer that tore his soul, especially those close to him. Perry Sachs, his closest friend, was out of reach and dying, maybe already dead, and he could do nothing but wait and try to exorcise the recurring image of finding a corpse in the dive suit. He stood motionless, doing the hardest work of his life: waiting. It took all his willpower not to fall to his knees and start ripping at the ice with his hands. It would be a useless act, but it seemed better than standing and staring down a very long hole in the ice.

A tear ran down his dark cheek, but Jack felt no embarrassment.

Gleason approached. "He must be free of the water by now. That will help."

Jack nodded. "The plane?"

"Still taxiing straight and true and slow. This was ingenious, Jack. I never would have thought of it."

"Griffin brought me around," Jack replied. "I just hope what we're doing is enough."

"We'll know soon, buddy. We'll know soon. If anyone can survive, it's Perry. He'd survive just to annoy Enkian."

Jack chuckled. "Yeah, that's Perry all right." He lifted his head. Sarah sat at the computer, waiting for it to come back online. Enkian had several men working on the generators. Jack hoped they knew what they were doing. Gwen and Griffin stood off by themselves. Gwen stood slump-shouldered, looking like a deflated balloon. Dr. Curtis was near the middle of the Chamber, pacing in a tight circle.

"What do you think is up with Larimore?" Gleason asked. "Do you think he's the one who did in the generators?"

"I don't know," Jack said. "He's missing. It doesn't make sense. Why would he do that? What does he stand to gain?"

"Beats me," Gleason said. "But I have some serious questions for him."

"If Enkian lets him live," Jack replied. "If he lets any of us live."

Jeter sat to the left of the president, who was leaning over his end of the long conference table that dominated the situation room. To the president's right was Admiral Dwayne Kelly. He was seated in the chair normally occupied by General McDivett. Around the table were key advisors from the State Department, the military, the CIA, and more.

"Mr. President," Admiral Kelly said. "This is a little hard to believe."

"I agree," President Calvert said. "It is nonetheless true." He looked around the room. "You'll notice some familiar faces are gone. That's how much influence this group has. They've infiltrated not just our administration but *every one,* going back many years. Maybe to the founding of our country."

Jeter saw the unbelieving stares. That had been the devious beauty of the generations-long operation—it was incomprehensible.

"But, Mr. President," the secretary of defense said, "if what you say is true, then how do you know that one or more of us are not part of the group?"

"I don't. Not completely. You are all being investigated, so expect a visit from the FBI. We've already done deeper and more specific background checks on all of you and everyone else in the West Wing. I'm sorry for the intrusion, but it can't be helped. To preserve national security, I'd have my own grandmother grilled. And so we're clear on this, if you're involved with this nameless group, you had better speak up now. Treason is still a capital offense."

Jeter bit his lip. No one moved or spoke.

"Very well," the president said. "You've been briefed. I want suggestions, and I want them fast. How do we deal with the mess in Antarctica?"

"That's a tough one," the admiral said. "Antarctica is a military-free area. No nation is allowed a military base on the continent. The Coast Guard runs icebreaking operations down there, but they're not equipped for an assault operation. And you said that misinformation had been dispensed about the C-5 crash to throw off the search. The integrity of the operations down there may be compromised."

"It makes sense," Calvert said. "It seems Antarctica is the goal. That's where you'd want operatives. So who do we trust?"

"I can think of one man," Jeter said. The president looked at him. It was a different gaze than he had grown accustomed to. Jeter now saw suspicion in his boss's eyes, despite Jeter's honesty about the matter. That was the problem with conspiracies. One never knew who to trust.

"Who might that be?" Calvert asked.

"The Coast Guard captain that raised a stink about the search, the one whose radio transmissions NSA picked up. From the logs of his transmissions, he seems untainted."

"But what can the captain of an icebreaker do?"

"I don't know," Jeter admitted. "But he's close."

Jack seized the line the moment Perry's helmet emerged from the ice shaft and pulled. "Order the plane to stop!" Gleason did, and two seconds later the cable stopped moving. Jack heaved with all the strength he could manage. His damaged ribs ignited with pain, and the wound on his arm ripped open again. Jack ignored it all; his attention was on the man in the dive suit. He pulled until half of Perry's body lay on the ice.

Gleason was by his side. "Let me disconnect him." A moment later, the umbilical that had towed Perry to the surface hung limply over the hole.

Jack dragged his friend to the side, away from the hole, the gantry, and the other equipment. Before he had the helmet off, Gwen was at his side. Jack worked the releases and gently pulled the helmet away. Perry's face was light blue.

"Move," Gwen snapped.

Jack was rooted in place.

"I said, move!"

Jack yielded.

Gwen removed the glove of her right hand and touched Perry's neck, positioning her fingers over his carotid artery. She didn't move. She didn't speak.

"Gwen—" Gleason began.

"Hush!"

Jack's stomach dropped like a meteor when he saw her lower her head.

Her head snapped up. "I have a pulse. Get the FAWS." She slapped Perry lightly on the side of the face. "Come on, Perry, come on." She slapped him again. "Perry, can you hear me? Come back to us. Come back."

Perry coughed. "Hands are. . .c–c–cold."

She turned to Jack. "Get this suit off him."

"Hold it," a voice said. "Stand back."

Jack watched Tia and Enkian approach, a handgun in the man's grip.

"He needs help," Gwen said.

Enkian raised the gun and pointed it at Gwen's head. "Stand back."

Gwen did.

"Watch them," Enkian ordered Tia. She raised her weapon.

Enkian bent over Perry then reached for the dark plastic bag attached to his waist. He tucked his pistol in his parka and gently opened the bag. He removed the brick Perry had retrieved, turned it over, and ran his fingers along the letters pressed into its wide surface. "Marduk," he muttered. He looked at Tia and smiled; then he stood and caught the gaze of his small army. He raised the brick over his head.

The Chamber filled with cheers.

Jack had had enough. He knelt beside his friend and un-latched the torso portion of the suit from the legs. It was time to get Perry out.

The light from the Chamber seemed wrong to Perry, but he couldn't figure it out. He wasn't thinking clearly. All he knew was that he had opened his eyes to the face of Gwen James and it was a pretty face. A second later he drifted off, his mind muddled with disjointed and confusing thoughts. He wondered how the little fish was doing.

❖❖

"Give me some privacy, gentlemen," Captain Thomas Mahoney ordered as he entered the communications room. The place emptied in a moment. Remaining behind was the senior communications officer. "You said you had an eyes-only for me."

"Yes, sir. Over there." He nodded to a computer monitor. Mahoney sat down and saw an e-mail with his name on it. He knew it was encrypted. He clicked on OPEN, and a password request window appeared. He entered a code known only to him. When the message decoded, he read it and felt a wave of confusion that was replaced immediately by resolve. He deleted the message. "Thank you. Carry on."

Mahoney marched to the bridge and saw Ray Seager standing at his post. "XO," he said sharply, "you're with me."

"Aye, sir."

He turned and strode down the companionway toward his quarters. Behind him came the fast steps of his executive officer.

Once in the privacy of the captain's quarters, Mahoney filled in his officer.

"Begging the captain's pardon," Seager said with dismay, "but this is impossible to do."

"That's true," Mahoney agreed. "That's why they called on the Coast Guard."

CHAPTER 31

Perry awoke slowly, blinked, and tried to order his thoughts. His whole body ached, and his headache remained. But his lungs felt good, filled with air that was cold but sweet. He tried to move but couldn't. He was paralyzed.

"Take it easy, buddy," Jack said. Perry turned to see his friend sitting in a chair next to him. Since he had to look up, he realized that he must be lying on the ice. "We've got you tied down."

"Tied down?" His voice sounded weak to his ears. Things were becoming clearer.

Gwen appeared. "We have you in the FAWS."

Perry was puzzled. "My brain has been a little oxygen deprived. FAWS?"

"Forced Air Warming Suit," Gwen explained. "Remember?"

Perry did. He had ordered several such suits for the mission. "It's coming back. My hands and feet are still cold." He shifted his weight in the sleeping baglike device. He could barely move.

"They're supposed to be," Gwen said. "The suit warms the torso first. That's where the important organs are. If we warmed the hands and feet first, then your blood would rush to your extremities before we wanted it to."

"That's what she says," Jack joked. "I think she's just afraid you'll disrupt the party."

"My invitation must have been lost in the mail," Perry said.

"Yeah, go with that," Jack said, then he softened his tone. "You had us scared, buddy. I'm glad you're back."

"You know how I like to make an entrance." He met his longtime friend's eyes. The gaze said enough. "How long have I been out?"

"Two hours or so," Gwen said. "You deserved a nap."

"The brick?"

"Enkian has it," Jack said. "Things have gotten a little weird while you were gone, a little stranger."

"I didn't think that was possible."

"Oh, it's possible, all right." Jack explained about the power loss, the sabotaged generators, and the missing Larimore. "Gleason had to rip the batteries out of the backup suit to power the FAWS."

"He's still missing?" Perry said. "There aren't that many places to hide."

"They found him about an hour ago," Jack replied. "He had slipped out to use the head. A guard went with him. They found the guard dead, his neck broken. His gun was missing."

"He had a gun?"

"Yes, but he didn't get to use it. Tia and the others found Larimore hiding in a fiberglass crate in the cargo area of Tia's plane. Apparently he was going to wait there until they flew out."

Perry thought about what he was hearing. "You think he killed the power then hid on the plane to make his escape?"

Jack nodded. "No one can survive out here without power. In some ways, it's a decent plan. If Enkian and the others wanted to stay, then someone would have to fly for parts or maybe a whole new generator, or at best, they'd just leave, and he'd be on the aircraft with them. Ironically, he was hiding in the aircraft we used to pull you up. That's when he was found."

"Ingenious and stupid," Perry said. "I can see a dozen problems with that plan."

"I think he's rounded the bend, if you know what I mean," Jack said. "He's in no shape to try anything like that again. They roughed him up pretty good."

"The power's on now," Perry observed.

"Yeah, Enkian's men got the lines spliced and the repairs made about an hour after we brought you up."

"I wouldn't have lasted another hour," Perry said.

"True," Jack agreed. "Larimore almost killed you."

"You know, I was entertaining thoughts that he might be part of Enkian's group." Perry turned away from Jack and directed his attention to the center of the Chamber. Things had changed. "What's going on over there?"

"That's the weird part," Jack said. "They've been unloading rocks, of all things. Rocks! They've put them in a circle. I think they're planning some kind of ritual. It's giving me the creeps."

"I'll tell you what creeps me out," Gwen said. "They have Sarah and Gleason training some of their men to use Slick. I don't think they're going to need us for much longer."

"I envy you," Enkian said. He had approached Perry as Gwen was helping him out of the FAWS.

"Don't," Perry said. Jack handed him his parka. He still felt cold but well enough to leave the confines of the warming suit. He stood and swayed, his head spinning. "I'm not in the best position here."

"You have seen with your own eyes what I have only seen on the monitor, what my father and his father and his father back more generations than I can count have longed to see. You have touched the tower."

"I can have Gleason put the batteries back in the other suit if you want to pay your brick mountain a visit."

"Don't be snide with me, Mr. Sachs," Enkian said. "I am a proud man and have no patience. I let your friends treat you because I owed you something for bringing me the brick. As far as I'm concerned, my debt is paid."

"Why are you here?" Perry pressed, too tired and sore to care about offending.

"To reclaim what is rightfully ours," he said.

"You have title deed to the ziggurat?" Perry said, his legs buckling. Jack stepped to his side.

"We are tied to it," Enkian admitted. "Tied in a way you cannot understand. It is the work of my people from ages before recorded history."

"Well, now you've seen it. So what's next? Taking up occupancy is going to be difficult, with it submerged in a pressured lake under ten thousand feet of ice. Trust me, it's not even a nice place to visit."

"We're taking our continent back," Enkian said. "This land was once ours. It will be ours again."

"That seems unlikely," Perry argued. "No one owns Antarctica. No country and certainly no person. You may have captured this base, but that's a long way from taking all five million square miles of it."

"You will be surprised."

"What can you do with it?" Jack asked. "I don't care how big a strip mall you build, people aren't going to come down here."

"Those who know—those who believe—will come." He stared as if his eyes could burrow into Perry's skull. "There is much here: water, obviously, but under the ice there is a continent of untapped minerals."

"That's the problem, isn't it? That whole ice thing, I mean." Perry returned the stare.

"I'm a mining expert, Mr. Sachs. I know how to move dirt. I can move ice."

"What? You're going to strip mine the ice?" Jack asked.

Enkian never took his eyes of Perry. "We prefer to call it *open-face mining*. I have the equipment that will uncover the ziggurat.

It will take a few years, but it can be done." He smiled. "I'm under no obligation to explain anything to you, Mr. Sachs, but I'll leave you a few things to think about. One reason this area is so cold is albedo. Are you familiar with the term?"

Perry nodded. "It's reflective power—the amount of light that's reflected from a surface."

"Very good. The ice reflects a tremendous amount of sunlight, far more than it would if the continent were bare ground. Change that, and the ice begins to melt."

"How can you change the physical characteristics of ice?" Perry asked. Then the answer hit him. "You're going to color the ice?"

"You are sharp, Mr. Sachs. But we will only do so where we want the ice to melt. Coal dust—and I have many sources for that—dark aggregates, dyes dropped from aircraft like fire retardant from firefighting planes, and. . .well, you get the idea. Also imagine what might happen to shipping lanes."

"Do you think other nations are going to just turn it over to you?"

"As a matter of fact, I do. We have been planning this for more than a few years. I have been honored with refining the plans and implementing them, largely because of your fine work."

"Give us the keys to that plane out there, and I'll consider that payment in full."

"I think I'll keep you a little longer," Enkian said. "But now that you're back among the living, you should be warned: I have no compunction about putting you or your friends at death's door. Or through it." He walked away.

"Cheery fellow, huh?" Jack said.

Dr. Curtis moved closer. "That looked interesting," he deadpanned.

Perry shook his head. "I can't get the pieces to fit. Tell me, Doc, can that really be the Tower of Babel?"

"How can I know?" Curtis said. "I would not have believed a story about what I've seen, yet there it is, mocking everything I've been taught."

"Maybe it's just another ziggurat," Jack said.

"Perhaps," Curtis agreed. "But even that is beyond all expectation. Human habitation on this continent is so far beyond the pale of contemporary science that I can barely comprehend it. Of course, others have suggested it."

"They have?" Perry said.

Curtis frowned. "There have always been those who preach that science is blind to the existence of previous civilizations. Occasionally they offer some evidence, but none of it can be scientifically verified."

"Such as?" Perry prompted.

"Well, there's the Piri Reis map of 1513," Curtis explained. "The map shows a portion of Antarctica, the Queen Maud Land to be specific."

"1513?" Perry said. "Antarctica wasn't discovered until 1818. That's a three-hundred-year difference."

"That's part of the puzzle, but even more intriguing is that the map shows the area as ice-free. That means that Admiral Piri Reis drew his map based on older maps that had to be made—if we use current scientific dating—prior to 4000 B.C. You can see why the scientific community dismisses the idea out of hand. Mapmaking was not a developed art then."

"At least as far as current thinking goes."

Curtis nodded. "Of course, the natural assumption is that no ice means the land could have been inhabited, but something happened to change all of that."

"What was the writing on the brick?" Perry asked, wrapping his arms around his chest and moving his weight from leg to leg to increase circulation.

"Cuneiform," Curtis said. "It's a name, Marduk, and that's what troubles me."

"The name?"

Curtis nodded. "There's an ancient body of work from Babylon called the *Enuma Elish*. It speaks of the Tower of Babel, saying that the name Marduk was stamped into every brick."

"Marduk was a Babylonian god?" Perry asked.

"Yes. He's one god of the Babylonian pantheon."

"Pantheon?" Jack said.

"All the gods of a particular religion. We believe in one God, so the idea of many gods sounds odd to us, but most ancient people had belief systems with multiple deities. Usually, each one was associated with a numen."

"Now you're losing me, Doc," Perry said.

"Numina—or numen in the singular—are supernatural powers associated with a place or a natural phenomenon. So every city had a god, the sun was a god, and there was a god of storms. You get the idea. Initially, the Babylonians worshiped a mother-goddess. The most ancient sculptures we have are of pregnant women, a symbol of fertility and promise. Male deities were introduced much later."

"You said Enkian and Tia were named after ancient gods," Perry prompted.

"That's right. Enkian is from Enki and Tia is from Tiamat. Now there's some irony."

"Why is that?" Perry asked.

Curtis took a deep breath and released it. He looked weary, and Perry knew the man had a right to. "If I remember my mythology correctly, Tiamat was the mother of all living. Her name comes from the Akkadian and means *sea*. She was involved in a battle with Marduk, who slew her, cut her to pieces, and made heaven and earth out of her two halves."

"Nice," Jack said.

"I'm guessing it is one reason Tia defers to Enkian. Enki was the god of wisdom, spells, and incantations; Tiamat of ocean water. In the Babylonian accounts, Tiamat is consort to Apsu, the god of freshwater. Their union produced many gods, including Ea, who is also known as Enki. Tiamat is often portrayed as a dragon, which explains the tattoo. You can see the connection between the two."

"Wait," Jack said. "That means that Tiamat is Enki's mother, right?"

"Right, but it's more complex than that. Marduk is Ea's son, who ultimately kills his grandfather and Tiamat, his grandmother. . .so to speak. But don't read too much into that. I imagine our unexpected guests have just taken on the names. Marduk became the chief of all the gods, and his eminence was so great that he claimed fifty titles."

"If Marduk was such hot stuff, then why didn't Enkian take his name?" Jack asked.

"Probably because he believes there really is a god named Marduk," Curtis explained.

"Hold on," Perry cut in. "You said Enki went by another name?"

"Oh, yes," Curtis said. "Remember, these gods and their stories were held by different groups. The stories vary some as do the names."

"Say the name again."

"Ea. It's spelled E-A."

"I wonder," Perry said. "We did some work for a mining company called EA Mining."

"He said he was a mining expert," Jack added.

"If that's his firm, then he has a lot of money behind him," Perry said. "They're global, and they're wealthy." He paused and then added, "I think I want to see what they've done to the Chamber."

CHAPTER 32

O f the fifty men Enkian had brought with him, thirty or more hustled about the Chamber, carrying boxes and unloading them. The contents were unexpected. Perry saw gray-blue stones removed from packing crates and set up on the ice. They formed three concentric rings of twenty-two stones each—sixty-six in all. Smaller stones composed the inner ring and were less than two feet high and a foot in width. The next ring was comprised of stones a third larger than the first, and the last ring was made of stones three feet tall and two feet around. Some of the men worked alone; others, especially those handling the large rocks, labored in tandem. The other men stood by with guns at the ready.

Enkian had taken a position in the center of the rings, directing their placement, calling for corrections, and snapping orders. Tia stood by his side.

Perry walked to one of the large stones and noticed that the top had been chiseled flat and a circular half-inch deep depression was centered in each one. More stones were brought in, but these were smaller and rectangular like bricks. They were of different shades and textures but were all the same size. Enkian took a step to the side as two men knelt on the ice and began to take one stone brick and lay it upon another in a staggered array. From his position outside the outer ring, Perry studied the stones. One was silvery; another, jet black; another, white as ice; and still another, green. Row was laid upon course until a small pyramid shape with a flat top rose from the ice. The last block laid was like gold. Then it hit Perry: It *was* gold. And the silver brick was true silver. The others were what they appeared to be—onyx, granite, and more. Perry counted sixty-six stones of every kind.

"This is weird," Jack said.

"Beyond weird," Perry added.

"Is that really a brick of gold?" Curtis asked.

"I think so," Perry answered. "If Enkian is the owner of EA Mining, he has access to every type of mineral in the ground."

More boxes were brought in, but these were different from those that had been brought in before. They had rigid plastic sides. Perry moved as close to one as he dared and watched the worker unsnap the metal latches and swing up the lid. Inside was packing material that had been carefully wrapped around an object Perry could not see clearly.

"Your curiosity is whetted, I see." Perry looked up to see Enkian approaching from a few feet away, Tia on his heels with her head bowed. The worker Perry had been watching carefully removed the packing material and then moved away. Enkian took his place, gently lifting a cylindrical object from the case. He held it as if it were alive, cradling it in his hands as a man would a child. Inside the clear plastic container, Perry saw a clay cylinder. "Behold the prophecy," Enkian said. He set it in the depression of the closest stone.

"Behold the prophecy," Tia repeated.

"I don't understand," Perry said.

"You never will," Enkian replied, then moved to the next stone, where another worker was unpacking an identical cylinder. Again Enkian picked up the package tenderly, said, "Behold the prophecy," and set the cylinder on the nearest stone.

Gleason, Griffin, and the others joined Perry. "This is making me real uncomfortable," Gleason said. "What are they doing?"

"I think we are about to see a pagan worship ritual," Dr. Curtis said.

Enkian stopped at each stone and repeated his previous action, Tia never more than one step away, her head down as if condemned to permanent humility. Minutes turned to half an hour until Enkian set the last clay cylinder in place.

He returned to the center of the rings. Tia followed. Wordlessly, Enkian's small army formed a fourth ring around the three stone circles.

Enkian stepped behind the altar and removed his parka, tossing it to the side. Underneath he wore a long-sleeved undergarment. He peeled it away along with the thick T-shirt he wore beneath it, baring his chest to air kept several degrees below freezing. If the bite of the frigid air bothered him, he didn't show it.

Perry leaned forward to verify what his eyes were telling him. Enkian's chest was a latticework of scars from shoulders to waist. Tia turned to a man in the first circle and held out her hands. He presented her with a long-bladed knife, which he had removed from what appeared to be a handcrafted rosewood box. The handle of the knife was encrusted with jewels. Tia knelt before Enkian, bowed her head, and raised the knife for him to take.

"I don't like the looks of this," Gleason said.

Perry narrowed his eyes as he watched the scene unfolding before him. No one paid attention to them. It was as if they had ceased to matter.

"Self-mutilation," Curtis whispered. "Not all that unusual. Many ancient cultures practiced it."

"Elijah and the prophets of Baal," Perry mused.

"Who?" Griffin said.

Curtis, ever the professor, explained. "An Old Testament showdown. The prophet Elijah faced off against four hundred and fifty prophets of Baal and four hundred prophets of Asherah. Elijah had laid out a simple challenge: If Baal was real, then let him show it by sending fire from heaven to consume an offering; if the Lord God was real, He would answer with fire from heaven. When Baal didn't answer, the prophets began to cut themselves to encourage his response. It didn't work. We know who won."

"You mean this is normal?" Griffin asked.

"Not normal," Perry said. "There's nothing normal about this. It's just not new."

Perry watched, stiff-jawed, as Enkian took the knife, approached the central stone altar, and threw his head back. He said something Perry couldn't understand. Perry looked at Dr. Curtis, who just shrugged and said, "I don't recognize the language."

Enkian began to sway. He muttered. He whispered. Only the name "Marduk" was recognizable.

Suddenly, Enkian stopped, lowered his head, and placed the point of the knife at the top of his sternum.

He pressed.

He drew it down.

Blood began to seep, then pour down his chest, mixing with the dark hair of his chest. He uttered no cry of pain; his face showed no agony. A red line zippered down, and Perry thought for a moment the madman was vivisecting himself in full view of all. No one showed surprise. Tia stood by, her eyes fixed on the gore before her as if she had seen it a hundred times before. *Maybe she has*, Perry thought.

The knife inched its way down Enkian's sternum to the soft abdomen, stopping just above the navel. He removed the knife and set it on the altar, then bent over the stones and laid his bloody chest on the rocks.

No one moved.

Minutes later he stood erect. He raised his arms, oblivious to the crimson stream that continued to trickle down his body. He groaned. He hummed and the others joined him. The sound roared in a crescendo amplified by the concave interior of the Chamber until Perry's ears hurt.

"I think I can fly the plane," Griffin whispered in Perry's ear.

"What?"

"I think I can fly the plane," Griffin said, a little louder. "I took lessons in college. I've flown solo several times." When Perry turned to him, he flushed. "It was just a single-engine Cessna, but I think I can deduce the difference between a single-engine and twin-engine."

"Deduce?"

Griffin nodded. "I'm talking about the smaller plane, of course. Still, the difference should not be insurmountable. Once we're airborne, I can figure out the distinctions on the way to McMurdo."

Perry shook his head. It was hard to believe he was hearing this. He had to admit that stealing the Casa 212 had crossed his mind. But he was unable to come up with a plan that would afford them the necessary time to make their way to the craft, start the cold engines, taxi far enough away, and take to the air without being cut down by a fusillade of gunfire.

"I appreciate it, Griffin, but I don't think they'll let us wander very far without killing someone to show their displeasure."

"We have to do something," Griffin complained.

"I agree. . ."

Enkian raised his voice. "Most honored are you above all the gods. Your decree is unmatched by men and gods. You, Marduk, are the most honored of all gods. Your decrees are unquestionable. For now and forever, your declarations are unchangeable. No one from the gods can transgress your boundaries. Marduk, you are our avenger. You are our avenger. . .our avenger. . .our avenger."

"Avenger!" the men shouted. "Avenger!"

"I'd be a lot more comfortable if they'd use a different word," Jack said.

The chant grew louder until Perry was sure the prefab dome of the Chamber would collapse from the vibrations. Sarah and Gwen were white with fear and held their hands to their ears. Griffin looked shell-shocked, and Dr. Curtis stood as rigid as a marble column, his jaw slack. Jack was surprised but unshaken. Gleason just looked puzzled.

Enkian fired his hand into the air, and the chant turned to silence in an instant. It was as if all the air had been sucked from the room. All eyes were fixed on him.

He lowered his hand and spread his arms wide. "For millennia we have waited for this day." His voice was fairly strong, despite the wound and his chest being bared to subfreezing temperatures. Perry felt cold just looking at him. "The prophecies told of this day, the Time of Return, the Time of Revenge."

He stepped to the closest clay cylinder. "Here," he said, "it was recorded. Here on these cylinders the words of our ancestors remain alive. They are ours to protect as those who came before us protected them. They looked forward to this day." He stopped and looked at Perry and the others. "Come forward."

Perry hesitated.

"Come forward!"

"This must be like the invitation in a Baptist church," Jack quipped.

"I doubt it," Perry said as he walked toward the circle.

"All of you!" Enkian snapped.

The outer circle of men parted before him like earth before a plow's blade. A few steps later, Perry and the others stood in the inner circle. Tia moved forward, her eyes hard like the stones of the altar. The message was clear. No one was to touch Enkian.

"Do you know what this is?" Enkian asked. Perry looked at the cylinder then at the self-inflicted wound on his chest. The gash was not as deep as Perry first thought, but it was deep enough to cause sufficient pain to drop a man to his knees. Enkian seemed to pay it no attention. The other scars—Perry guessed there were close to fifty of them—were evidence that Enkian had learned to live with pain.

Perry answered. "Not really. A clay cylinder of some kind." He could see its smooth sides were occasionally marred by cracks and missing clay. There were no letters, but tiny, exquisitely drawn pictures ran in vertical rows.

"It is the story of life," Enkian said. "The true story of life. It is the oldest writing in the world, penned—as it were—in the days of Gilgamesh."

"Gilga-who?" Jack said.

"Gilgamesh," Dr. Curtis answered. "From the *Gilgamesh Epic,* one of the many ancient flood accounts. It was written in cuneiform on twelve clay tablets about four thousand years ago. It's the Babylonian version very similar to the Bible's story of Noah's flood."

"Very good, Doctor," Enkian said. "Your Bible lifted the story from our more ancient accounts."

"I doubt it," Curtis said. "It's more likely the other way around."

"Your fellow scholars would disagree with you."

"It wouldn't be the first time," Curtis said. "And I also find it interesting that one of the main characters in the story of Gilgamesh is a man named Enkidu. Coincidence?"

"Many great men have taken the noble name of Enki," Enkian said. He looked at the cylinder. "This came to me through my father, and his father before him, and his father before him. These cylinders predate the *Gilgamesh Epic;* they predate the Bible. They are the only true record of my past. They are both prophecies and histories."

"Prophecies?" Perry said. "Are you telling us that these clay cylinders predicted the discovery of the ziggurat?"

"Discovery?" Enkian laughed. "It was never lost, Mr. Sachs. Never. My people have known its location for centuries. The account has been kept alive for millennia. We were just waiting for the time to. . .mature."

"That cylinder tells you when the time will be mature?"

Enkian looked at the cylinder with the gaze of a man who held the world's most precious possession. He nodded. "This one in particular. There are sixty-six of them, each kept in a glass container like this. The chamber is filled with an inert gas that doesn't react with the dried clay." He stroked the clear container. "They're all special. Each tells a portion of the story—of the Flood, the Tower, the Dispersion, or the Revelation. This one holds the future of my people. This is more valuable than all of my possessions and all of my businesses. It is irreplaceable."

"Your people?" Perry asked. "Just who are your people?"

"We are an ancient people. My fathers built the ziggurats. More importantly, they built *the* ziggurat, what you call the Tower of Babel. Have you heard of the Piri Reis map?"

"Dr. Curtis explained it to us," Perry said. "It's a sixteenth-century map showing a portion of Antarctica."

"More specifically, it shows an iceless Antarctica," Enkian explained like a teacher with a slow child. "It shows the continent that lies beneath the ice sheet, a continent no man had seen until a joint Swedish-British expedition did a seismic profile in 1949. Piri Reis based his maps on older maps. Maps my people had in their possession."

"You're saying the ancient Babylonians built the Tower of Babel on this continent," Griffin interjected.

Enkian's face darkened. "No, Dr. James, that is not what I'm saying. We are not Babylonians. The Babylonians are descendants of ours. We were those after the Flood. Mr. Sachs and Dr. Curtis hit on it. Their Bible gave them enough information to be close to the truth."

"Just close?" Jack said.

Enkian ignored him. "After the Flood, my people adopted a noble goal, to build a new civilization. Civilizations are built on shared goals and common interests. We built a tower to reach the sky. . . ."

"And God sent you packing," Perry said. "We know the story."

"Not God, Mr. Sachs," Enkian said. "Gods. Read the Mexican account, read the Babylonian version. The gods became displeased. My ancestors did not honor them as they should have. That is a mistake I will not make."

"I think you've already made a big mistake," Jack said.

"What you think means nothing to me," Enkian said. He looked back at the cylinder. "The languages were confused, just as your Bible says. In fact, it is from that event we get our English word *babble*. Not only were the languages confused, but the people were scattered, literally transported to other areas. Those who were left continued building a civilization and great cities. They became the Babylonians. Others raised up vast empires wherever they were planted. Have you ever wondered why there are so many stone structures in the world?"

Perry spoke for the others. "It's crossed my mind."

"Incas, Mayans, Egyptians, Babylonians to name a few," Enkian lectured. "Add to that stone monuments like the Callanish stones in Scotland's Outer Hebrides, the Avebury stone circle in England, the famous Stonehenge near Salisbury, England, and hundreds more. Stone is not lifeless; it is the foundation of life. Descendants of those first people erected monuments, some more successfully than others." He looked down to the ice. "Below is the greatest of them all, the original."

"I still don't understand how the tower could be so far south," Perry said. "It was built in Mesopotamia."

"And of brick, not stone," Curtis added.

"The material is the gift of the earth," Enkian said. "We made stone where no stone was."

"You speak as if you were there," Jack said. "You don't look that old."

"I was there in my forefathers. Their blood courses through my veins. Their knowledge has been passed to me. I have taken their past; I return to them a future."

"You could make millions writing pithy sayings for fortune cookies," Jack said.

"Don't trifle with me, Mr. Dyson."

"You still haven't explained how the tower came to be at the bottom of the planet," Perry said quickly, drawing Enkian's attention.

"Hapgood."

"Oh, please," Griffin said with disgust. "No one buys that nonsense."

"Dr. James," Enkian said. "There is a man-made structure two miles below your feet. If I had told you that was the case before you came here, you would have declared that nonsense."

"What's a Hapgood?" Jack asked.

No one spoke.

"Explain it, Dr. James," Enkian ordered.

"Charles Hapgood of Keene College, New Hampshire," Griffin said. "I believe he taught history of science or something like that. He published a book in the early fifties putting forth an impossible idea. He said Antarctica was at one time two thousand miles further north and, obviously, much warmer."

"Then how did it get here?" Sarah asked. Her voice was shaky.

Griffin explained, frowning as if the words pained him. "He believed in something he called 'earth crust displacement.' He said the crust of our planet shifted over the Earth's core. I believe he described it like the peel of an orange moving over the meaty part of the fruit. No orthodox geologist buys it."

"Albert Einstein liked the idea enough to write the foreword to the book," Enkian said.

Griffin didn't respond.

"Why tell us all this?" Perry asked. "We're not part of your group."

"Because I can," Enkian said.

"So what's next?" Perry said. "You have the hole in the ice, and you know the ziggurat is down there. What next?"

Enkian turned to Tia. "Bring him." Tia walked away, taking two men with her. She disappeared through the air lock that led to the Dome. A few minutes later she reappeared with a bound Larimore staggering before her. Even across the Chamber, Perry could see the man had been badly beaten. He was surprised to see him alive.

Tia pushed the commander through the circles until he stood by the altar and a few feet away from the ice shaft.

The beating must have been fierce, and Perry was moved with pity. Larimore's left eye was swollen shut, and his nose was broken and twisted. Dried blood was caked beneath his nostrils and at the corners of his mouth. He leaned to one side, and Perry assumed that they must have beaten his body until ribs broke. He dragged one foot behind him.

Perry felt sick.

"Here is the man who tried to kill you, Mr. Sachs," Enkian said. "Have any words for him?"

Larimore spoke first. His voice was hoarse and weak. "I'm sorry, Perry. I. . .I. . .didn't mean to cut off your generator, just those to the Chamber and Dome. I hit the wrong one. I thought. . ." he broke in a spasm of coughing. "I thought I could force them to leave. I was going to stow away and get help."

"After you made your escape," Griffin complained. "Save yourself first, is that it?"

"Let it go, Griffin," Perry said.

"But—"

"Let it go."

"He could have killed you."

"He didn't."

"It was an accident," Larimore complained. "I had to act when I did. Everyone was focused on you under the ice. It was then or never."

"It still looks like never," Griffin snapped.

"I understand," Perry said. He turned to Enkian. "Let Gwen help him. He needs medical help."

"He killed one of my men."

"So did Tia," Perry said.

"That's different," Enkian said. "She was acting on my behalf. Commander Larimore was working against me. I can't overlook that."

"There should be a sacrifice," Tia said.

Enkian nodded. "As usual, you are right."

"What kind of sacrifice?" Perry asked.

No answer came. Tia stepped to Larimore and delivered a crushing blow to his jaw. The man dropped to his knees.

"That's enough!" Perry shouted and started forward. He was immediately jerked back. Several men from the circle had grabbed him, pinning his arms to his side. He looked to Jack. Four men had wrestled him to the ground before he could move a step. It took all four of them to hold him down. Gleason was held in place by a gun barrel at his temple.

Tia stepped to Larimore's side and planted a vicious kick to his kidneys. He cried out in pain and fell forward. Then, with a strength that belied her size and gender, she grabbed Larimore's hood and dragged the half-conscious man across the ice, dropping him next to the ice hole.

Perry watched in horror as she pulled the commander's feet to the opening and positioned them over the hole. She motioned for the two men who had brought Larimore in. They each took a bound arm and lifted the man from the floor. Larimore's head moved limply from side to side, and Perry could tell he was barely conscious.

"Don't do this!" Perry pleaded. "There's no need. I'll take responsibility for him."

"Very gracious of you, Mr. Sachs, considering he almost killed you."

"You're no better," Perry said.

"No, but I am in control." He turned to Tia. "Do it."

In an act of cruelty Perry never could have imagined, Tia stepped to the semiconscious Larimore and gently patted his cheek until he came to. She stepped back and waited. It took a moment for the groggy navy commander to take in his situation. At first his eyes widened and he started to kick, but he stopped abruptly. He looked to Perry. "It really was an accident."

"I know."

"Maybe I'll meet your God—"

"Now!" Tia ordered.

Commander Trent Larimore disappeared into the ice. Perry tried to drive the image of a man falling through nearly two miles of ice from his mind. He prayed the death would be quick. He turned angry eyes to Tia, who seemed disturbed.

She looked at Enkian. "He didn't scream."

Enkian shrugged then faced Griffin. "Tell me, Dr. James. How's that for contamination?"

Griffin bent over and vomited on the ice.

CHAPTER 33

W hat's wrong with her?" Enkian asked.

Perry followed Enkian's gaze and saw Sarah on the ice. She was having another attack.

"People faint," Gwen said. She crouched next to the heap that was Sarah.

"Somehow, I think it's more than fainting," Enkian said. He looked at Perry and raised an eyebrow.

"Narcolepsy," Perry said. "The stress of watching. . . The stress triggers it."

"You brought a crewperson with a neurological disorder to this environment?" Enkian said with surprise. "I thought you a better leader than that."

Perry started to explain then dismissed the idea. He owed this monster no explanations. He watched as Gwen moved from crouching to kneeling. She moved Sarah's head to the side to make breathing easier and stroked the woman's dark hair.

Suddenly, Sarah's eyes sprang open. She mumbled something then sat up. A second later she was fully awake and on her feet. She looked embarrassed.

Enkian waved at the men who held Jack to the ice and those who restrained Perry. "Let them go. If they do anything foolish, kill them. I've grown weary of their antics."

"So who's next down the hole?" Perry asked.

"Amusing as that would be, Mr. Sachs, I still feel I owe you something for bringing back the brick." Enkian stepped to the dark object that rested on the stone altar. "You have brought my ancestors to me. It goes against my better judgment and the advice of Tia, but you are all free to go."

Perry wasn't sure he heard right. "Free to go?"

"Yes, you may leave as soon as you like." Enkian looked up, and Perry could see the man was serious.

"You're giving us a plane to fly out of here?"

Enkian bellowed with laughter. "Of course not." He looked at Tia. "Give them a plane, did you hear that?" She nodded and returned the smile.

"Then how do we leave?" Perry wondered.

"You walk, Mr. Sachs. You walk."

"We're hundreds of miles from any installation. We can't survive out there like that."

"That's not my problem," Enkian said.

"People will be looking for us soon," Perry said. "We've been out of radio contact too long."

"They think you're dead, lying at the bottom of the ocean."

"Why would they think that?"

"I've seen to it, Mr. Sachs. I have people everywhere and in high places. Your plane was reported crashing into the sea. No one is coming. The world thinks this is an empty place. There is no need for anyone to visit. The only aircraft flying in here will be mine."

"Let us at least take the snowmobile."

"No, no snowmobile. I'm being overly gracious as it is."

"You call a slow death overly gracious?" Jack asked.

Enkian shrugged again. "Everything is a matter of perspective. To be honest, I don't want your corpses around. I could drop you down the rabbit hole, but like I said, I feel a small degree of gratitude toward you for bringing me the brick."

"How can I lead my people onto the ice knowing they'll all be dead in a few hours? The wind is kicking up. Our cold weather gear won't protect us for long if those wind speeds climb much higher."

"You are probably right, but if you stay here I will have all of you killed and dropped down the shaft. The choice is yours: death here or death out there."

"Doesn't sound like much of a choice."

Enkian shivered. The cold was finally getting to him. How he had remained so long without his parka and undergarments was beyond Perry. Their captor frowned as if inconvenienced by the chill. He turned to the altar, set down the glass container, and motioned for his clothing. Tia walked to the man who held the garments.

Perry's mind churned like a blender. He looked toward the open loading door and saw the dim white ice lit by a sun that hovered just above the horizon. Wind whipped up ice crystals and swirled them through the air. Death waited outside that door, death by cold, a cold that would freeze the lungs and seep into the internal organs until they no longer functioned. He knew what would happen. Those less fit, those who carried less body weight, would be the first to go—Sarah first, then Gwen, then Griffin, then. . . He clamped his eyes shut and drove the image away, but it returned. As if perched on some hill, Perry could see the lifeless bodies of his friends laid out in a line as if held together by string. Images of the katabatic wind assaulting the still corpses with airborne razors of ice swirled past his mind's eye.

Perry's heart began to ache as if the deaths had already occurred. Turning, Perry glanced around the Chamber. Fifty-plus armed men stared back. There would be no fighting their way out of the situation. He looked at Jack, who returned the gaze. He could tell Jack had no ideas either. His eyes drifted to Tia, and he was convinced that she was a trained and merciless killer. He doubted if even Jack with his lineman's size could handle her.

He thought about what Enkian had said, that no one was looking for them. Perry felt alone, more alone than he had ever felt and more hopeless than he could imagine.

Enkian slipped on his thick undershirt, then his thermal shirt. In a moment he would don the thick white parka. To Perry the man was the personification of evil. What bothered him most was the thought that evil would win, that this madman would get away with it all.

The images came back, haunting him like some ghoul that possessed his mind. Despair was knocking on the door, and defeat was climbing in the window.

The struggle to conceive of a way they could survive on the ice continued. Maybe they could make it to the crashed C-5. A few of them had made it through a rugged night there once before, but damp reality extinguished the thought. They had barely made it back on snowmobiles. Seven of them walking the distance was impossible.

The only way out was by air, and Enkian was certainly not going to allow that to happen. Not if he had. . .any. . .choice.

There was a tickle at the back of Perry's brain, an urgent nudging. For some reason he was thinking of an event he had read about in the Bible, an event familiar to all Sunday school children. In the midst of a great storm the wayward prophet Jonah had said, "Pick me up and throw me into the sea. Then the sea will become calm for you, for I know that on account of me this great storm has come upon you."

That was how Perry felt. None of his crew would have been here had he not asked them to be. None of the dead strewn around the fallen C-5 would be such if he had not accepted the challenge of the mission. He didn't mind dying, but he could not stand to see anyone else meet their end. "Toss me into the sea," Perry mumbled. He looked at his feet.

"What?" Jack asked.

"Toss me into the sea," Perry said.

"I don't follow, pal."

Perry watched as Tia lifted the white parka jacket and Enkian begin to slip his arms in—

Perry sprang forward and dove for the altar, his eyes fixed on the one object that Enkian held as dear as life.

A warning was shouted.

A shot was fired.

Out of the corner of his eye, Perry saw Tia shove Enkian to the ground and cover him with her body.

Perfect.

Perry hit the ice hard, landing on his side, the cylinder in his hand. As Perry slid he pumped his feet, trying to find purchase on the ice. He didn't want to rise to his feet; he wanted to slide three feet further.

He heard voices, another shot, a man's panicked voice, but he ignored it all. He rolled on his belly, pushing with his legs and clawing with his one empty hand.

The hole was two feet away. . .one foot. . . In what seemed an eternity of seconds Perry reached his goal, stretched out his arm, and held the cylinder over the open mouth of the ice shaft. His hand was shaking, and he could barely breathe. He waited for the gunfire, but no more came.

"Stand down! Stand down!" Enkian was screaming. "No one moves."

The advancing footsteps stopped.

"Back off!" Perry shouted. "I'll drop it. I promise you that. I'll drop it." His eyes drifted from the cylinder to the hole, not wanting to look but unable to stop himself. Two thirds of the way down the two-mile shaft, Larimore's dead body floated. Perry was glad the shaft was too dark for him to see that far down.

The Chamber's activity had come to a halt. No one spoke. No one moved. Keeping the cylinder hovering over the shaft, Perry wiggled and twisted until he was on his knees. He looked around. Enkian was still on the ice, Tia by his side on her knees, her eyes drilling Perry. Jack and Gleason were several steps closer. Three of Enkian's army lay doubled over on the ice. Apparently, Jack was going to take on the whole bunch.

"It seems you have me at a disadvantage, Mr. Sachs," Enkian said calmly, but there were rough edges to his voice. "May I rise?"

"You may sit," Perry said. Enkian did. "Tell your mascot to sit."

Enkian did so, and Tia lowered herself to the ice. All around Perry were men with guns pointed at him. His mind was racing. *What part of this seemed like a good idea?* he asked himself. He took a few deep breaths.

"Tell me why I should not have you shot," Enkian said.

Perry pretended to drop the cylinder.

"No!"

"That's why," Perry said.

"You have my attention."

"Here's how this is going to work," Perry said. "My friends get the twin-engine plane. They get in and fly off safely. If that happens, I give you the cylinder, and you get to keep me as a bonus."

Enkian smiled. "You don't have a pilot."

"Griffin can fly the plane."

Looking at Griffin, Enkian smiled. "Right now I don't think he could walk to the plane by himself."

Perry threw a glance at the scientist, who looked as if he was about to faint. "He'll make it."

"You have more faith than I do," Enkian said.

"You're right. You had better not think about it too long. It's been a rough few days, and my strength isn't what it normally is."

"You know, if you drop that, I'll kill you on the spot. Maybe I'll just start killing your friends until you come to your senses."

"For what? So we can march out onto the ice to die? We're dead if we stay; we're dead if we walk out. This is the only way.

And if I see a gun raised in their direction, I may let go. I'm ready to meet my Maker."

"That would be the God who worked your ancestors so many years ago," Jack said.

Perry saw Enkian begin to break down. The man's eyes darted around, and his lips moved as if they had a life of their own.

"I let your friends fly away, and you return the cylinder to me, is that it?"

"That's it."

"How do I know you won't drop it the moment they take to the air?"

"You don't, but I am a man of honor," Perry said. "You have my word."

"And if that's not enough?"

"Then you can kiss this thing good-bye."

Enkian muttered, then he swore, then he screamed. "All right! All right! Tia, take them to the plane."

"No," Perry said. "They go by themselves. After they've checked for fuel, and I get a word that everything is good, and I hear the plane leave, then you get this back, and you can do whatever you want to me."

"It won't be pleasant, you know."

"I can live with that," Perry said.

"Or die with it," Enkian countered.

"Perry," Jack said, "why not order them all into the Dome? We can lock them in and all of us can fly out."

The thought had crossed Perry's mind, but he had doubts he could push Enkian that far.

"That won't happen, Mr. Dyson," Enkian said. "I'm willing to risk letting you and the others go, but I will not give up the base."

"Even if it means losing the prophecy."

"I know where the ziggurat is. I have more men coming, more equipment, more buildings. The plan is underway. It would be the second greatest tragedy of my life to lose the cylinder, but the greatest would be to lose the tower. We're in a bit of a stalemate, aren't we?"

"Jack, take the others and get out of here," Perry ordered.

"I'm not leaving you."

"You have to do this. They need you. Now get out of here. If this thing slips, then we're all dead."

There was a pause. "Perry. . ."

"I know, buddy, I know."

CHAPTER 34

Perry had shifted his position from kneeling to prone, his arm extended before him, his forearm cantilevered over the abyss. Despite the warm clothing, the cold was seeping in. He shuddered.

He heard a soft crunch behind him. "Enkian, you had better tell the munchkin behind me that I can drop this faster than he can catch it." Perry turned his hand over so the cylinder dangled from his palm and fingers.

Enkian gave a wave, and Perry heard retreating footsteps. Jack had led the others out what seemed like an hour ago. It had only been a few minutes—fifteen tops—but it felt longer. His arm was hurting, and the cold was bringing back horrible memories of being trapped in the dive suit beneath the ice. For some reason, he thought of the fish with multicolored lights. He was a stranger down there; the fish would be one up here. *God made us to excel where we are.*

"You know, Mr. Sachs, I'm having a little debate with myself. A part of me doesn't think the cylinder is worth all this trouble."

"Would that be the cylinder you said predates the Bible? The one entrusted to you by ancestors that stretch back a few hundred generations? I'm betting you took some kind of oath to protect all of these and this one in particular. You are a tradition-bound man, Enkian. You won't betray that."

"Don't be so sure," Enkian said, but the words lacked conviction.

A roar rushed into the open loading door—the sound of twin engines coming to life. It was music, sweet in timbre and tone.

"Sounds like Dr. James got the engines going," Enkian said. "I wouldn't have put money on that."

Perry chose not to respond. Minutes passed without change. The engines had to warm slowly since they had been shut down for several days. The cold was a constant danger to the mechanical equipment. A short eternity later the pitch of the engines changed as more power was applied to them. The engines roared then died away as the aircraft taxied from the buildings.

"Godspeed," Perry said. Although he couldn't see the craft, he could imagine it lifting from the ice to cut through the thin air. On board were Gwen, Griffin, Sarah, Dr. Curtis, Gleason, and Jack. Relief washed over him.

"Sorry for the delay, pal," a familiar voice said, "but we had to top off the tanks."

"Jack!" Perry cranked his neck to see his friend approaching. "I told you to fly out with them."

"I was going to, but I had already seen the in-flight movie."

"Unbelievable," Perry said.

"Yeah, that's me," Jack quipped. "It's things like this that keep me the lovable international man of mystery that I am. Besides, I don't think you would have left me behind."

"How far is the plane?"

"It's out of gun range if that's what you mean," Jack answered.

"That's exactly what I mean."

Enkian rose from his seat on the ice. "I've kept my end of the bargain. Now let's see you keep yours."

"Jack was supposed to be on that plane—"

"I don't care!" Enkian screamed. "He made his choice. Give me the cylinder."

Perry was about to relent when he heard another sound, the

sound of big engines. From the way Enkian snapped his head around, Perry was sure it was unexpected company.

"See what that is," he ordered Tia. She sprinted to the door.

"Tell me that's what I've been praying for," Perry said.

Jack moved to the door and returned a moment later. "We're having guests for dinner," he said. "Four aircraft are on approach. C-2A Greyhounds if I don't miss my guess."

Tia approached Enkian. "Military airplanes. Four of them, the kind that carry troops."

"Four?" Enkian said. "How far out?"

"Not far," she said.

Enkian looked at Perry, who still held the precious container over the open expanse. "Give me the cylinder."

"You know what's going to happen," Perry said. "Each of those planes carries enough men to handle you, and there are four of them. If they charge in here with guns blazing, not only are a great many people going to die, but this cylinder and all the others are in danger. Bullets from automatic weapons are going to shred a lot of them. Can you stand that kind of loss?"

"We can hold them off," Enkian said.

"Really?" Jack shot back. "You really think you can?"

"We have you for hostages. They'll be outside in the cold."

"They'll wait," Perry said. "More will come. It's over, Enkian. Give up and save your prophecies, your heritage."

Enkian raised his hands to his head and pulled at his hair.

"Look at your troops," Jack said. "They don't seem to have the confidence you do."

"These men will die for me."

"Some might," Perry said. "Then again, some might be smart enough to know when they're outnumbered."

"Tia?"

"The plane," she said. "It's fight or flight."

Enkian looked at the sixty-five cylinders set on the stone pillars, his arrogance dripping away. He closed his eyes and swore softly. When he opened his eyes, he was staring at Perry. He turned to Tia. "Clear out. Make sure every cylinder is loaded on the aircraft. We leave right away."

Tia screamed her orders and men began to move, each taking one or more of the cylinders. In minutes the Chamber was empty except for Perry, Jack, and Enkian.

"Will you give me the last cylinder?" Enkian asked.

"It's the only thing keeping Jack and me alive."

"I will have it again, Mr. Sachs. I don't care who I have to kill."

"Just leave us your address, and we'll FedEx it to you."

Outside, jet engines began to whine. "You're a brave and dedicated man, Mr. Sachs. I hate that in an enemy."

"Don't you have a plane to catch?"

Enkian straightened and walked to the loading door. Outside the wind whistled around the opening. He paused for a moment, looked at Perry, then at the cylinder. Two steps later, he was outside.

"Give me that," Jack said, taking the object from Perry's extended arm.

"I can't tell you how close I came to dropping that."

"In some ways, I wish you had."

Men in heavy white parkas swarmed through the opening like ants out of a hill. Each wore goggles and a black knit mask, and each pointed an M16A2 in every direction. They filled the Chamber with amazing speed.

"On the ground! On the ground!" a tense voice ordered.

Perry looked at Jack and shrugged. Both men went to the ice. A half second later the barrels of two automatic weapons were pointed at their heads.

"A guy could develop a complex like this," Jack said. "Personally, I'm getting tired of looking down the nasty end of a gun."

"It will all be cleared up in a minute," Perry said. "I hope."

The sound of boots pounding ice continued for long moments. Occasionally, a "Clear" would echo through the area. Perry could imagine them searching the air lock, moving into the Dome, checking each room.

"Let 'em up, boys," a deep voice said. The gun barrels disappeared. Perry and Jack pushed off the ice and rose to their feet. In front of Perry was a middle-aged man with a serious expression. He pushed back his hood, revealing close-cropped sandy hair and sun-darkened skin. He removed his goggles, and Perry found himself staring into blue eyes that narrowed as the man studied him. "I'm hoping you're Perry Sachs."

"I am," Perry said. "This is my partner, Jack Dyson."

The man studied Jack for a moment. "You play any college ball?"

Jack shook his head. "It interfered with my cooking classes."

The man looked at Perry.

Perry smiled. "He gets asked that a lot."

"I see. I'm Captain Thomas Mahoney, United States Coast Guard, at your service." He gave a small bow.

Perry held out a hand. "I can't tell you how good it is to see you." He started to say something else when one of the troops approached. Like the captain, he wore a white parka.

"The place is empty, Captain," he said struggling to catch his breath in the thin air. "These are the only two on the premises. We found two bodies outside."

"Enemy," Perry said.

Mahoney nodded. "This is my XO, Ray Seager."

"They went thataway," Jack said, pointing over his shoulder with his thumb.

"The big plane? The Boeing?" Mahoney asked.

"Yes," Perry said. "Another plane left a short time before that."

"We saw the Boeing leave. One of our aircraft followed, but the Boeing is much faster. Ultimately we'll lose him, but we'll pick him up in other ways." Mahoney looked at Jack again. "Pardon me for saying so, but you two look just a step above roadkill. I'm going to have a medic look at you."

"We'll be fine," Perry said. "The smaller plane is being flown by an inexperienced pilot."

Mahoney nodded then turned to Seager. "Get on the horn. Get an experienced pilot to talk him into McMurdo."

"Well, gentlemen, my orders are to bring you safely home, and since I'm only a few years away from retirement, I don't plan on messing that up." He paused and looked around. Perry watched him take in the scene of sixty-six stone pillars circling a bloody stone altar. Next his eyes drifted to the gantry and the wide hole beneath it. He walked over.

"Careful," Jack warned. "It's a long way down and no way up."

Perry thought of Larimore, and sadness reached deeper into his soul than the cold ever could.

"What now?" Perry asked.

"As I said," Mahoney replied, "my job was to find you and bring you home. The major portion of the team will stay behind to secure the premises and await further orders. We, on the other hand, have a long flight back. That will give you plenty of time to tell me your story."

"I don't think you'll believe what I have to say," Perry replied.

Mahoney laughed. "I don't think you'll believe what *I* have to say. By the way, we'll be flying courtesy of the navy. Be careful what you say; they're not real happy that a Coast Guard captain is calling the shots."

"Before we go, I need to tell you something, Captain." Perry looked at the ice shaft, took a deep breath, and told of Trent Larimore. "I don't know if he was part of the problem or a hero, but he deserved better."

Mahoney stepped back to the hole and, to Perry's surprise, bowed his head. He raised it a moment later and commanded Seager to bring the men in the Chamber to attention. Perry watched the Coast Guard captain stiffen his spine. "Commander Trent Larimore, United States Navy, died serving his country. We commend his soul to God and his body to the sea. Present arms!"

Unlike any traditional salute, Mahoney raised his right arm, fingers straight, in a slow tribute, held the position for several long seconds, then slowly lowered his arm.

"As you were," he ordered. Then he turned to Perry and Jack.

"Can I give you a lift?"

EPILOGUE

Have some more pie, Jack," President Calvert said.

"I'm on a diet."

Perry smiled as Calvert looked at Jack. "You're kidding, right?"

"Yes, Mr. President. It's a fault in my character. And I would love more pie."

"Try the cherry," Calvert said. "It doesn't matter how bad things are in life, cherry pie makes it better."

Perry took a bite of pumpkin pie, one of the six kinds on the large table. He, his parents, Jack, Gleason, Sarah, Griffin, and Gwen were all jammed into the White House kitchen at the president's request. Dr. Curtis was eating his third piece of pecan.

"Offices are for diplomats and politicos," the president had said. "The kitchen is for friends."

It had been two weeks since Captain Mahoney had snatched Jack and Perry from the ice. Two weeks of relaxation and reflection. Perry had gone home to Seattle, which by comparison to Antarctica seemed balmy.

"I'm glad you all could make it. I've wanted to meet you. You have done a wonderful service for your country. Unfortunately, I can't give out any medals. This remains top secret."

315

"I don't understand that," Dr. Curtis said. "The discovery is monumental."

"It is," the president agreed. "And the last word hasn't been heard on that. It's just that we're in a dicey situation. You were rescued by a team that flew in on navy transports and included a Special Forces unit. That in itself isn't bad, but they flew out of an area we'd just as soon the world didn't know about. The Antarctic Treaty doesn't allow for military bases on the continent."

"So we're in defiance of the treaty?" Griffin said.

"Yes, we are," the president answered. "So are six other countries. And that, my friends, is the end of that conversation."

"May I ask about your situation here?" Perry said. "I understand that Enkian had men entrenched in the government."

"He still does," Calvert said. "And not just our government. I've received reports from most European and Middle Eastern governments that Enkian had made inroads there. Even China, of all places."

"How could he achieve that?" Sarah asked. "It seems impossible."

"All things are possible, given enough time and patience," the president said. "This wasn't an overnight plan. It spans generations."

"And to think he got away," Jack said. The president didn't respond. "He did get away, didn't he?"

"Have some more coffee, Jack," Calvert said. "It goes great with the pie." Then he winked. "Life is like pie. Anyone can open a can of cherries and pour it into a store-bought crust, but the best pies have a little something added by the baker, something only the baker knows. Secrets can be tasty."

"I think we get your drift, Mr. President," Perry said.

Henry Sachs leaned over the table. "Perhaps this falls under that category of tasty secrets, Mr. President, but your chief of staff is not with us tonight."

"He's on vacation," Calvert said. "Spending time with his wife and daughter. If you promise not to talk to the media, I'll let you in on something—he's resigning when he gets back. The Secret Service agent that picked up his daughter was rock solid. That was lucky."

"Or providential," Perry said.

"Yes, of course."

"When we last met," Henry said, "you told me a few others were connected to Enkian and that they were not as noble as Mr. Jeter turned out to be."

"Jeter is noble; he was willing to risk his life and that of his family to expose the conspiracy. He's a true patriot. That's what we're finding. The heads of state that I've been speaking to have told me that several people connected to Enkian found loyalty to their country more important. You can only push an honest man so far." Calvert leaned back and took a sip of coffee. "As for the two close associates that found Enkian's dream more important than their own country. . . . Well, they've both retired and moved out of the country—far out of the country."

Perry knew better than to ask, so he inquired about a different matter. "Enkian was in charge of the world's largest mining company. What happens to his assets?"

"The courts have seized them," the president said. "They will arbitrate everything. My guess is that the company will be split up and sold off to competitors. His mines in other countries will be released to the local governments. It's not for me to say for sure, but it's a good guess."

"And what about Lake Vostok?" Griffin said. "We had just begun our research."

"You gathered a great deal of information," Calvert said. "The data revealed some interesting things."

"Is the lake still growing?" Gwen asked.

"Yes," Calvert answered. "Ice is melting in the Arctic and Antarctic, and it seems to be melting from below. We are keeping a close eye on it. The data from your work, data you haven't had opportunity to analyze yet, shows the lake to be warmer than expected. Geothermal activity is probably the culprit, but more testing needs to be done."

"And what of the artifacts?" Dr. Curtis questioned. "The one below the ice and the one discovered by Dr. Harry Hearns?"

"Unfortunately, the one in the iceberg found by Hearns has broken off and sunk to the bottom. I imagine someday scientists will be taking a closer look. As for the ziggurat, well, it's still there."

"When do we get to go back?" Griffin wondered.

"I'm not sure," Calvert said. "This whole Enkian thing has muddied things up. We have some explaining to do to the Russians. Their research station is the closest. The UN may get involved."

"It could take years," Griffin complained.

"I'm certain it will," Calvert said. "I'm certain it will."

The informal meeting ended twenty minutes later when the president excused himself to take a phone call. Secret Service agents led them down the corridor and out into a pleasant Washington, D.C., night. Two black Lincoln Navigators were waiting for them. Perry climbed into the first and was joined by Gwen and Griffin. The others loaded into the second vehicle.

"Well, that was interesting," Gwen said. "I've never had pie with a president before."

"Me either," Perry admitted.

The car pulled from the curb. "I found him evasive about the future of Vostok," Griffin said. "If the call comes, will you go, Perry?"

Perry thought for a moment. The time he'd spent at the bottom of the world was the most grueling of his life. He had suffered pain, hardship, and cold, and had nearly died under two miles of ice. "Yeah, I'd go."

"Me too," Griffin said. "Do you really think they'll call us again?"

"I hope so," Perry said.

A moment later, Griffin spoke again. "I have another question for you, Perry."

"Shoot."

"I've been thinking. Maybe I should at least hear a little about your faith before I continue to denigrate it. Do you know anyone who would be willing to tutor me?"

Perry smiled. "It just so happens that I do."

The call never came.